WITHDRAWN

The LIGHT at the BOTTOM of the WORLD

LONDON SHAH

HYPERION

Los Angeles   New York

First Edition, October 2019

1 3 5 7 9 10 8 6 4 2

FAC-020093-19256

Printed in the United States of America

This book is set in Adobe Caslon Pro/Monotype

Designed by Marci Senders

Library of Congress Control Number: 2018966316

ISBN 978-1-368-03688-7

Reinforced binding

Visit www.hyperionteens.com

For my fellow Pathans.
We too are worthy of taking the helm.

EYSTUROY, THE FAROE ISLANDS,
NORTH ATLANTIC OCEAN

Hope had abandoned them to the wrath of all the waters.

The great Old World floods had done more than exile humanity to the depths of the oceanic abyss. They had also ravaged humankind of all faith and, like expiring pockets of air, sucked out any belief they would ever again live in peace.

How else could it be explained?

Ari sat deadly still, copper-skinned knuckles frozen around the submersible's controls. The air had left his lungs; a rock, more jagged and leaden than the surrounding submerged mountains, formed inside his chest and thrust up into his throat. His eyes flickered as he absorbed the shifting deep around him.

The ocean was on fire.

They faced a tsunami of mighty vessels. Savage. More ferocious than a battery of starving barracuda. Powerful current producers, lasers, and explosives shot and rippled in every direction from the vessels' stocky underbellies. All around, the water wrinkled as merciless weaponry pinned his people's crafts in spheres of contained pressure. The vessels exploded before his eyes. Waves unfurled and rocked his sub. And still, he could not move.

Here, where harsh winds ravaged the ocean's surface hundreds of feet above them, where the North Atlantic Ocean skirmished with the winding

Norwegian Sea, the hostile environment had mostly protected the people of Eysturoy from them. The location had been chosen for the surrounding high ridges that shielded his community from the most perilous elements. Its wild and rugged terrain, always reduced to a dense darkness at the first sign of trouble, was often enough to deter the predatory fiends who'd annihilate his people in a fierce heartbeat.

But the adverse surroundings had proven no obstacle for the beasts today.

Huge beams floodlit the area as the hostile intruders highlighted the precipitous landscape. The revealing light accentuated every cliff, and lower down it snuck behind rooftops sitting on the submerged plateau, exposing the inhabitants. Family, friends, neighbors.

Ari peered into the vast and seething swells of the sea where the unbearable cost of the human and Anthropoid clash already drifted aimlessly within its rolling waves. Bodies. People he knew. Lance—the gentlest of all his friends. Gone.

His father's words were merely an echo now: *Trust in the community's defenses, son. Do not leave the home—never let anger get the better of you.* And his recent threat: *This is your final warning, Ari. Put yourself at risk again and I will send you to Gideon's in London.*

So he was supposed to let matters continue as they were? Accept the losses?

Lance. His insides lurched. He bared his teeth and his nostrils flared.

Why must they hide? Always they were cowering in the dark hoping they weren't discovered. Why not blow the enemy's crafts apart, feed their bodies to the great whites?

He blinked and swallowed, his breathing raspy now. A heat burned its way through his insides, inflaming his loss. His desperation. His hands shifted on the controls.

Ari charged headlong into hell.

Omnia mutantur,
nos et mutamur in illis

∝

*All things change,
and we change with them*

CHAPTER ONE
LONDON, CHRISTMAS DAY, 2099

The Old World Heritage Society demands a respectful distance be kept from all revered ancient London sites. This respect can take a deep dive into one of those endless chasms in the wild because honestly, I just don't understand what's so sacred about ruins.

I turn down the blaring punk rock music ricocheting off the submersible's interior and peer into the murky green-gray depths once more for any hint of a watchful Eyeball; the tiny spherical cameras could be anywhere. The current looks clear. I steer past the fluorescent face of Big Ben and edge closer to the center of the former Houses of Parliament, toward the soft illumination of the Memorial Candle. A small number of patterned rabbitfish remain transfixed by the commemorative shaft of light. A traditional reminder of the looming anniversary, the lilac ray beams up through the city's waters as far as the eye can see.

God, how I love staring at it every year.

Sometimes the Memorial Candle is all of humankind echoing up through layer after layer of current and wave and pressure, breaking through the liquid skin of the surface and reminding the universe: *Hey, we're still alive, still going down here!* Other times the glow is a greeting across forever, a trillion Old World hugs and laughter and memories and dreams reaching down through the ages, lighting our way.

Sixty-five years tomorrow. Only sixty-five years ago all of this was air, not water. Like, there was *nothing* all around. Nothing in between structures, below people, or above their heads. Humanity carried on outside as if they were safely inside. Imagine being out in the open without the security of the water, exposed to the whole universe like that? Surreal!

My Bracelet flashes. I check the caller ID on the plain flexi-band around my wrist. "Accept."

Theo's holographic face materializes above my Bracelet, his smile reaching his pale-blue eyes. "You on your way, Leyla? There's a money pot with your name on it. We have a clear window—pair of Eyeballs passed by not ten minutes ago, so we're good for another hour. You'd think they'd take Christmas Day off, but nope."

The money pot. I straighten, pushing my shoulders back. I really, really need it. Being a driving instructor doesn't pay nearly enough, and if I get the reply I'm waiting on, then I'll need every penny of the pot. I *have* to win today's sprint.

As if he's guessed what I'm thinking, Theo nods. "You've got this, I know it. And I know you don't want to borrow, but—"

"Hey, I'm fine, really I am. But thanks. On my way now."

"Great, we're all gathered by the bridge. Everyone's here. And, erm, Tabby's getting, you know, 'impatient.' Ouch, Tabs!"

His twin sister's face squeezes into the frame, with Tabby rolling her piercing blue eyes. "Ignore him, Leyla. Hmm, bet you're out by the Memorial Candle, all lost at sea again and—"

"Oi," Theo says. "Just cos *you're* a bot, doesn't mean everyone is. Ouch!"

Every time Theo says "Ouch" I actually flinch as I grin; Tabby's nails are always pointy and red, as if she's drawn blood in the jab.

"I'll be there in a minute," I say. "And, Tabs, leave Theo alone!"

The Clash's guitar riff resumes its rightful place at full decibel as I rise. The current is calm. I push the throttle all the way forward and hurtle toward Tower Bridge and my friends.

Light from the countless solar spheres a thousand feet up on the ocean's surface highlights the watery depths. Beneath me, early morning London is a giant interlocking puzzle of domed titanium buildings interspersed with acrylic transport tunnels—all shadowy shapes and misty lights. The inky body of the Thames passes by, the memory of a river. Londoners feel attached to the legendary trail of deeper water, and its former banks are kept perennially lit. The city glimmers around me. Festive and commemorative signs are everywhere. I approach Tower Bridge where the sprint will begin.

The sight of the bridge always lifts my spirits. I've spent more time hanging out here with the twins than any other location in London, our grouped subs giving the adults plenty to moan about.

Rapid movement near the Tower of London to my left catches my eye and I squint: Is someone watching me? But it's just a glistening oarfish slipping out of one of the upper windows of the White Tower. The creature panics, heading straight into the crab-like machines laboring on the tower's moss-ridden walls, before its flat silver body dives out of sight. I dip and zoom through the construction's middle, seaweed hanging off every remaining part of the smashed-up bridge deck, and spot the other subs waiting for me.

The twins are in their blue twin-seated craft, a joint seventeenth birthday present given to them earlier this year. I can just about make out their faces. Even in this murky environment, their platinum-blond hair is clearly visible, and the world is instantly that much brighter.

I peer at my competition. Eight subs of various sizes and models—all the usual contenders. I mustn't underestimate Malik; he's been paying me for lessons, and he's getting faster every week. We each chip in with the money pot, and the winner takes it all. Losing always hurts, because I know the coming week will be tough minus my contribution to the prize pot. I used to sprint solely for the thrills, but things are different now. And this week's festive pot is much bigger than usual.

"All right, let's do this." Keung, contender and organizer, addresses us all via group broadcast. "The check-in cars are ready and waiting.

Stop points are: St. Paul's, Clio House on Trafalgar Square, and finally, the Island Housing Project. Usual rules apply—anyone misses a single check-in and the sprint is forfeit for them, et cetera, et cetera. Theo's monitored the route for Eyeballs, and we should be all right for traffic violations for the next hour. Any questions?"

None. We move to line up at the walkway of the bridge. I give everything the once-over.

"Okay . . . Ready?" Keung asks.

Here we go. As usual, I'm driving Tabby's compact but powerful single-seated scarlet number. The cockpit offers a 360-degree scope of my surroundings. Perfect. The more I can see, the safer I am. I hope. I scan once more for the telltale blip of an Eyeball hovering in the depths, despite Theo's assurance. I can't afford a traffic violation; three of those and my driving instructor's permit is revoked. Thankfully he's never wrong, though, and there's no sign of the titanium spheres.

Theo's a technical whiz kid and will happily spend entire weeks fiddling around with the bits on the huge table in his room. It'd drive me up the walls if I didn't get out into the waters regularly. He's studied and recorded the Eyeballs' movements—the *exact* routes and shifts of the remote cameras.

"And in three . . . two . . . one . . . GO!"

The vessels move. The water churns and heaves, and my sub sways. *Bismillah.* I glance below, push forward on the joystick, and dive until I'm just above the enormous solar-fuel storage pipes. Phosphorous fibers are strewn over them, the celebratory illuminated strands mingling with the green algae worlds inhabiting their surfaces.

The music resumes with an album from the last decade, and I race toward St. Paul's, climbing, falling, and swerving in time to the beat. My mood soars, my heart expands.

I hurtle over a colossal protein plant before whizzing above rows of obsolete rooftops jutting out from the ground like Old World gravestones.

The brilliant white light of the tall streetlamps illuminates the shadowy grid of streets like ancient moonlight from forgotten skies.

St. Paul's looms into view. The check-in car hovers above the cathedral, its lights on the antiquated landmark's partial dome, and a humongous halibut descends inside via the open roof. The destruction was the result of an Anthropoid attack two decades ago—one of the terrorists' most brutal. I flash until the car acknowledges my attendance. Lights appear in the block of flats next door, the cube-like resin-and-acrylic structure blinking into life. London's waking up.

I tear away in the direction of Trafalgar Square and zoom through street after street, passing block after block, over all the ruin and decay and life of the city's seabed.

My biggest weakness when racing is I'm easily distracted. It's maddening. A sight here or there and my thoughts drift and I'm lost at sea, as Tabs puts it. Not good.

Traffic's still at a bare minimum this early, only the odd craft around. I get to Clio House in record time. The giant construction is Great Britain's largest historical-reenactment hall yet, but I prefer the twins' Holozone; it's more private and we never have to dress up! I check in and move on.

A quick glance and there's a car way behind me, its lights low. It might not be a contender, but I'm not taking any chances, not today. There's a flash of illumination below as the first Underground train of the day whooshes through the transparent tunnel, startling the nearby creatures as usual. I dip toward it, skimming the debris on the ocean floor. The corroded skeleton of a bus thickly carpeted with moss and a telephone box trapped under an enormous statue—a man riding some kind of animal—lie coated in breadcrumb sponge. Both have attracted a group of inquisitive herring. I press on.

Last check-in now. I head straight for the towering shadows of the Island Housing Project. The lofty housing looms ahead.

The towers were built to reach out above the waterline after the floods, part of another failed global initiative. Scientists hadn't foreseen the devastating levels the water would finally settle at, and the housing was fully submerged—now with no connection whatsoever to the world above.

The check-in car's waiting above one of the rooftops. The whole roof is witness to Old World hope, rigged with all manner of survival resources, including a helipad. I hurtle away, headed straight back for the twins at Tower Bridge. A glimmering shoal of salmon split and dart out of the sub's way, flickering in unison. My eyes narrow as the water ahead clears. I stiffen.

It wasn't the sub that caused the salmon to scatter.

A bulky shadow rises from the depths, pausing in front of me.

My pulse races. It's oily black and as wide as the sub. I don't recognize it, which means it could be anything. It turns its head and swims straight for me. Two narrow milky-white slits for eyes stare as it advances. *What the—*

I swerve, gripping the throttle and joystick tight, and luckily miss the animal by inches. But the turn is too sharp, and the sub lurches before spinning out of control. I take deep breaths as I counter the spinning by repositioning the wings.

I mustn't let the panic win. I'm safe. I'm at home, in London. This isn't the wild, and there's nothing to fear.

At last the whirling slows down, enough for me to notice the creature's shadow slinking away back into the depths. I shudder. Movement ahead catches my eye and a circular yellow sub speeds past me, toward Tower Bridge. Malik. *No.*

I push the throttle all the way forward, pull back on the joystick, and climb waves that have turned choppier. *Come on.* I see the bridge, its pulsing lights beckoning me. Malik is directly below me now, racing toward it. I head into a forty-five-degree dive at full speed. I hold my breath. *Come on, come on* . . . Malik is fast.

But I'm faster. I pass his sub and keep pushing forward as I level. *Please let me be the first.* My eyes scan the scene, spotting only the twins' craft. I lean right, soaring over the bridge and working my lights like mad. My Bracelet flashes, the twins' voices bursting into the sub.

"YOU DID IT!"

Yes. My shoulders relax. If the solicitor's firm gets back with a yes—*please, God*—then the money's as good as spent, and I'd have been in trouble without it.

I run a diagnostics and the sub's fine. *Phew.* And I know I didn't hit the creature, thank goodness. What even *was* that thing? I should spend more time on practicing stabilizing the sub when it whirlpools like that. Conquer that panic somehow. *A freefall.* It's the only way.

No. I'm never, ever trying a freefall again. One terminated attempt months ago was enough terror for a lifetime.

As we wait for everyone to finish, the twins and I finalize plans for when I join them later this morning. The idea is mostly to feast, play endless games in the Holozone, and watch the live draw for the London Submersible Marathon—the annual obstacle race through the capital.

The arduous course is a big deal—*huge.* But there are only a hundred places, so nobody really expects to land one. Imagine having the chance to race an obstacle course as big and dramatic as the London Marathon! To ensure the actual route itself remains a secret, additional race boundaries are randomly installed throughout the city, and every year the exact obstacles and challenges are always concealed, too. It's an incredibly tough undertaking. Thrilling, but seriously demanding. And *always* perilous.

"Enjoy this morning with your family, won't you, Leyla?" Theo says.

My insides do this wild flip thing as I remember I'm this close now to the best present ever—some real McQueen family time—and I can't stop grinning as I head home.

I speed up once more, belting out the lyrics to the '20s pop-rock playing. At last I steer onto Bankside, slowing down as I pass my long block of flats. The one-story basic construction isn't much to look at but remains watertight—I'm lucky. I do a quick scan of the immediate area to ensure there are no vessels lurking in the shadows today.

The sub grinds to a halt by my own bay on the parking wall, and I dip its nose into position, maneuvering until I hear it lock into place. The vehicle's seal emerges from around the edges of its body, a large oval shape of robust, watertight material extending to meet the seal surrounding the dock. I shift around in the seat, my smile wide. I'm *this* close now. With the seals joined and the vessel safely locked and watertight, any trapped water is sucked out. The craft's dome then slides back just as the hatch to the building releases, granting me access. I unbuckle and jump down into the compact space. Once the exterior door is secure again behind me, the interior hatch is released and I rush through into the long and gloomy corridor.

Covering my nose to block out the wretched damp, I sprint along the resin floor, passing rows of gray metal doors on either side. The pale-blue walls are full of cracks, the paint chipped, and blotchy mold spreads in all directions.

Soon as I gain entry to the flat, Jojo leaps around, wagging her tail. "It's almost time, baby." I shed my jacket and pet the Maltese pup.

I bounce on my toes in the narrow hallway outside the lounge, catching my breath. Any second now. Jojo's too intrigued to remain still. The fluffy white puppy circles my legs, only taking a break to watch the thin lounge door with her ears cocked.

Heavenly notes rise from behind the door, melodies of Christmases past. Jojo takes a step back, her brown eyes fixed on the entry. I scoop her up and take a deep breath.

It's time.

The door slides open. I step into the compact room and my hand flies to my mouth, fathoms of warmth spreading inside me. Jojo leaps down, wagging her tail and jumping around, but I can only focus on one thrilling sight.

Papa stands by the expansive window.

"Salaam, Pickle! So what do you think?" He smiles his usual lopsided smile, his bright hazel eyes twinkling. He points at the faded-red festive jumper he's wearing.

My pulse races; I stare, unblinking. "Salaam, Papa. I . . . I think it looks pretty fab." Warmth flushes my cheeks.

The "festive" design he's wearing is actually a map of some far-flung solar system that fascinates my papa with its remoteness and possibilities. All the colorful planetary spheres look like baubles, though, and over time it's become his "Christmas" jumper. It was a gift from Mama, before I was even born.

I should say something, but I watch, speechless, the corners of my mouth stretched.

"There's my little queen."

I turn toward the soft voice. My petite mama stands by the far wall, beside the towering turquoise vase she painted for Papa, smiling with arms outstretched.

"Come on, my beautiful gul—come give Mama your strongest hug. My little Leyla."

"Salaam, Mama." I move closer. I feel both light-headed and super awake at the same time. A comforting heat radiates from my chest and ripples throughout my body. Her green eyes, sand-colored skin, and lengthy ebony hair are seriously uncanny; we're identical. *My Kabuli peree*, Papa always calls us—his fairies from Kabul.

Like always on special occasions, Mama's wearing a traditional Afghan kameez. The vivid hues of the long, flowing dress seem to seep into the air around the room, instantly brightening the dreary space. An Old World rainbow after the rain. She tilts her face and smiles. Tiny beads dangling from the silver tika that sits on her forehead dance with the movement.

"You want to do the honors, Pickle?" Papa winks.

I might cry as I dart to the cabinet, careful as I pull out the most brilliant snow globe ever. It's a McQueen family tradition to bring it out on special occasions. I hold it high for them both to see, and Papa's face especially lights up. I cup the globe's smooth surface.

These small-scale spectacles, mostly of the Old World, are avidly collected. The more ancient the scene inside, the dearer the cost. Sometimes it's a row of houses on a bustling street, a hillside with trees and flowers, or a busy children's playground.

I prefer the less desired watery scenes.

I shake the globe and catch my breath. Tiny rainbow fish and sparkly jellyfish bob in the turquoise ocean around an inviting submarine, a warm glow emanating from its windows. It's so utterly perfect. A whole world right here in my hands.

The Christmas carol ends, and a favorite festive song replaces it, loud and merry. I laugh, setting the globe down as I nod along to the music. Everything is heavenly. I might burst any second now. It's too much. Could joy actually bubble over and spill out? God, I hope not, because I want this sensation to last forever. I break into dance moves, shaking my body on the spot beside an excited Jojo. Papa chuckles. Mama smiles.

I beam. They both look so happy. My skin tingles. It's all sheer magic. I'd never expected to feel *this* good.

The melody resounds in the small space. "Are you waiting for the family to arrive-rive-rive-rive—"

I stop mid-twirl as the song falters.

"Are you sure youuuuuuuuuuuuuuuuuuu . . ."

Jojo growls at the harsh electronic notes. I clutch my stomach. My eyes widen; I spin around to Papa. He's talking, but the words are indistinguishable.

He flickers into vivid colored lines.

Then he's gone.

"No! No, no, no . . ." A sudden coldness spreads inside. I turn to Mama. There's no one there.

13

"No, not yet, it's too soon. *Please.*"

Jojo stops barking and stands still. It's dark and quiet. I blink rapidly to cut short the prickly sensation at the back of my eyes and try to swallow past the ache in my throat. The weight of my chest will crush me. The water outside causes rippled, ghostly shadows on the moldy walls. The auxiliary lighting comes on and casts a thick gloom over the still lounge.

I'm alone.

CHAPTER TWO

I press my face against the window in the dimmed lounge and stare out into the patchy darkness. Jojo, cradled in my arms, whines.

"Hey, no need to feel afraid, you daft mutt," I whisper, trying to swallow away the lump in my throat. "It's only a power cut. I've got you now, baby. Everything will be all right, you'll see." I kiss her on her button nose.

I glance over at the far wall again. I'll be lucky if I hear from the solicitors today; it's Christmas Day, after all. But there's a small chance, and I pray the power cut is a short one.

I pull the colorful blanket closer around us both, Papa's light citrus-and-herby scent still very much present in its threads. I spent months crocheting the bright squares from various unwanted woolens. Papa insisted it was the best Eid present he ever received. My chest tightens.

Of all the moments for the power to fail, curse it. It had taken Theo days to perfect the clips once he unearthed them from Papa's album files, to ensure both cuts would look like one real scene. Still, it was only a projection. To think I'd secretly entertained the idea Papa might *actually* come home this morning—a compassionate release by the authorities.

I hang my head. Mama's spirited laugh from the footage plays in my mind. I was only three when it was recorded, so I can't recall the actual memory. I take a deep breath. "God bless you, Mama. Rest in peace." Mama suddenly passed away in her sleep a year after that recording.

"Hang in there, Papa, wherever you are," I whisper, placing my hand on the window and fixing my gaze on the familiar unknown stretched out before me. *Detained in a facility in London* is all I've been told of his where-abouts. Somewhere out there in the city, in its obscure and cloudy expanse, is my whole life. The routine ache pulls at me, tugging away at my insides and latching on to every thought. His absence is unbearable.

I tap my feet and glance over at the far wall again. *Come on.*

White emergency lighting beams through the green-blue of the early morning waters that stretch high above me. A lengthy form shoots past, startling Jojo. She tucks her head into my jumper. The shape slows down. An eel. It wriggles against the window and swims away, rising to follow the taillights of a four-manned security sub. All around the water fluorescent and phosphorous lights flash by as a mixture of police, ambulance, and structural integrity vehicles speed past.

"Looks serious, Jojo." I nuzzle the puppy, trying to ignore the obvious dread: Could the power cut be Anthropoid related?

A large Newsbot—resembling a sphere of crushed wreckage and blipping lights—whizzes by the window. Moments later a number of them, each bearing the logos of various news stations, race through the waves trailing the vehicles. It's serious, then.

A *ping* sounds as the power returns, and the dim auxiliary lighting in the room is replaced with sharp illumination. The communications wall of the lounge flickers back to life, information tailored to my interests displayed across its surface. *Yes.*

In the kitchen I command the Tea-lady on and hurry back to the wall with a steaming cup of kahwah. A calming blend of saffron, cinnamon, and cardamom fills the air.

An alert pops up: I've not paid my monthly Explorers Fund install-ment. I bring up my bank balance, pulling a face as I check it. I wave the alert away and skim each message as I dress Jojo.

The Landrovers are up to their usual scams and are "this close to discovering legendary dry land," if only they have my "regular financial support." I scowl. *Yes, quick as you can, five hundred pounds and Bob's your uncle: dry land.*

Firstly, there's no dry land up there—only a few mountain peaks. Secondly, discovering dry land wouldn't even begin to solve my problem.

There's another alert from the authorities demanding I end the constant petitioning and complaints regarding Papa's arrest. *Not bloody likely.*

I shake my head and throw my hands up as I reach the end of the morning's post. There's no message from the solicitor.

"Jeeves?" I call out to activate the Housekeeper.

"Good morning, Miss Leyla. How may I assist you today?" The voice coming from my far wall never changes, as people find it familiar and reassuring.

"Jeeves, a file was playing this morning when the power went out. Is it possible to replay it?"

Jojo's already trying everything she can think of to shed her festive outfit.

"I am sorry, Miss Leyla, but the power cut destroyed the file. Anything else I can help you with?"

I'll never get to watch the whole thing now. I swallow past the disappointment. "What caused the power failure? I want to pay some Christmas visits—the twins and Grandpa. Has the power cut affected my routes?"

Jojo gives a triumphant yelp as her festive hat rolls off her head. She catches me glaring and scampers.

"Miss Leyla, the power cut was due to an incident in Marylebone. Although authorities initially suspected foul play, emergency services now report an earthquake as the cause. Your intended journeys are not affected by the subsequent travel restrictions. Would you like me to order you a cab?"

Foul play. I gulp. The Anthropoids can go back to whichever hell they came from.

They're genetically modified humans. They were designed by desperate Old World scientists to breathe freely underwater, bear massive pressures, and possess great strength—all so they could help the survivors after the disaster when machines wouldn't be enough. But instead they developed heightened levels of rage and loathing, bloodthirst and barbarity. And they turned on us.

Their sole aim is to destroy. They're incredibly sly. In the water a genetically designed transformation takes place. The layer of skin acting as gills is an undetectable permeable design—making them even more dangerous to us. They've proven a truly terrifying mistake that humans have been paying for ever since.

Only last year one of them seized the opportunity to take innocent lives when a submersible caught in an earthquake hit trouble. Instead of aiding the family of four, a Newsbot caught the Anthropoid using specialized tools to cause vehicular damage. Within moments the sub's body had been pierced, and by all accounts the family inside succumbed to the pressure before the water had even filled the vessel.

If it weren't for Prime Minister Gladstone's relentless efforts to find and stop the Anthropoids, many more lives would be lost to the deadly creatures. As if the natural environment isn't enough of a threat already every time we're out there.

"No need for a cab, Jeeves, I have Tabby's sub. Have you run today's search of Papa's files? I submitted what you'll be looking out for."

"I have indeed, and nothing to report, Miss Leyla. Anything else?"

I sigh. "Keep running the daily scans, please."

There has to be *something* in them that can help prove Papa's innocence—even though the connections I ask Jeeves to look out for have become increasingly vague. It's been three whole months since Papa's arrest, and I've found *nothing* to shed any light on the vile accusations against him.

I pass by a now stark naked and contented Jojo. "Oi, you muppet. I'll have to dress you on the way there now. Try and be good today, Jojo!" The puppy hangs her head, before jumping into the hammock Papa made for her and swinging away. "Oh no you don't, you lazy sod. We're headed out to the twins' in a minute."

Not many people own real pets. They're as expensive as antiques. I'm incredibly lucky. Jojo was a gift from someone Papa helped a couple of years ago when their substandard property started showing signs of pressure damage. Papa lent them what little money we had, for a deposit toward a safer dwelling. It's one thing replacing a virtual pet—that's heartbreaking enough. Losing a real one's unimaginable.

My Bracelet flashes: Gramps! I transfer the call to the far wall, and Grandpa's face fills the space. Jojo wags her tail at the sight of him and he chuckles, his light-green eyes almost disappearing between the heavy bags beneath and the bushy gray eyebrows shading them.

I move closer. "Salaam, Gramps! Everything all right?" I narrow my eyes. "You look paler than usual."

"Shalom, child. And nonsense, I feel as fit as a fiddle!"

Grandpa moves back from his own communications wall so I can see him in his study. He lifts his cane and performs a brief and woeful jig meant to pacify me but succeeds only in worrying me further. I stare at his beloved, weathered face. Within a fortnight of Papa's arrest, Grandpa suffered a heart attack and still hasn't fully recovered.

"As long as you're eating properly, Gramps. Any drip-dry cupboards when I'm over this evening and you'll be in serious bother."

"That's why I called, Queenie." Grandpa drags a chair over and sits in front of the screen. He lowers his gaze. "The son of a good friend has stopped by, and I'm afraid I'll be rather busy today. Could we meet up after he's gone?"

"Oh, I see. . . . All right, but you must enjoy the day, Gramps, whatever you do."

"I promise to. I'm sorry, child. I shall miss you, of course. You'll still be busy, I hope?"

"Oh yes. Headed for the twins' as soon as we're ready."

"Good, good." Grandpa's expression grows serious now, concern etched into his face. He smooths the gray-white jumble of hair on top of his head. "Remember, you promised you would stay alert out there." He's trying to keep his tone light, but his eyes cloud over. "You haven't noticed anything else untoward, have you?"

On several occasions over the past few weeks I've had this feeling I'm being followed. Each time, I seem to catch the glimmer of a vessel's lights just before they're dimmed. Voicing my suspicions to Gramps was a bad idea, though. He rip-currented me by insisting I need someone to watch over me.

I most definitely do *not*.

"I told you, I can look after myself, Gramps. Please don't worry. But . . . if I *am* being followed around, do you think it could be related to . . . you know—to Papa?"

Grandpa's traumatized by Papa's arrest. I can't risk upsetting him by talking about it, and yet that day is the only thing I can think of whenever we chat.

None of it makes any sense. Grandpa was with Papa at the time; they're both astronomers and worked together at the Bloomsbury laboratories. Police stormed the building and took Papa away. Despite Grandpa's frail health, he's worked tirelessly since, desperately trying to get some answers as to exactly which prison Papa's being held in and how they can accuse him of such a terrible crime without a single shred of evidence. Why is the case "too sensitive to allow family and friends contact with him"? No, none of it makes any bloody sense at all.

Grandpa shifts around in the chair. "Anything is possible, child," he says, his voice low. "If you do suspect someone is on your tail, head straight to a safe place. *Please.* You're a smart scone, Queenie. You must remain careful." He straightens, his gaze flitting around the room behind me. "I wish you would have a rethink about moving in with me, child. It would only be until your papa was back. But you shouldn't be—"

"You know I love you, Gramps. But I can't move in with anyone." I wring my hands. "I'm really sorry. But it would just feel like I'm giving up on Papa. He's going to return any day now, inshallah. In fact I'm waiting on a solicitor's reply right this minute."

Thank goodness I'm sixteen and have a choice. A month younger at the time of the arrest and I'd have been declared a ward of the state unless I moved in with friends or family. I need to stay focused on helping Papa, be here for when he returns.

Grandpa turns to the side, distracted. I think his visitor has entered the room. "I have to go now, Queenie. You must pop around soon as I'm free. Enjoy yourself at the Campbells' and give that scallywag Jojo a big hug from me."

I bite back my disappointment; another exchange that hasn't revealed anything new about Papa's situation. "Will do, Gramps. See you soon."

The room is small anyway, but sometimes, like now, the walls really close in. I unfold a large canvas screen beside the album wall. Hanging inside the screen are all my cherished hand-drawn maps from over the years, Papa always budgeting to buy me the paper. They're of all the waters around Great Britain.

I trace a little note pinned to one of the maps. I fished it out of Papa's bin when I searched his room, looking for answers after the arrest. It's just a work memo containing a few everyday reminders for himself and coordinates for Cambridge—Papa traveled all over for his work—but it's handwritten, and seeing Papa's handwriting comforts me. Besides, the authorities took most of his belongings and I'm not throwing away what's left.

Movement on my wall catches my eye as an avatar pops up in the corner with a company logo: *Dickens & Sons, Purveyors of Legal Advice & Services*. The solicitors—finally!

I wave the message open. "Play."

"Miss McQueen. Thank you for your enquiry regarding legal

representation for Hashem McQueen. Unfortunately, we are unable to take on your father's case. We advise you to continue with your search for suitable representation. In this ongoing climate, where our numbers continue to drop and our very survival is at risk, the charges of exploiting the seasickness by aiding and abetting citizen suicides are indeed grave. Good luck, and good day to you."

What . . . ? No way. *No*. I shake my head. "Reply."

I fold my arms and glare at the wall. "Mr. Dickens, my papa is innocent. The police have made a terrible mistake. He *never* encouraged seasickness sufferers to take their own lives. He helped them wherever he could. There's absolutely *no* evidence to back the accusations up—surely that counts for something? *Please* reconsider. You were my last hope. Whereabouts in London is my papa? Why won't they let me visit him? Nobody's arrested and then never heard from again. Please, help us."

He never came home, I want to add. *One day three months ago he went to work as usual but never returned. What's going on?* I swallow past the hard lump in my throat. My chest is suddenly constricted, my ribs like prison bars. I gulp for air. "Send." The message disappears.

The grid of information on the communications wall dissolves. "Rule, Britannia" plays as the wall displays a picture of the Great Briton of the Day. The solemn voice begins:

"Today's minute's silence is in honor of the venerable William the Conqueror, who among other achievements compiled the *Domesday Book*. Inside its pages, time has been preserved forev—"

Oh, not now. "Sleep, Desktop."

I rub my arms and then wrap them around me, staring into nothing. It's true that the seasickness takes many lives. It's a horrific disease the waters brought with them. It comes on slowly; you have to watch out for the signs. First, people stop talking about the future. It doesn't seem to offer them anything anymore. Some will gladly go hungry just so they can spend the money buying Old World relics instead. Many start obsessively following the Explorers' progress and can't accept that an exact date for returning to the surface isn't yet available. And then there's the sadness that swallows sufferers whole. That's when some take their own lives.

I know one thing for absolute certain, though: Papa *helped* any sufferers he encountered. He tried to give them hope. He *knew* hopelessness was at the core of the seasickness, and he always did everything he could do to instill optimism in everyone he ever knew.

I walk over to the window and gaze out at the shifting waters. How do I help Papa now? Dickens & Sons were my last legal hope.

A persistent shape, first far off and then drawing closer, teeters on the edge of my vision. I swing my gaze and gasp; Jojo leaps down from the hammock and darts over, straight into my arms. She remains still, totally transfixed.

A dolphin. It must be at least two meters long. I place my hand on the window. What does the creature feel like? If only I could touch it. It looks so happy and carefree.

Apparently most sea creatures had different natural habitats and patterns of migration before the disaster. Many are now attracted to the lights of vessels and buildings, but I've never known a dolphin to come this close before. It swims even closer. It's a bottlenose, gliding effortlessly as if it *is* the water, as if a part of the ocean before us has taken form.

"Look, Jojo, it's smiling at us," I whisper.

The creature stops. It turns its head and follows whatever has caught its attention until it's out of sight. I suck in a quick breath and slump against the window. The corners of my mouth lift and my insides flutter.

Hope is all I have right now; it's as unending as the oceans—and I must hold on to it.

I just need a miracle.

CHAPTER THREE

The stars twinkle above us; a midnight-blue sky that every so often rewards us with a shooting star. A gentle breeze whispers through the greenery, the moonlight casting a subtle incandescent glow. Everything about the scene is utterly magical.

"Camping" is so cozy, definitely my favorite of the Holozone programs. Jojo stays alert, gazing upward with a low growl. An owl's hoot breaks the silence.

I reach for dessert, despite having eaten too much already. It's early evening; I've been at the twins' for hours, and Christmas dinner seems like ages ago. Luckily one of our favorite restaurants was moving through the area, and the blanket spread before us now bears an assortment of scrumptious sights and smells. I pile the plate with some mango pudding, a coconut bun, ice cream, and a banana fritter. Mmm. Theo grins at my hoard.

I raise my eyebrows. "All I know is, Ramadan's for fasting—and all other occasions are for feasting. Also, do you have any idea how much running I had to do during *Ripper's Revels* earlier? Ripper himself was after me! I've never played so many back-to-back games."

"Lightweight." Tabby grins, chewing on a juicy rib.

Theo leans forward for some jelly and cookies. "Reckon anyone from London will win a place this year?" he asks.

We've been chatting about the London Marathon for an hour now.

I shrug. "You never know; we had a *lot* of northerners participating last year! Imagine . . . traveling through all that water to be here for the event." I shudder.

Theo fixes his gaze on me. "Leyla, I was thinking . . . maybe you could join us next time we leave the city to—"

I shift, scowling. "Not this again, Theo."

"Please," he says. "Mum could make you papers in no time because you'd be traveling with us; no need to wait two years until you're eighteen."

I glare at him. "Why do you always have to bring this up? Crossing the borders can get stuffed. I'm not interested in the rest of the country, accept it." They couldn't *pay* me to venture out there in the wild. All the unknown spaces and creatures and endless dangers lurking everywhere. I wrap my arms around myself.

Tabby tilts her head to one side, her eyes narrow. "You can't avoid leaving London forever, you know. And you're missing out on so much, Leyla. You need to see all our hotels; the footage doesn't do them justice. Theo's got all kinds of tech wizardry going on."

Vivian Campbell, the twins' mother, took over the family hotel business after her husband's untimely death two years ago, when the stretch of tunnel his train was traveling through collapsed. Each hotel is designed to mimic a specific Old World era, furnished in relics and memorabilia of the age. They've even become tourist spots in their own right. Theo's only real interest in the family's business is the high-tech illusions he lays on for the guests.

"*And* you've missed all my nationwide comps," Tabby continues, lathering cream and jam onto a scone now. "I've another one in Wales, in the new year. Wish you could see me give them a good bashing."

Tabs is gifted at several martial arts disciplines. I've watched her practice and I'm certain I developed sympathy bruises each time.

"She's not kidding." Theo holds his hands out in front of him as if to protect himself. "She's been training in here with samurai and ninja warriors. Her opponents are in for a shock. Yesterday she had us battling on board a ship on the Aegean Sea. Apparently we were saving the Roman general Julius Caesar. Those pirates never saw her coming!"

Tabby smooths her hair. "Not one of those gormless gits had the balls to take me on."

I finish eating and draw my knees up to my chest, resting my chin on them. My hair falls around my legs. "It's just not my cup of tea." Better to stick with what you know—always.

It goes quiet. Jojo chews on her tartan dress. She yelps and jumps when Müller, the Campbells' latest Housekeeper, materializes beside her. He's wearing only football shorts. He sticks his chest out, flicks back a golden ponytail, and acknowledges me with a wink. I can't help giggling.

The twins take it in turns choosing a new Housekeeper every few months; all the programming remains the same, just the image and personality change. Tabby's choices are always funny. Currently it's a famous German footballer from the '20s.

Tabby looks Müller up and down and blows him a kiss.

The Housekeeper returns it before addressing her. "Your Highness—"

Theo snorts and we all start giggling now.

"You requested an alert for the viewing of the marathon draw."

"I did," Tabby says. "Thank you, Müller, that will be all."

He flickers out of sight.

"Cease Play," orders Tabby, and in an instant the Old World vanishes before us.

We're in the gleaming space of the Holozone, the largest room in the Campbells' home. The virtual installment was a gift from the twins' late father for their thirteenth birthdays.

We jump up and remove our sensors and lenses. The siblings tower over me despite only a year between us. As we head to the lounge I spot their mother, and Tabby and Theo go on ahead while I pause to speak to her.

Vivian, a carbon copy of Theo except with shorter hair, tilts her head at me. A sad smile lights up her kind blue eyes. "Stay over, Leyla. You could watch the anniversary commemorations here with us instead of going to that overcrowded pub tomorrow."

"I'd love to, Viv. Except . . . Papa and I *always* watch the anniversary broadcast at the pub and even though he won't be with me this year, I still need to do it. I'm not going home just yet, though. We're all watching the marathon draw first."

Vivian nods sympathetically and her eyes dim. "You want to be more careful than ever out there, love. Those beasts wreaked hell in the Faroe Islands last week." She shakes her head.

I grimace. "I saw that. It was a horrific attack."

A shadow passes over Vivian's face. "I simply don't understand how they dare get so close to our communities." She shudders and wraps her arms around herself. "Sometimes it seems as if there's just no hope for us. We were never made for this world. We were created for day and night. Not a perennial darkness. Is it any wonder"—she lowers her voice—"so many suffer from the seasickness. Such *hopelessness* . . . There's no cure for that. Meanwhile those horrors are multiplying, breeding like sunfish."

I tuck my curtain of hair back from my face so I can ensure Tabby is out of earshot. "Viv, *please*. What if Tabs heard? She's still recovering. . . ."

Vivian bites her lip and throws a hesitant glance in the direction of the lounging area.

"We might survive that evil," I continue. "There's more to living down here than the Anthropoids. We've endured a massive change in the planet. And well, I know it's obviously *nothing* like living up there, but . . . we're still alive. I really think that should be the main thing, Viv—the fact that we still *are*, not *where* we are."

Vivian looks at me, uncertainty in her gaze. "Oh, sweetheart, you're young and so naive to still carry hope in the face of such dispiriting facts. But you mustn't worry about Tabitha—Theo and I are committed to keeping her spirits up. Don't take up that burden on top of your own, love. I would never reveal my worries in front of her." She lets out a long sigh and her shoulders droop. "I'm well aware the seasickness could return any moment and reduce her once again to some shadow of what—"

"Come *on*, Leyla!" Tabby shouts, beckoning me from the open living space ahead.

Vivian and I turn to see Tabby and Müller dancing together rather suggestively.

"Tabitha!" Vivian admonishes and dismisses the Housekeeper, and we both let out a much-needed laugh.

"Oh, before I forget! Here you go, love." The twins' mother produces a tiny vial from her pocket. She leans over, opens the bottle, and pushes the tip to my nose. "Oh, just smell that. *Real* Old World earth! Not that replica rot they try and fob you off with down at the markets. Happy Christmas, sweetheart."

I give Vivian her gift. I found a turn-of-the-century garden gnome at the markets several months back. The millennium baroque is her favorite Old World period—she was even recently awarded honorary member of the Millennium Baroque Committee. Despite all its cracks and glued parts, the gnome still cost a small fortune; thankfully I was allowed to pay in installments. I knew she'd love it.

"You know, just sometimes"—her eyes grow wistful and bright as she hugs the gnome—"when I'm able to ignore the waters, it kind of feels as if I'm part of the Old World, you know?" Her Bracelet flashes. "We'll continue this later, love. It's wonderful to have you around." She kisses my forehead and moves to take the call.

I join the twins in the lounge. The Campbells' home is a sleek and glossy space. Floor-to-ceiling windows wrap around the open-plan living area that alone is larger than our entire boxy flat. Each mansion in the affluent neighborhood is uniquely designed. The pearly smooth sphere of a Maid-bot passes by me and gets to work polishing a cabinet displaying a host of Tabby's martial arts trophies and awards. My heart flutters; Tabby's placed her gift from me right in the center of the shelf. The detailed origami model is of a twelve-year-old Tabby dancing with her dad, capturing her most favorite moment with him.

A breath hitches in my throat every time I remember the twins will *never* see their dad again. I can't even imagine how that must feel. An unbearable thought.

Theo's face suddenly lights up. "Your present! I haven't given it to you yet!"

"Another one? But we've already exchanged gifts and you spent hours creating the holographic scene for me."

He frowns. "Fat lot of good the family scene did. Rotten luck that, the power cutting off when it did."

I squeeze his arm. "I don't need to have watched it all to know I loved it. Best present *ever!*"

Theo dashes off and returns in seconds. "Ta-da!" He holds up a long thin gift.

I unwrap it carefully, not wanting to ruin the lush paper; it would make a perfect origami model. "A brolly! Oh my gosh, thank you, it's stunning!" The umbrella's frame is bronze-colored and the fabric purple. "I've held one once before, all rusty and broken, when the Royal Preservation Society held an open day. But this is just *beautiful.*"

"Okay, it's not a real brolly," Theo says and winks at me. "It's—"

"Only a flipping weapon!" Tabby announces, her face gleaming.

My mouth falls open. I've never carried a weapon before; I stare at it, shifting around in my seat. A secret weapon. Designed to look like an innocent umbrella. I'm kind of thrilled.

"You can't be living on your own and not have some sort of self-defense, Leyla," Theo says. "I saw Miss Petrov come out of the Tax Office in Civic House twirling a parasol, and it came to me—I could design you a weapon disguised as an accessory! And I know you love the idea of rain. Oh, and that see-through tip is a brilliant light." He puts a reassuring hand on my shoulder. "It's very safe when not activated, so don't worry. But it's either this or you move in with us. All right, let's get you familiar with it."

Within minutes the brolly is adapted to my unique handprint, and I know how to use it. It has an immobilizing spray that I can top up with the thinnest canisters I've ever seen, and a tase function that I'm sure I'll never use. Tiny indented buttons along its length control the different parts. The brolly's fantastic. Scary, but fantastic. I grin and Theo mirrors it.

I leap into an embrace. "I *love* it. You're amazing, Theo. Thank you so much!"

He smiles and waves my words away.

"Marathon Draw!" Tabby shouts just as the screen switches to Elvis, and the corners of my mouth lift instantly.

We all cheer. He's Papa's favorite presenter, too. His attempts at the American accent alone are always hilarious. The Black impersonator is at the BBC Studios, wearing a white satin jumpsuit open down to the navel, where it's cinched with a rhinestone-studded belt. Thick gold-rimmed glasses cover his eyes. He straightens his glittering collar, runs a hand over his glorious pompadour wig, and points at the camera with a brilliant smile.

"Well, hello there, y'all lovely people of Great Britain. Merry Christmas! Of course I'm Elvis, and I'll be back hosting the 2099 London Submersible Marathon in just two days' time. Tonight, I present the live draw. So let's do this, folks. Only three minutes to go. You can watch the upcoming *Today's Terrors of the Deep*"—he grimaces at the idea—"or nip to that loo, and grab those drinks and snacks!" He curls his lip to say, "*Thank you very much*," and laughs heartily.

Today's terrors flash on-screen: a cunning current near Ireland that will drag you halfway across the world where blind critters feast for days on your corpse, and a creature that looks like a cross between a mammoth eel and a demon. I shudder and jump up. *Not today, thanks.*

I make a dash for the loo, then grab a snack for Jojo. When I get back, the draw's begun. A host of random numbers flash on a grid beside Elvis, changing too fast to read, and once he stops the screen, the highlighted number is matched against a register of all the entrants.

"Nobody we know!" Theo says, just as I'm about to ask.

Only one hundred names will be drawn. The odds of knowing a contender personally are tiny, but there was Jack Taylor two years ago. I try not to think about what happened to him.

The Campbells' Butler comes in with drinks. The robot's red "eyes" take in my presence, and he greets me with a nod. I relax as I sip my drink and get swept up in the draw.

Elvis calls out name after name, impersonating the original twentieth-century artist when he can. Before we know it, we're almost done. He checks his latest number against the register, and we see the name just before he announces. "Entrant number ninety-four, Camilla Maxwell!"

The room erupts. "We know her!" we all shout at once.

We cheer the place down and message Camilla to congratulate her as Elvis draws the remaining names until finally, all one hundred contestants have been selected. The presenter breaks into song and dance, swiveling his hips. We turn to each other in celebration, drinking and analyzing the results.

I try not to let the disappointment get the better of me. It was always a small shot anyway.

"Can't believe Camilla will be taking part!" Theo says.

Tabby waggles her eyebrows. "Amazing how the chief historian's daughter's name is drawn the first year she ever enters, isn't it?" She shakes her head, grinning. "Anyway, the media's going to go absolutely barmy! Camilla will be the marathon's perfect, shining star this year, just you watch. She'll hate the attention, poor thing. *Argh*, so exciting! Only two days—"

"Well, y'all are the luckiest folk around because everyone's back in the game!" Elvis's voice suddenly booms over our own, though with less verve than it normally carries.

We pause and turn to the screen.

"That's right, folks, the final draw will be repeated!" His expression then turns uncharacteristically somber. "Fellow Britons, in the true spirit of the Marathon Committee's pledge for full transparency, I can explain the disregard for the previous draw for hundredth place. It transpires the entrant has, in the time since applying for this most prestigious of Great Britain's sporting events, been identified as an Anthropoid—and dealt with accordingly. There is no cause for alarm, and today is a day for national celebration, y'all!"

My stomach churns, heavy, and from the looks on the twins' faces they feel the same way. If an Anthropoid managed to dupe the registration process, then we're not as safe as we think. . . . We're still vastly underestimating their cunning.

Anticipating viewers' concerns and a dip in excitement, Elvis cuts to a live statement from the committee's director, Mariam Khan, who reassures everyone this situation will *never* be repeated. The broadcast then replays several of the marathon's promotional clips. The presenter returns and with much flourish is soon preparing to once more select the final lucky entrant.

Tabby folds her arms. "How *dare* those beasts try it, though."

"Bloody hell." Theo shakes his head. "But at least they caught its identity in time! And Elvis is spot on—let's not give them the satisfaction of ruining the draw for us."

"True," Tabby says. "And, Leyla, you absolutely *have* to watch the marathon here with us!"

"Promise I will. Least we'll all be rooting for the same person this year!" I say, checking the time. Jojo's looking a little tired; it's late and her Bliss-Pod's at home, too large to fit into the sub. "Tabs, I'll need to start thinking about heading back soon."

"Aw, stay longer, Leyla. And at least let Jojo stay over if you're not going to. You'll be back around here tomorrow anyway. There's a—"

"Leyla Fairoza McQueen!" Elvis says.

We all look at one another. Silence. I shake my head, frowning.

Theo's mouth falls open. He turns to the screen. "Rewind. Stop. Play."

Elvis grins as he plays out the now much-hyped redraw for the last, coveted place. "And last of all, folks—*it's now or never*—entrant number one hundred is . . . Leyla Fairoza McQueen!"

The silence in the room continues for another three seconds.

And then we scream. It can't be! We jump up and down. And shout. I feel hot. The twins' pale faces are flushed with color. I can't believe it. I can't think clearly.

It was my first ever entry as I only turned sixteen a few months ago. Nobody *ever* really expects to win a place!

Elvis is reading out instructions to the chosen contenders, but I'll have to rewatch it later. My Bracelet flashes: congrats from an ecstatic Camilla, and then a message from the Marathon Committee. I must register with them at Westminster in the morning. They'll need to carry out further health and vehicle checks, in order to complete the full registration.

Contenders always talk about this moment, and it's true—it's so utterly surreal. The mere two days between the draw and the race itself is meant to add to the thrill, but I can't even think straight! With the odds against getting picked, many entrants hardly practice once they've entered. Others have a whole timetable for training, though—even enlisting professional help. Thank goodness for my weekly sprints. But still, we're talking a whole *obstacle* course. . . .

Oh my God, I'll finally be able to pay some bills and come up to date with my installments toward the Explorers Fund!

"Tabs," I whisper. "Erm, your car. Is it all right to—"

Tabby rolls her eyes. "Don't be daft! I'd be honored if you drove it in the marathon! Good job you've had some practice in it, you need something you're really familiar with."

"Thank you so much. Oh my God . . ."

We all scream and jump up and down again. My Bracelet won't stop flashing now—congratulatory messages from acquaintances and distant family members in Tokyo, Pretoria, Berlin, Kabul, and New York.

Grandpa's left a very worried message, his voice small. I move to a quieter corner and message him back. "*Please* try and not worry, Gramps. I *know* it will be hard, and that it's a challenging and difficult course. But there'll be tons of safety measures in place, and I'll be all right. Speak to you soon. Please stop worrying!"

Tabby beckons me over, her eyes and mouth wide. "Don't forget, the prizes are mega! I know it's a tough one—the *toughest*, but if you could somehow rank in the top five, you'd nab yourself a brilliant prize, Leyla! They're always—" She stops as the screen catches her eye, and she lights up. Theo and I both turn to see and groan.

It's Finlay Scott, the last London Marathon champion, drinking champagne, surrounded by adoring fans. He congratulates the contenders and wishes them well.

"Remember," he says, tipping his glass. "Whatever your heart desires . . ."

I catch my breath. Suddenly every sound around me is drowned out and heat spreads from my chest to my face. Just like that, there's a shifting of the tides.

I turn to the twins, breathless. "He's talking about the Ultimate Prize. . . . Don't you see? I have to *win* the marathon. So I can ask for Papa's freedom."

CHAPTER FOUR

I navigate the submersible through the blue-green waters around Westminster. The midday current is calm with normal visibility, despite the increase in traffic today. Jojo stayed at the twins' last night because we ended up chatting way past her bedtime.

My Bracelet flashes now, and Tabby's face pops up. I transfer her to the dashboard so I can see her as I steer toward Lambeth and the pub.

"Any nerves?" she asks. "We still can't *believe* you'll be taking part! Mum's so worried. It's both terrifying and so flipping exciting. It's unreal!"

I nod away at her words. "Same. It still hasn't sunk in! I awoke thinking it might've been a dream, until I checked my inbox; it's full of interview requests from various media and potential sponsors and such."

"Milk them for every penny! Are you done with the Marathon Committee?"

"Yes, just completed my tests and registration with them, and on my way to the pub now. Ugh, it was so busy out here this morning. Contenders, organizers, and media all cluttered the water everywhere you turned."

"Ha!" Tabby chuckles. "Oh, did you notice news stations aren't as hyper as they usually are? I mean, normally on the day after the marathon draw the media's focused solely on the race and contestants. But they're *obsessed* with the Anthropoid entering this year's draw, ugh."

35

"I know! I saw Channel Three hysterically debating it nonstop. They were asking if we're doing enough to protect ourselves. . . ." My voice trails off. "Tabs, do me a favor, please? I think a past champion asked for the freedom of a loved one, but I can't be certain. I'm sure I read about it somewhere, though. See if you can find out?"

"Oh, I can do that right now!" Tabby says and disappears.

It's entirely up to the champion. They can either accept first prize—for the past decade it's been a home or submarine, both always seriously luxurious and impressive—or they can ask the PM for a personal request: the Ultimate Prize.

The water is calm and clear as I pass through Westminster. Papa could be in any one of these buildings. So close and yet so far. Why won't they just tell me exactly where in the capital they're holding him?

I pass over the regular ginormous wreckage on the seabed here. The looming frame of an ancient passenger jet wreaked havoc drifting through the area after an earthquake a few years ago, before becoming stuck in an ancient town square. Tiny fish dart in and out of its rust-and-seaweed shell now like shooting arrows.

Wireless Man's dreary tones interrupt the mid-twenty-first-century crooning great The.Real.L.Cohen, as he informs us of a vehicle collision that has luckily ended in no fatalities.

Traffic accidents used to be the number one cause of death until they stopped designing vehicles with positive buoyancy. In the early days, anytime you got into trouble, your vessel climbed the water and you surfaced. Not only did the crafts usually climb too fast too soon, but safety was the last thing the troubled driver met up there.

The ominous voice goes on to remind us of the perils lurking in the depths. Like I need reminding. I drive on.

A huge shadow looms ahead as the giant concrete body of a tower block comes into view. A skin of algae wraps around its exterior, and random flickering scales from a shoal of cod illuminate the windowless black spaces that stare back through the water like soulless eyes. I shudder. Only the faintest trickle of natural sunlight penetrates these depths, and the interiors of old London are cloaked in darkness. Good job we have all the exterior lighting, which has now been intensified by the preparations for the marathon. Neon banners announcing the event flash on every structure and street corner.

Tomorrow, London will be crowded with dignitaries from all over Great Britain. Obstacles have to be in place and running smoothly, and cameras are dotted everywhere. The challenges are fierce and relentless. A single moment of distraction will cost the contestants dearly. *God help me.*

I cruise down a coral-covered former high street. Anemones cling to the slimy surface of a long-gone department store, and seaweed hangs from its windowsills. I put on a mellow soundtrack and continue toward the pub.

The streets below are truly antique. The Old World's presence is vital to our existence, the chief historian always insists. The ancient sights are especially beneficial to those suffering the seasickness. They are our only link to the past—to who we were.

But maintaining Old London is proving increasingly difficult.

I dive low, hovering in a residential street. Tiny terraced cottages line the road, preserved in its crumbling state. I blink, staring. Are any of the children that might have lived and played here still living, breathing, somewhere?

The hazy shapes of several crafts charging past jolt me out of my thoughts as they all speed on far beyond the legal limit. I flinch and instinctively slow down.

Blackwatch vessels. I hold my breath.

The Blackwatch are the only people to regard themselves above traffic laws. Above *all* laws in fact. The all-knowing, all-powerful force is the pinnacle of the nation's defense and security measures. Guarding the PM is just one of their duties; the rest are shrouded in secrecy.

Always remember to avoid any and all contact with the Blackwatch, Pickle, Papa always said, his voice heavy and his gaze far away. *Never attract their attention.*

I promise, Papa. I only breathe again once the menacing subs have passed. I straighten in my seat and hurtle through the green-blue currents toward the pub.

The soothingly familiar environment of the Moon Under Water relaxes me instantly.

It's the first time I've visited the Victorian-styled pub since Papa's arrest. We always popped in for Sunday brunch and sat by the warmth of one of its lush fireplaces, sipping our hot drinks. We played guess-the-song as Papa's Bracelet played intros. The ache is immense now.

Several locals stop to congratulate me on my marathon selection and wish me luck as I tuck into hot twisted churros. Many pub goers are more subdued than usual. Though the anniversary always leaves everyone feeling their lowest, the incident with the Anthropoid almost infiltrating the marathon is also at the forefront of their minds now, and *Anthropoid* can frequently be heard whispered around the room.

Commentary from the footage on screens echoes around the space. There are repeated mentions of "Operation Ark" and "the Resurrection Council." Low boos sound in the room as images of the asteroid approaching Earth flash on the screens. They still have several years before it hits, the prime minister at the time insists. Human beings will survive, no matter *how* much sea levels rise. The best scientists around the world are planning the most suitable course of action and preservation, the PM assures Old Worlders.

My gaze wanders around the room. The stuffed bull's head above the mantelpiece stares out defiantly over the large, well-lit space. Not *everyone's* focusing on the replays of the disaster. A boisterous local construction team share sea monster sightings as they play darts. A group of off-duty train drivers in the nearby booth discuss ancient transport over a pint. "I'm telling you," a woman says, "Old World trains were spotless, and everyone chatted, knew one another. It was safe as houses. And they never broke down—not once. Zero delays!"

Loud voices carry over from a group of teens, all Keep Great Britain Tidy volunteers, sitting a few booths down. A teenage girl with a map of the Old World tattooed on her head *really* doesn't like the latest boy band; she's "old school and proud," she tells the rest, only listening to music from the '60s–'80s.

On-screen, footage now switches to computerized graphics. I tense. The asteroid hits Earth. It's as good as the end of the world. Billions die instantly. Continental shifts occur. All the water previously held in deep subterranean reservoirs is released at an alarming rate. Soon the entire planet is submerged. Only 10 percent of Britons survive the disaster.

It's always very difficult to watch, no matter how many times you see it.

In the corner of the room, children listen, enthralled, as adults read them tales of magical outdoor adventures the Old World kids got up to. Elsewhere, there's a kerfuffle and a disgruntled voice rises. I whirl to look as security moves in on a booth and shuffles an inebriated man away.

A passing woman shakes her head at the drunken man's antics. "No manners anymore . . . Not like the good Old World days when they used to—"

An ominous sound, like a very loud and long foghorn, resonates around the pub. It repeats three times. The room hushes. A dart falls short of the board, hitting the floor.

I stand along with everyone else. All around Great Britain, everyone will be observing the three minutes of silence in honor of the billions of people who didn't survive the global disaster. I watch the screens, the horrific pictures. Utter destruction that led to the catastrophic loss of human, animal, and plant life around the world.

Leaving an entirely different planet in its wake.

The silence ends with a repeat of the horn. There's a shot of Prime Ministerial Sub One as it hovers beside the Memorial Tree at Queen Mary's Rose Gardens in Regent's Park.

King George VIII was the last royal to broadcast on the anniversary. Since his death, the royal family has become much quieter, issuing a commemorative statement instead.

The Prime Minister, Edmund Gladstone, his face heavy and shadows under his warm green eyes, addresses the nation. "The past *must* be remembered," he expounds. "It must be kept alive. The past is the only torch guiding us forward out of this darkness. This *hell*." His expression darkens. "You will have heard by now of the terrorist attack last week in the Faroe Islands. A particularly brutal onslaught that cost many lives. I won't stand idly by and watch as our species dies out. I swore to protect you all, and by God I'm going to." He looks distraught.

The official to the PM's left shifts in his seat. His always stern expression hardens further. I shudder. Captain Sebastian, the principal private secretary to the prime minister—or his right-hand man—always appears as if there's no escaping his scrutinizing gaze. He reminds me of the cunning seadevil—an anglerfish I once saw on *Today's Terrors of the Deep.*

The PM's face hardens. "This—this amphibian alien *must* be eradicated. Their creation remains one of the biggest mistakes in preparation for the floods. How shortsighted and irresponsible for the Old World scientists to expect two hundred unnaturally created beings to actually *aid* us post-disaster. Thirty-five. *Thirty-five* scientists and technicians lost their lives that day, brutally mutilated, tortured, and murdered, when those monsters freed themselves and escaped the laboratories. And we have been paying for their existence ever since. Far too many of us have lived through the same devastating loss at the hands of the Anthropoids. . . ."

The screen switches to footage of the Memorial Fountain in Kensington Gardens. The inscription on the fountain's plaque is distinct:

In memory of Eva and Winston Gladstone, beloved sister and darling nephew, sleep peacefully, Edmund Gladstone 2087. They suffered considerably. Anthropoids never attack without causing maximum pain.

The screen returns to the PM and his cabinet. The shifty Captain Sebastian glowers as he traces the lengthy scar running across his left cheek. An encounter with Anthropoids, some say.

Prime Minister Gladstone's voice drops low and flat. "Not a day goes by where I don't think of Eva, my sister. And my dear nephew."

Everyone listens to the PM in silence, nodding away and dabbing their eyes. Like so many, Edmund Gladstone has suffered personal loss at the hands of the Anthropoids.

The PM's expression shifts to a defiant one. "We were not born on this earth in order to slink away in its bladder like bottom feeders."

Pub goers clap heartily; many punch the air. The official to the PM's right, Lord Maxwell, Great Britain's impeccably dressed chief historian, straightens, proud. I imagine he must have celebrated his daughter Camilla's entry into the marathon with so much pomp and ceremony. My Bracelet flashes; it's Tabby again. As her face materializes above my wrist, I gesture for her to stay silent until I'm in an empty corner of the pub.

"You were right, Leyla!" She nods energetically while also trying to peek around me to see what's going on at the pub. "The '87 Birmingham Champion requested the freedom of her cousin and the prime minister granted it instantly!"

Yesss. "If I can just win the Ultimate Prize, Tabs, it'd solve *everything.* With a pardon, Papa would be out straightaway. No trial, no more waiting and not knowing. He'd be free!"

"If anyone can do it, it's you, Leyla. Wait, is that the Taylors?" Tabby's brow furrows.

I turn to catch the distinctive bright red hair of the Taylors—family friends—in the background behind me. It's Mrs. Taylor and little Rebecca Taylor, whose brother Jack died in the '97 London Marathon.

"Oh, God . . ." Tabby lowers her voice. "Just don't let your guard down during the race."

Jack Taylor's vehicle malfunctioned after he crashed into a building during the marathon two years ago. All around Great Britain, people watched as the flame-haired boy's submersible spun out of control, cracking and crushing under the pressure before sinking out of sight. It took several days to locate all the wreckage. Jack's body was never recovered, most likely dragged away by some predator. Rebecca couldn't accept her brother's absence, and Jack's been her imaginary friend ever since.

I do what I can to reassure Tabby I'll stay alert throughout and won't take any risks.

It's impossible to avoid the risks, though.

And yet I can't fail tomorrow.

I just *can't*.

CHAPTER FIVE

The observatory stands in the heart of Berkeley Square—a long white structure elevated several meters off the seabed. Inside the stately building's banquet hall, crystal chandeliers dazzle against the rich burgundy of the room, and paintings of past Britons adorn the walls. The London Marathon contestants sit at round tables for the traditional breakfast, while dignitaries sit at the front on two long tables running the length of the entire room.

I dip my head and my hair shields me from a nearby remote camera. Scores of the smooth, spinning eyes hover in every space around the hall, darting between the contestants. All around Great Britain, every moment of today is being beamed live into homes, public buildings, hotels, pubs—everyone's watching.

My plate remains untouched. I shove it to one side. In its place I fold and crease one of the Order of the Day documents into a new origami shape.

I yawn. No matter what I tried last night, I couldn't sleep. In the end I gave up trying and got up, and after praying and reading the Qur'an, I went over the rules. The same thought played on a loop throughout the night: *I have to win, I have to win, I have to win.* I'm *this* close to helping Papa. Finally within reach of seeing him again.

Camilla Maxwell, sitting beside me, offers me a weak smile that looks more like a grimace. As Tabs predicted, Camilla's entry into the race has added glamour to the event. The morning news was full with debate over what the chief historian's only child, his "pampered princess," might wear and how she'll cope. I follow her gaze to her father, Lord Maxwell.

Dressed impeccably as always, the chief historian's dark coat is decorated with a timepiece on the breast pocket. A bow tie hugs his long neck and a top hat adorns his head. His brow creases as his gaze moves from Camilla to me.

Camilla used to regularly hang out with the twins and me. Before Theo and Tabby had their own Holozone installed, we'd visit Clio House, the massive historical-reenactment hall. Camilla's dad's a patron there, and she was nearly always around, eager to discuss the scripting with anyone who shared her passion for writing. Since Papa's arrest, it's clear her dad doesn't want her to have anything to do with me. He narrows his eyes as he watches us now. Stuff him.

Camilla looks pale. I lean over and squeeze her arm. "Written anything lately?" I whisper.

"A short story about a little girl whose submersible malfunctions and falls down a deep trench; she soon realizes the 'trench' is actually the mouth of a monster." Her shoulders droop. "But it was declined. They're dead serious about the 'retellings only' bit."

"Ooh, monsters. Wait, you submitted an original . . . ?"

She nods slowly, chewing on her lip.

Warmth spreads in my chest. I've no idea why. I mean, it's sad news—her manuscript was rejected. But she wants to tell her own unique story. And now I love her. And pity her a little, because this means at some point she'll be receiving an origami gift from me.

I lean over again. "Queen."

A smile tugs at the corners of her mouth.

Finlay Scott, the last London Marathon champion, makes his way to the podium. Amid loud cheering and admiring glances from the contestants, he elaborates on how his life changed exponentially when he won the marathon last year. He pats his golden quiff—combed to perfection—and pauses for reaction. Cameras and microphones hover in the space around him. Tabs practically worships him and has a poster of him beside her bed, winking away and stroking his hair as he looks down at her. *Ugh.*

I stare at him now. The plonker could have asked for *anything.*

Keys to the nation with the freedom to travel anywhere in Great Britain and special access to the forbidden Old World heritage sights are just some of the things past champions have requested. But Finlay Scott declined a spacious and incredibly sturdy home to request superior citizen status as his Ultimate Prize. He's now treated as a VIP at all times, sitting among the dignitaries at every national event.

Up next is Prime Minister Gladstone. His gentle face brightens now, his green eyes shining as he mentions a special announcement.

"My fellow Britons, it brings me great pleasure in announcing there will be a referendum on the renaming of the country and capital city," he declares. "Returning to the rightful former titles of Britannia and Londinium will open up a direct verbal link to the past. It will remind us all of our heritage, and fortify a sense of never giving up on who we once were."

The room breaks out into cheers and enthusiastic clapping.

I shift around in my seat. Will renaming cities and countries reduce the seasickness numbers? Will it help us against the Anthropoids? The referendum doesn't make any sense at all. Another one of the chief historian's odd ideas, no doubt. As if on cue, Lord Maxwell dabs his eyes, nodding energetically.

All too soon, the PM instructs the contestants to say their goodbyes to the family and friends in the drawing room adjacent to the hall. "No past, no future," says Prime Minister Gladstone, and everyone echoes his personal motto.

I make my way across the room, playing with Mama's antique kara wrapped around my arm. The silver cuff had been one of her favorite pieces of jewelry. Today feels like the right day to wear it. I take a deep breath as all competing contestants enter the drawing room.

A sea of faces and infinite voices meet us. Family, friends, trainers, sponsors—everybody cheers, claps, and rushes to greet us, all speaking at once. Cameras and Bracelets capture the moment, and everywhere you turn last-minute advice is being doled out.

Jojo jumps out of Tabby's arms and darts into mine soon as she spots me. Tabs points a red nail at me, listing off everything I must and mustn't do. Theo winks surreptitiously.

I grin. "I've no idea what I'd do without you two. I'm so lucky to have you, and I love you both tons!"

Tabby hugs me before she's distracted elsewhere. I place the paper model I was making into Theo's palm.

His eyes widen as he stares at the Jedi. "Bloody brilliant. Ei-Shin Kenobi?"

"Yes. Theo, thank you for everything, especially since Papa's arrest. Honestly."

His eyes light up and he wraps me in a comforting embrace. "Your papa will be home one day; I can feel it. It's not the end if you don't win today, okay? We'll think of something else, another way to help him, promise. Remember, this isn't a sprint. Watch your back out there, Leyla." He turns his head and groans. "Neptune help us, look who's walked in."

Finlay Scott has graced the drawing room with an appearance, taking pictures with the contestants and their families. Tabs hurries over to us, her eyes sparkling and narrowed in contemplation. "He's even more lush in person. Oh how I want to play with him." She moves toward him.

Theo turns to me, his voice low. "I swear this isn't envy talking, but he's such a tosser. I don't get how everyone worships him. Have they gone bonkers? Who wears a fake military uniform covered in medals and a cape?"

"I think he's a bit of a dick, really." I grimace. "I heard he charges fans to stroke his quiff, but if he thinks you're 'hot enough,' he lets you do it for free. It's awful, I know, but whenever I see him I really want to hurt him a little bit. There's just something about him, you know?"

"I think that's what he brings out in Tabs as well," he whispers. "Only she has very specific punishments in mind—and they always include a dungeon. Like, what the hell." Color floods his face, and he shakes his head. We both grin, and I move on around the room.

A tall, willowy girl bursts into tears in her parents' arms, the nerves proving too much.

Newsbots hover around a woman in a silver jumpsuit as her fitness team stands by, checking her vitals. She jogs on the spot at an alarming speed before offering the cameras a dazzling smile and wink, and pointing at her nametag: Sal. I gulp; hopefully her reflexes are a *lot* slower when she's driving, or I'll have my work cut out. She catches me watching and wrinkles her nose, whispering something to her team. They all stare at me, shaking their heads and muttering. I hear Papa's name and "seasickness."

I raise my eyebrows and move away, scanning the room for Grandpa. His friend's son has extended his stay, and we've still not met up since. My heart lifts when I spot him sitting in a quieter corner on the far side; his face is heavy as he embraces me.

"Queenie, it's okay if you get wet feet and withdraw. You know that, don't you? All those obstacles . . . It really doesn't bear thinking about. The contestants will do *anything* to win the Ultimate Prize. I wish you'd told me you had entered for this madness."

"Sorry, Gramps. I didn't want to worry you; the chances of winning a place are tiny! And . . . I *want* to do it. More than ever. It could mean having Papa back. Please don't worry."

He sighs and presses a hand to his forehead. "If things don't work out the way you're hoping they will, you mustn't be downhearted, child. We're never giving up on your father, understood? Concentrate on the challenge ahead, keep your wits about you, and throughout the race you must put your own safety above winning, Queenie."

I wring my hands and nod. We embrace again. Holding Jojo close, I take a walk around the room.

Camilla Maxwell sits on one of the regal chairs, staring into the space and nodding in acknowledgment at her father's words as Lord Maxwell whispers in her ear.

Across the country, Britons will be trying to guess who'll succeed and fail, which distractions will prove most successful, who might try and cheat—all manner of bets are always placed.

What the— I stumble forward. It's the annoying silver-clad Sal who sneered at me. The fitness fanatic shoves me aside as she poses for the cameras.

"Hey!" I scowl. Jojo stiffens and growls.

The woman leans in, baring her teeth. "You're ruining my pictures. Now stay out of my way if you know what's good for you. And that goes for the marathon route, too."

"Huh? Not bloody likely. I'm free to stand wherever. And are you really threatening me already? That's not very nice, Sal. You must be feeling intimidated by me."

"You?" She twists her mouth into an ugly shape. "You're the daughter of a wicked, murdering wretch. You shouldn't have even been allowed to take part. How dare you?" She looks me up and down.

Wicked, murdering wretch? Don't people get bored with repeating the same cursed thing over and over, dammit? My fingers itch. If only I'd been allowed to bring my new brolly. Sodding security rules. This would've been a rather fab opportunity to test out the brolly's tase function.

The woman glares at Jojo and shakes her head. "And why is this beast allowed in here?"

"You say one more word to me, or so much as even *look* at my puppy again, and Jojo here will bite your rotten silver tongue right out of your rotten silver mouth. It makes her happy, and she's really good at it, too."

The woman screws her face up. Jojo growls again, and silver Sal backs away.

There's an announcement: All contestants are to leave the observatory in their racing cars and follow the convoy escorting them to the starting point at Regent's Park.

Everyone moves at once. The twins rush over, wishing me luck one last time. Tabs takes Jojo. I gulp. *Here we go.*

The journey to Regent's Park is somber. The legion of vehicles moves at a slow pace as everyone follows the official subs, which gives me time to think. Hopefully the prison guards know Hashem McQueen's daughter is taking part in the marathon and have allowed Papa to watch. He'll see I'm all right and it might comfort him. What might my parents say to me if they were here now?

Love you, Mama. Be at peace. Love you, Papa. So much. Wish me luck.

I focus on the route straight ahead of me.

We arrive at Regent's Park, where there'll be a short opening ceremony followed by a prompt start. I twist and turn in the cockpit. Illumination glimmers all around, as if some massive bioluminescent army from the deep has invaded London.

A bright orange vertical boundary encircles all observation areas, ensuring they remain clearly visible to contestants. Watching on screens at home is never going to be enough for some, and the spectators are out in force in vehicles of all kinds. Their subs hover above expansive rooftops or rest on specially made structures, all safely behind the vivid fencing.

Last-minute checks are being carried out, and everywhere I look, banners hang, bearing welcoming messages, sponsors, coats-of-arms, various Latin phrases. Security subs hover around the space. I count sixteen Eyeballs alone in the space of a few minutes, despite their varying guises as they bob around in the depths. The larger Newsbots are frenzied, darting in every direction. My pulse beats faster the more I see.

Contestants are ordered to gather in a huge circle, giving us a clear view of the opening ceremony in its center. We're asked to perform a last-minute systems check.

Tabby's single-seated craft is compact, with the cockpit sitting in the middle at the top of the twin-winged vehicle, and the robust exterior is a pearly scarlet. Bright identifying stickers have been attached to our vessels. I'm number one hundred. Everything looks shipshape, and all systems are running perfectly. As I tie my hair back, movement in the depths captures my eye.

Thanks to Theo's fascination with technology, I recognize the large "Pike" swimming beneath us. They're actually biomechanical contraptions that can open fire from a league away. You're safer behind them where they can't "see" you. Last year a small fishing craft accidentally caught several during an illegal trawling operation. None of the fishermen were identifiable afterward. The Pike are just one of many heightened security measures today, as Anthropoids always attempt an attack on marathon day. Several arrests have already been made throughout the city.

Despite my nerves, the opening ceremony is spellbinding.

A fountain appears in the water as if out of nowhere. You'd never guess it was a hologram! Vibrant ribbons pour from its mouth, swaying to piano sounds. As the music soars, more ribbons flow out of the top, like a rainbow flame. My mouth curves into a wide smile, and I turn the volume up in the sub.

Next, violins and harps play as compact submersibles, visible only as multicolored light specks, perform a synchronized swim. The captivating lights twinkle as if bioluminescent Noctiluca are performing a precise dance in the center.

Circular bots enter the arena to the sound of flutes. They emit spurts of every color throughout the water. The assorted shades intermingle and change into new colors and patterns like a drifting, mingling paint palette. The accompanying music is soft and bewitching.

At last, the area clears. There's a drumroll. The sleek submersibles of the country's leading hydrobotics display team, the Red Arrows, shoot by overhead, leaving lengthy trails of red, white, and blue in the water. *Oh crikey.* I shift in my seat. Any second now. *Wait for it. . . .*

Trumpets sound, and all manner of lights flash everywhere. Once all contestants are ready, they'll sound again to indicate the start of the race.

A clearing of the throat, and then the familiar voice takes over the waves. Elvis.

"And hello there, you awesome Britons, and of course our viewers around the world. Welcome to the 2099 London Submersible Marathon! I'm Elvis, your host for today's event. It's an honor to be asked back again. What can I say, *thank you very much.* Last chance to put those kettles on, nip to that loo, and grab yourself some grub, because it is all about to kick off. All right!" Elvis laughs his deep laugh as he welcomes viewers. As well as commentating, he'll inform us of any emergencies and potential rule changes.

I edge to the starting line with caution. I glance into the cockpit of the surrounding subs. Big mistake. The contestants eye one another nervously, menacingly. They jostle in the space, all eager to secure a pole starting position and shoot off the second they can. The charity subs will be at the back, behind the serious contenders. The starting line is indicated by a row of yellow lights that beam up through the waters so all contestants can spot them.

Several minor altercations are already taking place near the front as contestants aggressively guard their positions. I pinch my lips together; the start will be slow with a ton of stop-starts. Not my cup of tea. A sharp blue light flashes inside one of the cars.

"Oh my Gawd." Elvis tsk-tsks. "It's already getting wild out there, folks. And that there is today's first penalty! A twenty-second delay for number twenty-four for crossing the starting line early. And we now have an *ecstatic* office junior here at the BBC who predicted the first penalty would occur before the race had even begun. Courtney, you done good, girl!"

Behind the yellow beams of the starting line, the acute blue lasers of the marathon boundaries are just visible. The route winds around the city, going as far east as Tower Bridge before making its way back to Regent's Park.

This is it. I have to stay within the parameters, evade all distractions, conquer all obstacles, dodge any rogue drivers, and maintain a constant speed throughout—all the time ensuring I remain near the front.

I must come through for Papa. Finally I can do something concrete about his situation. There's nothing to fear. I can do this. I was born to race. *I'm ready.*

I rotate my shoulders, ignoring the tight sensation in my stomach. I offer a prayer as I squeeze my palms open and closed to steady my trembling hands. *Relax.*

The observing groups, who'd all been flashing their lights and spinning around in their submersibles with excitement, now remain still. The trumpeting sound repeats, and the yellow beams flash. Elvis's velvety tones barely contain his excitement.

"Aaaaaaaaaand they're off!"

CHAPTER SIX

It's pandemonium.

I suck in my breath as the competing submersibles all move at once. *Damn.* We vie for position in a frenzied rush that leaves a million bubbles in its wake. The rest shove, squeeze, and force their way forward through the flashing yellow beams of the starting line.

A few collide in the initial scrum, bouncing off each other and spinning wildly. A couple become entangled in each other's wings and roll together off the race path, crashing through the sharp blue boundary lines, incurring penalties. Some manage to move forward, frantically blocking potential overtakers at the first bend. The remaining racers are busy dodging those insistent on making their first moves at any cost.

I crane my neck in every direction and edge forward, groaning at the influx of vehicles all struggling at once for space and direction. Sod all the churning; it's affecting local visibility. The water above is clearer. The observing crowds and ton of distractions are all lower down, so there's a time limit on the higher depths. But I'm not joining the barmy crush in front of me now. I thrust upward.

"What do you reckon, folks? I'm thinking some of these high-risers are sure gonna incur that penalty!" The commentator's voice fills the space. "Keep sending in those thoughts now, y'all."

I gradually rise above the battle. *Phew.* With only a handful of vehicles around at this level, visibility is vastly improved, the current calmer. All right, then. *Bismillah.*

I hurtle through the yellow beams. The blue of the boundary parameters farther down is now weak, only just visible through the blue-green waters. Throwing a glance at the Heads-Up Display, I set the timer and press on.

A huge sub dives ahead of me. The ginormous streamlined vehicle, resembling a colossal eel, causes rolling waves that rock my craft. I push the throttle forward and speed through the surge it leaves behind, zooming on as fast as the vessel allows. This is my best chance of making some distance before I run out of time as well and have to join the others.

All I can spot below is the lighting. Everything else is a shadowy blur as the city whooshes past beneath me. The sub tears through the water. Loud bleeping: the timer! I tilt the craft's nose at a forty-five-degree angle and continue forward. Can I make the depth limit in time without having to head into a straight dive? Five, four, three—*yes*. The HUD confirms I'm now within the required depths.

I frown, taking the scene in. The boundaries might be clearer down here, but everything else is chaotic. *Stay calm.*

Easier said than done. I'm at Euston Square. At street level, the structures and distractions are seriously jarring. My sub rocks in the choppier current. Lights blink in my face. Newsbots dart through the chaos, spinning away as they battle for the best footage, rising and diving to wherever the action takes them.

An observation post built on a specially made tower flashes all manner of lights as spectating submersibles greet passing contestants. I nod as I scan the route; rising higher paid off. Though it's far busier down here, not many racing cars are this far along yet. I speed up and make some headway, only to slow down upon taking my first corner; the circuit ahead is busy with a vehicle-rescue team. All too soon other contestants catch up, forcing the vessels into a crawl. The emergency team leaves and I peer into the water to determine why we're still barely moving. *Oh great.* The novelty subs also caught up with everyone—and I'm stuck right behind them.

The group, often sponsored by companies and wealthy patrons, moves together, showing no intention of overtaking one another. The driver of the car in front—a charity entry designed like a '50s hippie camper sub, decorated in bright flowers and illuminated PEACE and LOVE signs—is busy displaying hydrobotics all over the place, trying to garner as much publicity as possible. The observers love it.

I jostle and maneuver forward through the colorful throng. Several drivers aren't having it and try to block me. I focus and push on until at last I've squeezed past the bulk of the traffic. Enough dilly-dallying.

I dart past a red dragon-shaped sub, swerving sharply so as not to hit a bulky polka-dotted vehicle by its side. I dive beneath it. A plaice swims out of the aperture of a rust- and moss-ridden pillar-box, straight past me and into the chaos of the route. *Stay focused.* I press on.

Brilliant—the novelty subs are gone. I rise and shoot forward. A quick glance over my shoulder and I see another craft has also come through, hot on my tail.

Full throttle, I charge through the water. My mouth curves into a smile. This is more like it. After all the frustration, the unhindered speed is exhilarating.

"Well, dip me in the ocean and hang me out to dry, folks, number one hundred sure can fly. Just look at that sub tearing through the route. *It's now or never...*" Elvis breaks into song, and then my details are relayed for viewers. He reads out messages of support and adulation that are coming in for all the contestants, including "Wow, you go, Leyla!"

The route is narrow, the traffic heavy in places. I focus, forcing a course for myself at each turn, my frustration with the initial delay lessening as I pass the others. Music plays in my head as the misty shadows of buildings whoosh by. Nothing else matters. Onward, full speed ahead through clearer waters.

Around a tight corner now and I'm soon at Bloomsbury. I speed above the ancient British Museum, around another corner, and jolt. Swerving sharply, I cry out, before dipping to avoid a headlong crash with another car. *Blimey!*

My vehicle spins. I grit my teeth and focus on controlling the wings to counter the force. At last the craft is stabilized. I blow my cheeks out and peer at the other sub.

It's a regal-looking car, an ornate cream affair resembling a Victorian carriage. It hovers in the water, not going anywhere.

Camilla Maxwell sits still inside her stately submersible. I squint; why isn't she racing? Why is she hovering here? And right on the corner, too. Someone will be hurt if she doesn't move! I flash my lights. *Well, go on then, quick as you can.* The chief historian's daughter shakes her head. I peer closer, taking in her expression. *Oh.*

When the fear takes over, it paralyzes you. I know this feeling.

Camilla's moment of dread could lead to something terrible if she doesn't move out of the way, though. I check the time, stamping my feet. Sod it—there's only one thing to do. I turn to face the carriage-like craft from the side and tuck the wings away. *Look lively.*

I charge forward and ram the horrified girl's car.

"You have to move, and make it dead quick. I need to get going!"

I hit the decorative sub again and Camilla reacts, throwing her hands up. She turns her ornate sub around. A Newsbot is ecstatic, darting around as it catches it all.

"All right," Elvis says. "There's no giving up around number one hundred—Miss McQueen's having none of that. Thanks to her swift actions there, number ninety-four seems to have overcome her wet feet and is back in the race. The daughter of our esteemed chief historian, y'all."

I race on, shooting past Camilla. Hopefully she'll be all right for the rest of the race. Damn the fear to hell. I know that cursed dread so well.

Focus. I speed through Holborn's wide streets and above empty squares.

Better to risk further menaces down here than to rise again. I narrow my eyes at the commotion ahead as I pass a group of subs. A rescue mission is taking place. Emergency teams are at the scene, the Newsbots buzzing around in the flashing lights. A hefty breakdown submersible pulls the impaired vehicle along. It's the large, eel-like sub that nose-dived into the race right at the start. The devastated driver sits weeping inside.

"And that's the third of the many planned disruptions, folks, and as you know, a favorite staple of the race—as number eighteen just found out. And number seventy-one is now struggling at the back. Watch out for those system flares, y'all, they'll stall ya!"

Lights flash to my left. The congregation of residents from Chancery Lane observes from the roof of their lengthy apartment block, the bright barriers glimmering all around them.

Ahead, two submersibles block each other's progress. The translucent Underground tunnel beneath them stands several meters off the floor. I suck in my breath and dive below it. Soaring back up, I race over the dome of the legendary Old Bailey.

A silver submersible beside me flashes its lights. Inside is the irritating Sal, indicating I drop behind. *Nice try.* I continue on. The vessel comes threateningly near; any closer and I'll *have* to fall behind, simply to avoid contact. I hold my position, though, as we both race on and give no indication of letting up. A Newsbot loves it. The tiny 360-degree eye on top of the sphere whirls and spins away, a red light on its body flashing as it captures our every move. Just when I'm considering giving in so I can avoid a mishap, two more Newsbots drift close to capture the action and Sal immediately checks herself. After offering a menacing stare and offensive gesture she swiftly moves away, the news stations on her tail.

Residents of homes along the route are pressed to their windows in the hopes of seeing some of the action. Colorful lights flash inside the rooms, and figures move around the spaces—marathon parties. I rise higher.

"There goes the devilishly scarlet number one hundred. What do you reckon, folks, will the glossy red prove its driver her *good luck charm*?" Elvis sings, then chuckles. "Send in those thoughts, now!"

Other cars are visible here and there, each contestant battling the route. The Bank of England, a ruin of crumbling stone walls and columns, whooshes past beneath.

The route winds through Whitechapel. Playing *Ripper's Revels* in the Holozone with the twins on Christmas Day seems like ages ago.

"And that's another two contestants out of the race, numbers three and forty-four. Don't underestimate those challenges, y'all! Well, folks, we're being inundated with special mentions and requests to hear me sing." Elvis sounds ecstatic. "But it's the London Marathon, people—priorities! Oh, okay, perhaps a *very* quick line for all you fine folk out there, but then that's it, y'all." The commentator clears his throat to offer a short chorus, sighing afterward. "And that was straight from my heart to yours, know what I'm saying?"

I can't help but grin; he's totally barmy and utterly ace.

The water is murkier now. I race through as fast as I dare, and traffic decreases as I pass car after car.

Tower Bridge—finally. I allow myself a tiny sense of relief. I've made it this far, and from here on the route heads back west again.

I check the HUD as I begin crossing the length of the bridge. Within seconds a huge pressure materializes behind me, startling me. *What the hell?* It pushes me in all directions, trying to force me out of the boundary lines. A car in front swerves all over the place until the driver loses control, spinning into the boundaries.

It's some kind of wave simulator. I've felt a similar force before, at Brighton Pier. The beach resort has a wave machine, generating waves in all directions, allowing the fake sea to appear more realistic.

The waves on the bridge lash at the screen, making it almost impossible to see. I have to stay in control. The onboard computer will come through for me. Halfway along the bridge now. Bots appear on both sides, firing the dreaded flares. I focus on keeping my balance as I dodge the challenges. Careening off course is costly. *Steady.* Another car hits the boundaries. *Almost there.* The waves are strong. The craft lurches with the force. My neck aches. At last, I reach the other side.

"All riiight. And in record time!" Elvis's voice is full of admiration. He reads messages of support coming in, including "I want that raven-haired rocket's number!" The commentator breaks off to focus on an altercation between several cars that have crashed out of the barriers near the back.

At London Bridge, contenders whiz by way too close to each other, really taking risks now. A pearly-bronze car, designed to resemble some kind of wildcat and complete with raised paws, veers perilously close to me to avoid a conger eel caught in its path. I cry out, swerving to avoid it, when out of nowhere, a system flare hits me full on. I freeze.

How can anything be *so* red? The color floods the car as it holds the vehicle in its grip. I twist in the seat, blinking rapidly, before taking a deep breath and gathering my thoughts.

I shouldn't panic. It's only a flare and it'll soon wear off. While it's active, though, it will render the onboard equipment almost useless. I'm basically stuck here until its effects fade, and the most I can do is hover. I groan, hitting the seat. Several cars race by.

After what seems like an age, the effects of the flare clear. I check the controls to confirm: All systems are back online. I thrust the sub forward and continue on to London Bridge before anything else slows me down. *Finally.* I speed through the route, careening past faint rail tracks before rising another fifty feet and heading toward Covent Garden. Steering through a group of contestants, I zoom over Somerset House and the rustic cages of ancient transport settled in its square below.

Spectators flash their lights and spin their vehicles around, having a smashing time. Several queue by submarines that hover far above us where refreshments and sub-battery top-ups are available throughout the event. I hurtle through the route as fast as I dare, speeding over the enormous pile of debris and ruin lying opposite the old Royal Opera House. One of its algae-covered columns buckled recently, the familiar fluorescent warning beams flashing away.

A sub on my tail is getting too close. *Ugh.* It's the annoying Sal in her silver vessel again. And the vehicles directly ahead mean I can't yet move out of her way. She swerves alongside me, and this time she's far more determined to cause trouble. She tilts her craft's wing, and her vessel edges toward mine, forcing me closer and closer to the sharp blue lasers of the marathon boundaries. *Oh hell.* If I set them off, I'll incur the gravest penalty of the race, and at this stage I'd never recover time-wise. I try to call her bluff and move closer to her myself but only make matters worse. She's not budging. It's impossible to overtake the vessel in front; there's just not enough room now, and I could hit the boundaries trying. *Argh!* What to do?

A group of bots appears out of nowhere, firing at us.

I instinctively duck down in reverse until I'm out of firing range, then pause to check the situation. I managed to dodge them! As I peer up at Sal's sub, it takes a hit. Immediately a net snares the silver vehicle. They will let it go, eventually. But instead of waiting it out, Sal fires on the bots. A bright neon substance shoots from her car. As soon as it hits the contraptions, they're useless. One by one the bots release the net as they succumb to the liquid. *Uh-oh.*

Despite the inspections for any illegal modifications to racing cars, someone always tries getting away with something. Within seconds, security submersibles are at the scene, escorting her away—an instant disqualification. I pass by and Sal is *furious.* She beats her fists against the cockpit. The nearest spectators love it, flashing their lights with joy.

Elvis tsk-tsks. "You sure as hell won't succeed if you can't conquer that water-rage, y'all. No destroying the distractions, folks. *Don't be cruel. . . .*"

Leicester Square, with its array of vast domes providing entertainment and escape, proves largely obstacle-free. An army of tiny spirally bots is on the warpath, but there are many targets. I remember them from the last marathon and dip lower. The closer to the seabed you are, the less likely these particular bots are to follow you, preferring to remain in the chaotic heart of the race. I rise again, focusing straight ahead of me, my mouth pursed. I dodge and swerve my way through the old junction of Piccadilly Circus.

Westminster is cloaked in shadows caused by the naval submarines overhead. I speed around 10 Downing Street—the headquarters of the government—as passing above the sprawling dome is strictly forbidden, and zoom past the desolate but lit-up Houses of Parliament. As I approach Westminster Abbey I have to dodge several increasingly agitated contestants near the ancient church.

Flares and irritating mechanical traps swarm the area around Buckingham Palace. Camouflaged bots hide among the plant life and rusted metal of the former royal palace gates that twist in every direction, clinging to the stone-and-seaweed walls of the palace itself. I hold my nerve, evading the challenges and zooming over and onward.

Past the old moss-carpeted Harrods store in Knightsbridge now.

I zoom over the ancient Victoria and Albert Museum, pressing on until at last I enter Kensington Gardens.

After some shoving and scrambling with another contestant who tries and fails to intimidate me into letting him overtake me, I arrive at the Peter Pan statue. Ghostly holograms appear in the water. My mouth curves into a smile.

The children are having fun. Several are playing cricket, some hold hands in a circle as they sing, and others skip or sit smiling as they pick flowers. The children appear so happy and at home in the water. It's heartening. *Careful.* It's a cunningly placed diversion, meant for those easily distracted. Like me. I move on past the projections, over Hyde Park, and on to the once-triumphal structure of Marble Arch. My palms are getting sweaty, my pulse quickening.

Crowds watch on Oxford Street to my right. Teams of flatfish are visible in the lights of the observing vehicles as they forage among the boulders and stone.

"All riiight, people, and we arrive at the spot where Finlay Scott came into his own last year, refusing to be intimidated. Many contestants have made it this far, only to panic here. Who will shine, who will crumble? Time to see exactly what our contestants are made of. Oh, *the wonder of youuuuu*." He sings and laughs heartily.

I gulp greedily for air. I need to relax. The first few vehicles to make it this far are now seriously aggressive. I swerve as a circular golden-colored sub passes way too close to me, determined to get ahead at all cost. The route is narrower here than at any other point in the race. This is where I'd intended on breaking away. I jerk the sub left and right, but the contestants block one another's every attempt to outdistance the rest. The water above me is just as busy. I eye the traffic. Can I do it?

I flip over and dive low—very low. Moving forward, I peer through the dome to ensure enough distance between the seabed and myself. *Keep going.* Skimming the floor by a hairbreadth, I dart past the cars, before turning the vehicle right again. *Yes.* Running the thruster at full speed, I catapult the sub onward.

"What a maneuver from Miss McQueen!" Elvis exclaims. "Aaaand several more messages of support coming in for Leyla McQueen now, including 'We love you' and 'You go, raven rocket!' Well, the contestants are sure gonna need all the good vibes you can muster—things are really heating up out there now, folks!"

Baker Street. The end is so close now. From here on it's a straight race to the finishing line back at Regent's Park. I wipe my palms on my legs and take longer, deeper breaths. I can't make any mistakes.

Within seconds I pull ahead of the gold car that surpassed me earlier. At last I'm in the park, approaching the Memorial Tree that stands right in the center of the boundaries. The board in the distance has a huge zero lit up; nobody's passed the finishing line yet. . . .

Contestants are forbidden from passing over the symbolic Memorial Tree. I crane my neck to plan the best route around it and notice the car beside me. *Damn.* The number fifty-seven sub is plain at the front, with its rear resembling a Roman chariot. Two decorative wheels cling to its sides. It aims to approach the tree from the left. Fine, I'll pass it from the right. *Oh hell.* Several heavyweight bots lie in wait to the tree's right. I recognize their design and function from the last race. They trap you in unforgiving time-costly nets. Left it is, then.

As I race on, aiming for between the tree and the other car, number fifty-seven also speeds up, leaning in sharply now.

If it continues to tilt at the current angle, it will hit me.

"Well, folks, what's gonna happen? Is number fifty-seven—a Mr. Paul Martin—really willing to risk a potentially fatal collision? At that angle a hit would damage *their* chances more than number one hundred's. In fact it would be disastrous for number fifty-seven. Reckless! Exactly what are these two willing to do to win the London Submersible Marathon?"

I keep a constant watch out for the car racing on my left. I thrust forward with everything I have, startling a shoal of glimmering sardines that split around the vehicle. Hurtling through the weighty current, my gaze constantly switches between the path ahead and the car careening in my direction from the left. The chariot sub needs to fall back. Or alter their angle. There's no escape. The car speeding toward my own is guaranteeing a horrific crash. On the edge of my vision, somewhere to my right, I register movement in the distant water—a bulky fish, drawing near, I think—but thankfully Elvis's voice keeps me focused on my immediate danger.

His tones are heavy with disbelief. "This is suicide. He *must* know this? He needs to stop, or we're looking at another marathon death, folks!"

My mind races. We will collide, and he'll at the very least sustain terrible injuries. I'll suffer damage to the left wing and possibly tail, but I'm all right with that. I *must* win. The other driver has made his choice, and I have to do what needs doing. *Oh, Papa.*

In the last few moments, as the finishing line approaches, I yell and rise out of the way of the car racing toward me, seconds from certain impact.

My chest opens and several hundred million cubic miles of water pour in and crush and snap and drown the dream of Papa returning home tonight.

I feel nothing. Numb.

I turn slowly, expecting to see the chariot-styled sub charge forward and over the finishing line to victory.

Except it's not there.

I can't even *see* the other vessel. What happened? Where did the car go?

And then all becomes clear as my gaze shifts to movement on my right. Number fifty-seven was speeding at such a sharp angle that even my rising out of its way couldn't keep it on course. It was leaning too far right.

It's trapped in one of the time-costly nets fired by a sly bot. A bot I'd mistaken for a fish. Every thought crashes into my head, all at once, and my pulse races.

He's in a net. Nobody else has caught up yet.

And I'm free to move.

A cry bubbles up inside my throat and escapes my lips. *Relief.*

And the audacity to still hope.

My eyes prickling, and my face and neck flushed, I turn the vessel around until it's facing the finishing line.

And I race.

And the giant zero switches to a dazzling one.

CHAPTER SEVEN

The observatory buzzes in anticipation of the Ultimate Prize request. I gaze at the sea of captivated faces—family and friends of the contestants—all turned toward me as I sit on the stage with my fellow finalists. Gone are the tables of the marathon breakfast, and instead everyone is seated in rows in front of the stage.

The voices fall silent. Only the whirl of Newsbots as they spin away in the grand room, and the swish of microphones darting to hover in every conceivable space around me, can now be heard. Lights flash and cameras zoom in for their close-up. Everything is set to capture the moment.

I take a deep breath and stand. Unable to keep the smile off my face, I nod at the presenter—a woman dressed head to toe in mint green and looking like she's just stepped out of the ancient 1950s—to confirm I'm ready to make my request. A microphone hovers just above my head. I turn to Prime Minister Edmund Gladstone, who's seated to the right of the stage.

"I request the freedom of my father, Mr. Hashem McQueen, please, sir."

The crowd oohs and whispers; some boo—and there's a cry of "Murderer" from somewhere at the back—but many clap, too.

Everyone's attention instantly shifts from me to the prime minister. Sitting to his right is the shifty-eyed Captain Sebastian. His right-hand man leans in toward the PM with plenty to say, his poker-faced expression giving nothing away as he speaks.

The PM then also confers with Lord Maxwell on his left. The chief historian nods in concentration at whatever Captain Sebastian is saying.

I bounce on my toes. Will they release Papa *today*? It's quite possible! When the order comes from the very top, surely they wouldn't bother with too much paperwork?

Captain Sebastian suddenly turns his steely gaze in my direction. I gulp as he locks his cold, calculating stare on me. He narrows his eyes as if deep in thought. As ever, a finger traces the scar running across his left cheek. I swiftly fix my gaze on the prime minister.

The PM beckons Mariam Khan, the director of the Marathon Committee, who's sitting a few seats along. Khan immediately joins Edmund Gladstone, nodding earnestly at whatever he has to say. At last she stands and walks over to the stage, making her way to the podium. My insides flutter as I picture Papa's face. I feel light-headed. Finally!

Khan greets the audience, both those in the room and everyone watching around the country and world, before going on to summarize everything the London Marathon stands for as she builds up to awarding the Ultimate Prize.

"And it is in *this* spirit, in the committee's drive to ensure that this— the most prestigious of all British sporting events—remains synonymous with everything good and right, and stays reflecting the *best* of British core values, that the prime minister regrets to inform both this year's champion, Miss Leyla McQueen, and the Marathon Committee, that he cannot in good faith grant her requested Ultimate Prize. Naturally, on behalf of the committee, I fully accept and understand how difficult and brave a decision the honorable prime minister has had to make."

I blink rapidly. I don't understand. I know what she just said, but I don't *understand* it. I'm not sure what's going on. My chest begins to tighten.

Some of the crowd cheer at the director's words, while a few brave low boos. But overwhelmingly, there's silence—and some discomfort on the faces turning to me now.

It starts to sink in. My request has been denied. That's what's happened.

I recoil. My throat grows dry and a freezing cold wave crashes into my insides. Again, Papa's face flashes before me.

Khan continues. "Please join me, fellow Britons, in congratulating our new London Marathon champion, Miss Leyla McQueen, on a *truly* admirable win—affirming our nation's pride!"

A pause and then enthusiastic clapping and cheers break out.

"As is customary, in the absence of any Ultimate Prize, the Marathon Committee awards Miss McQueen with not only the respectable sum of money reserved for the champion, but this year's default prize. And what a most splendid first prize it is! Miss McQueen, may I present a one-off vintage Wright vessel!" She gestures toward the screens around the walls.

Captain Sebastian immediately narrows his eyes.

I bow my head.

More applause and whistling. The other prize-ranking contestants surround me; they speak, patting my arm and hugging to congratulate me before they turn to the screens in anticipation.

Why was it denied?

Why?

I turn to the prime minister; his eyes soften and his mouth turns down in regret. My gaze returns to the faces before me.

Papa will not be coming home today.

I need the ceremony to be over. My insides are too heavy, pulling at me.

This was probably the most realistic chance I'd ever have of getting my papa back.

The poised presenter walks to my side. She gives a small smile that's more resentful than celebratory. "What do you think, Miss McQueen? Shall we see the marvelous feat of engineering that you are so *lucky*"—her perfectly arched eyebrows waggle a fraction—"to have won today?" And then the hint of a sneer.

She's clearly another one who thinks I shouldn't have been allowed to race today. I would tase her. God forgive me, but if I had my brolly right now, I think I'd definitely tase her.

My hair shields me as I dip my head and stare at the floor. Somewhere in the background, footage of my prize plays on the screens. The crowd oohs and ahhs. I bite my lip. A submarine—when I was hoping to be reunited with Papa tonight.

The presenter reminds everyone that contestants will receive their prizes the next morning at Westminster once the paperwork and any necessary preparations have all been sorted.

There's a subtle prod in my back. One of the production crew, a young woman, furiously indicates for me to show my face.

I lift my head and stare vacantly at the crowd, rubbing the back of my neck; my breath hitches when Jojo's gaze meets mine. The puppy leaps out of Tabby's arms and heads for the stage. The presenter tries stopping her, but the crowd objects and she refrains, smiling and shrugging. I scoop Jojo up and bury my face in her fur.

"Congratulations, Miss McQueen," the prime minister says. His soft voice carries across the stage as he walks over to me with a warm smile.

He hands me a certificate and trophy. Light bulbs flash and the hovering cameras go manic as I'm congratulated. The PM shakes my hand as he faces the cameras.

"I wish to say a personal thank-you to Miss McQueen. She demonstrated the most honorable racing I've ever had the privilege to watch. Despite knowing that rising out of the way of a certain crash might cost her the championship, she still acted in the best interests of a fellow human being."

My eyes prickle. *Don't you dare.*

The PM nods. "If we all look out for one another this way, there will be no danger to our numbers. And *nothing* may ever defeat us. On behalf of the entire nation, I thank you, Miss McQueen. An example to us all." He claps for me.

The room erupts in cheers and applause. The PM returns to his seat.

It doesn't matter. None of this matters. Papa will remain locked up somewhere.

I stare into the space ahead. The presenter leans in for a comment. Her fixed smile soon wanes when she's met with nothing.

I breathe a sigh of relief, and Jojo relaxes in my arms when the hovering equipment and frustrated presenter move on down the line to the first runner-up.

Following prize allocation is an announcement: Contestants must remain in the observatory for all pictures and interviews. At long last, someone shouts, "Cut!"

I stumble off the stage. As I do, I catch Captain Sebastian move to a corner of the room, aggressively waving away a Newsbot as he does. I pause to watch. He speaks intensely into his Bracelet, his features twisted with tension.

And then he suddenly whips his head in my direction and looks straight at me.

The look he throws my way could freeze the entire waters. My legs and insides quiver.

Why didn't they grant my request?

What is *really* going on?

Where is Papa?

CHAPTER EIGHT

I exit the hatch and drag my legs along the gloomy corridor to the flat, Jojo in my arms. I wince as I move my head around. The constant twisting my neck during the marathon is kicking in now. Maybe the Medi-bot will help.

Ahead, in the hallway, I lift the champion's trophy. I close my eyes, walking through the realistic images of the holographic projections flashing up and down the lengthy space. In one image, I'm rising out of the other contestant's way in the last seconds before impact. I look around and none of the news highlights show my Ultimate Prize request being rejected. Funny that.

Papa's face flashes in front of me for the umpteenth time and I flinch; my chest is tight, all twisted inside. The entire marathon and prize-giving ceremony are just a blur now. I reach for the door's security scanner. My hand freezes in midair.

The door is already ajar.

Oh God. I inhale sharply; my lungs ache in response. The puppy tenses. What to do? I push the door fully open, my hand shaking. Jojo leaps down and runs in, ignoring my hushed calls. Inside, my brolly lies on the floor. I grab it. The stand it usually hangs from is on its side, my belongings everywhere. My heart has stopped, I'm certain. I take long, deep breaths; pain stabs at my chest.

The puppy returns whimpering but not growling. I turn to the lounge with my brolly ready.

The door slides open. I gasp and shuffle back a step. It's as if I've left my mind outside in the corridor and am not really seeing, feeling. I don't know where to look.

Everything is destroyed.

All my belongings are smashed, ripped apart. Every bit of furniture is on its side, stuffing from upholstery and cushions everywhere. Pictures from the walls lie in pieces on the floor.

I stand in the doorway for several moments. Finally I edge into the kitchen and bedrooms. The entire place has been turned inside out. I gasp in Papa's room, a sour taste in my mouth. On tiptoe, I reach up for the high shelf and relief washes over me; the Qur'ans are still in place on it. Thank God they didn't fling them to the floor. I shudder at the thought.

I turn back to secure the front door; the lock wasn't forced. What does that mean? Something cracks under my foot as soon as I enter the lounge. Mama's beloved Afghan tea set is sprawled about in sharp, jagged pieces, no longer taking pride of place on the shelf. My origami models mix with the rubble, shredded. *Why?*

I draw in breath. *Oh no.* A heap of turquoise pieces now rest where Mama's vase used to stand. She crafted it for Papa after they were engaged and he adored it, refusing to ever put anything inside. It was a feat of beauty in itself, he always insisted. I scoop up a handful of the smaller shards. They glisten in my palm. I let them slip through my fingers.

I hesitate. "Jeeves?" The wall flickers to life, thank goodness.

"Good evening, Miss Leyla. May I congratulate you on your outstanding achievement today in—"

"Please run the flat's security data for today."

I shuffle through the space, my arms wrapped around myself. I shake my head; a million memories all eerily tainted now. Mama's drawings of her favorite poets, Jalaluddin Muhammad Rumi and Robert Frost, are slashed. The folding screen catches my eye; it's been ripped off the wall and thrown on the floor. *No.* I step over the carnage and grab it, holding my breath as I open it. My shoulders slump in relief. All my handmade maps are still inside. Hours and hours of drawings, ever since I was a child. I prop the screen up against the wall.

Something smooth sticks out beneath the sofa—the Medi-bot. I pull the rectangular-shaped aid out. It's crushed on one side, the trays all damaged. There'll be no pain relief. Jojo's hammock lies in pieces beside it, and I pick up one of the wooden parts. Who would smash a puppy's hammock? Papa crafted it with his own hands, insisting the lazy pup would love it, and she did. I throw the wood back. Nothing makes sense.

"There is no available security data for today, Miss Leyla. The security system was disabled today at five thirty p.m."

Someone is responsible for this, and for wiping the data clean afterward. But who, and more importantly, *why?* My heartbeat whooshes away. I can feel it in my chest, ears, neck. My legs won't stop trembling. I need to sit.

"Who disabled the system, Jeeves?"

"The system was disabled by you. Your personal ID was used. It—"

"What?" Everything is wrong.

"Your personal ID was used to override the internal system. Miss Leyla, is there a security problem? Would you like me to alert the authorities?"

I frown. "Yes, please."

Mama's handwoven wall hanging catches my eye. The tapestry is ripped to shreds. It was passed down from her great-grandma. I press a hand to my head. *Think.*

"Miss Leyla, you are scheduled for a visit from the police at eleven a.m. tomorrow. You are advised to find a suitably safe place for the night if security has been compromised and—"

"I'll be fine. Jeeves, please run another search of every single file of

Papa's. Alert me to any document I haven't opened myself."

It only takes a minute. And I already know the results.

"Miss Leyla, all of Mr. Hashem McQueen's files have been thoroughly examined. There are no documents you have not marked as read. Anything else I can help you with?"

"No," I reply, my voice quiet. "You can't help me, Jeeves."

Everything is wrong. The flat. Papa. If only the PM had granted my request, then Papa would probably be on his way home now.

I step over my belongings, grinding my teeth. Strangers entered our home, going through our personal things. How *dare* they?

How dare anyone force themselves into our only private space in the whole world? It *has* to be linked to my sometimes being followed around outside and to Papa's arrest.

My face warms. I have a right to know what's going on, dammit.

I call Grandpa. No answer. I message him again, and finally the screen flickers to life.

Except it isn't Gramps I'm looking at—it's a complete stranger.

My pulse races and my stomach rolls. Have they got to Grandpa, too?

It takes me a moment to focus and realize the guy's around my age, maybe a little older. He's staring back at me, eyes narrowed.

"Who are *you*?" I demand. "Where's my grandpa? What have you done with him?"

His eyes, honey-brown, watch me intently. He folds his arms. He's a golden-copper shade and all muscle and angles and wariness. "Your grandfather is safe," he says, his voice low and husky and slightly irritated. "Why would you assume I wish to harm him?"

"WHO ARE YOU AND WHERE IS MY GRANDPA?" I shout.

He shakes his head and juts his chin out. "I am a friend, and Gideon is okay. He's busy taking an important call. He will be here any moment. What is so urgent?"

"Wait . . . *you're* his friend's son visiting for Christmas from the Faroe

Islands? Gramps said he had a visitor staying over. And why are you answering his calls? I need to speak with him. It's urgent!" I look behind me at the state of the room and turn to face him once more. *"Please,"* I say. "Call him. Somebody . . . somebody's destroyed my flat."

A muscle flexes by his jaw, and he runs his hand through long, dark hair that falls to his shoulders in waves. He tries to peer around me at the room, and when he meets my gaze again, his eyes flash a fiery amber shade.

"I will call your grandfather," he says, and promptly leaves.

What on earth? I pace the room trying to make sense of things. It's impossible.

"Queenie! Are you hurt, child?" Grandpa comes into view at last, his eyes wide.

Oh, thank goodness he's all right! "Gramps, who is that guy? Why's he—"

"Queenie! What happened? Ari said something about the flat? Are you hurt? Please, child, tell me everything at once."

I show Grandpa the destruction. "Why would somebody do this to my flat, Gramps? I know you know! Please tell me what's going on! I know everything's somehow related to Papa's disappearance. You can't deny it anymore!" My gaze is unwavering, the heat burning my face.

His face falls as he absorbs my words. "Enough, child." He holds up a hand, shoulders sagging as he nods in defeat. "I will tell you what I know. But you must wait until I get there."

"No, Gramps, *please.* No more waiting. Tell me now."

I've waited long enough. Not knowing is killing me.

He takes a deep breath, exhaling slowly. "I'm sorry, Queenie. I should have told you. I will try and explain, child. But first let me remind you that in the absence of your father, I'm your guardian. You must understand that whatever I do, I do it with your interests at heart. You're in danger, and you need protecting. You refuse to move in with anyone. You left me with no choice. When someone started following you a few weeks ago, I turned to my old friend Ben for help. He agreed to send his son to ensure you're keeping safe." He pauses when the guy reenters the room, visible in the background. Grandpa gestures to him. "Leyla, this is Ari. He isn't here for me; he's here to ensure your safety. Ever since he arrived, he's watched out for you."

I screw my face up. "What? You asked somebody I don't even *know* to come watch over me? I already told you, I don't need anyone's help! And why didn't you just tell me the truth? Also"—I take in this Ari guy who right now looks like he'd rather be anywhere but here—"why would he agree to this? Why would he want to watch over a stranger?" I move closer to the screen and lower my voice. "That's not healthy, Gramps. Please ask him to stop."

Ari straightens and folds his arms.

Grandpa's eyes dim. "He didn't really have much choice, Queenie. You heard about the recent horrific attack in the Faroe Islands?"

I nod and my stomach goes all funny. "What's that got to do with anything, though?"

Ari leaves the room. Grandpa watches him leave, his own expression heavy.

He turns back to me. "Ari is from the Faroe Islands. His community was the one attacked. He lost someone close to him during the onslaught. His father knew I was concerned about you being followed, and afraid of how Ari might react to his friend's death, so he sent him here to keep him busy—and you safe. He's come a long way to help us. And I won't apologize for taking steps to protect you, child. I only wish I'd told you."

I pause, swallowing. "Do you trust him, Gramps?"

"I trust Ben, his father, with my life, and I trust Ari with yours. And as you know, right now we need people we can rely on, Queenie. He knows whatever I know of the situation."

"More than I do, then," I say, unable to keep the bitterness out of my voice. "*Why* do I need someone to watch over me? I need answers, Gramps. I mean it. Where's Papa? What's really going on? If you don't start trusting me with what you know, then I promise I'm going to ask anyone and everyone. I shan't stop asking questions until—"

He tries again to persuade me to wait for him to come over but eventually sighs and nods. His face is heavy, and his shoulders drooping. My nails find their way into my mouth.

"It breaks my heart to tell you this now, Queenie. I tried so hard to keep it from you, to keep you from the pain. But you are right, I have an obligation to tell you the truth."

I stare unmoving, unblinking.

"Your father was never arrested by the police, child. It was—it was the Blackwatch that came for him."

I suck in my breath, my hands covering my mouth. The ominous Blackwatch. The all-powerful force meant to protect the PM. Papa dreaded them. . . . I can't stop shaking my head.

Pain breaks through Grandpa's expression. "We were working, when the laboratories were suddenly cloaked in darkness. Within seconds, they were inside the premises. At first, we both presumed it was an Anthropoid attack. Your father put up a good fight before they finally identified themselves and aimed their weapons at us. One of them went for your father. I tried to help but was punched in the chest. The last I saw of him, your father was unconscious. . . . Two soldiers gagged and tied him, then hauled him out of the room. And then my world turned dark."

I flinch. "No! No, no, no." I stumble back.

Grandpa grimaces. "I'm so sorry, child. They left me behind. Your father is not in Westminster. I—I'm afraid he's not even in London—"

"No, don't say that!"

"Unfortunately, it's true. We know your father was taken out of the city. But nobody yet knows exactly where in the country they're keeping him. He seems to have disappeared. Do you understand, Queenie?"

I open my mouth to speak. My lips quiver and I shut it again.

Grandpa shakes his head. "Whoever was behind this farce of an arrest, they falsified the accusations. We've always known that. It has to be someone very high up for Blackwatch to do their bidding. And this makes it very difficult for us to go public. I'm afraid it's no surprise that your request to have your father freed was rejected. It's a mess, child. We've been working on it nonstop, trying to determine why they've taken him."

I stare into the space, willing myself to absorb the meaning behind all the words. But all I can see is Papa bound and gagged.

"I'm so sorry, Queenie. And now—now they've done this to your place. You're no longer safe on your own."

I swallow and force my voice out. "'We'? You and who else, Gramps? And the *Blackwatch* . . . What could they possibly want with Papa? And why have the police lied all this time and led me to believe it's an ordinary arrest?" The way he shakes his head and his exhausted gaze tell me he's already puzzled over the same questions countless times. "Grandpa, what if this goes as high up as Captain Sebastian? I'm *certain* it was him who persuaded the PM not to grant my request—I was watching him! And after the ceremony he looked *really* tense and angry. What if it was linked to the state of my flat? Sounds far-fetched, but I think he's somehow connected to all this. And he just gives me the creeps—always staring, always watching."

"Sebastian is unsavory, a blight on this nation, child. He's also highly slippery, too cunning to be caught out. But yes, there's no doubt in my mind he plays a big part in this."

I gasp at the confirmation, before steadying myself. "Oh, Gramps, you should have told me the truth. From the very beginning. All my visits to the police station, enquiries, petitions, the endless pleas to the authorities, searching for clues, begging for legal representation—when all that time I could've been doing something that might have actually helped Papa. I thought *everything* depended on the marathon. Oh my God, I contemplated letting someone get seriously hurt just to ensure I'd win the race so I could ask for Papa's freedom. They could've died!"

"I was wrong to keep the truth from you, child. Forgive me. I didn't want to worry you, and I was trying to protect you. You mustn't lose heart. We will *never* give up on your papa."

I swallow and take a deep breath. "I know you meant well, Gramps, and you've been bearing this burden all on your own. But you could've just trusted me with it, you know. Made it easier on the both of us. I'm stronger than you think. At least I *finally* know the truth now."

An hour later the news is on. Even background noise is better than being alone right now. There's a reminder of the Anthropoid threat to the city. I turn away.

Grandpa's words play over and over in my head. The images make my insides ache.

He pleaded with me to either allow him to come over now, or for me to stay at his place until we've sorted something out. Neither suggestion seems to solve anything, though. Not properly. I press on my temples. My head feels like the water looks after an earthquake, all sand and grit—too murky to allow for any sense of direction.

At last I know what happened that day. How can I help Papa now? There's nothing he wouldn't do to help me. I wrap my arms around myself as a memory surfaces.

There were a number of food production setbacks eight years ago when the Deptford Farm crops were destroyed in an Anthropoid attack. The terrorists also hit the huge central banana plant next door, and both bananas and the paper their stems and leaves produced were rationed for months until imports were sorted. Too young to understand the full implications, I was only worried about the shortage of paper and how it might affect my love of mapmaking. One of the country's largest protein plants was soon after damaged in an earthquake, and suddenly there was a nationwide food crisis.

Papa regularly went hungry so I'd have enough to eat, but I was too young to realize. He would make excuses at mealtimes, come home and apologize for having been so ravenous he'd eaten at work.

If Grandpa hadn't noticed his weight loss and forced him to stop . . . I try to swallow away the hardness in my throat, ease the heaviness in my chest. It's not working. There's just so much to think about. And, as for this Ari guy, I really don't need anyone to watch over me! I can look after myself. My name echoes from the news. I glance at the state of the room. I'll need to make a few lists.

It's impossible to focus, though.

The authorities have been lying to me, letting me believe Papa was in Westminster. Who can I trust? There isn't a single reason why the Blackwatch would be interested in Papa. They protect the PM—and do God knows what else. But my papa has nothing for them. Why did they take him? What do they think he's involved in?

There's nothing—not a single memory, action, or shred of evidence—of anything dishonest about Papa. Absolutely *nothing* to indicate he ever unwittingly became involved in anything dodgy. Either they've made a terrible mistake, or somebody has framed him. But that still doesn't explain why the authorities are lying to me.

My eyes prickle, the rocklike lump in my throat increasing in size as I try to make the room safer for Jojo before she wakes up. After some further growling at all the chaos, she finally jumped into her Bliss-Pod, where the soothing sounds and lights worked their magic, and she's now snuggled asleep inside the large pebble-like shape.

On the news they mention how the top-five ranking contestants will receive their prize deeds and keys of ownership at the Marathon Committee offices in the morning. The excited woman then summarizes the five prize-winners and their prize lots.

I slump yawning onto the hard, seatless sofa, rubbing my neck.

The newsreader mentions my name. And then there I am on the podium, accepting the champion's certificate and trophy from the PM.

Does he know his precious Blackwatch took my papa?

Something glimmers beside me on the sofa, tucked into the stuffing. I reach out, finding the family snowglobe. My throat grows drier, tighter. Whoever broke in must've thrown it. I pull it up and cup its smooth surface in my hands.

Papa won't be returning anytime soon. That's the truth. I drag my legs to the window, my movements stiff. Not everything from the walls has fallen. Mama's oil painting of Oscar Wilde, my favorite of all her artwork, hangs lopsided, its canvas defaced like everything else. Mama loved everything about him. Why shred a canvas? Do they think Papa's hiding something?

Did they find what they were looking for?

In the background, the newsreader goes into detail about the submarine I've won.

I was hoping to be reunited with Papa tonight. But after all that, he's not even in London. The thought of him being out there, somewhere in wilder waters . . . I gaze out at the shifting forms of the dark and turbulent environment. The late evening current sends waves heaving onto the building.

Who did this to the flat? If it's the authorities, what more do they want? They already have my whole world.

Where are they keeping you, Papa?

The newsreader sounds really enthusiastic now as she shares the specs of my prize vessel. I pause, listening to the details for the first time. My heart stutters at her words. Everything stills for a second. And then just like that it surfaces, riding in on the furtive current and crashing into me, reckless and alarming.

A wild, outrageous idea.

I look down at the globe, tipping it until the glitter falls inside the glass dome. The rainbow fish swim and the tiny submarine bobs away in the turquoise liquid.

I gaze, unblinking, into the all-encompassing vastness outside. I hold my breath, clutching my chest. Its weight will crush me.

Where are you, Papa?

I press my face against the window and shudder at the inky void before me. Such a mystifying expanse. Such a *dense* darkness.

The current gathers speed and the waves around Bankside swell, growing bigger and stronger. A storm is gathering force.

I close my eyes, take a deep breath and exhale, and give in to the unthinkable thoughts.

CHAPTER NINE

"**T**he name's Deathstar. I'm the mechanic who's been caring for the beauty you've won, and I'll be giving you the tour of your prize vessel. So friggin' chuffed to meet you!"

The mechanic's eyes sparkle and he grins widely, bouncing from foot to foot as he guides the twins and me toward my prize sub. We walk along one of the lengthy walkways inside the principal base in Mayfair. In the water between these walkways sit rows of government vessels. The humongous enclosure is never-ending. A camera, controlled by a woman trailing way behind, whizzes around us. Publicity doesn't end with the race.

On the way here we stopped off at the Marathon Committee's offices at Westminster. All top-five ranking contestants took pictures with the PM as he formally handed over the documents and any keys to our prizes. As I'm champion, a tidy sum of money was also transferred to my account. The PM asked us all to be responsible with our newfound fame and prizes. I wanted to ask him why the Metropolitan Police have been lying to me all this time about my papa's arrest. And why his own personal guards took my papa away. I didn't ask him anything, though; I can't risk attracting even more attention.

Sounds—drilling, cutting, motors of all kinds, people instructing and reporting—echo in every direction. An army of robots hovers over the arsenal of vehicles, maintaining and inspecting them.

"*So* chuffed you won!" The mechanic shouts to be heard over the din as he continues to guide us. "Second-place's maneuver was nasty at the end there!"

The twins walk quietly beside me. I alerted them to the robbery last night. We've agreed to discuss it later at the flat, away from prying eyes.

My Bracelet has been flashing all morning. Among the messages of congratulations, Grandpa is worried about me. I canceled the visit from the police, telling them I was mistaken. They're the last people I want near me now.

Theo whistles as he looks around the space. Tabby grabs one of the beams that pass under the balcony above us. Metal structures form staircases and balconies all around the sides of the place. Tabs swings gracefully, landing nimbly on her feet. The camera makes sure to capture her.

The mechanic beams and gestures my presence with heavily ringed hands. "Can't *believe* you're here in person. Sorry, don't mean to creep you out or anything, but you're one awesome racer!"

I grin and check on Jojo. The puppy was only allowed entry on condition she's kept in her travel box.

A commotion in the far corner catches our attention. Cameras and a group of cheering people surround a woman who's posing for pictures against a bulky white sub that looks like an enormous beluga whale. Deathstar whistles and claps in its direction.

He turns to us, eyes shining. "A returning Explorer!" he explains. "Can you believe it? These people risk their lives to ensure we'll be able to survive on the surface soon. Amazing!"

I'm filled at once with dread. I wonder where she's been, what horrors she's seen.

We walk on and I move closer to the mechanic. "So, Mr. Deathstar." I lower my voice. "Is the sub working? I mean, can—"

He stops, his hand hovering in my face. "Whoa, whoa, whoa, Sunshine. 'Is it working?'" His eyes widen and his tattooed face breaks out in laughter.

The rings in his nose and up the sides of his earlobes jingle. "Of course she's working. What do you think I've been up to this last year? She might not be a naval vessel, but she's sturdy, all right. You can't do better than a DeepFlight sub, best on the planet. And never let it be said that Deathstar doesn't take care of his beauties! Oh, and it's just Deathstar, no need for the Mr." He pauses, gesturing toward himself. "Kind of ruins it a bit, don't you think?" He secures the ponytail hanging down his back and carries on walking.

Vessels of all kinds are lined up like mammoth bullets. If only I could touch them.

"She's almost twenty-five, your baby," Deathstar says. "A seventies Wright MIK twenty-one. A vintage beauty."

We turn left onto another walkway and the mechanic pauses, whistling as he gestures ahead.

I gasp. Everyone stops and stares at the sight.

"A real gem and according to some, designed by Adam Wright himself," Deathstar offers in hushed tones.

I open my mouth, but no words come out. *Oh my God.*

The submarine is *massive*. Its matte surface is gunmetal gray, a single row of circular viewports dots its middle, and the entire tip is wrapped top to bottom in transparent acrylic. I better not be dreaming. I turn to the twins; they're watching my reaction. We all break into spontaneous grins. My mind races, but now's not the time to voice any of it.

"Wow," I finally say. I spin around to the mechanic. "Deathstar, tell us everything!"

His face lights up and he claps his hands as he launches into the specifications while Theo hangs on every word, mesmerized.

"Thirty-five meters, two-story—though you have a little surprise on the top. Ten leagues, twelve in small bursts, brand-new reactor . . ."

Once he's relayed the general details, I walk the length of the vehicle. I move as far back as possible in order to take the colossal vessel in, from the four rudders and propeller at the tail end, to its smooth bow at the front. On the very top, its substantial fin is seriously impressive. The whole thing looks so bloody magnificent. Papa will love it!

I hurry back to the mechanic, who's still sharing specs with a captivated Theo. Once I've touched the craft, it will be real.

"I want to go inside," I plead. "When can we go inside?"

"She wants to touch everything." Theo grins. "Leyla has to know how it feels."

"Just waiting for them." The mechanic nods in the direction of several people carrying papers and gadgets of all sorts, all headed for the gangway leading to the top of the vessel. "Sorry, can't spend too long touring her this morning, what with all the paperwork and other official stuff that wants doing. You can pop in anytime to visit her, though."

The group beckons us to follow. We all enter the submarine.

Warmth flushes my face and my lips part when I stand inside the passageway. How can the place feel so familiar? No detailing of the craft's interior resembles anything I've ever experienced before. Yet the space welcomes us, embraces us. Blimey, it's the total opposite of my own building's corridor! I hold the travel box carrying Jojo up so she can see.

"Can I take her out now please? I won't let go of her."

Deathstar agrees and Jojo is soon in my arms, peering around, mystified.

The officials head downstairs for the control room where they'll wait for us.

The mechanic guides us along the narrow passageway. Pipes of all sizes run along its length. Despite its industrial appearance, it's a homey space—a mixture of copper, steel, bronze, and iron, and cozy hues of mustard yellow, browns, and reds. My mouth curves into a wide smile as I crane my neck in every direction.

"Tanks, the fresh water system," the mechanic continues as he points out what lies behind each door. The doors themselves are walnut, several inches thick, and round at the corners. "Storerooms. Galley's next, hopefully with everything you'd need, but can't stop right now, I'm afraid."

The floating camera whizzes away in the spaces around us.

We approach the wide pair of doors at the tip of the craft. All door-frames have a small security monitor fixed to them, and I can assign clearance procedures to any room I wish, Deathstar explains.

"And up front we have the saloon, of course."

The doors slide open and we all inhale at once.

The living quarters are open and cozy—a world away from my boxy, cold flat. Fixed furniture, a warm cherry wood that matches the floors, is dotted around. There's plush violet seating to the left of the room; I push my hands down on the deep seats and laugh. All around, muted greens, yellows, coral, and burgundy dominate in the upholstery. The walls are a dusky assortment of color.

It's a lush and heartening space. I sigh. It's beyond perfect. Papa will think so, too.

The translucent tip creates a huge viewport that makes up the entire nose of the vessel. Intricate detailing has fashioned large, magnificent arches on the see-through acrylic. *Wow.*

"Same view downstairs, miss. Control room's directly below us," calls out the mechanic.

Built into the wooden wall cabinets by the seating area is an absolute rocking multimedia and communications system. Several antique framed pictures hang beside it, and charming accessories are dotted all around. A lavender armchair stands by bookcases—one of which remains stocked with the previous owner's private book collection. I can't believe it.

I've spent forever getting told off for opening books at the London Markets just so I can smell that addictive smell. Antiques—and books especially—are *far* too expensive to ever hope to buy. But now I can sit in the lavish chair taking in the dreamy scent of pages from my *own* books, and Papa will stand in the tip of the vessel, gazing out. I glance around and sigh.

"Batteries under there." Deathstar points to a hatch in the floor. "Not to worry, though, the Navigator knows where everything's stored. That reminds me, they're waiting for us. Need to press on! There's another storage area, a room for any crew and staff, two small-scale bathrooms, two compact bedrooms, and the main bedroom," the mechanic explains as we move on. "But I'm afraid there's no time to inspect any of them now." He brightens as if he's suddenly remembered something. "I think we can quickly squeeze in one of its surprises, though!"

The twins and I exchange quizzical expressions, grinning. Deathstar winks and points to a twisty staircase that leads even higher. I climb the stairs. Though there are only a few, they wind out of sight.

I turn the corner and a platform comes into view. It's enclosed by a clear dome all around and above it, allowing a 360-degree view of the surroundings. Oh *wow*. A tiny room at the top! There isn't enough height to stand, but two or three people can sit, watching the world go by.

The mechanic calls out. "Sorry, but they're becoming restless, must go."

We climb down the winding iron-and-maple-wood staircase to the lower level.

Deathstar points left. "That way's the reactor and the engine room. Triple backup systems, I'll have you know." He beams as we hang on to every word. "Plenty of time to learn all about that later, and now this way."

Theo pauses beside a door with a window and whistles. "It has its own airtight chamber? *Yes.* Leyla, you have your own moon pool!" He punches the air.

I can't believe it. I peek through the window. It's a wide room, quite bare and sleek. Robotic equipment is attached to the ceiling. On the floor in the center is a *huge* door covering the moon pool. Once the room is pressurized with enough air, the door to the pool can be opened onto the ocean remotely, with the greater pressure inside stopping the water from getting in. Submersibles will be free to enter and exit the submarine. I shudder at the thought of descending into the wild through the opening.

"That's right," the mechanic confirms. "Not pressurized at the moment, though; it isn't cost-effective unless she's out there. Want me to set it up?" He turns to me, his eyebrows raised.

I stop tracing the row of copper bolts around the edges of the doors and swallow before I speak. "Yes. Whatever you need to do to have the submarine fully operational."

Thank goodness for the prize money; I'll need it all. I swiftly avert my gaze to protect my thoughts. It's getting harder to keep them contained.

"Understood. Right, your submersible's having its last checkups and will need powering up before handover, but I can confirm it's running smoothly."

I now have my very own submarine *and* nifty submersible. I'm dreaming!

Deathstar briefly runs through the main changes he's made renovating and updating the vessel. He's an utter genius, and I tell him so. His face goes crimson against the silver piercings.

"No worries, you earned it." He beams. "You were something out there. And working on this beauty's been a dream come true. Always wanted to buff up one of the Wrights, and the donor left a generous sum for the job. Okay, we need to head in."

The control room is at the end. The hovering camera isn't allowed in.

Theo whistles as we enter, his eyes shining, and runs over to the busy panels, checking the displays. I try and note as much as possible. It's a sleek and uncluttered space. Dials of all kinds, flashing lights, buttons, LCD displays, phones, keyboards, speakers. All around us, another means to control everything about the vessel can be found. Theo spots a separate workstation in the far corner.

"High-res forward-looking sonar, the very latest," a technician busy testing a dial points out to him. "Gives a clear view ahead for at least a tenth of a league, sea conditions permitting, of course." The dial she's checking bleeps and she nods, satisfied, and moves on.

The next few hours fly by. The onboard Medi-bot measures all my vitals and a health-monitoring chart is created. My DNA is taken and recorded along with iris scans and fingerprints, each result uploaded into the security system. I request the same be done for Jojo. I'm tested on my driving knowledge and offered a training program I can undertake any-time.

An elderly official turns to me. "We now require your choice for Navigator. If you need any ideas, Winston Churchill, Hermione Granger, Spock, and Storm are currently trending," he says. "And Captain Nemo and the twenty-fifth Doctor seem to be making yet another comeback."

Theo's grin is wide, and he bounces from foot to foot. He lowers his voice. "I can merge Navigation duties with Housekeeping—kind of like a super-Housekeeper, if you want, Leyla?"

No way! My very own Housekeeper? *Wow.* I've only ever had the stan-dard Jeeves.

I smile at them both. "I'd like you guys to choose my Navigator for me, please."

They brighten and huddle away from me, whispering. Reaching a swift conclusion, they write the name down for the officials and refuse to tell me.

"We want it to be a surprise," Theo insists.

I fidget, beaming.

"I shall begin updating the navigation system at once," a technician assures me, and sets to work in the background.

A bearded official waves his hand. "Miss McQueen, before the vessel deeds may be issued, we need a name for the vehicle. The previous one was deleted per the donor's request. Again, should you find yourself at a loss for ideas, we can recommend several: the *Victoriana*, *Waterloo*, *Nautilus*—"

"I know what I want to call it." I scribble the name down and hand it to the man, who glances at the paper and narrows his eyes.

"Are you certain? I mean, this isn't even—"

"Yes, no doubt about it." I return the twins' inquisitive looks with a mysterious smile.

Finally we're done with all legalities and necessities, including the official photographs of the handover. We make our way out of the vessel.

"It's bloody brilliant," Theo says, nudging me and smiling. His face grows serious. "And don't worry about your place or anything you lost, Leyla; we'll soon have you sorted, all right? We need to make sure you're *really* safe—both inside and out there. It's madness."

I look at the twins, and then glance at the camera whizzing around us once more, waiting until it's at a safe distance. I need to be extra careful. Theo and Tabby both raise their eyebrows and lean in.

"It doesn't matter," I say, "about the state of the flat or anything else, really. Because as soon as the vessel's ready, I'm leaving London to search for Papa."

CHAPTER TEN

"They were definitely looking for something specific in your files, too," Theo says quietly. His brow is furrowed as he swiftly checks and then swipes away file after file on my far wall.

Tabby and I fix our stares on him.

"They searched *everywhere*," he continues. "Your personal docs, public records, contacts, even your finances. They're after something. And now we know more about your dad, it *must* be connected to his situation. Erm, and that's not the worst part. The security override? It came from a governmental source. In Westminster."

The government. My hands and legs tremble, and my insides turn cold.

Tabby shakes her head. "What the actual hell is going on? And whatever it is, surely you don't need to leave *London* because of it? I don't get it, Leyla. I mean you've always *dreaded* the thought of trav—"

"Please, Tabs," I say. "We've already gone through all this. I'm definitely leaving to search for Papa. I'm going to ask Grandpa for help. I think he knows even more than he's finally let on and I'm going to ask him to set me on the right course. He kept saying 'we.' They know Papa's not in London; they might know more. It's a start at least."

Theo looks wide-eyed at the destruction around the room. "You know I'll back you on anything you decide, but traveling alone with Anthropoids out there . . ." His expression clouds over.

"I know." I move closer. "I can't bear to even think about *them*—or any of the actual traveling beyond London part, really. But I've no choice. Papa's not just arrested, but *missing.* And the government is involved somehow. They're lying to us. I have the submarine now, so I can go search for him myself."

Tabby throws her hands up, her color pale. "Even if you do manage to find out where they're keeping him—then what? Leyla, you think you can outmaneuver the *Blackwatch*?"

"No. But I'll finally know *where* he is and hopefully *why*, too. And then I'll take it from there. Beats waiting around here." I point to the chaotic lounge. "I'm not exactly safe here anymore, am I? I can't search for Papa if I disappear, too."

"But this Ari guy you mentioned, he's looking out for you now," Tabby says.

I shrug. "Didn't stop the flat from being ransacked, though, did it?"

"No." Tabby sighs. "Imagine if you or Jojo had been at home. You could've been hurt. . . ."

I sit on the cushionless sofa and hold my head in my hands. I wish I knew *everything* being kept from me.

Theo shakes his head. "And now they've tried to access your private info. . . . I can kind of understand why your grandpa kept things from you for as long as possible. This is seriously messed-up stuff. Look, I'm going to send you a program soon as I get home. Activate it the second you get it, Leyla. Once it's uploaded, with only a one-word command, your messages, files, everything can be deleted. I mean *really* gone. Trust me."

"Wow, thank you."

He waves it off. "It's nothing, last year's project. This year's is bigger and better, only I've not had the chance to test—" He breaks off when the far wall flashes. "Just a tracer I was running," he explains, moving closer to the communications wall and checking the stream of data.

I get up and walk over to the window, stepping around one of the large piles of wrecked belongings. Tabby joins me.

Wireless Man blares out around the flat, congratulating somebody in Surrey on killing a basking shark that had dared to drift into urban waters, scaring the residents.

"Sleep!" Tabby shouts at him, sounding more like she's hissing.

It goes quiet as we both stare out at the water.

She shakes her head. "Surely you don't have to *leave*, Leyla? We could try—"

"You have to leave, Leyla," comes Theo's voice from across the room. It's subdued and tight. "You need to leave as soon as you possibly can."

A cold nausea sweeps through me. Tabby and I exchange similar looks of dread before joining him. I follow his gaze to the coded text glimmering on my wall.

"What is it, Theo? What does it mean?"

He turns to me, swallowing before he speaks. "It means the Blackwatch themselves have you in their sights. You've been marked as a security threat." He shakes his head. "There's nothing left for them to do after that, Leyla— except to take you in." Theo covers his mouth and turns back to the wall, deep in thought.

Tabby's shoulders rise and fall. "Hell, no . . ."

The quivering in my legs is instant. I stagger back a few steps and Tabby grabs me.

"I knew it was bad," I whisper breathlessly. "But I just didn't realize *how* bad."

Tabby helps me to the sofa and we sit. She takes my hands, her expression steely now, her eyes glinting. "You're not alone. Look at me, Leyla. We love you, and we're going to get you out of here before they come for you."

My chest aches. "I can do it," I say, nodding. I turn to Theo. "Does it say *why*? Why they're watching me, what they want from me—why they took Papa?"

Theo shakes his head. "Nothing. I'm sorry . . . You were right. Leaving really is your only option now." His voice is low, tinged with disbelief. He rubs his face. "Okay, you'll need to contact the mechanic in charge of your sub. Grant me instant clearance and full access to it, for a start. Its defense and security systems are pretty cool already, but I think we can improve on them further. We have to make sure you're prepared."

I nod away eagerly. I'm not sure if I'm trying to reassure them, or myself.

"Are you out of your mind?!"

"I have to get out of here and find Papa."

"Are you *completely* out of your mind?!" Grandpa lowers his raised voice.

We're in his study and it's late evening. Ari's out, thank goodness; Gramps might trust him, but I can do without a scowling stranger hanging around. His bright amber gaze is too intense, and I just don't like him.

"You've only ever known London, Queenie—it's a whole other world out there. We need to do *something*, but wandering around Great Britain on your own isn't the answer. Can't you see that? Why must you be as stubborn as the seas!" He isn't backing down as he continues to pace the room with his cane: *tap-shuffle, tap-shuffle.*

I chew on my lip; I *have* to do this. But I also can't bear to upset him. "What do you propose we do, Gramps? This is the *only* answer. Everything I thought the government would never do—*could* never do, that things could never get that bad, that someone or some law would stop them before they did, has already happened. They took my papa away without having to prove why to anyone. They've lied nonstop about it ever since. Nobody's going to come and magically save us. I'm taking the submarine and going to go look for him. But I don't know where to begin. And you know until I'm eighteen I can't travel long-haul without a guardian unless I have papers."

His shoulders sag. "They slapped me with a travel ban after your father's arrest. The ban also blocks me from underwriting travel papers for others. It's no longer safe for you here. I understand that, child. But you traveling around Great Britain on your own would be like rising up and breaking out of the surface of the water, only to find yourself in the center of a merciless tempest. Why can't you understand, you can't simply—"

"No, why can't *you* understand, Gramps—aut viam inveniam aut faciam, remember? You taught me that: 'I will either find a way or make one.' I'm leaving regardless—whether I have papers and a destination or not. I must leave before they take me, too, or who'll help Papa then?" My voice breaks and I hush, steadying myself.

Jojo jumps into my arms and buries her nose in my cardigan.

Grandpa moves closer, wrapping me in an embrace as he leans against the wall. I huddle against him. Gramps always smells of tobacco and vanilla. Along with Papa's, it's one of the most magical smells in the world. Sometimes scent alone can change your whole mood, can even transport you somewhere else entirely. Scents are spells, and I love Gramps's smell so much.

I'm reminded of when his heart attack temporarily incapacitated him, just after Papa's arrest. That was the darkest time for me. The two dearest people in the world to me needed my help and there was nothing I could do. I put my head against him as he lay weak and helpless, and promised I'd always be there for him. I sigh, my gaze wandering around the study.

Images of Mama, Papa, and me are everywhere you look. All manner of quotes cover the walls, including one of my favorites, *Gam zu l'tova*—"This, too, is for the best." Beautiful scientific models cover his shelves. A silver menorah graces the wide windowsill.

Grandpa shifts. I hug him tighter. "Papa's somewhere out there, Gramps. He needs me, I know it. I can feel it. Please trust me. Don't keep

95

anything else from me, all right? I know you want to protect me, but I *am* capable. I must search for Papa."

He gazes up at the ceiling and sighs heavily. "Before I even considered it you'd have to first promise me you'll let me put in place any security measures I deem necessary and—"

"Anything! I promise!" Finally. *Thank you.*

"If you *must* leave, you will head for my cottage in King's Lynn and you don't move from there until I've joined you. Understood? I'll be with you soon as I can leave without causing suspicion."

It's a start. "I'll stay put at the cottage until you get there, promise. And then I can plan my next step. But, Gramps, your travel ban?"

"I'll break it. It's important that you're safe, child. So many obstacles to overcome . . . How will you travel without papers? I can only think of Vivian Campbell, but it would be placing her at risk when—"

"No," I say. "I can't ask Vivian." Grandpa's right—it would only cast suspicion on the twins' mother. They'd never approve her sponsor application, and they'd most likely place the Campbells under close observation.

"And Sebastian will be right behind you the moment you slip up. . . ."

"Let's not worry about what *might* happen, Gramps. We can sail that trench when we come to it. I can't let the fear stop me from trying. And . . ." I raise my eyebrows. "We're forgetting something. The Explorer Permit. They're not going to deny the champion of the London Marathon a place with the prestigious Explorers."

Taking a long breath, I release as much tension as possible as I exhale. Every time I think of my plan, a most profound terror surfaces.

Terror, and a glimmer of hope.

CHAPTER ELEVEN

The nightmare that's haunted me since childhood is always the same.

I'm about four or five years old. I stare out of a small window. I know that for leagues around there's nothing but deepest, darkest waters. I'm frozen to the spot, Papa's voice distant, calling out to me from somewhere. I'm too afraid to move a muscle, though. Because then I might miss something and will never know what's out there in the emptiness—and the not knowing is so much worse. I know I ought to breathe, but I'm always too afraid in case it disturbs the inky void outside. Something stirs. I can't see or hear it, but I feel it, brooding in the unknown depths. My insides constrict, my chest crushing. The pain is excruciating, and yet I still don't call out for help, for fear of interfering with whatever lurks in the bottomless abyss.

This time when I awoke from the nightmare, I could've sworn there'd been more. That someone had been *in* the water, suspended there in the wretched space.

The water doesn't always arouse fear, though. The positive feelings are equally intense. Just sometimes, the water is promising and nothing is impossible. The constant soft, cradling *thump* that I feel more than hear, the ceaseless pulsing that gently reverberates right into the heart of me. As if the sea itself is alive and breathing. The emotions they stir within me at those times . . . a cocooning magic.

Of all the times for the nightmare to haunt me again, it had to return today, dammit.

I glance at the far wall for any sight of a waiting message, but there's none. *Come on.* I can't move until I've downloaded the permit, and the Explorers Administration promised they'd get back to me noon latest.

I've spent the last few days finalizing preparations. I've studied the submarine's control manual nonstop, memorizing the vessel's details over and over. Tabby's been back and forth to the submarine, loading it. The cash prize is proving really handy. The sub itself is ready to sail. All the necessary programs have been installed and triple-checked over the last couple of days, including Theo's latest modification—an anti-tracking device. Everything is coming together for me to leave this evening.

New Year's Eve is my best bet at sneaking out of London unnoticed. Everyone's always distracted by the New Year celebrations, and this year they'll be huge because it's not only a new year, but a new century. The authorities will be stretched throughout the night.

Jojo's already at the hangar with Grandpa and Theo. We've gone over the plan countless times. I'll leave via Dartford Tunnel, the shortest, relatively safest way over the borders.

"Anywhere but Epping Forest." Tabby's warned me repeatedly, the others immediately agreeing. "It's bloody well dodgy, and we're always advised to stay well clear of it."

Once across, I'll head to Grandpa's cottage at King's Lynn where I'll be safe until I know my next move. The entire time I'm on board the submarine I mustn't contact anyone unless it's absolutely unavoidable, Theo explained. More than likely, all communication conducted by the twins and Grandpa is being monitored, and any contact between us could draw the authorities to the vessel's location. But I'm more concerned about getting them into trouble. Once I reach Grandpa's cottage there's a secure line there, and I can communicate with everyone again.

Blackwatch's intensified surveillance of me is hard to miss. The subs are no longer discreet about following me, and it's becoming increasingly difficult to shake them off. At least I haven't seen Ari anywhere; Gramps finally saw sense and sent him away, I think. I don't need *anyone* watching me.

I wrap Mama's soft pashmina tighter around my shoulders. The faintest scent of jasmine and musky attar still lingers in its silk and wool fibers. My grandmother sent it all the way from Kabul, in Afghanistan, as part of a huge wedding parcel when Mama was getting married. The corners of my mouth lift.

The waters can't halt human connections. The desire—the sheer will, to reach out, to anchor one another, is too stellar. People will always find a way to keep from losing one another—from losing themselves. The human spirit didn't drown. It was swept up and carried along; it flows still, the stream coursing its way through everyone's lives.

I just have to find a way to beat the dread, that's all.

I walk over to the album wall to download the pictures but can't resist glimpsing a few first. I swipe them into view, one by one.

There's an image of Mama and me, in Kensington Gardens—her favorite place in London. At the time, it was "winter" in the never-ending indoor gardens. Mama has me in her lap. I wave past the image and pause instead at one of my favorite pictures of my parents.

I wasn't born yet, and they were living in a single room, only able to afford basic amenities and tasteless reconstituted food. Despite their struggles, though, their expressions are blissful. Papa was studying at the time. Mama was the creative one, painting and taking photos.

In one image, Papa's surprising Mama with their tiny room transformed into the closest thing to a studio he could create for her. In another, they're huddled together under a woolly blanket wearing silly grins as they point to Mama's first portrait painted in the new "studio." It's of my great-grandpa Kasim McQueen—an American who visited Afghanistan and fell in love with both the country and my great-grandma and never went back. The painting is striking. So was Mama. She always carried an expression of sheer wonder and exuberance.

What would she say to me now if she were here? I wrap my arms around myself. What's it like to receive a hug from your mama? I gaze once more on both parents' faces, then download the images and delete the album. I jump when the communications wall springs into life. It's time for the Great Briton of the Day. The solemn voice lists off the lessons learned from the Battle of Waterloo as Lord Horatio Nelson's face fills the wall. The broadcast is interrupted by a message alert: the Explorers Administration. At last! I play the message:

"Miss McQueen, we are greatly honored that this year's London Marathon champion has expressed an interest in joining the ranks of so many pioneering Britons before her. You have nothing to prove so far as navigational skills go. And so it is with deep regret we inform you that on this occasion your Explorer Permit application has been rejected. We received a request from the authorities to deny you this undertaking. Captain Sebastian felt it was asking too much of somebody in a situation such as yours, what with your father's unfortunate circumstances. . . . Please do accept our most humble apologies. Good day, Miss McQueen."

I stare openmouthed at the wall.

No permit.

I have to leave now, and I don't have the means to travel legally. I shiver.

How *dare* he? I hate Captain Sebastian so much. Why deny me? Exactly what he is up to? It's all I can do to stop bursting into tears. I can't give in now, I just *can't.*

There's only one thing for it: I'll just have to hope and pray security forces or border patrol never stop me.

All I know is I'm not spending another night in London. If they come for me, Papa is lost to me forever—I'm certain of it.

There's a sour taste in my mouth, and I try swallowing it away. I close my eyes, and all I see is a vast and terrible unknown ahead of me. An endless abyss of monstrous creatures and earthquakes and the all-destructive Anthropoids. And now I can add to that the threat of being stopped and discovered traveling illegally.

Can I *really* do this?

My insides heave. I scramble to the bathroom and hurl, throwing up the little I've eaten since last night. Damn the trembling in my legs. I take deep breaths. I *must* conquer the fear; I've no other choice. I *have* to leave this place so that I have some chance of finding Papa.

I wash and pray, asking for guidance and success for my trip. Retrieving any files I want to keep, I then activate Theo's deletion device and wipe away the rest. Within minutes everything is gone. As if I never even existed here. I gulp at the air. *Focus.* I can do this.

I check the flat for the final time. I mustn't leave a single thing behind that might lead anyone in my direction. The compact space is empty. And not at all like home.

Goodbye, flat. Wish me luck.

I open the front door and, stepping out, close it behind me. Ignoring the thumping in my chest and the quivering in my legs, I press on down the damp and dismal corridor. The tiny bells in Mama's anklet jingle with each step. It feels right to wear it today. I tug at Papa's "Christmas" jumper wrapped around my shoulders like a snug shawl and don't look back.

CHAPTER TWELVE

I've never said goodbyes before. Not like this. I can't remember Mama passing away. And though I waited and waited for Papa to come home from work, he never returned. In either case, there were no goodbyes.

Inside the hangar, ashen-faced, Grandpa manages a small smile as he indicates the letters gleaming on the side of the submarine. "I take it that was your idea."

I nod at the name of my submarine: the *Kabul*. It looks perfect. Mama's place of birth in Afghanistan and the city of Papa's ancestors. I think Papa would love it. Every time he called me his Kabuli peree—his fairy from Kabul—his warm hazel eyes would shine even brighter.

A fair amount of activity is going on in and around the vehicle. Deathstar and several other crewmembers walk up and down the gangway, entering and exiting the vessel, making preparations for departure. All manner of last-minute checks are being carried out. The twins are inside somewhere.

Grandpa takes me to one side, and we sit on some portable wooden steps. He reaches into his pocket. "This is for Jojo."

It's a red collar with a silver bell. I shake the bell and smile at its chime.

"It was meant for Benjy," he continues. "I was going to give it to him after the floods, when everyone was safe and we'd settled into the new place."

I stare at him. He rarely talks about the time of the planet's transformation, and I hardly ever ask. It's such a difficult subject for him. "Gramps, you've never mentioned Benjy before."

"Benjy was my dog."

"But you never said . . . Why've you never told me you had a dog?" I lean closer, inhaling his familiar warm and sweet scent.

"What good would it do, child, to wallow in the past? *Everyone* lost something. We all lost somebody. And the animals suffered as we did. They panicked, ran kicking and screaming. Some tried to protect their loved ones till the very end. They drowned. Cats, dogs, cattle, wild creatures, billions of animals all over the planet, drowning."

My heart drops, sinking lower and lower.

I've watched countless graphic simulations, all the live recordings, documentaries, and endless replays—we all have, and still do—of what happened. But they're nearly always framed by someone else's gaze. To hear a firsthand account from Grandpa, knowing it's his own experience, is something else. No wonder he doesn't like to talk about it.

I swallow and slip my hand in his. "And Benjy?"

"Benjy . . . he vanished when the tremors began. We searched everywhere, and then we had to leave for the holding centers." He shrugs, shaking his head. "I don't know. Maybe he made it and spent the rest of his days with a loving family." He pats my hand at the thought.

My mouth trembles. I lean in even closer. "Gramps, did you ever wonder if your biological parents survived?"

He takes a shaky breath, his eyes weary and far away as he wraps an arm around me. "Constantly, in the beginning. Even though all evidence pointed to the contrary. And then it was confirmed a few years later—my parents were just two of the billions that died during the disaster." He takes a deep breath and exhales it in a short puff. "People had hoped taking to the seas would save them from what was to come, but eventually all such last-hope vessels found their way to the bottom of the world."

Image after horrific image flashes before me; I shudder. This is the most Grandpa's said about that time.

He waves a shaky hand in the air. "And that's when my aunt Esther took off with me—the moment she heard of my parents' plans for us all. It was such a *confusing* time for everyone. It was chaos, everywhere. There wasn't a scam people didn't think of. And then there were doomsayers, and mass suicides, and of course those that welcomed the news, were excited at the prospect of such a dramatic change. The poor couldn't afford to be excited by it, though; they never welcomed it, child." He shakes his head.

I gulp. "How come you were fostered? Why didn't you stay with your aunt Esther?"

"After the disaster, she became my only living relative. And she died six weeks later. Toxins from the water leaked into places, spreading disease and death. So *many* were lost in those weeks immediately after. Nobody had anticipated just how much water was held deep in the planet's mantle. When the rock's impact released it, the levels just kept rising, child. Where they would stop was anybody's guess. Too many buildings didn't hold up to the devastating reality, the pressure on them far more than had been accounted for. Traffic accidents . . . So many unforeseen matters." He lets out a long, heavy sigh and squeezes my shoulder. "Respice, adspice, prospice."

I swallow past the heartache, nodding. "'The past, the present, the future.' And I will, Gramps, promise. I'll try to look in *every* direction, as best I can—always." My voice is hushed. I squeeze his hand. "Do you miss it—the Old World? Did you spend years wishing everything would go back to how it was? Does that world seem like a dream now?"

"The memories remain very real. I've never quite forgotten the fear. And the nightmares never really left. Of *course* I wish we still lived on the earth's surface. But you know, Queenie, the Old World wasn't quite the utopia it's made out to be. The reality was very different. The changes in the climate . . . It had become a frightening place. Certainly a far cry from the Lost World." He chuckles.

The Lost World is one of the Campbells' hotels. I visited it recently when the twins took me for a sixteenth-birthday treat. Located in Notting Hill, it reflects life in the first three decades of the twenty-first century, just before the whole planet was reordered in 2035. It's the most blissful place I've ever experienced. Every single thing is perfect: trees grow, birds sing, flowers bloom, the sun shines, children play outside. It looks and feels like magic.

Grandpa tucks long strands behind my ears. "You made me so proud, what you did in the race, child. I don't think I've ever been more proud of you. 'And fill your hearts with love and selflessness . . .'"

"I know this, wait, Sri Sathya Sai Baba?" I bite my lip. He smiles, nodding. "But, Gramps, is it selflessness if you don't want someone's death on your conscience? Is that a selfless act, or were you looking out for yourself?"

"I never, ever want you to doubt that you are a loving human being, Leyla Fairoza McQueen. Do you understand?"

I nod.

His face eases into a smile, his eyes glistening as he taps me on my nose. "Meeting your papa was the best thing to happen to me. He doesn't need to be related to me to be my son. He *is* my son. The McQueens *are* my family. You remember the day you took my vintage Dragon out for a spin?" He grins. "You were only twelve. I think I almost had a heart attack when I glanced up to catch you driving past my study in the sub. I saw my whole world come crashing down before me. I told myself I'd never see you again."

"I'm so sorry about that, Gramps. It was such a smashing shade of purple, I just *had* to have a go."

He chuckles. "You were deeply apologetic when you brought it back an hour later, but practically floating with exhilaration as well. You know, your mother was exactly like you, Queenie. Nobody could ever tell Soraya she wasn't allowed to do something. Once she got an idea into her head . . ." He gazes off into the distance, a deep sadness in his eyes. "Your mother would have been so proud. I'll be looking out for you; we all will be." He clears his throat. "It's a dangerous world out there, and I must do what I can to keep you safe, child. Please understand that whatever I do, it's only with your survival and success in mind."

"I know that, Grandpa, don't worry. I understand."

"And you have everything you need, yes?"

Not really, Gramps. I'll be traveling illegally . . . I nod in reply and shift around. How dare I get mad at him for keeping things from me when I'm now doing exactly the same to him.

"Good. You will find your father, and I know he would want to explain things to you himself. As much as I want to speak to you about some matters, it isn't my place."

Like what? My curiosity's piqued. I've always known Gramps isn't telling me *everything*—even when he finally told me the truth about Papa's disappearance—but hearing him confirm it now sends my mind spinning. What's so important that only Papa can tell me? I open my mouth, but then close it again. I can wait until Grandpa joins me at his cottage. We chat some more. Finally, it's time. I gulp hard and hold on to him, reluctant to let go.

Despite once losing everything, his family, friends, his home—the *world* as he knew it—Gramps never lost hope. His eyes shine with tears now. "See you at my cottage. Shalom, Queenie."

I kiss him on the cheek. "Salaam, Gramps. See you soon."

I swallow and turn to the gangway. A couple of technicians and Deathstar are walking down, and they tell me their job is done. The *Kabul* is good to go.

"You take awesome care of yourself, and of my baby here." The

106

mechanic grins as he gestures to the sub. "The Navigator will alert you to anything that might need attention in the engine room, but you'll be taken through it step by step if that ever happens, so no worrying. Oh, and you might want to secure the moon pool door—as of six minutes ago I'm no longer this baby's daddy, and she's stopped listening to me." The corners of his mouth droop.

I shudder as I picture an opening into the abyss. "Don't worry, I'll never have the moon pool door unlocked." I thank the genius with a hug.

I pause by the entrance and wave at Grandpa. Taking a lengthy breath, I blow my cheeks out as I exhale.

And then enter my submarine.

I make my way toward the muffled voices coming from the saloon. Tabby's telling Theo off about something. They hush as I approach. Tabby's lips are pressed flat, her arms folded. She holds my gaze and smiles.

Theo offers a half smile and clears his throat. "You're here, Leyla. Great. Everything's ready. Come on; need to update you. We love the name, by the way."

We take a tour of the whole vessel apart from the now pressurized airtight chamber. I peek into the smaller connecting chamber beside it, spotting the submersible. It's a compact twin-seated vessel, its exterior protected by an impenetrable titanium cage.

I remember my picture and reach into my bag. It's one of my favorite images—passed on to me from Papa—and I gaze at it as I hang it outside the moon pool room. How surreal and yet strangely affirming that this image of a scene from back in 332 BC should hang here; how different the world!

The print depicts Alexander the Great being lowered into the sea in a glass diving bell. Apparently he made several dives this way. The painting was part of a quintet created for Akbar, the great Mughal emperor. And now a print hangs in my submarine—the *Kabul*, no less—in London, on the eve of the twenty-second century. I know ancient Persia was a very long time ago, but sometimes it also feels as if the human race just blinked and now we're *living* inside the seas—never mind being lowered in glass diving bells from the sides of boats. No wonder Papa often refers to time and space as magic!

"Leyla!" Tabby cuddles Jojo in her arms as she stares at me. "You don't have the time to be distracted right now!"

We move on as she goes over everything with me. She's already unpacked and put away almost all of the boxes. The kitchen and stores are stocked.

"Don't forget what I said about my modification," Theo reminds me. "In theory, the anti-tracking device should kick in once you get going, ensuring you don't pop up on the Traffic Ordinance Council's system. But I've not had the chance to test it in practice. Your Navigator's going to run a test when you're underway, to make sure. If it comes back negative, stop off at the Brighton Pier resort in Belvedere—it's more or less on your route anyway. My friend Sam knows you might show up. If there's a problem with it, she'll sort it."

As he leads me to the control room, Theo's expression suddenly brightens, his eyes shining. "Go on, ask for your Navigator!" he urges, strapping a new Bracelet onto my wrist.

I falter for a split second. What if I really don't like their choice? "Navigator."

Oscar Wilde himself appears before me.

I stare. "No way. NO BLOODY WAY! Oh my God, you guys!"

He's exactly as he appears in the archives. Dressed flamboyantly, he wears fashionable Victorian clothes: a velvet waistcoat, plush jacket, and knee breeches. I peer closer—no glimmer. It's amazing! Mr. Wilde acknowledges my delight and greets me, bowing with a flourish. He assures me in a soft voice and warm accent that there's nothing to worry about, that I'm not alone in this.

I turn openmouthed to Theo, who throws his hands up, grinning.

"All right, I modified him quite a bit after they uploaded him. Mr. Wilde here is your *super*-Housekeeper."

I'm mesmerized. He looks *so* real!

Theo's expression turns serious. "The Navigator doesn't know the route out. No specific journeys were logged because we couldn't risk the officials knowing your exact plans. It's the first place Sebastian would have his people check, and we need to give you as much time as possible. So you need to fill Oscar in now, Leyla."

I nod. "Mr. Wilde, we'll register our journey now, and then you'll have our exact route." Am I really chatting with Oscar Wilde as if he's a real person? You bloody bet I am! Warmth floods my cheeks.

"*Oscar*, if you please," my Navigator insists, in that debonair way I always imagined he would. "And take your time, my dear lady. If you are not too long, I will wait here for you all my life." He bows his head.

I recognize the quote and squeal with joy. There's much more to come, Theo promises, filling me in on the Navigator's capabilities.

"I *love* him. Thank you so much. Oh my God, you're utterly brill!" I hug Theo, and we register the intended journey, indicating all the security bases that need avoiding along the way.

Jojo darts out of the control room, and Tabby rushes after her, calling to her.

I turn to Theo. "Promise me you won't worry too much."

He squeezes my arm. "*We'll* be fine. You need to focus on you." He suddenly leans away from me, pinching his bottom lip. "Leyla . . ." He clears his throat. "There's something you need to know. You'll— You won't—"

Tabby walks in with Jojo. She glances at us and holds Theo's gaze.

"I won't what, Theo?" I ask.

He reddens and waves his hand. "Promise me you won't get distracted from the plan."

I reassure him as much as I can, even though I think he meant to say something else before Tabby reappeared, but I've no idea what. Then, as if without warning, it's time.

Tabby is pale, her face tense, her usually bright eyes clouded as she moves closer to me. "I love you, I hope you know." She swallows and reluctantly hands Jojo over.

I embrace her. "Don't be daft. Of course I bloody know." We both grin tearfully. "I love you, too. Everything's going to be all right, you know. Try not to worry."

Tabby rolls her eyes. "Still believe in all that hope and magic stuff, Leyla?"

"You should, too," I insist, nodding.

Tabby looks so wistful and serious for a moment it makes my heart ache. "*I* believe any dad who raises his child to believe the world is full of magic and that there's *always* hope—no matter what—truly deserves for her to rescue him one day when he needs it."

"Oh, Tabs!" We hug again.

Theo's eyes are wide as he embraces me. "Leyla. Promise us you'll be careful. *Promise.*"

"I promise. Thank you so much. For everything, you guys. I love you both so much."

We all huddle together in a silent embrace.

I want to scream as they walk away. The twins climb the stairs. The sound of the main access hatch shutting securely after them is almighty. They're gone. I'm alone.

All of a sudden, my surroundings are too much, too heavy and demanding. My legs wobble as panic claws at me. *No.* Not now, dammit. Oscar appears. I jump at his sudden presence; I'll need to get used to that.

"My dear, we are clear for departure."

The enormous steel-and-wood cradle beneath the vessel slides slowly forward toward the huge door at the end of the hangar. *Whoa.* Deep breaths. I push my shoulders back. It's time to get out of here to safety, and then to go looking for Papa myself. Once I'm at Grandpa's cottage in King's Lynn, I can plan my next move. He'll have no choice then but to tell me *everything* he knows. And it will lead me one step closer to Papa. It *has* to.

I head for the saloon, requesting Oscar's presence. Jojo has wandered off to explore before I can stop her. I peer out of the windows; several mechanics wave about, instructing one another as the craft moves. The twins and Grandpa have placed themselves in full sight. My pulse races. I hold my hand up one last time and they return the gesture, before receding from view.

Goodbye . . . Oh God.

The door rises. The mechanic beside it flashes a thumbs-up in my direction, and the vessel leaves the hangar behind.

Once inside a second enclosed area, the door shuts securely behind me. The chamber begins to flood. I pace the viewport, crossing and uncrossing my arms. Hopefully the Navigator knows exactly what he's doing. I hold my breath as the water levels rise around me. At last, the exterior doors open. The sub abandons the cradling frame, moves forward out of the base, and enters London's waters. I suck in my breath.

The craft rises at once. *Bismillah.*

My heartbeat whooshes away in my chest and ears. I peer in every direction. All kinds of laser lights blink across the rooftops. The New Year's celebrations have begun. Beams—in every color, shape, and size— pulse through the liquid space in time to music that will be playing on screens until well past midnight. Lights ripple from distant homes as parties are already underway. The entire city glimmers. Forever lit up, London wraps its arms around its citizens. My heart stutters; will I be able to return once I find Papa?

Higher now and the city is barely visible below. I stand still, absorbing everything. The deep, rhythmic hum inside the vessel is both heard and felt. The swell of the sea rising and falling is different in a submarine, heavier and yet smoother, almost soothing. The current is choppier, though. At this height it would prove challenging to control a submersible. Smaller, more agile vessels come into their own when navigating the streets, but the turbulent upper waters are too challenging for them. Heftier transport can travel high enough to even catch a little natural light.

Farther up now, and it may as well be the open sea.

Oh God. I shiver, taking quick breaths. I'll have to find a way to counter the dread.

Something moves beside the craft. A small shape, rising and dipping. For the second time in days, a brilliant dolphin appears, the vehicle's sidelights casting a silver gleam over its body. It swims playfully alongside the submarine before moving around to the front and blowing bubbles. My mouth curves into a hesitant smile. The marvelous creature can only be a good sign.

Maybe what lies ahead might not be as daunting as I fear?

CHAPTER THIRTEEN

"**A** calamity, my dear lady," the Navigator ceremoniously announces. "The test to ascertain the performance of the anti-tracking device has returned negative—the modification's ability to function appears to be blocked in some way. If one were to hazard a guess, they might propose that the magnetic storm currently raging on the surface may be interfering with it."

Damn. I'll show up on the Traffic Ordinance Council's systems, and I've no doubt the authorities are going to use it to track me—if they haven't already. Trying not to let the setback get to me, I instruct Oscar to stop over at the Brighton Pier resort in Belvedere before heading for the borders. Soon as Theo's friend has fixed the tech, we'll be on our way again.

Time for a warm drink. The galley is fabulous, bigger than the kitchen in the flat. Alder cabinets with copper handles fill the space, and bronze pipes run everywhere. Ancient styling hides the latest technology and gadgets. Just off the kitchen, plants hang from the ceiling on cords: my very own hydroponic garden!

Back in the saloon I sip the hot chocolate as I check out the huge ornate bookcase full of books. *My* books now. I can smell and hide in those pages as often as I like. My smile widens. Inside each cover is a whole other world. And all of those worlds—strange and familiar, weird and wonderful—and all the different characters with their hopes and dreams and their adventures and quests are right here on this one bookcase. *Magic.*

I grab a rolled-up picture of Papa and me; its frame was smashed in the robbery. It's my fifth birthday in the photograph—my first without Mama. Papa tried to make it as special as he possibly could. I'm clutching a doll of a Swazi princess that I'd wanted for over a year. It was vintage and so it took Papa longer to save up for.

I hang the picture on the wall, beside a ticking clock displaying a complicated clockwork system in a style I've never seen before. A thought dawns on me and I feel lighter.

Just for once, for the first time since Papa's been gone—and despite knowing his situation is graver than I first feared—a feeling of despair hasn't followed a memory of him. At last I'm doing something concrete about his absence.

I sit in the lavender armchair by the bookcase and review my updated journey out of London under the light and warmth of an elaborate bronze floor lamp. We're almost over Canary Wharf, right on track. We drive on toward Belvedere and the indoor beach resort. The sooner the modification is sorted, the better.

Jojo's full of beans and keeps wandering off to explore, ignoring my calls. She's even left half of her dinner, the daft thing. All the excitement is proving too much for her.

The evening waters stretch endlessly on all sides. I move to the viewport, standing several feet back from the overwhelming windows. The choppy waves roll by, coursing around the bow as the *Kabul* plows through. It really is impossible to spot anything in the dark. The only illumination is from the solar spheres and the submarine's fore light. I gulp; it's like pushing through a vast nothingness, not knowing *what* you might encounter.

If only the familiar, brilliant white light of the streetlamps somehow reflected up here as well. And how strange not to be confronted by the shadowy shapes of buildings towering above me. Some of the sea life is also different. The craft's harsh lights captivate groups of vividly patterned fish.

All the warnings about the unknown terrors of the deep surface; I shiver.

Where's Jojo, for goodness' sake? I call out for the puppy and am met with a faint, happy bark from somewhere but no return. I summon Oscar instead.

The Navigator appears in a fabulous number: a ruffled shirt and seriously decorative breeches. He pats his hair as if conscious of his appearance.

"Any problems, Oscar?"

"No problems, my dear. We are on course for the stopover at the Brighton Pier resort. Though authorities are present in the area, there are no reports yet of any possible obstruction to our trajectory. May I assist you with anything?"

"Look at it," I whisper.

He joins me in observing the passing environment.

"It's—it's quite scary, isn't it?"

He turns to me with a quizzical expression. "Why is the scene frightening to you?"

"Well, when it's too dark to see, just about *anything* could be hiding out there."

"My dear lady, the true mystery of the world is the visible, not the invisible."

His voice is whimsical; I like it. "But if you can *see* it, how can it remain a mystery? It's visible, so you know what it is. How can that be as scary as not knowing? No, Oscar." I shake my head slowly as I absorb the scene. "I can't imagine anything worse than not knowing."

The submarine gives a slight heave; I tense. Food. That's what I need.

I take a plate of steaming Kabuli pulao back into the saloon along with a snack for Jojo, if the overexcited puppy ever decides to show up. Scattering two plush cushions from a pile at the side of the viewport, I sit cross-legged and tuck into the delicious rice and meat, its spicy saffron aroma taking over.

Is it a good idea to eat a yummy meal while you peek out at a never-ending mass of water and imagine yourself sinking? Probably not. Virgos like to worry, Papa told me. They like keeping it real. Hmm, maybe not that bloody real, though. I avert my eyes.

Rice flies from my mouth when Oscar appears beside me without warning. I *must* get used to that.

"My dear lady, Belvedere approaches."

"Thank you, Oscar."

The vessel presses on. As I watch, something bobs into view in the distant light. It drifts into the sharper illumination alongside the vessel. What on earth is it? *No.* I jolt, crying out. My hand flies to my mouth, and a cold chill spreads inside.

It's a bloated corpse. It's decaying; an adult, I'm sure. Hair fans out around their face, their mouth open and eyes fixed with a hollow stare. The harsh light of the vehicle compounds the already pitiful state. The body is tangled in ropes and a thin material: a homemade sail. My throat goes dry. The poor, poor person.

They must have tried to survive on the surface.

Since the planet's transformation, there've been random and violent storms up there. Fatal waves wreck anything and everything. Even the engineers maintaining the solar panels and spheres, satellite dishes, and oxygen pipes wear protective clothing when visiting the surface. We're safer down here. I don't understand; why do some people risk *everything* to try and live up there before it's safe enough for us to do so?

The body meanders onward in the cold light spreading from the craft, rotating as it goes. It's soon out of sight. An image of Papa unconscious at the labs flashes before me. An ache pulses in my chest. I head for the passageway, hugging myself.

"Jojo!"

I begin checking those rooms that allow instant access. The puppy's muffled, content sounds carry up from the lower level. That muppet. I climb downstairs to more of Jojo's familiar sounds. What on earth? They're coming from the control room. It doesn't make sense. How did Jojo access the room?

I enter the control room. Jojo's fine, thank goodness. She's eating some kind of treat beside the sonar station. The puppy wags her tail in greeting.

"Jojo? How'd you get in here? And where did you get that biscuit?"

I glance around. Is there a second entrance point? Impossible.

Something flits right on the edge of my vision. *What the—* My pulse quickens.

Did I imagine it? No, I definitely saw something.

I move past the communications board, making my way around the room. What the hell is going on? I hold my stomach, dragging my feet. Again, something catches the corner of my eye. My hands tremble; if only I had my brolly on me. I jerk, swinging my gaze to the right. My palms sweat. There's nothing there.

I turn the corner by a huge locker and jump, shrieking. My eyes wide and my mouth open, I freeze in position.

Standing still, and with an unreadable expression in those fiery amber eyes, is Ari.

CHAPTER FOURTEEN

"I don't believe it. He actually put someone like *you* on board with me," I say, pointing at Ari. "I can't believe Grandpa would do this to me. I thought he'd sent you away!"

His gaze flickers and he folds his arms across his chest. "'Like *me*?'" he demands. His voice is low and husky.

We're still in the control room, going around in circles about the fact Gramps snuck him on board the submarine the day before. *He's* the security measure Grandpa insisted on. Oh, how I regret my hasty promise! And thanks to the no-communication rule, I can't even vent at anyone. Turning around is out of the question; it's just begging to be noticed by the authorities.

His eyes narrow, waiting for an answer. He runs his hand through his long, dark hair. Around his neck is a tiny beaded leather string, and a knife hangs from his waist. Why would he need a knife? I shudder; what does he think we'll encounter out here? He's wearing a black top and casual bottoms. *Stop staring at him.*

"Yes, like you," I say. I'm uncomfortable with him but realize it sounds pathetic. He's definitely not Theo, though!

He scowls and a muscle flexes by his mouth. "I promised Gideon Abraham I would protect you." He speaks carefully and assuredly.

"Except I can take care of myself!" I try to gather my thoughts. I'm stuck in a vessel with him. This is really happening. Jojo walks around his legs, wagging her tail. The little traitor. "Jojo? Come here, baby." After several calls, the puppy finally walks over. I squint as I scoop her up. "What have you done to my dog?"

He cocks a thick, dark eyebrow, and one corner of his mouth lifts ever so slightly. A faint twinkle appears in the coppery eyes. He's laughing at me, the dick. "Jojo and I have got to know each other very well. She loves her biscuits."

Is he really taunting me with my own pet? Enough. I pace the room trying to think of a way out of the situation and come up with nothing. I look up and the stowaway's watching me with an expression of distrust. He hid on board my property and *I'm* suspect?

I narrow my eyes. "So you've been following me around to 'protect' me from others following me around? Don't you have anything better to do?"

He clenches his jaw. I recall Grandpa's words about Ari's own circumstances and regret implying he doesn't have much else to do. And if he's only here on his father's orders, then it must be hell being somewhere you're not wanted.

But still, why did Gramps have to ask a total stranger to accompany me? And such an infuriating one . . . Oh my God, the twins—they knew! *That's* why they were so awkward when I entered the vessel, hardly meeting my gaze. I think Theo was about to tell me when Tabby stopped him. I groan. Grandpa must've just told them what he'd done. They should have warned me!

He saunters around the room, his movements fluid and easy. Everything about him is strong. His build, his shoulders and arms, his hands. His eyes are something else. Mesmerizingly bright and permanently suspicious. *Oh my God, stop staring at him!*

I straighten. "There's no need for you to do that," I say, as he reads a dial.

"I'm just checking engine status. I can't command the sub, so there's no need to be afraid. Gideon could only ensure security clearance for access."

Afraid? Is he for real? This stranger should *not* be here; it's my sub. "I have no reason to be afraid; it's not me hiding on board someone else's vessel."

He raises an eyebrow. "Hiding? You would have discovered me sooner if you had been more alert."

Argh. Oscar appears. Ari stiffens and his hand moves faster than a sailfish for the knife around his waist, before it falls away.

The Navigator tilts his head in my direction. "We are approaching the resort, my lady."

I turn to the maddening one. "Gramps told me you don't have much choice, that you're just doing this for your dad. But the *second* we get to King's Lynn, you leave my sub."

"That's fine by me. This is the very last place I want to be. My family needs me, too."

"I don't need you. I can take care of myself. Anyone tries to stop me from finding my papa, they'll be sorry they crossed my path. I haven't just left without a sodding clue, you know. I can jolly well look after myself."

His face tightens. "You have no idea."

"Then tell me!"

"I know what people are capable of. You can't beat them." His voice is low and resolute.

"Beat who? You mean the Anthropoids?"

He holds my gaze.

"I might never encounter *them*," I continue. "Anyway, I'm stronger than I look."

He's about to say something but seems to change his mind and shakes his head. "They are without a single cell of humanity. I've seen what they're capable of; you don't want to know. You can't reason with them." His expression darkens as he pauses. His hands curl into fists, his bronze skin flushing. The briefest hint of fury glimmers in his eyes, like the simmer of magma in the volcanoes along ocean ridges. He takes a breath before continuing. "I've left my family for this. Do you understand that? My family. Nothing in my existence is of more importance to me than them. I have been given no choice in the matter, though; I must do this for my father. I'm here until you reach your grandfather's place, and then I am done."

He turns his back on me and busies himself as the vessel starts descending.

Grabbing Jojo, I only now notice the target board propped above some lockers. Several knives are embedded in its center. *What the hell?* I hasten out of the control room. Even if Grandpa does trust him completely, it's seriously weird to have to share my space with someone I don't even bloody know. I could just scream.

The submarine gradually drops. *Whoa.* I rush back up to the viewport, gulping air to combat the slight heaving sensation. It's very different to the diving motions of a submersible.

Soon the vast white dome-shaped structure of Brighton Pier is visible. Lights pulse and beam, and shadows reign in the surrounding depths— security subs patrolling the area. The resort is always a popular New Year's Eve destination for families and therefore a prime Anthropoid target.

Ignoring the usual car parks, I find a submarine hatch on the side of the building; the *Kabul*'s bridge extends a few meters, docking at the resort. I'm used to submersibles connecting directly, and the bridge between the submarine and the building sends a tremor down my spine. Imagine passing through and something goes wrong?

Security beams flash away outside. If the anti-tracking device weren't so important, I wouldn't have stopped at all.

But with the threat of Captain Sebastian discovering my departure any moment, I need to ensure I remain as invisible as possible out here.

CHAPTER FIFTEEN

Theo's friend, Sam, is already waiting for me in the parking area. She's wearing the resort's familiar white T-shirt with *Brighton Pier* blazoned in blue across the image of an Old World pier. She holds her wrist up and her Bracelet confirms her identity.

Her freckled face beams as she hoists a rucksack onto her back and chats away without pausing. "Is it true you're going traveling? Theo said. You'll never catch me going out there, far too dangerous with those beasts around. And— Oh, *helloooooo*."

I follow her gaze and frown. Ari's left the sub to come and check on me, *argh*. I give him a dismissive wave. He scowls and stays hovering.

"Phwoar. Who *is* he?"

"What, nobody! I don't even know him!"

"Erm, he just exited your sub?"

"Whatever. I honestly don't even know him!"

"Okaaaaay, then. Oh, congrats on the marathon! You rocked it! Oh my God I hate Paul Martin *so* much—didn't even deserve his second place, really. He could've hurt you real bad if you'd not risen out of his way! Total shit."

"The biggest." I grin. "Thanks. Hope you haven't been waiting too long." I brush past Ari, and he follows us inside the craft.

"Just got off my shift actually—perfect timing!" Sam launches into questions about the vessel as she takes in her surroundings. "I'll need the control room mostly, and then a few minutes in the engine room after. Whole thing shouldn't take more than an hour. Can't believe you have one of the old seventies Wrights." Her face lights up on sighting the interior of the sub and she whistles. "She's magnificent. German engineering, Japanese tech on all Wrights—*nice*."

My grin widens. It may as well be Theo standing before me. We make our way to the control room and Sam gets to work. Ari seems to have disappeared, thank God.

I pace the room. I should just do it. I'm wasting time thinking about it. I have a whole hour. Why wait here when I could be at the beach? I needn't be long—in and out.

Sam is engrossed in her work. "Navigator was right. It's definitely the magnetic storm, messed with the tech. But I'll have it fixed in no time."

Great, a quick visit and then I'll be out of here. I inform Oscar and Sam, change, and exit the vessel for the beach.

As I make my way to the center of the resort, there's notice of another earthquake; Richmond Park in southwest London was hit this time. Hopefully nobody was caught up in it.

The noise and music grow louder as I get closer to the resort itself. A quick ticket to the beach, and soon I'm gazing on the place where I spent several amazing days with Papa when he surprised me for my fourteenth birthday. Warmth spreads in my chest. I stand there a moment, taking it all in. It's beyond fab.

The largest leisure space in London, it's as if the outdoor landscape goes on forever in every direction. You can't tell where the distant scenery ends and the projections begin. I remove my shoes, digging my feet into the sand, and make my way along the beach. A little boy flashes me a toothless grin before returning to his sandcastle. I squint in the bright glare of the "sun."

The tranquil blue skies are busy. Kites fly, and doves and seagulls coo and squawk as they glide through the air. I hold my arms out, the rare hot air heavenly. My skin tingles.

What must it have been like to have different seasons and weather in the world? To have varying temperatures, sights, and smells. To feel the wind on your face, a raindrop on your head, hold out your hand to catch a snowflake and watch it melt in your palm. What *had* it felt like?

Music and singing carry over from a brightly lit bandstand as I walk past. Huge, twisting slides are in full use, and in the far distance, holiday goers climb the gray rock faces. The merry-go-round flickers bright orange, red, and yellow as both adults and children ride the donkeys around and around.

I face the vivid aqua waters. If only the real thing were as translucent. Imagine being able to do it all: explore the depths of the water, swim on its surface, and then when you were done, move onto the land and look up at the sky. Old Worlders had been able to do all that. So many worlds in one. Is that why people will do anything to return to the surface? I guess Deathstar's right; the Explorers are amazing, risking their lives to find ways for us to have that again. I really shouldn't complain so much about the hefty monthly installments.

Right, time to get going, but first I dig my feet deeper into the warm white sand, stretching and curling my toes. I bend down, scooping some up and letting it run through my fingers. The ground quivers faintly beneath me.

I peer closer. Grains of sand jump up before my eyes as I feel another tremor. Is that normal? I straighten, glancing around. Nobody else seems concerned. Maybe it's a new addition. Perhaps they've installed—

The sky flickers, and then the birds begin to disappear.

A seagull flying low over the distant horizon vanishes, only to reappear frozen in flight. I take a step back. If it's only a technical failure, why does the ground feel funny?

At once, the whole sky—along with every cotton cloud, kite, bird, and the shining sun—turns to rigid lines of vivid color. I shiver. Others notice the changes, looking and pointing above them. It's very wrong. In the absence of the blue skies, the entire arena has taken on a whole different aura, an uncomfortable and surreal tone. My stomach rolls.

Alarms ring out. The lighting dims inside. I glance upward and freeze.

The colorful stripes are gone. In their place is the see-through roof of the resort. All around us the vast, dome-shaped cover, never before seen from the inside by holiday goers, is now fully visible. With no holograms or projections to disguise it, the real thing is terrifyingly jarring against the safe and staged interior. The dark evening waters sway as they beat against the structure. Somebody cries out, and chaos ensues.

People abandon deck chairs, and those gathered around the Punch and Judy show and the candyfloss and ice cream stands disperse in seconds.

An animal, the biggest I've ever seen, swims over the roof of the resort and down to one side. A giant moving shadow. I stand rooted to the spot, a cold stinging in my chest. It's some kind of whale, gliding to and fro. Every time its dark form comes closer, the bigger it appears, its empty eyes staring. Ominous red lights flash all around me, and then an announcement:

"Brighton Pier is under Anthropoid attack."

Oh my God.

"Please evacuate the building in an orderly fashion," the voice continues. "Do not stay. Please remain calm but exit immediately."

The place fills with terrified screams. The warning keeps repeating itself. The resort's staff call out loud instructions as they try to organize an instant evacuation.

Another tremor now, this time stronger. Figures fall off the donkeys in panic, unwilling to wait for the merry-go-round to stop. Cries for help carry from the distant rocks where the climbers now dangle helplessly on ropes.

I shake. I stamp my feet to regain the strength in my legs. It makes no difference. I take deep breaths: *Think.* It's impossible. How will they attack? Weapons fired from a distance? An explosion? An attack in person? My mind races from one terrifying possibility to another. Nausea rises, threatening to choke me. It hurts to swallow. *Anthropoids.*

We are the tiny decorative fish in a sad Old World fishbowl. Trapped.

The shadowy creature rams the roof again. *Focus.* Jojo . . . Will she be all right? Will the vessel survive the attack? A cry nearby. The little boy who was building a sandcastle earlier sits bawling in the chaos of screams and sirens. Way above him, a winding slide rocks.

I finally stir and hurry toward him, grabbing him and running away. The slide comes crashing down and panic only increases. The boy's shrieking mother spies her son. She snatches the toddler off me, and they speed away. Another tremor.

I jolt. What am I doing? I need to leave. *Now.* I join the throng running along the beach, headed for the hatches. I try ducking through the crowd. No luck. It's too large for the narrow stretch, and I can't move fast enough.

I head for the swaying trees. There are far fewer people there, moving much faster. I drag my feet, forcing one in front of the other. Jojo and Sam . . . What if the submarine—

A tremendous rumble lifts me off the ground. I soar through the air.

Vivid colors pulse around me, and an onslaught of noises all merge into one: Alarms, shouting, crying, and from somewhere so very far away, something that sounds like Jojo barking. I hit the floor. My whole being screams silently.

The huge palm tree above me cracks and swerves down in my direction, just as a dark void washes over me.   ◆

CHAPTER SIXTEEN

The boy is around the same age as me, not more than four or five years old. We happily gaze at each other. When he places his hand on the window, I giggle and mimic the gesture. As I watch, he jerks his head back, his concentration elsewhere. An expression of absolute horror breaks through the previous joy. I cry. I can't stop the tears as I look on his terror-stricken face. Everything darkens. Somewhere, a soft, deep voice speaks urgently. Papa's skeletal figure appears, shackled by heavy chains. He moves forward, reaching out to me, but the clanging metal stops him. His emaciated form is too much, the hollowed eyes defeated, the soul crushed. I scream and scream, but no sound escapes. And the redness . . . the redness is everywhere, beckoning me to focus.

I force my eyes open, blinking. Muffled sirens and other sounds, a deep, husky voice among them, resonate from every direction. The world around me pulses vivid red. For a second I'm back in Tabby's sub in the marathon, hovering until the effects of the flare wear off. Above me, copper tracks dotted with light bulbs run the length of the space—the ceiling of the submarine. I'm on the sofa in the saloon.

Jojo whines. I turn toward the sound and pain stabs at me. Ari sits a few feet away, Jojo cradled in his arm, her paw bandaged. In his hands he holds the first aid kit.

I inhale sharply as I suddenly remember. The attack! What happened? Did everyone get out? How did I get here?

Ari glances up. "You're awake, good. How do you feel? You need to get us out of here." His face is rigid, his voice wrought with tension. "I can't command the sub." His eyes shine in the throbbing redness of the room.

A resounding *boom* rocks the vessel.

"*Now,*" he urges again.

I manage to raise my voice above a whisper and instruct Oscar to make an immediate departure. The submarine hums into action.

I swallow. "Jojo."

He places the puppy into my arms. I gasp; she looks terrified and confused, and immediately snuggles closer to me.

"She'll be okay," he mutters as he watches us together.

"Why is she hurt? What happened?" I try to sit up. *Ouch.*

His mouth presses into a straight line. "She's okay, just hurt by falling debris. Look, you shouldn't be moving around. I need to tend to your wound. I only had time to clean it before the puppy needed my attention." The sub heaves and he scans the viewport. "I recognized the tremors and then saw you were already gone. I knew Jojo would be able to locate you faster, so we went after you. A rumble threw you, and we found you just as the trees began collapsing."

I again move to sit up but wince as pain jabs at my leg. Ari groans and sits down by the sofa with the first aid kit. He gestures to my leg. "I need to touch you; is that okay with you?"

I nod and he immediately tends to my leg. There's an obvious gash and it stings. Though his hands are huge, they're unexpectedly gentle.

What if he hadn't gone looking for me? Sam! I beckon Oscar and question him.

"Our visitor left a message for you, my dear lady: 'The modification is now fixed and running smoothly. There should be no further problems with it. Good luck!'"

Did she escape the resort in time?

Ari watches me as he secures a dressing on the wound, the orange depths of his gaze shifting as he narrows his eyes. Curse the color rushing to my face; he's so close, though. And it's as if he's trying to understand something. When our gazes meet, the muscles in his sharply angled face flex, a curtain draws over his taut expression, and he's unreadable once more.

"It makes it harder for me to ensure your safety if you go running off without letting me know." He says it very matter-of-factly.

"I don't *need* you to—"

The vessel lurches. I gasp and move to stand.

He shakes his head. "You need to rest for a while."

"I want to see what's going on. I need to see it."

I make my way to the viewport and he joins me, though unlike me, he doesn't pause a good distance from the windows. He continues walking right into the very tip. I gulp; how can he stand so close to the windows? He stares at the sight below us. I grab a pair of binoculars from their hook and slump down onto the cushions several feet away.

As the submarine pulls away, the resort is barely recognizable. Only an eerie shell exists now. The odd submersible escapes the madness, hurtling away at full speed. Defense vessels and bots of all kinds scurry around the place. I zoom in even closer on the binoculars and cry out.

"Oh my God . . . There are people still trapped down there! We need to go back. We have to go down and help them!" I stop to catch my breath.

He stares at me.

I shake my head. "Why did they do this? Why do they hunt us down like this?"

He pinches his lips together, his expression tense.

"I *hate* them," I whisper. "I hate them so much. . . ."

Whoa. My head grows light and I fall sideways. He's beside me in an instant. I wave him away. I need to see what's going on. He turns back to the view, swearing under his breath as he takes in the scene beneath us, his eyes shadowed.

A deep tremor rocks the submarine. My insides zigzag and coldness sweeps through me. It has to be an explosion. Jojo barks and scurries to me. The surrounding waters cloud with bubbles as further tremors and eruptions follow from below. I roll along the floor. Ari halts my movement, Jojo in his arms. I peer out. *Oh my God.* I cry out at the sight.

The mighty ocean smashes its way through the resort's curved roof, and the wild and very real sea pours into the building. An escaping submersible is caught in the downward flow and sucked back inside the resort. The huge whale that had been looking in on us all is also tugged down toward the doomed building with the unflinching force. It fights through the turbulence, though, and speeds away.

I stare, shaking my head nonstop. It's too much. It's *hell*. The submarine shudders.

"Rise *now*!" I shout at Oscar.

The vessel battles against the pull from beneath us, rising above the deadly maelstrom. The waves are frantic and the water churns, blocking the view. My insides heave; my mouth tastes funny. Did Theo's friend get away in time?

People are dying down there—the impossible pressure, the water smashing its way into their lungs. They'll be fighting for their last breath. So much horror. Such loss of life. My whole body shakes. I need to pull myself together. *Focus.*

Ari's expression is dark as his gaze meets mine, his mouth set grimly. I turn away.

"O-onward, Oscar," I instruct the Navigator, forcing my voice out and trying hopelessly to slow down my racing heart. "To the borders."

CHAPTER SEVENTEEN

I lie on my side, my eyes closed. The same scenes play over and over inside them. People terrified, running for their lives, the ocean crashing down on them, flooding everything and everyone in sight. I shudder and open them again.

Security is heightened further. Naval subs, bots, and unmanned patrol drones everywhere you look. Despite Theo's device now running smoothly, remaining discreet in the heightened climate seems impossible. We cannot be stopped, though. I need to get us across the borders and then on to Grandpa's place in King's Lynn. Once he joins me I will insist he tell me *everything* he knows about Papa's disappearance so I can work out where to begin searching for him.

At least Sam made it out, thank God; she messaged us to let us know. And the authorities don't know about her and so won't have been tracking her communications. I don't want her getting any grief from them. I check the news.

The attack on Brighton Pier is so far an isolated incident. Every news station is covering it and *Anthropoid Attack!* flashes away at the bottom of the screen. The chill returns, the tightness in my chest. I keep watching. I need to know. And then the pictures emerge.

There are a couple of them. Each figure caught by Eyeballs and Newsbots as they dart through the water, hungry for death and destruction. Bloodthirsty and inhuman. One even brazenly swims right up to a Newsbot. A long, pale face with limp, fair hair swaying in the water around her. There are three fingers missing from her hand. Gaunt cheeks sink inward, and her icy blue eyes are penetrating. . . . Her gaze *burns* with rage and loathing. I recall all the notices and warnings now: It isn't a *she*. It very definitely is an *it*. My pulse races as I take in the pictures. Crushed bodies float around inside the resort. It's too much.

I turn away, only now realizing Ari has entered the room. He stands rigid, his shoulders rising and falling as he watches the screen. He catches my eye and moves over to the wall, staring intently at the picture of Papa and me. I command the screen to turn off.

I chew on my lip. "There were others headed for the hatches," I say. "Maybe some of them might have been saved if they'd come on board the sub?"

He doesn't turn around. "My responsibility was only to you."

How can he be so matter-of-fact? "We might have saved someone. If you could've helped even *one* person survive that madness, then you should have. The pain their families are going to go through . . ."

He swings around, his mouth clenched as he looks down at me through hooded eyes. He shoots a quick glance back at the picture again, before returning his gaze to me. Although his expression is blank, there's something behind the flickering amber specks in his eyes. Something he's struggling with. He opens his mouth to speak, when he tilts his head, distracted. His gaze darts past me to the view outside, his expression expectant.

I turn around. Nothing. "Do you think Gramps will know we're all right? I don't want him to worry."

He nods. "I think he'll know." He glances over at the viewport again. "We're not alone." Though low, his voice is assured, as if there's never any question about anything he says. "It's a security check."

No. I check again but can't spot any indication of a nearby vehicle.

Please, God, let him be wrong! And then Oscar appears.

"My dear lady, we appear to have been graced with the good company of a security vessel," he announces.

Oh bloody hell. This is it. So soon, too. My pulse races.

"It's just a routine check," Ari explains, taking in my expression. "They'll need to see the Explorer Permit Gideon said you'd applied for. I had to leave for London in a hurry and don't have anything."

"No, you don't understand. . . ." I gulp, my eyes widening. "I don't have anything either."

He straightens, his face concentrated on my words.

"I applied for the permit, but—" I hesitate.

I trust Ari with your life, Gramps had said.

"Captain Sebastian told them to deny me. I never told Grandpa. I'm afraid we're traveling illegally. . . ."

Ari lifts his chin and cocks his head, thinking.

"My lady, there is a priority communication request," Oscar says.

Here we go. Ari and I both stare at each other with what must be the same faltering expression. I gesture to him to move out of sight.

I accept the security officer's communication request.

A voice infiltrates my vessel as a face appears on the screen. The officer asks for my papers. The official is irate in the wake of the attack and follows her request with quick-fire questions, hardly giving me time to answer.

Keep calm. I reach inside one of the walnut cabinet drawers and take a bendy, translucent card out. It's my old membership card for Clio House, the historical-reenactment hall. Why am I even doing this? *Because having security forces chase me should be a very last option.*

Okay, my trembling hand is most definitely going to give me away. I hold the card up against the scanner by the screen and give the officer my best smile.

Seconds later, she shakes her head. *Oh hell.*

"I'm afraid that doesn't seem to be registering as a working permit,

Miss McQueen. You are in a submarine, so I assume you are traveling long haul. I'll need to see papers or a permit that allow for that. Let's try one more time, shall we?"

Let's bloody not. My legs quiver. I stare at her. "That's because it's an old permit. I do have a new one, but I can't find it just now. . . ."

The officer watches me closely. My legs nearly give way. *Stay calm, dammit.*

Her eyes narrow and then recognition breaks through her expression. "You're Leyla McQueen! The London Marathon champion?"

I nod, sighing in relief. That's right—I'm a champion!

She straightens. "I'm afraid I'm going to have to ask you to accompany me back to the Mayfair Hangars, Miss McQueen—under the direct orders of Captain Sebastian."

Oh God.

I end contact immediately, and Ari rushes forward.

"Oscar, speed up. *Now!*" I shout. "And register security forces as primary hostile bodies."

"Yes, my lady!"

Ari nods. "And we should stay on course; if backup doesn't arrive in time, then we have a good chance of losing them without straying from our route."

"That's what I'm hoping!"

The *Kabul* thrums into maximum life and hurtles through the water, its nose piercing the current and frothing the surrounding waves. We *must* lose them immediately; it'll prove harder to outrun security when there are more of them.

"My lady, I detect four more security vessels on our tail."

Argh!

Ari rushes into the viewport, peering out. "Oscar, fire on them!"

"No, wait!" I shout. "We don't attack preemptively, only defend. Keep going, Oscar, and ensure all defense systems are active!"

The craft shudders.

"Oh, calamity! We appear to be under attack, my dear!" Oscar announces.

"Okay, rise! We need to rise, Oscar! Keep going until the security vessels fall away!"

It's the only way. Though the security forces' crafts are hefty and advanced, they're still not submarines. No matter *how* sturdy submersibles are, they're no match for the turbulent higher waters.

They turn out to be far more determined and resilient than I'd anticipated, but eventually we rise high enough for them to drop away.

"Stay at this height for another league, Oscar, and remain on course at full speed."

I wring my hands. So . . . Captain Sebastian has put a security alert out for me. *Why?* Because he suspects I'll be searching for Papa? What possible reason could he have for trying to stop that? I wish I knew what was going on!

Ari joins me, looking out into the waters.

The chase—and knowing I have to evade all authority vessels from here on—has left me feeling on edge and I move away.

I grab the brolly Theo gave me and slump into the cushioning sofa with Jojo. I want to know exactly how to use the weapon, just in case. Ari leaves the saloon.

I'm familiarizing myself with the brolly when Oscar reappears, his expression mildly concerned as he plays with an ornate ring on his finger. "My dear lady, I'm afraid a change to the trajectory is in order. Leaving via Dartford Tunnel is no longer feasible. Due to the Anthropoid attack on the city, its border-crossing points just closed. Nobody is to leave London for at least twenty-four hours. Instructions?"

My heart sinks and I sit up. "What on earth am I supposed to do now then? We need to cross the borders *tonight*. Security is stretched this evening, so we'll never get another chance like this! I must get out of London tonight!"

"Epping Forest," says Ari, striding back into the room. He has his target board and knives with him. "It's the least guarded route. Everywhere else is crawling with border patrol, and *all* security forces will have received the same instructions from Captain Sebastian. The forest is a back door over the borders—which is why it attracts all kinds. But it's your only option if you want to cross tonight. The sooner we reach King's Lynn, the better."

No kidding.

I tense as I absorb his words. *Anywhere but Epping Forest*, Tabby had said. But security is only going to increase going forward, so I *must* leave London tonight. I don't have any other choice. I swallow. "I'm not turning back. We cross via the forest."

Ari nods in agreement and I'm left wondering what he's prepared to see us through, just so he can return home as soon as possible.

He hangs his target board in the saloon and stands far back, ready to take aim.

I chew on my lip. "What about when you miss the board? Jojo's running around in here."

His brow furrows. "Why would I miss the target?"

He holds a blade in each hand. The muscles in his arms bulge every time he draws his hands back and aims. A certain energy radiates off him. The knives never, no matter how far back in the saloon Ari stands, miss the center of the board. I wish I could look away.

When he's done, he heads straight for the viewport and sits, eyes closed.

Jojo scrambles down and joins him.

"Jojo, come here, baby." I beckon the puppy with fervent hand gestures that she simply ignores.

Ari plays with her, smiling and delighting in her antics. I cross my arms. He speaks gently, constantly patting and stroking Jojo. She just thinks anything he does is flipping fantastic, daft thing. She's embarrassing herself, really. At one point, as the puppy tries to impress him with a series of naff acrobatics, he laughs heartily in response.

I tap my feet on the soft rug. A globe of the Old World stands next to me, beside the bronze model of a cat curled up. Leaving via Epping Forest is almost doubling back on ourselves. Still, we survived an Anthropoid attack, thanks to Ari, and a chase by the security forces. Perhaps it might get a little easier?

I consult my maps. Security bases lie on either side of my intended course, and rival shrub gangs also work the area. But if I stick between Dagenham and Barking, I should be safe. Hopefully. With a sinking feeling and a bad taste in my mouth, I instruct Oscar on the new directions and the sub turns northwest, toward Epping Forest.

It's not like Tabby to have warned me against passing over the forest without good reason. But one way or another, I'm getting out of London tonight.

I pray I've made the right choice.

CHAPTER EIGHTEEN

Everything always makes much more sense after a cup of tea. I sip the soothing liquid and nibble on a scone as I watch the sub pierce London's waters, in the direction of the forest.

Jojo's exercising. A juicy bone floats around the room, rising and dipping teasingly. No matter how fast the puppy is, the projection is always faster. Why didn't she alert me to Ari's presence? She's meant to be loyal to *me*. Her limp's entirely gone; thank goodness he tended to her.

I recall Grandpa's words: *He's here to ensure your safety.*

The tea does the trick. Making Ari a cup, I head to the control room. He's not there, and I trace him to the engine room.

A constant thrumming greets me as I enter the hot space. A maze of pipes curve all around, running along the sides and even above my head. Dials, levers, valves, and tanks, in all shapes, sizes, and materials, surround me. I walk on until I spot him.

He's shirtless, sweat gleaming across his back and shoulders. He pauses to check every valve, read each dial. His golden-copper tinted skin twitches as the muscles in his arms, shoulders, and back flex with the movements. How can anyone look both graceful and incredibly strong at the same time?

I quickly avert my gaze, slosh some tea in my haste, and moan.

He glances in my direction, his gaze as piercing as ever. Concern breaks through his expression.

"Is everything okay?"

"Yes." *Don't you dare blush.* "You know Oscar will alert us to anything that needs checking? And the readings in the control room are all looking fine."

He nods. "I just wanted to be sure. Some things only crop up once the vessel's underway. But so far, so good."

I place the cup down. "Erm, tea."

He stares at the cup, slight surprise surfacing in his eyes. When he catches mine, his gaze is swiftly shuttered once more. He passes by me to check a pressure gauge—barefoot and looking right at home. He smells like warm wood, leaves, and water. Perhaps a forest might have smelled like him.

"I don't like tea," he says. "I only drink coffee."

What the hell. Who doesn't like tea? And to think he's suspicious of others? "Well, that's too bad. I don't like coffee so I only brought tea on board."

"I have everything I need."

Argh. He isn't the only one who wishes he wasn't aboard my sub. He's maddening and I really don't like him. But there's something I need to ask. "What do you know about my papa? Anything I don't?"

The question catches him off guard, and he stares at me before leaning back against a tank, slipping his hands in his pockets. His face is flushed, his skin radiant and his eyes bright. "That depends," he finally says, his expression as guarded as ever, "on what you know."

"Papa went to work one day and never came home. The police told me he'd been arrested for aiding seasickness sufferers in taking their own lives—a rotten lie. Grandpa finally told me the truth recently, that it was the Blackwatch who took him away. The authorities said Papa was being kept in London—another lie. Grandpa knows he was taken out of the city. Not a single shred of evidence has been produced to back the accusations against Papa. And that's everything I know. You?"

His brow furrows slightly as he stares intently. Then he's guarded once more and shrugs.

"I'm only here because my father insisted I help his friend. Your grand-father's asked me to ensure you get to King's Lynn safely. Once you're at his cottage, I go back to my own life. That's all I know."

I hold his gaze, unblinking.

Finally the amber depths in his eyes flicker and shift and he sighs. "Did you ever question anything before your father went missing?"

"Like what?"

"Did you ever hear of others going missing before your father?"

I try to remember. "Sometimes, yes. Rumors here and there. But they were arrested because they'd done something criminal."

He raises an eyebrow.

I glare at him. "My papa's innocent!"

"I know," he says.

My mouth opens; I close it again. It's always *such* a relief anytime someone agrees!

"And," he continues, a bitter tone creeping into his voice, "just maybe those other people who disappeared were also innocent? Did you never wonder about that?" He removes his hands from his pockets and folds his arms. "You people . . . Always content with your own lives no matter what's going on with somebody else, somewhere else—as long as you're fine. Always believing everything you're told."

I shift on my feet. Why am I "you people"? He truly is maddening! "What do you mean? Why would I suspect ordinary arrests—"

He straightens, clenching his mouth and raking his hand through his hair. He averts his eyes, as if he regrets his outburst. "Look, I told you. I'm just here to make sure you're safe. When we reach the cottage in King's Lynn, I'm done."

I open my mouth, but before I've got a word out, Oscar appears.

"My dear lady, it would appear we have sailed into contested shrub turf. We are, most unfortunately, in the center of quite a rumpus between rival gangs."

We both rush back upstairs to the saloon. I shake my head as I absorb the information and peer into the water. Despite knowing about the danger, I still managed to walk right into it.

"Oscar, switch to defensive mode immediately and stay alert," I say.

"Hit them," Ari urges, baring his teeth. "Hit them all *now* so we can be on our way."

"Well, of *course* I bloody won't. The *Kabul*'s been updated with the best defense systems; we have to trust in Deathstar's and Theo's tech. Those subs aren't interested in us; they're fighting among themselves. If we race through it, they'll see we're not a threat."

His brow furrows as he studies me before pacing the viewport. Does he trust *anyone*?

I run through my options; this is where a submersible is so much more advantageous. You can't just swiftly rocket, nosedive, or backflip a submarine out of danger.

I instruct the Navigator, "Switch to infrared, ensure our defenses remain running. Don't dip, there'll be far more of them below. This height is challenging for them. We should rise another fifty feet, but then we might be spotted by patrols. Press on, full speed ahead."

The submarine pushes onward. Lasers ricochet off the vessel's body as it weaves around the crafts attacking one another. I jump when the sub lurches and summon Oscar.

"There is nothing of concern to report, my dear lady. The vessel is absolutely fine."

I bite my nails. "Still, rise a little higher, Oscar. Just twenty feet."

Shrubs are big business. And illegal. The demand for them outweighs the supply. The plantlike reeds grow randomly on higher ground, and everyone wants to claim the slimy flora. Dried out and smoked, it helps you forget to be afraid. For a while. But they've contributed to our numbers falling, as overdoses are fatal—and common.

Climbing works, and we leave the battle behind. Oscar confirms the sub is undamaged.

We cross the Thames by Thamesmead, almost back where we started. I swallow my disappointment. If I'm to get to the forest by midnight, I have to remain positive. We could never have anticipated the attack at Belvedere. We press on. Somewhere beneath us now is the Farm, one of the Campbells' most successful hotels, offering realistic mock earth, grass, fences, fields, and "outdoor" activities. You have to be quick to secure a place at the hotel. I always mean to visit it, just to see what it's like. Maybe once Papa is free and his name cleared, inshallah.

Soon the water turns greener and choppier, the churning caused by both a protein plant and power farm below, adding froth and increased buoyancy to the current.

The submarine plows on above the city, speeding over the once ancient site of the City of London Cemetery and Crematorium. Very few Old Worlders remain in their resting places.

Oscar appears. "My dear lady, Epping Forest is upon us."

I brace myself.

CHAPTER NINETEEN

W e'll maintain height for as long as we can, only diving close
to the forest at the first sign of border police. Despite patrol
being thinner here than at any other point of the M25, not many leaving
or entering London do so via Epping Forest. The place is a law unto itself.

Drifting branches and twigs hint at the location. Something moves on
the edge of my vision. I gulp; border police, already? It isn't them, though. It's
the most unexpected and welcome sight. I have to catch my breath. *Wow . . .*

It's a pyrosome; the largest I've ever seen. It floats in the water beside
us. The cylindrical creature must be at least ten meters long. It swerves its
gelatinous body as it moves alongside the sub, its pinkish-white color giving it an ethereal appearance in the vessel's light. It's like a water deity. A
group of eco-bots keeps the creature in sight. It moves away in dance-like
slow motion. As soon as it's drifted far enough from the vessel's glare, its
own blue-green light is visible; bewitching flecks in the darkness. I stare
after it, mouth open.

And I only now notice the vague shape in the far distance. Border
patrol!

I grab the binoculars and race up into the little platform at the very
top of the sub. Yes, most definitely a patrol car. It hovers some distance
above us. It's a matter of seconds before it spots us, if it hasn't already.
It's time to descend.

The submarine is somewhere above the center of the forest as it dives. I confer with Oscar over the best sensory system to use to negotiate the dreaded woodlands.

Ari stands, staring into the water, his expression dark and distant as he spies the odd fishing net on our way down. "We should stay as high above the forest as possible."

The more frustrated or agitated he becomes, the lower his voice drops.

"I know, but we *have* to descend because of the border patrol. If we stay close to the forest we can move forward without the threat of security stops. They aren't likely to wander that low. It's better than being an open target in the clearer waters above."

He takes in my decision and nods, but the hesitant expression remains.

I suddenly brighten. I totally forgot the submarine has the latest interactive mapping system! "Wait—I can just show you."

I activate the simulated sea chart. The room turns translucent blue as water ripples everywhere around us. Jojo stares, transfixed. It's as if we're *in* the water, a part of the ocean.

We see crevices, ridges, jutting ranges, earthquake zones, the marked habitats of deadly creatures, and even animals. I use my hands to zoom in and out of the different areas.

Ari turns in every direction, taking it all in.

"So we're right here." I guide him through the area, explaining all the obstacles.

He watches me closely. Through the now marine tones of the room, his gaze is more intense than ever. I tear my eyes away.

I bring up all the creatures hidden in the depths. The sea's wildlife fills the space. The deeper I go the more breathtaking the animals, totally outrageous life-forms. Everything from opaque shapes and transparent anatomies to bioluminescent beings swim around us, showering us. I laugh and reach out. I meet his gaze and it's relaxed, his eyes bright. I stare back. *Wow.*

He looks totally different when he drops his guard. . . . He remains mystifying. Unfathomable, yes. But so much softer, kinder. My insides flutter.

Heat floods my cheeks. I swallow, straightening immediately, and turn away. Only to let out a loud gasp when a gigantic creature surfaces on the map, its dark eyes empty as it swims toward me. A red warning sign follows the animal around. What is it? I've never seen it before. I rack my brains for the menacing creature's identity, but nothing comes to mind. Quivering, I inhale loudly and wave both arms out beside me. The sea chart vanishes, taking the water and creatures with it.

There's just so much I don't know. So many terrors lurk in the depths.

Ari moves over to the viewport, where I join him to check the view.

"It's not as scary as you think," he says, his voice subdued as he rubs the back of his neck. "The world—it's not as terrifying as you believe. It was just a sea creature."

Just a sea creature? "Have you never watched *Today's Terrors of the Deep?* There are some truly terrifying things hiding out in the water, you know."

"Then it is a good job you have regular reminders," he says, sounding reluctantly resigned. "Imagine if you forgot for a moment."

"And why on earth would we want to forget? That would leave us vulnerable."

"And you believe living in fear of everything helps you?"

"Who lives in fear? Being aware of the dangers keeps us alert. Always better to know."

He presses his lips into a straight line, and we stare out into the water.

I recall his words to me earlier. What was that all about? What did he mean about us always believing everything we're told? I sigh; once I get to King's Lynn, I'll make *sure* I get some answers.

The darkness has intensified outside. Is that even possible? I order the sub to stop diving and for full lighting capacity to highlight our surroundings. *Yikes.* I wrap my arms around myself as we take in the sight.

Beneath us, the undergrowth is an endless expanse of ancient trees, all uprooted and toppled over one another. The mass of plants—a mixture of long dead and evolved new life—ripples as if the ground itself is alive, whispering, plotting.

I maneuver us through the brooding waters. Other vessels are just visible here and there, glowing lamps drifting in the dense darkness. A wide net drops from the underside of a camouflaged and modified sub calling itself *Pan*.

Fishing is illegal for citizens. It causes too many traffic accidents. Only verified companies are allowed to fish, and stock is sold cheap so nobody is forced to place themselves in danger. But in the forest, anything goes.

The sea life is captivating. From the largest fish that glare through stony eyes, to the tiniest creatures darting around as they investigate the submarine's lights. *Oh my.* I've never before skimmed the remains of an ancient forest. It's another world.

I'll stay hidden as low and for as long as possible, rising to cross the borders when I see my chance.

The sub plows over and through the dense landscape. Dimmed lights can be spotted as vessels lurk farther below for whatever reason. Creatures of all shapes and sizes dip and graze as they move across the swaying plains. Strange long, wormlike animals crawl around the growth, side by side with fish I could swear are ancient insects. More shrub production. Farmers cut at bulky-leaved plants, the razor-sharp contraptions spinning away beneath their subs.

We're not too far from the northern end of the woodlands now. At last. We'll maintain this speed at least until we've crossed the borders. I lift my shoulders and let them drop, allowing myself a small sigh of relief.

Almost immediately, a robust craft—one of the larger submersibles—rises out of the depths and hovers in the far distance. Directly in the *Kabul*'s path.

CHAPTER TWENTY

The submarine decelerates.

"No, we mustn't slow down in the forest." Ari screws his face up as he peers out.

"I *know*, but Oscar knows what he's doing."

"My dear lady, somebody wishes to communicate with the *Kabul*. A private vessel."

A private sub wants to speak to *us*? What if they ask me what I'm doing here? How on earth would I explain driving this close to the forest? What if my plans are halted now when I'm finally so close to the borders?

Ari's eyebrows meet, and he folds his arms, his face tight. "Don't engage anyone. Don't believe anything they say."

"Huh?" I stare at him and shake my head. "This is *my* sub, remember."

"You can't trust anyone."

"What's wrong with you?" I snap. "Is *everyone* your enemy?"

"I want to be done with this and return to my family who need me," he says through gritted teeth.

"At what cost, dammit? It might be a genuine emergency. If it isn't, we'll just move on."

He pauses, his eyes meeting mine, his expression dark; then he swallows and looks away.

I take a deep breath. We *must* cross the borders tonight, while security forces have their hands full. My gaze wanders to the frameless picture of Papa and me.

I accept the communication request.

The screen fills with not one, but several faces all vying for monitor space.

A small, wild-haired woman at the front jumps up and down so she'll be visible and a thin man at the back grins nonstop, his mostly toothless mouth all scabby and pus-infected. Shrub addiction.

A bald man clears his throat. "Welcome! Welcome, dear friends, to our *simple* dwelling in the woods. So nice of you to visit us like this." He bows with a flourish.

I manage a small smile. "I'm sorry, are you in need of help? I'm in a hurry but stopped in case you need assistance of any kind."

They all turn to one another, nodding and smiling.

"Must people need urgent help in order to interact, nowadays?" asks the bald man, with a hint of displeasure. "No emergency here. We just fancied a chinwag, that's all."

"Oh. I'm afraid I can't stay. In fact, I have to be on my way right now, otherwise I'll be late, but it was really kind of you to welcome me like this." I smile.

They turn to one another, muttering.

"Little girl!" calls out the bald man, who seems to be their spokes-person. "Come now, don't be shy; we don't bite." They all shake their heads in protest. "We continue the peace-loving tradition of the Old World. We're the hippies, the legendary ancient tree-huggers, and you're now in our neighborhood. So follow us and let us all get to know one another."

The others nod, and someone calls out for them to all have a cup of tea.

The jumping woman is beside herself with enthusiasm. "Put the kettle on! Have a biscuit!" she calls out each time her face fills the screen.

"I love tea," I begin, and they cheer. "But I have to go now. Maybe another time?"

They pull long faces.

"She has to go? But where's she going?" The toothless man turns to a round, red-haired woman at the back. "She's not intending to cross the borders, is she? It's suicide!"

The red-haired woman wags her finger at me. Her voice is firm, her accent broad. "You don' wanna be doing that, love. There's crazies out there. I've seen it meself. You wanna be careful." She looks aghast and the bald man puts an arm around her.

"Our Laura knows what she's talking about, she's been to *the other side*," he says. There's a collective intake of breath as the group allows the fact to sink in. "Laura's one of the lucky ones. Nobody else from our family ever came back." His voice is loud and bitter now.

"The other side! The other side!" chants the small woman every time her face is visible.

"Thank you. I appreciate all the warnings, I really do." I nod. "But I'll be all right. I—"

"Oh, you'll 'be all right,' will you?" the spokesman says with a slight sneer. "So you'll 'be all right' when you meet one of the countless extremist groups—"

"Scary bunch," the toothless one interrupts, shuddering and wiping some pus at the corner of his mouth. "We only just dodged those nutters, Flesh Forward, the other day. Can you believe that? Human beings sinking so low as to start worshipping those beasts? A 'powerful and magnificent species,' that woman called the Anthropoids. No point resisting them, she insisted—said we should all join them in acknowledging their superiority over us, become willing subjects. The world's gone barking mad." He starts muttering to himself.

"And there's the escapees from Broadmoor." Sadness breaks through the red-haired woman's expression. "And believe me, love, you *really* don't want to bump into one of them after what those poor folk have been put through in that excuse for a prison."

"The Anthropoids! The Anthropoids!" the tiny woman chants with each bounce.

Everyone, including me, falls silent. I made a mistake; I shouldn't have stopped for them. Tabs was right about the forest.

The jumping woman, who's still now, so only a few disheveled hairs on her head are visible on-screen, mutters, "An abomination . . . abomination . . ."

I clear my throat. "They're mostly only rumors. Like this 'Broadmoor'; there isn't *really* a top secret torture prison—" Ari turns to me, and the bald man also makes to speak, but I press on, forcing my voice to sound certain. "It's a lot of scaremongering, that's all. I do have to go now, but thank you for the invitation and your concerns. I'll be seriously careful."

The rest of the group looks sad, but they nod with understanding. The spokesman, however, tsk-tsks and his face tightens. "You think you're too good for traditions, don't you, missy? Getting all high 'n' mighty and—"

Enough. I end communication and instruct Oscar to continue with our journey, and try my best to avoid Ari's now irritated stare. Moving on proves difficult, though.

The group blocks our path. Whichever way the submarine turns, they drive right in front of it, preventing us from speeding off. The sub could simply continue, but these people might be hurt if they don't move out of the way. And above us is border patrol.

Ari's expression is unyielding. "Why not fire a warning shot?"

"Look, can you please just *stop*?"

Reluctantly, I contact the insistent craft again. The spokesman folds his arms and gives a slight smirk and knowing nod. "Changed your mind, love? Follow us."

I purse my mouth. "Do you think this is 'peace-loving'?"

His eyes narrow. "Just maintaining traditions. *Someone* has to."

"Don't manipulate the memories of those gone before us. Stop using them like this."

His face hardens. I stick my chin out. The others look uncertain and even shrug apologetically behind him.

The thin man wipes his mouth, his eyes wide. "Oh, you've gone and done it now, lassie. You best be off right away. No backchat allowed, I'm afraid, nope." He glances hesitantly in the bald man's direction.

The spokesman shoots him a seething look back, scanning the group questioningly, before folding his arms and sneering my way. "Listen. You can't—"

"*Enough*. Be on your way." Ari moves beside me. His breathing is fast, his nostrils flared. His voice is dangerously low as he bares his teeth at them. "You have exactly one minute, or we fire on you."

I nod along with his words, though I'm not too sure about the firing bit.

Papa's gaunt face flashes before me; the hunger he silently endured so I'd have enough to eat. Shame on me. Wasting time here when I should be moving forward. I take a deep breath. *So close now.* I check the time. Has it really only been hours since I left the hangar? I could've sworn it's been several days.

The spokesman shakes his head. "Oh, you're going to regret threatening *us*, missy! Prepare to—"

I instinctively end communication. "Oscar. Defense mode on and rise now."

As I suspected, the water immediately fills with firepower. Thankfully it's old and weak.

Ari's beside me by the window. "Why aren't we returning fire?" He shakes his head and places his hands on his hips. "And we're rising? What about border police?"

"We're far bigger and stronger; we can get away without hurting them or damaging their craft. Besides, apart from their spokesperson, the group is actually well-meaning. And we've no other choice now but to ascend. Down here we have *all* sorts of obstacles. At least up there we only have the one. It's time to rise up out of this—this strangeness and risk border patrol in the clearer waters. Better what you know, always. And we're very close now anyway, won't be for too long. We should be all right." I chew on my lip.

Ari watches me. His hooded gaze—fringed by long dark lashes—is conflicted. Seeking something. *What?* He swings his attention back to the water, running his fingers through his hair. "Why do you have to be so stubborn?" he asks quietly.

Huh? I blink at his question.

He waves his hand. "You could have ignored them. Forced them out of the way!"

"Why would I do such a thing?" I snap.

He shakes his head and clamps his jaw. I fold my arms as I peer into the water coursing around the viewport. The submersible is still doing its best to block the *Kabul* from rising. They risk everything hovering above in its path. I order the sub to keep ascending.

Reluctant to test the higher, turbulent waters, the craft eventually drops back. I scan for border patrol. Not only is Epping Forest not a designated border-crossing point, but also no crossing is permitted for twenty-four hours. We press on.

We're now at the forest's northern tip. The Bell Common Tunnel will soon be beneath us and once we cross over it, we'll be out of London. *Finally.*

I pace the floor. "Keep going, Oscar."

Then, most frustratingly, my entire body trembles. I gulp for air, stumbling back.

Ari's beside me in an instant.

My insides quiver. The room goes funny, moving around me. The space sucks me in.

His brow creases. "What is it?"

I gesture to indicate that I'm all right and make my way to the sofa. Slumping down, I concentrate on my breathing. He stands beside me, staring, his thick eyebrows drawn.

"I'm fine," I insist, but he stays put. "It's nothing. I'll be fine in a minute." Except there's such a weight on my chest, it will crush me, surely.

I'm leaving London.

Everything familiar, everything I've ever known, will be behind me. Everyone was right. I know *nothing* about what's out there. Anthropoids on the rampage, random security checks, and strange people who at the very least could halt my search for Papa. Who the hell am I kidding, thinking I can do this?

My chest aches. I take deep breaths. "Oscar, maintain speed."

I grab my bag and rummage through it before emptying the contents onto the floor: sweets, tiny gadgets of all kinds, the odd paper model, miniature emergency kits. And handmade maps. The few I made especially small so I could always carry them around. They comfort me when I need it. I open one up, staring at it.

I close my eyes. All the maps I've created over the years, far too many to recall. Papa always marveling at them, trying to provide whatever I need so I can indulge. The excitement of making one . . . The thrill of discovery and pinning the exact location down. I *love* making them.

I frown as I open my eyes. The idea of exploring is *exciting*. Definitely terrifying beyond belief, too, but there's no doubt about it—I've also always found it thrilling.

Ari kneels beside me, his eyes narrowed as he checks the maps. "You made these?"

I nod.

"Why? Why would somebody who's spent her life afraid of leaving London—"

My face burns. Why did Grandpa have to tell him *that*?

"Of ever crossing the borders," he continues. "Why would she make maps? Maps not only of London, but the whole country?"

There are gold specks in his questioning eyes. Dark stubble covers his chiseled jaw; his face is quite perfect, really. . . .

I open my mouth, but no words come out.

"You were right," he continues. "You're stronger than you look. Your grandfather asked me to keep you safe. But not because you are weak. It's because *they* will do whatever they have to, to achieve what they desire. You are not safe around them."

I straighten. "I won't be safe again until I'm back with my papa."

I suddenly realize the time and command the screen on. Prime Minister Gladstone's making a statement. He looks as if he hasn't slept for weeks.

". . . And so despite the vicious and cowardly assault on the Brighton Pier resort, the traditional New Year celebrations and annual fireworks display in London will go ahead in defiance of the Anthropoids, and in memory of all those murdered today," the PM says. "The twenty-second century will see humankind regain their rightful place on the surface, and as such, at this momentous point in time, Britons will *not* cower in the face of terror."

The PM smiles, his face softening. "And now, a gift to all Britons, in honor of a new century dawning." Edmund Gladstone clears his throat and looks straight at the camera. "My fellow Britons, I give you Operation Renaissance—my promise to you."

The camera cuts to a huge mahogany table. A miniature model sits in its center. The PM's voice carries over. "This really is the future. We are one step closer."

The replica model is of 10 Downing Street—the headquarters of the government—but without its supporting titanium columns. Instead, Number 10 floats on the surface of the water. Facilities and transport infrastructure surround the miniature government building. The camera cuts back to the PM.

"Operation Renaissance is my belief in our brave and industrious Explorers who are working zealously to ensure we are close to returning home. Furthermore, a new batch of surface drones have been released; drones able to travel higher and farther than ever before. They'll soon have a thorough understanding of the ever-changing climate above and what it holds in store for us. Operation Renaissance is top priority alongside the usual: historians, preservation, Explorers, defense. It will not be long before we are on our way to living once more like the species we were—magnificent, advanced, and civilized. Not some scavengers cowering in the abyss."

"Marvelous, quite marvelous." Lord Maxwell, the chief historian, is sitting beside him rubbing his hands together and nodding vigorously. "At long last a tremendous wrong shall be righted. And, as chief historian, might I add how this very moment right here shall one day go down in the annals of history."

"Indeed, Lord Maxwell." Prime Minister Gladstone nods, his eyes shining. "We are human beings—*Britons* to boot. Once upon a time we ruled these very same waves that now take countless British lives. We must never give up on what we were."

If Explorers are really close to finding a way for us to survive on the surface, what would that mean for Papa?

The PM stands and walks over to a war table. "May I present the Battle of Trafalgar, 1805. A magnificent British naval victory of the Napoleonic Wars over France. *That's* who we were, and *that's* what we'll return to. A species to behold. We were conquerors. We won't be conquered by this deep darkness, and any evil that lurks within—not on my watch."

A few more words, and finally the prime minister is done. "No past, no future."

"No past, no future," the officials around him echo, and the national crest ends the broadcast. Captain Sebastian wasn't among them.

The countdown to the New Year starts on-screen.

I scoop Jojo up and stand by the tip of my submarine, staring into the liquid void. I rub my temples; instead of feeling soothed, I'm just irritated by the PM's words. What have his men done with my papa? How can we enjoy returning to the surface when our loved ones are missing?

The submarine rises even higher. The *Kabul* begins crossing over the Bell Common Tunnel. *At last.*

I hug Jojo close as 2100 chimes in. A new era has arrived. The twenty-second century. The future. It will bring change, inshallah. It *has* to.

The usual official laser light shows begin on-screen. Beams stretch and pulse through the water by the old Thames riverbank and in Edinburgh. For as long as I can remember, I've always watched the New Year's firework display on the communications wall as it beams live around Great Britain.

"Happy New Year, Papa," I whisper to the outside. *Hold on.* "Happy New Year, baby." I kiss and hug Jojo.

I turn to Ari, who's joined me in the viewport. "Happy New Year, Ari."

A glimmer of warmth flickers across his face. His eyes shimmer briefly, before fading. *Pity.* He looked so different just then, so much softer.

He stares into space, a grim twist to his mouth. "Your father's missing," he says. "Up in the Faroe Islands, in Eysturoy, we're not free. Death clouds everything we do. We live like prey in hiding. Dodging and defending, never knowing if the day will bring the murderers our way. We're not protected as you are down here. Tell me, when the people you love are tortured, lost, when their lives are taken by such inhumane means and there's nothing you can do about it—where's the happiness in that?"

His voice drips with unmistakable sadness, and I feel a heaviness in my chest. It's the most he's revealed about himself since hiding on board. He buries his thoughts and feelings so much. . . . I recall Grandpa's words: *His community was the one attacked. He lost someone close to him during the onslaught.*

"Who—who did you lose? Grandpa said you recently lost someone?"

His eyes flit across the water. His gaze grows dark, his voice hesitant, barely audible. "Lance. A friend. He lost his family in an attack last year. He . . . He never hurt anyone in his life. They attacked two weeks ago. Lance died." There's an ache in his eyes and voice.

I swallow. "I'm so sorry for your loss. Poor Lance. We *will* defeat those beasts, you know. The Anthro—"

"There's no hope." He swings his gaze back in my direction, his expression unreadable. "For any of us."

The sheer bitterness and resentment in his voice is hard and uncompromising.

I shake my head. "There's *always* hope," I say quietly. "We can always change things. I'll finally know the truth when Papa's with me, what's really going on. We can fix things and clear his name. And then maybe he can help you somehow? The authorities shouldn't get away with abandoning you like this. You should have as much protection as we have down here."

Jojo jumps down from my arms and heads for the Bliss-Pod. Time for bed. I follow to settle her in. "Auld Lang Syne" begins playing on-screen.

"No," Ari whispers under his breath, his voice deep and rueful as he gazes out. Is he speaking to me? Even blessed with the sharpest hearing, I have to strain to hear him. "No, the truth won't set you free, Leyla McQueen."

The certainty in his voice is startling. My insides sink. The sub may as well be descending into the deepest, darkest trench.

He's wrong.

The truth is *always* better.

I return to the window. There's an immovable weight inside threatening to engulf me, drag me down. Somewhere just beneath it is the daring to hope.

I'm on my way. Hopefully one step closer to Papa. I stand still and hold my breath as the M25 passes by below and the craft speeds over the London borders. I blow my cheeks out slowly. We've just left the protection and reassurance of the only home I've ever known.

The *Kabul* powers on, beyond.

CHAPTER TWENTY-ONE

Jojo is fast asleep. I sit on the sofa yawning, squeezing my eyes shut. When I look up, Ari stands watching me, a hint of concern on his face.

"You're very tired. Assign me command rights so you can get some sleep," he says.

Though the words are authoritative, his tone isn't. There's a surprisingly gentle edge to it.

I lower my gaze. I *am* drained, well and truly zonked out. After a fitful night's sleep that included the dreaded nightmare, I woke up early to get everything done on time for the departure. Today must be the longest day of my life. But let him take over the sub?

His gaze is steady. "You don't trust me."

Gramps trusts him with my life. He's already *saved* it once, along with Jojo's. And even though he's secretive and makes me feel apprehensive, I actually *do* trust him.

"You need to sleep," he insists. "You've done enough. You can take charge after you've rested. If you're tired, you'll make mistakes. Let me take care of things for now."

"Fine . . . but I don't want us traveling as I sleep." I look away.

He opens his mouth to speak. I cut him off by summoning the Navigator. Oscar has changed, now sporting a plum velvet-and-satin dressing gown, with matching slippers.

"Oscar, grant Ari full primary rights, please. And then find us a safe place for the night. We can continue on in the morning."

If only Ari would be open with me . . . I turn to him. "What did you mean earlier, when you said we were always content with our own lives no matter what was going on with others?"

He inclines his head and lifts his eyes to my face, the bright gaze piercing from beneath thick lashes. A muscle tics along his jaw as he watches me think.

"It's because of the government," I say. "Because . . . they don't protect you. . . ."

He gives a curt nod, his face giving nothing away.

"You said we believe everything we're told. What did you mean?"

"It's nothing," he says quietly, remaining still. "Forget it."

"Please, if you care at all about my grand—"

"Gideon?" He snorts. "I told you. My father gave me no choice. They're *friends*." He shakes his head, sneering at the idea. I'm more confused than ever, but I need answers, so I don't react to his words. "After they attacked us, I had to leave immediately," he adds.

"Because you'd have gone after the beasts who killed Lance?"

His gaze flickers, and he nods.

I shake my head. "Why do you blame *everyone* when it's just the gov—"

"Because you stay silent! Your only concern is with yourselves," he spits, raking his fingers through his hair. He folds his arms and takes a deep breath, as if trying to stay calm.

"Huh? Who? All Londoners? *Who* stays silent? How do you mean?" I prickle. "*We* only care about ourselves? It's *you* who's willing to hit out at anyone and everyone you meet!"

I grab the Bliss-Pod, hoping I haven't made a mistake assigning him primary rights to the sub, and hasten out of the room before he can reply. *Argh.* He's so bloody insufferable!

When I enter the master bedroom, though, I forget everything.

Wow. It's bigger than any bedroom I've ever had and decorated in an exquisite Far Eastern vibe. Japanese-inspired style is everywhere.

The walls are actually *papered.* Copper wallpaper glistens with the printed silhouettes of branches and twigs reaching out delicately over its surface. I brush my hands across it. Dark wood and pale blossoms fill the room. Velvets and brocade in olive and plum colors make the place feel sumptuous and warm. And it's actually carpeted.

It's the most perfectly blissful room I've ever seen.

There's a large, circular porthole as tall as me; the ebony waters surge past. I command the blinds to close.

Past the bed are screen doors that lead to a bathroom, and a smashing wardrobe space, all digitally managed and fully working. I shake my head.

I could never have even dreamed of this. It's a complete home. Everything Papa and I could possibly want or need tucked away inside. So utterly perfect. It's barmy to think it's ours.

A warm shower later, I crawl into the luxurious bed and all tension just slips away. The softness of the mattress! I wave my hand around, playing with the mood lighting for a while, exploring its different strengths and colors. First off, a cozy marigold glow.

Within seconds, I drift into a deep sleep.

"Look at it, Jojo," I whisper, hugging the puppy in the morning. I kneel a few feet away from the window, staring through it. Jojo's brown gaze brightens as she snuggles closer.

The sight is mesmerizing.

The submarine moves through a giant kelp forest growing on high ground.

Faint natural light seeping through makes all the difference, and the vivid colors of the looming plant life against the blue of the water is astonishing. The stipes stretch upward, fronds swaying along their lengths like a thousand arms. Striking sea creatures dart among the mass of gangly stems. The kelp bows to the weight of the vessel as it plows through.

"What do you think, baby? It's something else, isn't it?"

Jojo nuzzles my arm and I laugh, leaning in to cover her with kisses.

Ari's listening to music; low, soothing notes echo from elsewhere on the sub. Such stirring, melancholic tones. A piece searching for something. The music stops. The sub begins rising.

I play some more with the puppy, when she cocks her ears and jumps down from my lap.

"Hey, where are you—" *Well, of course.*

A towering Ari stands watching us. Jojo circles his legs, her tail wagging. I peer up from under the hood of my long black robe.

He's showered, his wavy shoulder-length hair glistening black. He's barefoot, wearing a black T-shirt and casual bottoms. The knife hangs from his hip as usual. I stand, my hand reaching for the pocket of my robe. I hesitate and let it fall away.

"You're awake. Good," he says. It really is such a *husky* voice. "There's something you must see."

He gestures behind me. The vessel stops rising. What does he want to show me? I turn around.

There are no words.

I suck in a quick breath. My heart seems to stop, and then it races.

It's the single most beautiful sight ever. Like, *ever.* It's otherworldly. Sacred. My whole body tingles. For the first time, I walk right into the very tip of the vessel and place both hands against the window.

It is the sun.

A plane of liquid light shines in every direction, the shimmering rays reaching down like glistening words of solace, as if to remind humanity the sun is still here. It embraces me, soothing me until I feel buoyant. It's a privileged glimpse into the Old World, this world, other worlds—the universe.

My eyes prickle. Blood rushes in my body, warming my face. My heart expands.

I'm alive.

I stare in silence for the longest time. I turn to say something. Ari's in the tip of the vessel now, holding Jojo up so she, too, can see. He murmurs to her in his low, comforting tones. I glance at the water again and gasp at yet another new sight. Lilac jellyfish are suspended in the glimmering light.

They're completely worthy of drifting along in the semi-luminous waves. If fairies were real, this is how they'd look. The diaphanous bodies are covered in pink-purple specks and move so effortlessly. Their arms sway, like purple ink released in the water.

I let out a long and blissful sigh. How did he know I've never seen the sun?

"It's—it's so . . . Thank you. I've never seen anything like it." I can't find the right words.

How do you describe magic? You can't. Sometimes . . . just sometimes, words aren't enough. Some things are beyond verbal language.

Ari turns to face me, hesitant. I meet his gaze. His own softens as he watches me intently. My mouth curves into a small smile. His eyes flash the fieriest honey gold.

Yes, he's rude, and aloof, and annoying—and most definitely keeps trying to steal Jojo away from me, but he's also . . . Again, I can't find the right words. I reach into my pocket.

He gazes at the golden parchment figure in the palm of my hand. A seahorse.

"I like to make them. Erm, here." I hold my hand out to him. "It's for you. Thank you. For helping Jojo and me."

He hesitates and swallows, before taking the paper model. He turns it over in his hands and looks back at me. His chest rises and falls as he stares. The gentlest warmth surfaces in the amber depths of his gaze as he holds my own.

Oscar appears in front of me and I jump. The Navigator opens his mouth to speak, when Ari suddenly stiffens, his eyes widening and his face turning thunderous.

He launches himself at Oscar.

What the—

Ari leaps straight through the Navigator and grabs me, pulling me down. He crouches over me. I shake. Jojo leaps around, growling and barking.

"Don't look," he implores, his tone urgent. "You mustn't look outside the window."

Oscar still speaks, but I can't make out his words. My mind races.

There's only one thing he'd not want me to know is out there.

I duck under his arm and glance up. Nothing. Not even the jellyfish. He saw something, though. Ari realizes I'm looking out and tugs at my shoulder to turn me away from the view. I swing my head over to the right.

I can't scream. I open my mouth and try, but no sound comes out.

It snarls. A predatory expression rages in its eyes as it meets my gaze. Its hair fans out around its face, the mouth open, allowing the water to freely enter.

An Anthropoid.

It stretches through the water toward us, pounding on the window. It jerks its head back and then, with startling velocity, bolts out of sight.

"Ari." The whisper barely leaves my lips.

He hears, holding me as I curl up on the ground. I can't breathe. He turns my face toward his, gently gripping my shoulders, telling me to take deep breaths. I shake my head. Every part of my body trembles. My heartbeat lashes away in my ears.

An Anthropoid. Looking deceptively human, except it's an abomination.

His eyes implore me to focus. "You're safe," he insists. "He can't enter the sub."

What are those rasping sounds? It's me.

I stare at him. "But it's one of *them*. They're beyond cunning. What are we going to do?"

We're still staring at each other trying to work it out, when we both sense an ominous change and our heads whip around to the viewport.

The *Kabul* has slowed.

Ari's hands fall away from my face; he grabs my hand, helps me up, and we run out of the room, calling for Jojo to follow.

Oscar repeats what he's been saying since he appeared. "My dear lady, there has been an Anthropoid sighting in the vicinity of the vessel."

Then:

"There appears to have been a security breach."

CHAPTER TWENTY-TWO

Ari glances back at me in the passageway. "The moon pool, did you secure it? I didn't have command rights at the time. Did you lock the door?"

My eyes widen. "Oh my God. Deathstar, the mechanic, he—he told me to secure it. I totally forgot! Oscar, is the moon pool door still unlocked? Are you able to secure it?" I pause, leaning against the wall, breathing fast. It's too hot, and my pulse hammers away. How could I have forgotten to take care of it? What have I done?

Oscar nods. "Why, of course, my lady. May I mention how this submarine has been fitted with the very latest in remote security applications? Why, one could—"

"Please lock the pool access door this instant, Oscar!"

"As you wish." The Navigator bows. "The door is now locked."

"And why have we slowed down?"

"The propeller. There appears to be something wrong with it, my dear. While it is still functioning, its thrust has noticeably decreased."

"Oscar, if it slows down any more, let me know, and try to find out more about what exactly is wrong with it. And you can check for heartbeats on board, right? Run a scan."

The Navigator tilts his head. "I detect a total of five heartbeats on board. Two without clearance."

Oh my God. I stumble back and Ari helps. Two. *Two of them.* On board the submarine right now. The passageway is closing in. I shake my head.

A noise sounds from somewhere below.

Ari turns to me. "Stay up here." His eyes beg me not to argue. "Remain locked in until I say it's safe."

"No."

He swears, shaking his head. He grabs the knife kept around his waist and holds it out front.

"Oscar," I whisper. "Is it possible to pinpoint the exact location of the unregistered heartbeats on board?"

He tilts his head to confirm. "Both unapproved guests are in the engine room, my dear."

Ari's expression darkens. "Lock yourself in the saloon with Jojo. Take this." He thrusts the knife in my direction. "I have other weapons."

"Keep the knife. I have my brolly. How are you going to fight them all by yourself? It's impossible—"

"You must go! *Please.*"

I head back to the saloon, locking the door as he approaches the staircase. My whole body trembles now. Jojo whines, burrowing her nose into me.

"It—it's all right, baby. It's going to be okay, you'll see."

My throat aches, as if a large stone has lodged itself there. I grab the brolly. A crashing sound makes me jump. I run to the door, putting my ear against it. What's going on? I beckon the Navigator for an update.

"My dear, there are three heartbeats in the engine room now. Two are unregistered, and the third is that of the gentleman, Ari."

I should've stayed with him. Nobody can survive two Anthropoids at once. I unlock the door and inch it ajar, holding the brolly out in front of me. It won't stay still; my hand shakes too much and the noises aren't helping. Angry, muffled exchanges, followed by shouting.

166

I edge along the passageway, forcing one leg in front of the other. Jojo insists on following me and no amount of silent gesturing will get her to return to the saloon. Indistinct sounds carry up from the lower level. I creep down the stairs.

Finally I can make out the words and I jolt.

"And what about *our* dead?" one of them shrieks.

More muffled sounds—Ari.

A female voice shouts, "You are wrong! They will be avenged!"

Then loud thumping and clanging, followed by groans and cries. *Oh God . . .*

I move along the passageway, willing the quivering in my legs to cease. No luck. I can't get all the footage, all the horrific images I've ever watched on the news, out of my head. The indiscriminate slaughter this species has carried out.

The engine room door slides open. My pulse pounds away as I slip inside. The hot space thrums. I flinch at each noise, moving around pipe after pipe and rows of tanks.

Stifled sounds emerge. Groaning and snarling. Struggling. I creep toward them. The brolly won't hold still; I'll never take accurate aim if I can't stop the shaking. There's somebody ahead. *Ari.*

My eyes widen. He's locked in battle with an Anthropoid. His T-shirt's ripped, and blood and deep scratches cover his chest and shoulders. Groans fill the air as their blows land. Each *thump* makes my insides lurch. Something on the floor to my right catches my eye. I freeze.

It's one of them.

It lies spluttering as it tries to move. It's a he, and it has Ari's knife plunged into its neck. *Oh God.* My hand flies to my mouth; I can't scream. I cower, breathing hard and fast. *Think.* Except I can't stop staring at it.

An actual Anthropoid, not several feet from me.

It looks so *human.* Except it isn't. I really am this close to one of the most vicious creations to have ever existed on Earth, and still it seems so human.

The beast is unbelievably strong. It refuses to die, despite the knife lodged in its neck. Jojo whines, her ears cocked. Does the puppy know? Does she suspect this is an impostor?

Focus. I turn to pick Jojo up. She isn't there. *Oh please no.* A loud clanging and heaving fills the space. Where's Jojo?

I peek around the corner, my brolly pointed. The struggle continues as punches fly in every direction. They move too fast for me to get a fixed aim on the monster, and even if I did manage it, I can't use the tase device—it'll also take out Ari.

He's on top of the beast when the thing flings him off, sending him sprawling backward.

Jojo barks from somewhere behind.

Ari swings his gaze in our direction and spots me. "No! Get back to the saloon, Leyla!"

It's too late.

The Anthropoid cranes its neck and sees me. Its sharp blue eyes shine when they catch sight of me. I back away.

It strides in my direction. *Oh my God.*

I scream.

An exhausted-looking Ari moves toward it once more. But as he passes by the spluttering form on the floor, it reaches out, its bloody hand taking a firm hold of Ari's ankle. Ari shouts for me to run just as the monstrous figure yanks him down, its eyes enlarged and nostrils flared. They both get up and launch themselves at each other, tumbling together out of the engine room and into the passageway.

I run, cowering behind a huge copper tank, Ari's bruised and bloodied state seared into my mind.

Where's the other beast hiding? Where's Jojo? Should I make a run for it? My whole body trembles now, my hands, arms, legs, everything fails me all at once. I wipe my sweaty palms on my robe; I'll need a firm grip on the brolly. Movement to my left catches my eye.

The Anthropoid. It walks toward me.

Jojo makes a desperate dash for the other side of the engine room.

"No! Come back, Jojo! Get behind me!" I point my brolly at the thing.

It ducks behind a tank and sprints toward a terrified Jojo. It's *impossibly* fast and grabs her, breathing hard and heavy. I scream. The woman is around thirty. A thin, gaunt face with sandy hair. She—*it* has high, narrow cheekbones and long arms and hands. It's dripping wet. Its eyes . . . Frosty and bright, they seem familiar now as they bore into mine with such ferocious intensity. Where have I seen those eyes before? It's such an icy look and yet I feel as if I'm burning alive. *So much hatred.*

It wraps its hand around Jojo, and I notice the missing fingers. It's the same Anthropoid that took part in the attack on Brighton Pier—the one caught on camera.

Jojo. She's visibly trembling in its arms. I swallow to combat the dry throat. It makes it worse. And the dread . . . the dread threatens to rise up and drag me somewhere deep down.

I clutch my abdomen; am I going to be sick? "L-let go of her. Please. Don't hurt Jojo."

It shrieks, a long and raging sound, turns to me, and says, "Why isn't *our* pain as important to you? Why should *we* suffer—watch our loved ones blasted to pieces—and not you? WHY?" It's screaming now.

Freezing nausea sweeps through me. And I can't look away.

I can't look away because along with the beast's brutality, its loathing and raging, the bloodthirst and all the frenzy, there's something else there, too.

I think it's pain.

I don't understand it, but it's there. And I can't stop shaking my head at the horror of it all. I scream as it glances at Jojo in its hand, swings its arm back, and hurls her through the air.

No. She flies across the room and hits a round silver valve attached to one of the tanks. A barely audible yelp echoes as she lands. She lies quivering. The white fur on her head reddens at once. *No, no, no.*

I scream and scream and stumble back as I call out to her. The brolly falls. Jojo just lies there. Before I can regain my balance, the thing closes the distance between us and grabs me. The room spins. And then all I know is pain.

Hands pummel me, agony radiating from my chest, shoulders, back. I gasp, fighting to breathe. My lungs are failing. Nerves explode everywhere. My limbs aren't mine anymore, refusing to obey me. I crouch into a ball on the floor, begging it to stop.

For a second I think it might.

For just a second, as its face hovers above mine, something unexpected flickers across it. . . . Something like sympathy.

But then rage rides in, sweeping away any hint of compassion, and it grabs my head and hits it against the floor.

A tsunami of pain. *Everywhere.* Dull pain pulsing inside my skull, a sharp cutting pain speeding down my spine, and hot, burning pain radiating throughout my body. I take short, quick breaths. *Don't black out.*

My pulse scares me; my heart will burst out of my chest if it gets any louder, faster. My sweat soaks the robe. The Anthropoid stomps on my hand, and several cricks fill the air. A strange sound leaves my lips, muffled as I bury my face in my arm. It's too much. My face burns with sweat. I can't escape its loathsome eyes, no matter where I look. The heady smell of hot metal is suffocating; the room has shrunk.

My fingers hang limp. "I—I'm *begging* you, please s-stop."

It shakes its head. "Never," it says, baring its teeth. "From now on we avenge each and every one of our dead."

"Y-you can't—you can't go around attacking us, and not expect us t-to retaliate. *You* hurt *us.* You t-terrorize us. We can't live like that!" I break into more sobs.

"LIES!" it screams.

Blood trickles down my forehead and cheek. Rust in my mouth; bitter and warm. The brolly . . . I can't reach it. I gulp for air.

"Oscar." I whisper it into my armpit as I lie crouched in a ball. I'm not sure what I expect to happen, but I'm desperate. "Oscar." It's probably not loud or clear enough.

"You summoned me, my lady?"

I bloody did. A sob rises in my chest, his voice a beam of light in the darkest depths.

The Anthropoid's eyes bulge, and its face scrunches up at the sudden sound of the Navigator behind it. It turns around to face Oscar.

It's hard to crawl when every muscle in your body has betrayed you. And I'm finding it near impossible to focus. I can't take my eyes off the beast's back as I shuffle the few feet and grab the brolly.

My hand shakes violently as I lean back to aim. The two limp fingers aren't helping. I recall Theo's instructions. *Now.* I press the tase button.

Nothing.

The beast tries to grab Oscar, its hands falling through the air.

I try again. The button's jammed. *No.* I inhale sharply. Huge mistake. It turns to me again and moves toward me.

I clench my mouth and repeatedly jab the button. *Come on!* It finally depresses. *Now.* I aim the brolly at it and press again on the tiny green button with everything I have.

A buzzing, zapping noise reverberates around the room. The thing shudders. Its whole body convulses as it stares at me, eyes wide and mouth open.

Using both hands to combat the trembling, I aim and fire again. Once more the room fills with the dull droning sound. I keep my finger pressed down. Finally, only several feet from me, the Anthropoid staggers back. It falls, hitting its head on a pipe before meeting the floor. It twitches.

I sit up, crying out and holding my head. Shuffling closer to it, I aim and zap it again. Somewhere, at the back of my mind, there's this feeling too much will kill it. I don't even care. The trembling is alarming now; I just can't stop shaking. It finally stops moving.

I aim for its heart and zap it once more.

I force my voice out. "Jojo?"

The puppy utters a sound in reply but stays where she is. Her once gleaming white coat is blotched a bright and baleful red.

"Oh, Jojo . . ."

I shuffle toward her, cradling her, stifling a scream as my limp fingers brush against her and radiate agony. I grab a pipe and haul myself up. The room spins. There's a hammering in my head and my neck aches. The spinning eases and I force my feet to move. The Anthropoid lies there. *Focus.* It's impossible; everything's fuzzy. Every muscle in my body seems to have gone rigid. I turn to the Navigator. It's an effort to raise my voice above a whisper.

"Heartbeats, Oscar . . . Is there an uninvited guest in the engine room?"

"There is not, my dear. There are only the heartbeats of my lady and Jojo."

A sob escapes my lips and my shoulders slump. I stare at the dead Anthropoid. *I'm glad.*

Holding Jojo, I open the door; the passageway spins before becoming clear. And I see them both. The monster—panting and dripping in blood—looms over Ari, who's up against the wall, its hands wrapped around his neck. *Oh God.* I freeze.

It's as if I'm watching it on-screen. Ari starts to slump down against the wall, the beast hunching over him as he does. And then Ari slowly reaches up and wrenches the knife out of the Anthropoid's neck.

I lose count of how many times Ari stabs it.

I don't even look away.

It's as if none of it is real. The knife goes in—blood comes out. Again and again.

The ferocious being finally staggers back. It jerks. The eyes bulge. All the muscles in its face tighten. It claws the air, choking, clinging to its artificial breaths for everything it's worth. Which is less than *nothing*.

Its mouth twists and blood splutters and seeps from everywhere. It reminds me of orcas in battle. Except orcas might have more compassion.

At long last, its hands stop scratching the empty space, and it slumps facedown onto the floor. The body twitches, then stills.

I can't stop shaking my head, and my body won't stop trembling. My breathing is too fast and raspy. A pool of blood spreads around the monster. I cling to Jojo.

Ari stands there looking at it, a stunned expression on his face. Cuts and blood mar his gold-coppery skin, his body already swelling. His chest rises and falls, exhaustion in every breath.

As he notices me, his mouth falls open, his eyes flitting between Jojo and me.

I killed the other beast, I want to say. But the words are stuck. And my ribs hurt from breathing alone, never mind speaking.

I swallow and point at the engine room behind me. His eyes narrow.

"Go," he urges, his voice barely audible. "Back upstairs. Lock yourself in the saloon and see to you and Jojo. Please, Leyla," he says, when I haven't moved.

I blink rapidly before dragging my feet toward the stairs, taking care to step around the expanding channel of blood.

I make my way up to the saloon, secure the door behind me, and lean against it.

An incessant drumming beats inside my skull, a dull, pulsing agony. I squeeze my eyes shut in the hope things will be clearer when they open. But no. A void rises inside. I push it back down. Right, the Medi-bot for Jojo.

I make my way to the cupboard, hugging the whimpering puppy close. Oscar speaks. What's he saying? My head is going to explode, surely. An unbeatable vacuum rises up, sucking me inside.

I catch my breath and slump down, hitting the floor.

CHAPTER TWENTY-THREE

"*Steady . . . and increase the thrust,*" *Papa instructs me. "Trust those instincts, Pickle. I'm right beside you.*"

I'm eight, driving a sub for the very first time. I'm hesitant but also desperately want to try it. I increase the speed, dip low, and zoom over the rust-and-coral-covered steel wall of the Thames Barrier. I'm free. "Look, Papa, I'm flying!"

Papa laughs, his heart in his eyes. "Yes, you are!" He beams.

"Papa? You're my wingman." I giggle.

His eyes fill with emotion. "Pickle, you're my entire world."

Everything falters just a fraction. I try to hold on. I can't. I'm pulled back, rudely plucked from such a perfect moment in time.

My eyes flutter open. The corners of my mouth curl up. Papa. And this time he wasn't suffering. This time it was a real memory. I blink rapidly. I'm on the floor in the saloon. My hand is wet. Red. My eyes travel down. Jojo's nuzzled close to me. Blood seeps from her ear, her eyes barely registering me. *Oh God.* I gasp as I remember.

I sit up and wince. Hurried footsteps sound from somewhere. The door opens and Ari rushes over. His expression is the heaviest I've seen, his eyes dark and troubled as he takes in the scene, his gaze darting from my face to Jojo, and back to me again.

"Slowly," he says. "You must have blacked out." He picks the puppy up and checks her wound. "Jojo needs stitches. I will see to her. How do you feel?"

I push my hair out of my face and yelp, jerking my hand away. I bite down hard on my lip. Ari's gaze travels to my misshapen fingers. Rage and concern take their turns, but it's the consideration that reaches his eyes.

I check the time. I've been out for over an hour. I grimace. How could I cave in at a time like this? Jojo gives a faint whine.

I take deep breaths. My head feels like it will implode. Everything hurts too much, and I can't think straight. I clear my throat. "Yes," I whisper. "Please see to Jojo."

He hands Jojo to me and I cradle her in my arms as he gets to work following the Medi-bot's precise instructions. He grabs the medical supplies from the cabinet. "There's only one Medi-bot?"

"I think so. Jojo first."

He cleans and prepares the puppy's ear. "What—what did you do?" I ask, keeping my eyes on Jojo.

"They're gone. I used the waste disposal unit."

"They're no longer on board?"

He shakes his head. I slump in relief.

The muscles in his face flex. "I've ordered Oscar to keep going. And to crush anything that gets in our way." Her stitching done, he gently scoops Jojo out of my arms and lays the bandaged and medicated puppy inside her Bliss-Pod to rest and heal.

He returns to me and picks the Medi-bot up again. I can't tear my eyes away from *his* wounds; my breath hitches. That thing really beat him.

He sighs as he looks at me. "You need a full scan, Leyla," he says softly, his expression tender. "Everyone must be checked after an attack for injuries."

My heart falters as I absorb his words. As I watch him, conflict clouds his gaze, shadowing his expression, and there's a telltale grim set to his lips. And I realize . . .

He's been in this situation more than once.

He offers his hand and I take it, so grateful for it as I rise to my feet; I squeeze it as the room spins a little but let go once it stops. He holds the Medi-bot in front of me, and a beam runs over my body. Within seconds, my diagnosis hovers in the air:

Concussion, two broken fingers in the left hand, a fractured rib, surface wounds. Treatment: Fingers to be protected with a splint—no realignment required; cleaning, sterilizing, and treatment of surface wounds; ice pack on affected rib; painkillers; rest.

My shoulders slump with relief. The concussion could've been so much worse.

The bot secures my fingers, binding them together. A quick jab from its needle and a painkiller is immediately coursing through my body.

Ari looks in on Jojo before walking over to the viewport, his bearing stiff as he sits. Bloodstains smear his shoulders, arms, and chest. I look down at the Medi-bot, walk over to him, and place it on the floor beside him.

I clear my throat. "You should use it, too. The *Kabul* . . . Is she secure?"

"Oscar carried out a full security sweep—twice. She's secure." He stares into space.

He's far away somewhere. There's something different about him, but there are so many other things I have to try and focus on right now.

I nod. "I need to check, see it for myself."

Grabbing my brolly, I hold it out in front and open the door. Silence. Only the submarine's usual thrum. I take a deep breath and edge into every room upstairs. Nothing. Nobody. I gasp and shudder as I catch sight of my reflection.

The robe fell open at some point, and my white nightdress is torn, crimson blotches everywhere. Even my face has scarlet smears across the cheek. Nausea sweeps over me. I avert my eyes.

I stumble away and creep down the staircase. My knuckles turn white as I grasp the brolly. The giant that Ari knifed is missing from the passageway, the corpse no longer where it fell. Though blood is still strewn about, there's far less than before. Something moves on the edge of my vision. I gasp and swing around, pointing my brolly.

It's just two Maid-bots working away. I didn't even know the sub had them. The bots spray something on the walls and floor and continue cleaning the place up.

I peer into the moon pool room through the window. Nothing. I have Oscar confirm the number of heartbeats on board. Three. He could be mistaken, though. I move from room to room. No sign of anybody.

There's only the engine room left to check. My finger hovers above the brolly's tase button as I step inside.

The Anthropoid really is gone.

I tremble. The dread swells and rises, gathering force until it crashes into me, plunging me back into that deep chasm of terror and pain. The frenzy of the beast. The *hatred*. And Jojo . . . It's too much. If only I'd been able to tase that thing before it hurt Jojo.

If only I'd locked the moon pool door.

I return upstairs. Ari remains in the viewport, gazing out. Clasping my hands tight, I swallow, fighting the tears that threaten to leak.

The next thing I know, Ari is walking over to me, his expression tight, his face all hard angles and concern. I look up at him. His eyes flicker.

He takes a step to close the gap between us. "Leyla—"

I take a step back. My shoulders rise and fall. My throat's dry. "I need to go take care of something." I leave the room without looking at him.

Once I'm in the bedroom, I close the door behind me and take deep breaths.

He's wounded because of me. Jojo's hurt because of me. I didn't secure the moon pool door.

Ari was right when he said I have no idea.

I look down at all the blood on me. I have to get rid of it. I can't stand it—not a second longer.

I become dizzy in the shower and have to sit to wash, and it all takes forever. Even on the gentlest setting, the spray hits my skin like a thousand giant needles. It *burns* my scalp. But I need to know I washed all the blood off.

When I'm finally dry and dressed, I walk over to the huge, circular porthole. The sub glides through the current. These waters are much wilder than anything I've ever known in the capital. All I see in the thick gloom is one horrific image after another. Holiday goers at the resort, drowning, terrified. Jojo's bloodied body, whimpering in pain. Grandpa's heart attack. The beast in the engine room. Papa, in God knows what state right now.

My heart is lodged in my throat. No amount of swallowing is easing the burden. *Pull yourself together.* The pressure in my chest intensifies. It's as if I'm holding an ocean inside. It crashes against my lungs, squeezing, trying to crush me from the inside out. *Don't you dare; there's no time for any nonsense.*

I slump down in front of the porthole. Pain, fear, and sadness all grapple for position, eventually merging as one unbearable, burdensome victor.

The tears flow hard and fast, my body convulsing. I couldn't help any of them.

At last, my sobs subside, and my breathing finally relaxes. I peer out into the shifting void.

Why did they do it? Why are they hell-bent on trying to eradicate humans? I shake my head. Why did it feel the need to hurt me like that? Why hurt Jojo? So much pain and destruction. Its frosty eyes flash before me and I shiver. And then there was something else. . . . And I don't really know what it was, but it was there, etched in its face, beneath all the horror. As if some part of it knew it was so wrong to do what it was doing, and yet the anger wouldn't let it stop. Where does that rage and hatred come from? Why did it—for one, brief moment—look at me with sympathy? Because it's an evil abomination and can't help itself? Or because of something else?

What's going on?

And Ari. What did he mean by the truth not setting me free? And people believing everything they're told? He's keeping something from me. But I also feel safe around him. I shake my head. I honestly don't know anything anymore. What was he going to do or say when he stepped toward me?

I picture his arms and chest. I wrap my arms around myself. The thought of a hug right now seems like the best thing in the world. A part of me wants to turn back. Go home to London. To Gramps. My heart flutters at the thought of him. Theo and Tabby—I already miss them so much. Turning around is such an absolutely comforting thought. Ahead is only uncertainty.

And Papa.

He needs me. I must keep it together, can't go losing it now. I won't give in until I've found him. He's all right. He *has* to be.

I summon the Navigator. He appears, sporting a midnight-blue frock coat.

"Oscar, we're still moving too slowly. What's the situation with the propeller?"

"It is stable, my dear. However, it has been sabotaged, which is preventing it from operating at full capacity."

The Anthropoids messed with the propeller. I stand, slowly pacing the room as I absorb his words. "How far away are we from our destination in King's Lynn?"

"A little over ten leagues."

What to do? The thought of being unable to speed up if we hit any more trouble is too much. . . . Without speed, we're helpless. *I'm* helpless.

Crawling through these waters is out of the question. We're powerless until we fix the propeller, dammit.

"Where are we right now, Oscar?"

"Above Ely, my dear. Just past Cambridge."

"Anything from our caution list between us and our destination?"

"A security base at Saddle Bow."

Great; the one thing I can't risk passing—and especially when I'm unable to speed away if trouble arises. Wait, Cambridge . . . Why does it ring a bell?

Papa's note. I rush to my drawer, rummaging through my things in search of the little purple box of papers I'd packed it in. Where did Tabby put it? I find it and check the note with his dear handwriting again.

It's just a few scribbled everyday reminders to himself, but it also has coordinates for Cambridge. Just beneath the numbers is a name: *Bia*. Papa circled it. The first thing on his list of reminders is: *Respond to Bia*. It's ticked off—something Papa always did as he got through his list of things to do. And that's it. It's not much to go on, but it's better than nothing.

I have a location and the information that Papa knew this Bia person. If we retrace our steps a little, we could stop over at Bia's in Cambridge, sort the propeller out, hopefully, and be on our way again. It's a long shot—the location could very well be something other than Bia's address, and they might not be in—and even if they are, they might not be able to help us. But still, there's a small chance. I'm not staying out here like this, dawdling powerlessly through strange and wild waters. I shudder.

"Oscar, are you absolutely *certain* the moon pool door is secure now?"

I should have had it welded shut back at the hangar. We don't need a hole that opens into the abyss. *Anything* could be hiding in the depths below.

A tremor races along my spine, and I'm transported back to my failed freefall a few months ago. My ill-thought-out attempt at conquering the dread. The submersible spinning through nothingness—headed for only God knew what. The fear. The not knowing that gripped me and froze my thoughts, turned my muscles rigid. I was incredibly lucky to abandon the move in time. *Never again.*

Ari's wrong. It's better to stay as alert as possible than to let down your defenses against the environment.

"Oscar, you can get us to Cambridge, can't you?"

"Of course, my lady. Why, one could rule the waves from—"

"Cambridge will do for now."

I register the new coordinates. The *Kabul* turns around as I return to the saloon. Ari's using the Medi-bot to give Jojo her next dose of painkillers. He moves over to the viewport again and sits, rolling his shoulders. Oscar stands beside him.

I pick the Medi-bot up and make my way inside the tip. "Your wounds need tending to. . . . I can do it if you want?"

"Why are we turning around?"

It's like an afterthought. There's no frustration in his voice. He seems shocked. Shocked, and also resigned. What's going on in his head?

"We're stopping off at Cambridge," I explain. "It's too risky to go on with a broken propeller. My papa knows somebody in Cambridge, and I'm hoping they can help us with getting it fixed."

He looks away, his posture rigid. I was expecting him to fight the decision. I wave the Medi-bot at him, my eyebrows raised. He nods, and I get to work cleaning the wounds.

Ari removes the torn T-shirt. Everything seems to still when I touch him; I'm too aware of my own heartbeat and of the strange sensation in my fingers every time they brush his burnished-copper skin. His broad shoulders and back stiffen at my touch, his muscles flex.

Ahead, the unfathomable environment courses around the sub.

"How about a game of chess, my dear lady?" Oscar announces suddenly, as if in a moment of inspiration. "I find it helps chase any melancholic mood away. Or perhaps we shall ruminate on the wonders of art? I daresay, my dear, I am quite the rogue when it comes to—"

"Not now, Oscar. It's not a good time. Something awful just happened."

Oscar bows his head, offering his sincere commiserations. The Navigator muses quietly on calamity and woe, happy to impart his own insights.

I spray Ari's wounds and work away. The swelling looks painful. I kneel in front of him, tending to the back of his hands.

When I look up, he's watching me; his eyes flicker, and his lips pinch together.

He knows I cried.

He searches my face, struggling with something. The amber gaze is conflicted—flitting between shimmer and shadow. Secrets seem to just ripple around him in an unnavigable flow.

What is it? I want to ask. Instead I dip my head, letting my hair conceal me.

Ari clears his throat. "Are you still in pain?"

I shake my head. "Thank you," I whisper. "For everything."

He shifts.

"I'm sorry," we both say at once.

My shoulders rise. "You didn't sign up for this. I forgot to secure the moon pool door, which let them board the sub and hurt you and Jojo. You should head home when we get to Cambridge. I can go on to Gramps's cottage on my own; it's not more than eight leagues from there, and I'll hopefully be able to speed the whole way. You need to go. Nobody else must get hurt. It's *my* decision to search for my papa, and you—"

"It was a mistake," he says. "There was a lot to think about, and you forgot about the moon pool door. We have all made mistakes."

I stiffen, before continuing to tend to his cuts and losing myself in my thoughts. After a while I quietly voice them, breaking the silence. "Do you think it's a good plan—my waiting at Grandpa's cottage until he gets there?"

He pulls back slightly. I look up and he's rubbing his jaw, thinking. "I think the most important thing is for you to be safe. Even if it slows down your search for your father. You can't look for him if you're hurt. Or if the authorities catch up with you."

"I just feel like . . . like there's so much I don't know, and waiting feels like I'm wasting time. I did promise Gramps, so that's what I'll do. But I can't wait to actually be on my papa's trail, you know?"

"Yes," he says softly, his brow creasing slightly. "And you're not afraid?"

I answer quietly. "I don't think there exists in this world a person who isn't manifestly terrified in some way. I think maybe we're all carrying the trauma from the disaster somewhere deep inside us. And the existence of the Anthropoids . . . it's only multiplied that terror a thousandfold."

Ari pauses and watches me, deep in thought. His chest and shoulders rise as he breathes. "What do you think would help heal people?"

"Some hope, of course." I shrug. "All right, we're done." The wounds are all treated.

The sub heaves, and our gazes dart to the water. We're descending.

Soon Cambridge is visible below. We steer over both ancient and modern streets intermingled with colossal, never-ending pipelines, and gigantic tanks of all shapes and sizes. The sub moves around a vast power farm; tethered to the floor and reaching high above us, large kites glide on the current like seagulls on the surface.

We both cock our heads at once when the *Kabul* slows down considerably.

I get up. "Oscar? Have we reached our destination?"

"Indeed we have. My dear, we are at the venerable former grounds of the antiquated Cambridge University." He pauses, tilting his head. And then: "There is a message for you."

"A message? From who?"

"A gentleman by the name of Charlie."

I frown, exchanging looks with Ari even as I say, "Accept." Who on earth's Charlie?

A thin white face appears on the communication screen, wearing a nervous smile. "Hiya. You realize yer cruising through private territory now, don't you?"

"I'm sorry, I had no idea," I say. "Nothing came up on the systems regarding private—"

"Where are you headed?"

"That's none of your business," Ari comes forward to say.

"Whoa, hold yer horses," Charlie says, holding his hands up in defense. "Only asking. Wait there. I have to report all unexpected drifters. If yer not here for trading, then—"

"I'm looking for somebody called Bia!" I blurt out.

Charlie frowns, his wispy eyebrows meeting. "You know Bia?"

"Well . . . not exactly."

What can I say? How much is it safe to share? Papa knew this Bia person, and that's all I have right now. I take a deep breath. I'm either about to do the right thing, or else I'm about to make a massive mistake. But I have to do *something*.

I give Charlie my name, Papa's name, and mention Papa knowing Bia. And then I tell him about our immediate predicament with the propeller.

He puts us on hold for a few minutes.

Though he's smiling when he returns, he seems a little pensive. "Sure," he says. "We'll take a gander at yer propeller. There's nothing the Johnson sisters can't fix. Follow the escort." And then he disappears.

"What es—"

A whole legion of camouflaged crafts materializes in the depths. They move in, lowering from above, rising from the seabed, and closing the gaps to the sides. They're all circular and compact, and the closest in color to the oceans as I've ever seen a vehicle.

Ari's mouth curls into a sneer. "I don't trust them."

Well, of course you don't, I'm about to say.

But he seems to have good reason right now.

We move on, following the vessels in front. Minutes later, as we pass some crumbling ruins, the submersibles slow and we're all hovering.

"Why stop *here*?" Ari stands beside me, hands on his hips.

I shrug. There's nothing below us. Only a rocky terrain surrounded by the usual fluorescent warning signs. I peer at the unfamiliar seabed.

"The subs below have fallen away. . . . I think they want us to continue descending. But why would they want us to rest the *Kabul* down there?"

"Don't do it." Ari brings his face close to mine. His eyes burn bright.

I stare into them. He really does have the fieriest gaze. Color floods my cheeks.

He bares his teeth. "It's a trap."

"My papa knows Bia. Erm, I think. We have to trust them. I'm not crawling around the water an open target. The *Kabul* has to be able to speed up—God knows where my search for Papa's going to take me, and it'll be hard enough, without me traveling in a substandard vessel. Descend, Oscar," I instruct the Navigator.

How strange . . . The flow of the current here, it shouldn't exist. It *wouldn't* exist if there weren't anything below to cause it. The pitch-black craggy surface approaches. It looks like a huge field of flattened mountain. A school of coalfish seems unperturbed as they move over it. And there's no depth-warning signal from Oscar. I wrinkle my brow. *What the hell?*

The submarine doesn't halt. It continues to descend.

The water glimmers as the vessel lowers. I straighten. "Oh my God, the glimmer—the ground's only a projection!"

The seabed seems to swallow the submarine. A vast structure materializes beneath us. Dark and rugged. It looks like one humongous rock. *A hiding place.*

We're led to a camouflaged side hatch. All around us are open waters. I stand in the viewport, wringing my hands. Ari is still, hands on hips, as he looks at me. His expression is cloaked once more; the usual muscle tics along his jaw as his words echo my own thoughts.

"Are you sure we can trust these people?"

CHAPTER TWENTY-FOUR

"**W**hy the hell have you brought knives?" My mouth falls open. "We need their *help*. We can't aggravate them." Despite the painkillers, my ribs feel sore every time I speak.

Ari hides the knife behind him somewhere, slipping it beneath his dark top. He rearranges the gray blanket-style shawl wrapped around his body. "We don't know these people."

I peek inside the Bliss-Pod I'm carrying to ensure Jojo's all right as we stand inside the *Kabul*'s bridge, waiting for the hatch to the place to release. When it does, we step through. It secures behind us again, and the inner door opens. Two armed men await us.

Ari stiffens and I press my arm against me to ensure the brolly's still hanging off it as we enter the building. We're standing in a huge docking bay, with rows of hatches.

I recognize one of the guys as Charlie. He can't be much older than me; he's thin and pale, with fair hair and kind hazel eyes. He smiles at the Bliss-Pod and the sight of Jojo, and steps toward us. I move back. Before I know what's going on, Ari has him in a neck hold, his face tight and the gleaming tip of his knife pressed against the guy's throat. My stomach rolls.

"Steady on!" Charlie's eyes are stretched wide. "The puppy." He points at Jojo. "Just wanted to see the puppy. We don't have any pets here."

Only now do I see that concentrated on Ari's neck is the other guy's laser weapon. My heart races. He's tall and hefty, and wears a permanent scowl.

I turn to Ari, pleading with my eyes. "Charlie was just checking on Jojo. He doesn't mean any harm." *Don't do anything stupid, or they'll hurt you.*

Ari shoots Charlie a threatening stare, before putting his knife away. The burly guy, who looks South Asian, steps back, though his weapon is still pointed in Ari's general direction. He wears a simple iron bracelet on his wrist—the Sikh kara.

Charlie quickly moves aside, rubbing his throat. He offers me a hesitant smile. "Thanks. Bia sent us to fetch you. I remember you now—yer the Marathon champion! Knew I'd seen you somewhere before!" His smile stretches. "You were my favorite to win. You were awesome."

"Thank you." I point in Ari's direction. "And this is Ari. We're really on edge right now, that's all. We were attacked. Anthropoids . . ."

Charlie's brow furrows as he exchanges a swift look with the other guy before turning back to me. "How? Did they get away?"

I glance at Ari; his gaze is steady as it meets mine. I take a deep breath. "We killed them."

I *wanted* it to die. I was glad when it did. I swallow the memory away.

"Too bloody right. Sorry you had to go through that," Charlie says. "Don't want you worrying while yer here, though. Yer safe as houses with us, and, er, Jas here is *always* on edge"—he jabs his thumb in the other guy's direction—"so don't worry about coming across jumpy." He grins.

Jas glares at him.

Safe as houses. Still, better to remain alert.

"Oscar?" I beckon the Navigator. The duo stare at him when he materializes. "Keep her on standby until you hear from me."

He nods. "My lady."

"You," Jas says to Ari. "Blade-boy. No knives from here on."

Ari's brow creases. His gaze meets mine, and I pull my best pleading

187

face. He presses his lips flat and removes the knives from somewhere behind his back. And then another one appears from his waistband. And yet two more are unveiled from just behind his shoulders. I stare at him.

"And the one around your ankle," Jas says.

Ari's eyes flash so bright and hot now, I can't believe Jas isn't on fire.

After taking Ari's last knife, Jas turns to me. "And you can leave the umbrella behind. Everything will be waiting right here for you when you're done."

"This?" I hold my brolly up. "But it's just my brolly." I stare at him wide-eyed. "It's— It's the only accessory I have." The corners of my mouth turn down.

Jas narrows his eyes.

"It's only a brolly." Charlie shrugs and waves his hand, and Jas relents with a curt nod. We're finally good to carry on.

I turn to Charlie. "Erm, you said Bia sent you. Is Bia a scientist?"

"Nope," Charlie says. "Bia's . . . just Bia. She's the boss!"

"Of what?"

Charlie opens his mouth but closes it again. "Of us, I guess." He chuckles, deflecting the question.

I exchange looks with Ari. *Please, God, let them not be some kind of cult. . . .*

Charlie pauses now, turning to me with a shy smile, his eyes warm and welcoming. "Want the scenic route through the shop—much shorter, too—or are you after peace and quiet?"

A shop?

"The quiet route," Ari says, at exactly the same time that I say:

"Anything that might take my mind off the attack for a few minutes. Definitely the shop."

Charlie looks hesitantly at Ari for a second, then nods at me. "Scenic route it is!"

We're led down a dimly lit corridor and through several sealed doors. Just how big *is* this place? At last, we pause by a guarded door. Two heavily armed men move aside, and we're granted access. We all step into an end-less room. My mouth falls open. *What the*— I stare, taking it all in. It's the last thing I expected.

"This here's the Trading Post," Charlie shouts over his shoulder as he walks through the expansive place.

My gaze darts from one sight to another.

Ari twists his neck in every direction and takes the Bliss-Pod from me. He rubs his jaw. "Erm, maybe be careful here? There are too many people around." He points to my ribs, and I nod.

It's like the London markets. Only so much more . . . *alive.*

Each colorful stall bears a huge banner stating its name in fancy let-tering. Ropes of ancient-style light bulbs connect the stalls, and neon signs decorate the walls of the enormous hall. Voices ring out all around us. Owners and customers alike barter, laugh, and argue. Salespeople, dressed in bright and bold fashions, whiz by on hover boards. All manner of mer-chandise hangs off their bodies as they dart here and there. I wrap my arms around myself; Ari's right, I'm definitely too sore for someone to bump into me.

"I don't get it," I say to Charlie. "Why's this place hidden? People would love it."

"The trading here doesn't go by any laws," he replies. His voice drops low. "And where anything goes, just about *everything* goes on. You wanna stay alert."

A bald girl skips out of a nearby stall, the Royal Infirmary, thrust-ing something into Charlie's hand. He stuffs the tiny bundles away with haste. "Top stuff," whispers the girl. "Bia will love it. Only come in this morning."

I crane my neck. My eyes widen at the Deli. Every shrub Britons are warned about is openly on display. Customers laugh and chat as they try the products—as if they're buying sweets! There's a woman slumped against the wall in front of us. Shrub juice dribbles from her mouth.

She adjusts the virtual glasses she's wearing and sighs as she escapes her reality. Charlie tells off a boy who's about to rummage through her coat pockets as we move on.

"This is Bia's?" I ask him. "The Trading Post?"

He laughs. "We wish! Nope, we just rent the place beneath it."

Bloody hell, the place goes even lower? What on earth do Bia and her people do?

We move on past the Flea Market. Delicate ancient china and jewelry dominate the goods. Most items are either chipped or cracked, but they're priceless. The Royal Preservation Society would *implode* if they found out they were on sale to the public!

Jas gestures to us all to pause as he stops at Hamley's. It's full of every weapon imaginable—both Old World and very modern. He takes an interest in the tiniest grenades I've ever seen. Not that I've seen many. But these look like pearly marbles.

"Half price on all treatments today, my lovely." A voice whispers in my ear and makes my heart stall in my chest. "Come take a quick gander."

Before I know what's happening, someone grabs my arm and we're moving. I freeze. I think I stop breathing. It feels as if I'm back in the engine room with the Anthropoid. In seconds we're inside a tent called the Salon. Surgical-looking equipment dots the shelves and almost everything is a cold milky color. I finally manage to pull my arm back, glancing up at a tall, lean man twisting the ends of his lengthy mustache as he peers down at me.

My arm automatically goes up, and I aim the brolly at him.

I clench my teeth and try to slow my breathing. "You can't just *drag* someone to your bloody stall."

"Aw, come on, me duck." The owner pulls the corners of his mouth down and his mustache lowers. "Delicate wrists like yours? They were *meant* for our newest epidermal tattoos. And you've my personal guarantee—absolutely no pain during the implanting. You're a reader, aren't ya? Clever lass, I can tell. I've just the thing for ya. A whole library of books inside those delectable slender wrists. Tell ya what, just for you, I'll throw in an art museum on your other—"

He moves toward me. I go blank. I don't want him to touch me.

My grip tightens on the brolly, and I press down on the button for the immobilizing spray.

Mist spritzes through the air as the spray leaves the tip of the brolly, surrounds his face, and settles into his eyes.

The stallholder inhales, blinking it away. He hisses and swears, and his hands dart to his eyes, pressing his palms into his sockets. "Ya little witch!"

I step away from him. "Don't you *dare* ever drag anyone like that again." I rub my arm where he grabbed me, a particularly sore spot since the beast kicked me there.

He grabs at the air, his eyes now red and watery. "Where are ya?" Instruments fly as he flails and knocks into things.

My heart pounds against my rib cage and thumps away inside my ears. How long did Theo say the effects would last? I duck and brush past him before he has time to grab me; my ribs ache. As I bolt out of the tent, I almost run into Ari, his eyes wide.

"Where did you go?" he asks.

I shake my head and hurry to join the others, just as Jas is done at the weapons stall and calls us over. Charlie turns to look at the sudden commotion behind us; I risk a peek.

Several concerned people surround the stallholder now as he shouts. "It was a little witch, am telling ya! I swear it on the Old World. She wants locking up, the bitch!"

"Someone's been at the shrub juice, I see," Charlie says, shaking his head at the increasingly angry man.

Ari's gaze darts from the stallholder to me, his eyes narrowing. I raise my eyebrows a fraction and shrug as we all walk away. I can't risk attracting attention here, but that guy was well out of order.

We leave the lively space and descend via an iron staircase.

"How much farther down does this place go?" I ask.

"Low enough. We *needed* something deep down. It's the only way we can be sure of—"

Charlie cuts off when Jas shoots him a hard, disapproving look.

"Oh bugger, I'm off again!" Charlie says. "Pay me no mind—I get confused sometimes. I mean who doesn't want secure digs, right?" he hurriedly adds. "And this place was always designed to be off the grid, what with the illegal gaff above." He opens a door for us. "It was the perfect place to set up the Den."

The Den? I straighten, trying to summon courage I don't really feel right now. I turn to Ari and he meets my gaze. The same doubt lurks in his. His hand moves toward me, his expression reassuring. But then he pauses and drops it before he touches me, and a deep russet blush spreads across his cheeks. Instead, he looks at me and nods as if to say it will be all right. I swallow and nod back, cursing the warmth in my own cheeks now.

Charlie enters a series of codes into the largest door yet, and we walk through. He halts before another similarly hefty door where a laser scans us. We're granted entry. I gulp, my grip on the brolly tightening as I take in the sight ahead. Ari tenses beside me.

I'm not sure if they can fix the *Kabul's* propeller.

But I *do* know these people are very definitely up to something.

CHAPTER TWENTY-FIVE

T he Den is considerably smaller than the place above it but far more intimidating. Technology of every kind dots the room. Real screens are lost among the sheer number of holograms, and information hovers everywhere you look. We pause just inside the doorway. The surrounding walls and ceiling reflect strange instruments.

I point at the odd apparatus. "What are they?"

Charlie whistles. "Only the most advanced scrambling and blocking signals!"

"Why? What do you guys do?"

He suddenly looks as if he thinks he's already said too much; he glances away and presses his lips into a straight line. If only Theo were here. He'd not only love the place, but I bet he'd know *exactly* what they're up to in an instant. How well does Papa know these people?

There are at least twenty-odd people around the space, all of them looking busy. Several work on the projections—sifting through what looks like endless charted data: coordinates, costs, and all manner of categorized info. An elderly, agile woman exits one of the many doors around the open space, heads straight for a giant wall rack and busies herself with the biggest armory I've ever seen. Why would they need weapons? She seems to be inspecting each piece, checking each one against a file hovering beside her.

Charlie takes Ari and me to a small group watching a news report. It's an interview with Captain Sebastian. A chill comes over me as I'm reminded of his involvement in all this.

Are they tracking me in some way? I must trust in Theo's modification.

We wait as Charlie moves to the front of the group and speaks with a Black woman. She turns around, and I immediately know it's Bia. She most definitely looks like she's in charge, her dark-brown eyes focused in a soft face. Bia, lean and statuesque, glances at both Ari and me. Her eyes linger on my face, and then she lowers her gaze and shakes her head, her expression tightening. I chew on my lip; have they changed their minds about fixing the propeller? She moves forward and beckons us all to a quieter area.

We take up a group of chunky, comfortable sofas, one of several seating areas randomly scattered around. Jas joins us, too. Ari refuses to take a seat and stands by, leaning on a structural post. Charlie brings food and drink. I shake my head at food but ask for a cup of tea.

I shift in my seat as Bia studies me; her oval russet-brown face is tilted, eyes searching. Long dreads hang down to her waist, and a bright orange silk flower is pinned to her dress. She crosses her legs.

"So you're Hashem's child," she says. "Can I see the note?"

I pass her the paper Papa had scribbled her name on.

She nods after reading it. "Very well. You need help, and I will not turn you away. But know this: I'm *deeply* uncomfortable with you being here. Once your vessel has been sorted—" She breaks off to turn to Jas. He leans in, has a hushed exchange with her, and leaves the room. "Then you leave immediately. Understood?"

I twist my hair and nod.

"And know that very rarely are strangers allowed inside the Den," she continues. "You're only here because I trust your father without question. This place is *years* of hard graft, girl. You never mention its location to another soul. Is this clear?"

I nod again, hoping I'll never forget. "How do you know my papa?"

"I just do. We've never actually met. But I have nothing but respect for Hashem McQueen. I've done what I can to help Gideon locate him since he went missing. And I know your father would not have you within ten leagues of this place. He wanted to keep you safe. And Hashem never felt you would be safe if he joined us here. That's all I can tell you. Don't worry about your vessel—people are seeing to it as we speak. And then, like I said, I would appreciate it if you left instantly."

Well, wow, my head's spinning. So many questions. "Are you a scientist?"

"No. And now I have to go, I have—"

"But why would Papa think this place is dangerous for me? What do you—"

Bia holds a hand up when a frowning woman hurries toward us and whispers something about an earthquake. They both look back at one of the hovering maps.

Bia stands. "My apologies, it's a busy day." Her eyes take in my face, strapped fingers, and the way I'm curling my arm around my ribs. She sighs, pinching the bridge of her nose. "I'm sorry about the attack. You did well to come out of it alive, and by all accounts they got what they deserved. Need anything, just ask someone." She gestures to the room.

"Thank you."

She nods curtly and moves away, conferring with the worried woman.

I take Jojo from Ari, and he sits down to tuck into the food.

"You're not eating?" he asks, chewing on a large rib with a hint of concern in his eyes.

"I'm not hungry." My head's too full of questions; I can't focus properly.

I check on Jojo. The puppy's wound is healing nicely. The effects of the treatment are wearing off, and she'll awaken soon. With any luck, she won't remember what happened.

Charlie comes over with my cup of tea. "Are you *sure* you don't want some grub with that? If you don't fancy what I brought over, I can cook up a mean omelet in no time. No trouble, I swear."

I shake my head. "I'm all right, honest. Thanks."

He hangs his head. "I'm dead sorry about the Anthropoids storming yer sub like that. It must have been hell." He wrings his hands. "You want anything, let me know." He breaks into a smile, and his eyes light up. "Can I watch Jojo for you while you have yer tea?"

I nod, cupping the warm drink. When I look up, Ari's gaze is concentrated on me. His own eyes are cloudy, his expression conflicted. I swallow. A beastly flush creeps into my cheeks out of nowhere, dammit. Thankful for the curtain of hair, I tip my head and take the place in.

I squint at the screens. All manner of geographical imagery, coordinates, names and locations, routes, and codes flash back. Who are these people? What are they up to?

A young woman walks by and looks Ari up and down. Her eyes shine. She pauses by a screen trying to look busy, but she isn't fooling anyone as she continues to stare at him. I prickle; how bloody rude. I turn and screw my face up at her; she sneers at me and goes back to eyeing him. Whatever. Why do I care?

I feign interest in a huge map of Great Britain on the wall and walk over to it. Multicolored pins dot its surface.

Ari's immediately beside me, his voice low. "I don't—"

"Trust them," I finish.

He pauses, and then his mouth twitches. He cocks his eyebrow, and the amber flecks in his eyes dance and tease. His whole face softens, lighting up. He towers over me; big, strong. Beautiful. *Secretive.* There—right there, just behind the bright eyes. A guarded look, always, all the time. And yet still I feel safe around him.

Charlie walks over. "We have mixed news on yer propeller, Leyla. It's going to take a while—possibly well into the night. Good news is it'll be right as rain once the Johnson sisters have worked their magic on it."

"'Well into the night'? I mean, thank you tons, I'm so grateful, honestly. But what do I do now?"

"I suppose you'll have to stay over," Bia says, walking up to us, brow crinkled and lips pressed in a straight line as she makes no secret of her discomfort at the idea. She holds up a hand. "But then you leave bright and early." She walks away, calling back over her shoulder as she points to a row of doors along the right of the space, "We've plenty of rooms if you don't want to be on the vessel as they work on her. I just pray your father never hears of this." She joins a few others by the huge map on the wall.

Ari and I move to a quieter spot.

"You're staying *here*?" he asks, his face tightening as his eyes flit around the room.

"Yes. I want to know more—like what they're up to hiding down here. Maybe then I might figure out how Papa's connected to them. I won't learn anything about them if I stay on the sub. And you?"

He squints as he glances around uneasily. "I don't exactly have any choice."

A quick trip to the submarine later and we have what we need for Jojo and ourselves, including further doses of painkillers. Despite Ari stating he's more than capable of protecting me, Bia sent an armed woman with us, too. "Nothing happens to you on my watch," she insisted. *I'd rather you just shared some truths with me*, I wanted to reply.

Back in the Den, we throw our bags into the small rooms we've been given—Ari's is a few doors down from mine—and join the others at the long dining table filling up with food. My tummy rumbles as my appetite returns. Everyone chats over one another as they eat and drink, and I'm soon scarfing down the delicious lamb casserole and warm bread.

It feels strange—*different*, being with Ari around others. I can't place it. Everyone else here are strangers, and I keep seeking him out every few minutes. And I feel as if he's doing the same. It's actually reassuring to know he's here with me.

After dinner, Bia agrees to secure a quick chat for me with the twins. She's unable to do the same with Gramps, though, she explains with a preoccupied look—she knows for sure he's under Blackwatch's surveillance as of a few hours ago. My legs tremble with what this could mean for Grandpa, but she assures me he'll already be aware. I have to trust she's right.

I catch up with the twins from inside the small room I'll be staying at, quickly summarizing everything that's happened. The sight of Theo and Tabby pulls at my heart. They're both in tears even though I sail over the more painful details. We move on to chatting about the Den and I lower my voice.

"Theo, these people are definitely up to something—you should *see* this place. What if it's connected to Papa's situation? How will I find out anything concrete if they don't tell me?"

Theo chews on his lip, his gaze hesitant. "It's not ideal, but there is something you can do if you think they're holding back from you."

We whisper for a while, before the chat turns to Captain Sebastian.

"Hopefully, with the anti-tracking device, you'll remain one step ahead of him. Nobody can hold the Blackwatch off forever, though. . . . But as we'd discussed, as long as you avoid attracting the authorities, steer clear of all security bases, and my modification continues to work, then you should try not to worry too much about it yet. I'm running scans all over the place trying to keep my ear to the seabed. And . . . you *must* keep that moon pool door locked when it's not in use." He sighs and shakes his head. "Thank God he's with you—Ari. I'm so glad you're not on your own, Leyla."

"Where is he right now?" Tabby asks, her expression suddenly changing for the first time since we started chatting. There's a glint in her eye and her mouth quirks. "He's . . . quite something, right? I saw him on the sub."

Theo whirls around to face her. "Tabs! Leyla and Jojo have just been hurt and—"

Warmth floods my cheeks.

"Are you telling me," Tabby says, ignoring Theo's stare, "that you haven't even *noticed* him, Leyla? *No bloody way.* Because he's noticed you. Oh . . . you *do* like him—I can tell!"

I want the stark, cold floor of the small room to open up and fold me inside it because I can't control the heat rushing up my neck. Both twins watch me closely now. *How has he noticed me?* I want to ask. What does she mean? I recall their betrayal and the distraction is heavenly. "Hey, you guys *knew*! Why didn't you tell me he was on board? I can't *believe*—"

"Because you'd never have agreed to it, of course," Tabby says, not at all remorseful. "And you've seen—you've bloody *witnessed*—how horrific it can get out there. You need all the help offered to you. I mean, there were *two* of those monsters on board!"

"Sorry about that," Theo says. "But yes, Tabs was right to—" The call is abruptly cut.

I return to the Den, where Bia explains time was up, and any longer would've resulted in the call possibly being traced. It's disappointing, but at least I *did* get to speak with them.

I spot Ari in the far corner; he's pacing the area, completely unwilling to hide his displeasure at being here. Jojo is cradled in his arms. He looks up and meets my gaze. For a moment, both of us pause. We just stare at each other. I don't know why I'm doing it.

Because you like him. Not at all . . . I hardly know him.

His eyes flicker now, questioning. Always questioning . . . He makes me feel safe. And happy. He makes me feel *good*.

I like Ari. I really, *really* like him. My cheeks and neck flush with warmth again. What did Tabby mean when she said, *Because he's noticed you?*

I jump when Charlie approaches me, yawning. "What's *his* story?" he says, nodding in Ari's direction. "He's a bit much, I reckon."

Ari squints at him from across the large space, and Charlie quickly averts his gaze. He slumps into one of the sofas, stretching his arms above him.

I take a deep breath as I watch Charlie. He might be just tired enough to let his guard down and tell me something of use. Like what my chances are of acting on Theo's words.

I sit beside him and lower my voice. "I guess you better be off soon, Charlie. I don't know about Cambridge, but traffic's a bloody nightmare in London after six—"

"Yer having a laugh, aren't you?" Charlie grins. "I stay here—have done ever since I met Bia. Even the boss herself doesn't budge from this place!"

In no time, Charlie's telling me when and where everyone sleeps.

I'll never get this close to finding out more about what's happened to Papa, and—despite wishing I could just hide somewhere instead—I don't intend on wasting this night.

CHAPTER TWENTY-SIX

I bolt up, trembling, and immediately command the light on. My eyes narrow at the strange surroundings. Sweat clings to my face, neck, and chest. I focus on calming my breathing and remember I'm in the Den, at the Trading Post. The quiet buzzing of the alarm still sounds and I switch it off, so utterly relieved now that I'd set it. I was having a nightmare. I was back in the engine room with the thing. This time I wasn't so lucky; the brolly refused to work.

I shudder and bring my knees to my chest. Remembering why I'd set the alarm for three a.m., I shake myself alert and grab my robe, ignoring the quiver in my legs. I edge the door open, and slip into the main area of the Den.

Low lights blink and beam. It seems to be empty, but I scan every corner, twice. I look around and sigh; where to even begin? I want to search *everything*, but that would require at least two people. And then I remember Theo's words to me back in the control room.

I can merge Navigation duties with Housekeeping, kind of like a super-Housekeeper, if you want, Leyla?

Of course! Oscar isn't only a Navigator; he's also my Housekeeper, connected via my Bracelet and programmed to be available twenty-four/seven—no matter *where* I am!

"Oscar?" I whisper into my Bracelet, and hold my breath.

The Navigator materializes before me. *Yes.* I set him on silent before he can say a word.

"Oscar, see if you're able to access their systems. Download any information that might mention Papa. Understood?" The Navigator nods and sets to work.

Meanwhile, I go through everything I can. It's mostly wipe-boards, so I start on those, trying to decipher all the info scribbled across an entire stack of them, with no luck.

"Oscar? Find anything?" I whisper, trying to ignore the nausea spreading inside.

The Navigator shakes his head and continues scanning their systems. I don't want to follow Theo's instructions for snooping unless I absolutely have to. Determined to find info by some other means, I take a long look around the room. A pile of large notebooks catches my eye.

I flick through several indecipherable volumes until I stumble on one where the content is straightforward enough. It's a thick book with pages and pages about the Explorers and their efforts to find a way for us to return to the surface. Why would they be interested in the Explorers, of all things?

I scan it, half-heartedly. There are copies of reports registered by Explorers over the past decade. Following each report is the official statement released to the public at that time. And . . . the two are *vastly* different. I straighten, more focused now.

There's a report from a scientist, Dr. Varsha Patel, dated September 2093, and one of the paragraphs is highlighted:

> *In conclusion, the commonly cited standard atmospheric oxygen levels of 21 percent do not correspond with my own findings (app. 1c). Despite breathing filtered air, I experienced adverse physical ailments attributed to the environment. The exact levels of the greenhouse gases, including water vapor levels, all*

proved significantly higher than is widely believed (app. 3c).
My equipment was rendered ineffective in a matter of hours
due to a violent magnetic storm. Within days I was forced
back into the depths with acute sunburn, and—despite my
respiratory equipment—my blood oxygen levels were critical
(app. 4b). The conditions on the surface are hostile and deadly,
and there is absolutely no indication of this changing in the
foreseeable future.

The public statement following this report was an entirely inaccurate interpretation of Dr. Patel's findings:

Though oxygen levels are lower post-disaster, enough oxygen
remains in the atmosphere that, with minimum effort and
adaptation, could prove more than adequate to sustain human
life.

That's it? The Explorer's report states the ecosystem is—at best—perilously volatile. And the air poisonous. The public statement has totally ignored the majority of the problems.

I don't understand it. At all. But there's no reason to doubt it—both the reports and subsequent statements are completely official. I flick through page after page, but everything I see says only one thing:

All this time, the government has been lying about the findings of the Explorers.

According to the Explorers' reports, there's never been even the *slightest* hope of us ever living on the surface of the water again. Not here in Great Britain—not anywhere in the world.

It's as if a mighty wave has rolled in, knocking me off-balance.

It can't be true. . . . And yet there it is.

After all that, all those promises, all the talk about us ensuring we're ready to return any day, there was never even the tiniest chance of it happening. Not in our lifetimes.

I realize I'm more shocked and terrified at the brazen lie from the government than the possibility of never living up on the surface of the water. I've never before bothered to read the monthly Explorer reports, never been interested in following their progress.

But *why* have they lied? What's the government really up to?

My legs start shaking. The possible scenarios—and the not-knowing—swirl round and around in my head until I think it might burst. I stumble back.

Straight into somebody's arms.

A hand clamps down on my mouth and twists me around to face them.

Ari. He jerks his chin to indicate the far corner of the space.

Charlie's entered the open area; I'd have never spotted him from this angle. Ari removes his hand.

Charlie goes straight to the kitchen and sets about making a warm drink. I dismiss Oscar via my Bracelet. Ari points to the nearest sofa. We cower behind it until Charlie leaves the space. I let out a long sigh.

"Sorry," Ari says quietly, indicating the hand he'd clamped over my mouth. "I was coming over to you when I saw him. What are you doing? You're putting yourself at risk."

I point toward the notebooks, and we make our way over. I finally find my voice and fill Ari in, whispering.

"So you see, all this time the government have been *lying* to us. Can you believe that? They're meant to look out for us. They're meant to *serve* us!"

Ari nods, his expression suddenly studious. "We should always question everything," he says quietly, his eyes burning into me. "*Everything*, Leyla."

Papa's voice rings in my ears: *The facts, Pickle. Always. Only cold, hard facts.* My papa. A great astronomer. My heart aches for him now. Everything in his absence is too confusing. So many truths revealed to be lies.

He would never accept the lies. *We* mustn't accept them. How *dare* they tell us we'll be living up on the surface very soon when we clearly won't be?

I meet Ari's questioning gaze. "Explorers have *died* trying to find ways for us to live on the surface. And yet the authorities still send them up there. No matter where you are on the globe, the surface is hell—it's a death trap. It's all here in the official reports. For one thing, we're breathing filtered oxygen down here. We'd have to wear masks and carry filtration systems all the time if we were up there. We'd be fighting the environment twenty-four/seven. Our numbers would drop even further. Yet they still encourage the idea. And all those poor people who work so hard to meet their payment to the Explorers Fund every month! For what? And, Ari . . ."

His eyes flicker bright with anticipation when I say his name, his gaze unwavering now.

"If the authorities can lie about that—if they could make people believe such a *huge* lie—then we have to ask ourselves not only *why*, but what *else* are they lying about?"

He's so incredibly still as he searches my face . . . as if he's holding his breath. A glimmer of something flashes across his expression, but it's gone before I can pinpoint it. Was it sadness? Apprehension?

"What's the government up to, Ari? What's *really* going on with my papa?" My voice cracks.

He moves closer to me until his face is inches from mine. In the dim glow of the room his eyes are almost hypnotic, and his face more mysterious than ever. It breaks into the *softest* expression and pulls at me. I step toward him just as he closes the few inches between us and wraps his arms around me. I breathe him in as I bury my face in his chest.

Deep breaths. His smell is how I imagine the Old World outdoors to have smelled. Fresh, foresty, wild. Despite the alarming discovery just now, this is the safest I've felt in far too long. And my insides . . . they just *flutter*. His arms feel so comfortable around me, and yet he's incredibly, undeniably exciting. It's like he's both home and the unknown. And though anything unknown always leaves me reeling in terror, Ari doesn't.

"I . . . I can stay on," he says, his voice hesitant and low. I hear him swallow before he continues. "Once we reach your grandfather's cottage. If you need me, I can stay longer. To help you search for your father." His chest expands against my face as he takes in a long breath, releasing it slowly. He sounds *exhausted*. "Too many families have been lost to their lies. Let me help you find yours, Leyla. I want to do this for you."

There is so much pain in his voice I can't bear it.

And I can no longer imagine going on without him on board. I whisper against his chest. "Yes . . . Please stay longer if you can. If your family will be all right without you for a while."

It takes a moment for me to realize his hand is ever so slightly stroking my hair in a reassuring gesture. I never want it to stop.

A sound in the far corner pulls us apart and I glance over. Nothing. My gaze returns to Ari and our eyes lock; the most tender look shines in his. His shoulders rise and fall. I feel the warmth in my face and swallow, remembering where I am.

I shake myself out of my thoughts and take a few steps back. Clearing my throat, I beckon him toward the sofa.

I fill him in on what Theo said. "Because I still don't have any info on what's going on here, or with Papa, you see. And Theo said we might have some luck with *that* system there," I say to him, pointing to the largest of a specific group of screens and trying so hard to block out the feeling of being against his chest. *Focus.* I flick my wrist to indicate my Bracelet. "Theo sent help, and it's specific to Papa."

Ari nods and we make our way over to the row of screens, pausing by the main one. I glance at the blinking visual display. If only Theo were here himself!

I follow his instructions and upload the coding he passed on to me. Immediately a bright white insignia appears on-screen, rotating forebodingly. *Oh no.*

"Theo said if that particular security crest appears, then there's a risk my transferring any info might leave a trace." I bite my lip.

Ari glances at the screen and back at my face. "What do you want to do?"

"Well . . . I mean we're out of here first thing in the morning, right? He said it could take them a while to discover a breach if this happened. We can't leave this place without *trying*. I just have a feeling these guys know more about Papa's situation. I want to risk it," I say.

"Yes?" Ari cocks an eyebrow.

"Yes. We continue to upload this coding, transfer the results, and then get out of this area before anyone else wakes up." I offer a quiet prayer that I've made the right choice.

It all seems to take forever. Anywhere Papa's name is mentioned on this tech, Theo's coding will capture it for Oscar to identify. At last we're done, and I can't move away from the screens fast enough.

We pause where we must part ways and I stare at my Bracelet, mumbling something that's meant to be *Good night*. Ari twists the beaded necklace around his neck as he nods in reply, and I hurry to my room.

When I climb back into bed, sleep is a million leagues away.

Possible mention of Papa in the downloaded info and the lie about the Explorers' progress both work together to keep me awake for too long. And the sense of Ari's arms wrapped around me doesn't lessen at *all* as the hours tick by. His words also linger.

He's right; we must question *everything*. Without Gramps and the twins with me, Ari's the only person left who I can trust. No governmental body or representative can be trusted. It's just one terrible lie after another. I must stay focused on finding Papa myself.

I trace my Bracelet. I *finally* have something, I'm certain. At Grandpa's place in King's Lynn I'll decide my next move based on whatever the download might reveal.

Please, God, let it be something hopeful, positive.

I try not to think about Bia and her people possibly finding out what I've done. If they *do* discover the security breach, I pray it's when we're leagues away from here.

God knows what these people are up to, and I wouldn't want to ever cross them.

I wake up light-headed. Ari's arms around me is the very first thing that pops into my head, and I just want to lie here thinking about it. Unfortunately the rest of last night also kicks in, and I hasten out of bed, yawning away.

We're out of here very shortly, and finally I'll have some answers. Grabbing Jojo's Bliss-Pod, I open the door and step into the main area of the Den, where Bia's words greet me.

"Did you *really* think you'd get away with it?"

CHAPTER TWENTY-SEVEN

My insides drop and I tighten my grip on the Bliss-Pod's handle as I take in the sight ahead.

Bia stands in the center, arms folded. Her expression is hard, her mouth set as she stares ahead, refusing to look at me directly. I swallow, but my throat is dry. Jas stands beside her, weapon in hand. Charlie rubs his arms as his confused gaze meets mine. Behind them several others stare accusingly in my direction. I scan the space. Those working on screens around the room keep looking over their shoulders at us to watch.

My legs quiver as my mind scrambles for what to say and do. There's movement on the edge of my vision, and I notice the two armed guards inside the space.

Everyone turns when a door opens and Ari exits his room, his gaze meeting mine before anyone else's. His face softens immediately, his color flushing. Then, as he reads my expression, he scans the scene. He clenches his jaw and straightens. He's ready to fight.

"Your Bracelet." Bia holds out her hand, her eyes focused on her palm. "Once you've returned what's mine, then we can discuss how you were made welcome here, taken in, and had your vessel seen to, and the *audacity* of you thanking us by spying on us—*stealing* from us. And why you thought you would get away with this grave mistake, girl."

I swallow again and force my voice out. "I—I only want to find my papa. Why won't you help me, tell me everything you know? Instead you're keeping secrets from me. I wouldn't have *had* to sneak a—"

Bia nods at Jas. And then everything happens so fast.

Jas turns in my direction. I call out in protest, holding the Bliss-Pod behind me to protect Jojo. Ari reaches me before Jas does, standing in front of me and brandishing a knife out of nowhere. The two armed guards rush toward him. Jojo barks like mad from inside the Bliss-Pod. Charlie shakes his head in disbelief. "Mind you don't hurt the dog!" he shouts.

It's all too much. A chill sweeps over me as I back away. My brolly slips slowly from my arm into my hand.

Just as one of the guards reaches Ari and points her weapon at him, and I'm raising my brolly in her direction, a low, unmistakably urgent alarm sounds around the space. Everyone freezes. An even deeper siren follows it. Red lights flash all around the Den.

For the briefest moment, nobody speaks. And then:

"Raid!" shouts Charlie. "The Post is under attack!"

Several heads whip up in the direction of the Trading Post above us.

"Stations!" shouts Bia, hastening to a far wall. "You all know what to do. They must *not* discover the Den!" Everyone starts rushing around the room.

Attack. Oh my God . . . Anthropoids are attacking this place right now.

"Who did you tell?" Bia looks over her shoulder and yells at me. "Who have you informed of our location? Speak up, girl!"

"*What?* Nobody! I only spoke with the twins, and I never mentioned your location!"

She turns around to face me, hands on hips and her eyes penetrating. "Somebody followed you here, then . . . This raid cannot be a coincidence. It's the Blackwatch out there."

The Blackwatch. My stomach drops. "It's nothing to do with me!" *Was* it just a coincidence the Blackwatch turned up while I was here?

She presses her lips together and shakes her head, turning back around. My legs quiver. There's a rumbling in the background, and then a low *boom*.

Ari rushes over to me, his eyes blazing with urgency. "Please listen to me now. It's a full-blown attack; I know the signs. We *must* get out of here. And this is our only chance. I will go check the sub; I have primary rights now, and I will make sure it's ready. You hide somewhere safe until I tell you the vessel is all set for departure."

A louder *boom* makes me jump. It's like the attack on Brighton Pier all over again. Only worse.

"All right, but I want to come with you!"

He runs his hands through his hair, his expression conflicted. "No, Leyla. You *must* stay down here until we're ready to depart. It's too dangerous for you up there. *Please.*"

I nod, a feeling of nausea rising inside. "Go, then. Hurry!"

He rushes toward the door, throwing one of Bia's guys out of the way as he does. I scan the room. All I can hear are various alarms and shouted instructions. Some people are by the armory, grabbing weapons, others frantically working away at the screens, while more are communicating via video chats. I never did find out what they do. I swing my gaze left to catch Jas hurriedly exiting an internal door. He squints at me and looks around for Ari.

The door to the Den slides open as one of Bia's people rushes in, and I see my chance.

Charlie told us there was another way down to the Den, a way that avoided "the scenic route," he'd said, referring to the Trading Post. I need to locate it so I'm ready to run when Ari tells me we're good to go. I glance at Jas. Then at the door still ajar. I look at him once more, and he lurches forward just as I run.

I race through the door. When I glimpse the blue of Jas's turban behind me, I continue running.

Everything's louder out here: sirens, shouting, and the *thud* and *boom* of firepower. My heartbeat thrashes away in my ears, and my chest squeezes tighter and tighter.

The corridors are dimmer than they were yesterday, and the ominous red pulses through the passageways.

When it feels like I've been racing down the same corridors forever, I have no choice but to pause and catch my breath. *"Please,"* I say, turning around to face Jas, who's still on my heels. "I only want to find my papa. Please let me go."

His eyes flicker, softening for a moment. But then he blinks and straightens. "Look, I have my orders—you must not leave the Den." His expression is rigid, but his tone almost pleading as he blocks my path. Despite his words, he hasn't pulled his weapon on me.

Jojo barks nonstop from inside her pod now.

"I'm really sorry, Jas," I say.

His bushy black eyebrows meet, and he opens his mouth. I whip the brolly up, and before he can get a single word out, press down on the button. He yelps so loud when the spray hits his eyes I almost drop the brolly. Groaning and trying to blink the substance out, he moves aside. As I push past him, Jas mumbles something. Then louder.

"Upstairs, then stay left and you'll find the docking bay." Tears stream down his face. "We're on the same side; it's not what you think. Look, just get out of here. Argh!" He rubs his fists into his increasingly red eyes.

"Oh, thank you so much, Jas! I'm really, truly sorry!" I shout as I run past him, deeply regretting my actions. At the corner, I turn right for the stairs.

I run upstairs as fast as I can. *Boom.* The ground shakes slightly beneath me, and it's an effort not to stumble. Murmuring soothing words to Jojo, I do as Jas said and stay left. Finally I open a door leading to the docking bay. It's frantic. People run and shout in every direction as they hasten to their vessels.

My hands shaking, I access the hatch to the *Kabul* and yell in my Bracelet for Oscar to let me in as I run through the sub's bridge. Within moments, the hatch to the sub is released and I'm safely inside.

I let out a huge sigh of relief at the submarine's familiar smell and thrum. I hadn't realized until now just how much I love it, how I already think of it as home.

Jojo scrambles out of her pod as I order the bridge connecting us to the Trading Post to retract. I run to the saloon, straight into the viewing port. And stifle a cry.

It's absolute chaos out there.

A chill comes over me as I take in the scene in the distance, hoping it remains well away from the docking bay.

All manner of submersibles light up the ashen depths, hovering and darting around. Laser beams shoot through the water. Firepower on both sides bursts brilliant and bright in the gloom, before succumbing to the water and sputtering out of sight. Will everyone at the Trading Post and Den be safe?

"Oscar, what's going on? What's the update with the propeller? And where is Ari?"

The Navigator tilts his head. "My dear lady, the *Kabul* herself is ready for departure. All defense systems are running. Her propeller has been serviced back to its former glory, and we are poised for voyage. It is most tiresome, then, to reveal that we remain stationed due to the mooring equipment anchoring the vessel to the workstation. It would appear those in charge of releasing the *Kabul* have—rather understandably under the circumstances—absconded from the vicinity! And so the gentleman, Ari, was left with no choice but to take a gander at releasing us from the workstation himself. He left just before your good self arrived. I was to contact you in a short while to inform you of departure and beckon you on board."

"Oh God . . ." I groan, watching the clash unfold. "What if—" An ice-cold current surges through me as the shadowy silhouettes of several submersibles involved in the attack register.

Bia was right. It's definitely the Blackwatch.

My pulse races. What if they identify me? What if they manage to stop us? Who would search for Papa then?

The Navigator cocks his head. "I say, this Ari fellow is as masterly as he is dashing; I do believe the *Kabul* is moving. Take heart, my dear; we shall flee this cumbersome folly at once."

I slump against the window in relief. "Oh, thank God! Oscar, *soon* as Ari's back on board, be sure to lock the moon pool door!"

Slowly but surely the vessel starts to pull away from the hatch. A hazy form in the distance heads toward us.

"Oscar, I see our submersible! Watch the moon pool and be ready to lock up the *moment* Ari's through!"

The silhouette drifts toward the submarine. Where are the craft's lights? I can barely make anything out—Ari could be hurt! As the form draws near it becomes gradually clear I was mistaken; it isn't our submersible, but some kind of sea creature. It comes closer.

And closer. My pulse races as the animal closes the distance between itself and the sub. My eyes widen and my mouth falls open as the realization settles. It isn't a sea creature.

It's one of *them*. An Anthropoid.

No. *No, no, no.* Not now.

I try to call out. *Oscar. Ari.* But no sound leaves my lips. I stand frozen. I close my eyes. *Think.* I can't.

I start shivering as my recurring nightmare sneaks up on me now. I'm a little girl again, gazing out at the water, so carefree, happy. And then someone is *in* the water, suspended there. The moment is all too brief. The water clouds, the current suddenly furious and furtive. And a terrible turmoil rides in on the waves. It takes over my body, restricting my breathing, my muscles and bones. It leaves nothing but destruction and despair in its wake. And a permanent dread forever afterward. . . .

Except *this* isn't my childhood nightmare—this is real.

I open my eyes and look out. I can't spot the beast. *Where is it?* My breathing turns raspy. I clutch my chest, my throat. Oh my God . . . the sub. Is the sub secure? Where's the Anthropoid got to?

A figure rises from the depths, right in front of the viewport. I scream.

Its eyes are wide, frenzied; its hair spans around its head, and the thing gestures wildly. Water flows in and out of its mouth, as if it were air. Unnatural.

I stop screaming. Then I slowly shake my head as I stare back at it. Its hair. Its face.

Its eyes.

Ari's eyes.

Ari.

I can't move, can't blink. It isn't real. *This is not real.* It *can't* be him.

And yet it is.

I don't understand. . . . I don't understand it.

A thousand feet of tremendous pressure are pushing down on him, but Ari's showing no sign of it. . . . He's moving freely. His lungs and ribs haven't collapsed, his bones haven't snapped, he isn't being crushed to death. He's shirtless. In freezing temperatures. All he's wearing are his usual black bottoms, no shoes, no socks. The beaded necklace hangs around his neck, the knife around his waist.

It can't be real. It's *not* true. Ari is human!

Inside, I'm sinking, slowly making my way down through an endless nothing.

Ari moves as close as possible, and places his hand on the window. His eyes search my face. *Desperately* searching for something. His expression pleads with me. But neither my mind nor my body will cooperate. I can think only one thing.

Ari is an Anthropoid.

I take a step back.

His lips part and anguish gushes out. Pain washes into his eyes and contorts his face.

My heart lurches then, a real physical tugging inside my chest. I can't bear to see him in any kind of pain. But still I don't move.

His hand comes away from the window. He stares at me.

And plummets out of sight.

A moment passes. A few more. Something shifts and stirs inside me and suddenly there are too *many* emotions, too many questions. I can't breathe. *Please, God, help me.*

I gulp at the air and push everything deep down until only the instinct to survive remains.

"Oscar . . ." I whisper. Then louder. "Oscar." My throat aches now.

He materializes in front of me, acknowledging my presence before turning to gaze into the water.

"The moon pool door, Oscar. Close it at once. Close it *now*."

I can't move as I peer past the Navigator and into the depths. I'm frozen, and yet I can't stop shaking inside. The water shifts and courses around the viewport and I squint. Nothing.

"The moon pool door is now locked, my dear," Oscar confirms. "I can assure you, the *Kabul* is currently quite secure in every respect."

The vessel backs away from the chaos and starts to rise.

All ability to process the situation has abandoned me. I'm a bot.

"Oscar? Revoke Ari's primary rights, all access—*everything*. Do it at once."

The Navigator turns from the windows to face me and bows his head. His gaze then shifts past me to settle somewhere behind me.

"Sir, I'm afraid I must recall all security clearances and privileges granted to your good self."

Oh dear God.

I turn around.

Ari stands there, his shoulders rising and falling as water drips from him, and a resentful look simmers in his eyes. My body feels heavy enough to sink the vessel.

I'm confined alone in a submarine with an Anthropoid.

But it's Ari, my heart whispers.

Still, I take a step back.

CHAPTER TWENTY-EIGHT

"**P**lease, Leyla," Ari says, holding up a hand. "Don't be afraid of me."

"You're—" I swallow and try again, my throat aching and dry. "You're one of *them*."

I have my back to the viewport, and he hasn't moved from where he stood.

"I am. But please—think about it. Up until a few hours ago you thought humanity would be returning to the surface any day now. That is clearly a lie the government has been upholding for years. Until recently you thought your father was detained in London—another lie. Don't you think it's possible they might also be lying to you about us? We're not—"

"All this time . . ." I slowly shake my head. I just can't *believe* it. "All this time I was with—with—"

"A *beast*?" He spits the word out. Then he looks away as if regretting his words. "Leyla," he asks quietly, his eyes clouded as he meets my gaze again, "are you afraid of me?"

I don't know *what* I'm feeling. . . . "*How* are you one of them, though, when you're you? How can *you* be an Anthropoid? It doesn't make sense!"

He folds his arms. "What I *am* makes sense to me. I didn't intend to deceive you. I *wanted* you to guess. Last night, in the Den, I thought you might finally realize."

I look away, recalling the moment. *We should always question everything,* he'd said, his expression intense and full of anticipation.

He rubs his face now. "Look, I will shower and change into dry clothes—give you some time. And then can we sit and talk about this?"

I nod, but only so I can be alone for a bit. He leaves the saloon. My head is spinning as I pace the viewport.

No, the truth won't set you free, Leyla McQueen.

Ari's words, spoken on New Year's Eve when he thought I couldn't hear him. They whoosh around and around in my head now. They play over and over. Everything he ever said and did, on repeat. All the words. All the images. All the *real* meanings behind them.

Ari is an Anthropoid.

He's the *enemy.*

I leave the viewport and curl up on the sofa, remembering his mouth, the water flowing in and out. He'd left via the moon pool door. He must've walked straight in there, into a pressurized chamber, uncovered a hole to the bottom of the world, and jumped in. No sub. No protection. I shudder.

Had he left the sub before? Maybe when I was asleep . . . Is *that* the real reason he wanted primary rights? So he could exit and enter the *Kabul* as he pleased? How could I spend so many days in such close proximity to an Anthropoid and not notice anything?

My heart stammers. . . . I hugged an Anthropoid. The most evil creation.

Except Ari's not evil.

I picture his face, here, on the sub with me.

The way he moves in a room. Fluid and agile. Graceful. *But of course.*

So many things make sense now. . . . The guarded gaze; a solid gold secret hidden behind amber specks that spark and shimmer. And then his unbelievable strength. The Anthropoid *beat* him, hit him again and again, and still he fought on.

For you.

I gasp and sit up. Ari killed his own kind for us. . . .

No, dammit. *No.* He's a beast. He's an *Anthropoid.* They are only evil. Anthropoids are incapable of human feelings. But Ari . . . he's shown us nothing but kindness, consideration, sympathy. He cared for us, was empathetic and brave for us. He *can't* be one of them!

Oh my God—does Grandpa know? Did he knowingly place me with an Anthropoid just because they're strong enough to protect me? Would Gramps do that?

I can't think straight. It's as if a giant eel has wrapped itself around my chest and is squeezing tighter and tighter. I keep bringing my Bracelet up so I can speak with the twins, and my wrist falls away when I remember it'll get them into trouble and could possibly give my location away.

How can Ari's lungs not collapse under so much pressure, when I feel like mine have caved in under the weight of this one truth alone?

Ari is an Anthropoid.

And yet you haven't asked him to leave.

He had every opportunity to hurt us, and all he did was protect us.

He isn't one of us. Oh my God, Ari really is one of *them.*

The weight of a thousand feet of water above me presses down now. It will crush me. Question after question. Demanding to be answered. I can't stand not knowing.

Jojo wanders in, and I shake the thoughts away, fetching her some biscuits from the kitchen. She sits in the viewport to eat.

Ari returns to the saloon.

"Does Grandpa know you're . . . Does he know what you are?" I ask immediately.

He checks Jojo's wound and joins me by the seating area, taking the seat opposite to mine. And nods. "Your grandfather is a good friend of my father's. He has always known our identity."

I whip my head up. "All this time Gramps has been friends with *Anthropoids?*"

220

How can that even be?

"Yes. We are not your enemy, Leyla." He leans forward, tension simmering around him now. "Do you even know what *really* happened that day the Old World PM finally met with the two hundred artificially created beings that would help after the disaster? There was *no* attack. Anthropoids didn't go 'mad' and strike the team and escape the compound. That is all a complete *lie*." His face contorts with loathing. "What actually happened is the PM felt sick when he met what the Old World geneticists had conceived. He couldn't *stand* it. He saw human beings, not some workforce, and he couldn't bring himself to go ahead with the plans for the original two hundred. It took a lot of persuading, but he managed to get all involved to agree: The Anthropoids were human in every aspect but their ability to survive underwater. He ordered they be set free soon as they went through a sterilization program. Except the water hit before it—"

"No way!" I wring my hands to stop them trembling. "You're saying all these years—"

"Leyla, let me finish, please? The PM declared it ethically wrong to use them as a labor force. It was decreed treasonous for anyone involved to ever speak of them to anybody. The two hundred would be freed, and they would die out naturally and nobody would be the wiser. As I was saying, a sterilization program was organized so they could never breed. The water hit before it could be carried out, though. Suddenly there were two hundred artificial humans free at large. The PM filed an honest account of everything, and to this day only subsequent prime ministers have access to that information—and have always been sworn to *protect* the Anthropoids. Until *this* government. They replaced the true history of the Anthropoids with one of barbarity and—"

"You can't alter an entire history of a species!" I close my eyes. "We would know if—"

"You *can*, though. You can rewrite history if you're in charge of the accounts that are passed down. They have used us ever since to push forward with their own twisted agendas. *That* is the truth. Not what the Anthropoid Watch Council puts out every single day. You're being lied to. We are *human*, Leyla. We are *you*. We lack nothing—we only possess more. We're you, but with the ability to exist underwater. That makes us 'beasts'?"

I stare, speechless, before finally finding my voice. "But even if that were true, the Anthropoids—"

"You. Say 'you.'"

"The Anthropoids are *beasts* because they terrorize us. You can't suddenly deny that! Attack after attack, day after day. They've caused such pain and horror and they terrorize—"

"An angry minority. Otherwise it's only ever in self-defense. And say 'you.' I am one of them."

My legs quiver. "I don't understand! They attacked *you*, your community—in the Faroe Islands. They killed Lance and—"

Pain breaks across his face, his eyes dulling. He shakes his head. "It was the Blackwatch, Leyla. They came for our community and they attacked us. It was all we could do to survive."

Enough. A sense of nausea rises inside. I can't hear any more. Because I have no idea who or what to believe. Does Gramps really believe all this? I can't even ask him. But that's not the point. I must think about what *I* believe, how I feel about it. And I'm just so very confused.

Because Ari does not come across as a liar . . .

So what on earth am I meant to be thinking right now? I feel like I can't breathe; I just want all this to *go away.*

His eyes lock on to mine. "Please believe me; I did not set out to deceive you or *anyone*. Your grandfather thought it best that I didn't reveal my true identity to you. You were not ready yet, he explained. Do you still want me to stay on, once we reach your grandfather's cottage?"

Oh, Gramps . . . Why didn't he just have more faith in me and *trust* me?

Why did he never tell me he *knew* Anthropoids—that he'd befriended some? I recall his words back at the hangar as we said our goodbyes:

Please understand that whatever I do, it's only with your survival and success in mind. . . . You will find your father, and I know he would want to explain things to you himself. As much as I want to speak to you about some matters, it isn't my place.

I nod as I hear the words again. I *know* Gramps has my best interests at heart; I can *feel* that. I just wish he'd told me everything. And what does he mean about Papa explaining things to me? Is Papa also friendly with Anthropoids? Has my whole life been one big lie?

I realize Ari's waiting for an answer.

Do I want him, an Anthropoid, on board with me?

"I don't know. . . . I've no idea about anything anymore."

I wring my hands and try to focus. Do I still want him with me? Back at the Den it meant everything to hear he wanted to stay until we found Papa. Now I find out he's one of *them*. I don't know what to think. I had set off on my own. I had full faith in myself. Why should that change? Once we get to the cottage and I know what I'm doing next, I'll— I gasp.

"Leyla?"

"The information we downloaded, I never asked Oscar to check it. Oscar!"

The Navigator appears, straightening his olive velvet waistcoat. "You called, my dear?"

"I'm transferring some data to you right now, Oscar. Please scan it for *any* link to Papa and tell me the moment you stumble on something."

The Navigator nods, receives the information, and disappears again.

Ari watches me and I realize I never answered him.

"What does it matter to *you* that my papa's found?"

Though I never say, *Why would an Anthropoid care about a human?* it's clear from the muscle that tics along his jaw in response that he knows what I mean. I don't care.

More silence. Finally, I gesture to the water outside. "Why did you risk getting caught out there in the water, especially when it was crawling with the Blackwatch?"

"Everyone fled when the place was attacked. There was nobody left to release the vessel from its moorings. There wasn't enough time to go back and try to break into the workstation; if we hadn't left when we did, you'd never have got out of there. The Blackwatch always have backup coming. I knew I could free the anchors manually, so I used the moon pool."

I try not to imagine him dropping into the darkness like that, but the images are unstoppable, vivid and terrifying. I nod and my throat starts hurting again.

The Navigator appears, and I jump up in anticipation. "Tell me, Oscar."

"There is but a single mention of Hashem McQueen on the information transferred, my dear lady. His name and coordinates. I have already passed the references on to your good self."

"Well? What's the location, Oscar?"

"The coordinates point to the Far North, my dear."

North. At last, some direction. "That's great, thank you, Oscar."

The Navigator bows with a flourish. "Indeed, I have nothing to declare but my genius."

I hasten to my maps, rummage through them, and flatten one out on the table.

Ari folds his arms, and when he speaks, his voice is so low it's barely discernible. "I would dive to the bottom of the deepest rift for my family. I *understand* why you need to find your father, Leyla. I am a human being. We are exactly like you in every way, except we can survive out there. I think you will need me with you."

A human being.

I rub my arms, knowing he is right about at least one thing: I *will* need him. I wouldn't be here now if he'd not set off on this journey with me. He has only helped us, and more than once. But to continue on with him, knowing what he is? Can I even do that?

Put Papa first.

At last I nod, though reluctantly. "If you're sure," I say quietly, following the coordinates on the map I have open before me.

I tap the map before shifting my gaze to the water.

"I am certain," he says.

All right, then? I wish my hands would stop quivering.

"Oscar? Please register those coordinates you sent me and instantly adjust our route accordingly."

The Navigator tilts his head as he reads the new route for the *Kabul*. "Oh I say, a new trajectory! My dear, we are no longer to head for King's Lynn?"

I press my lips together; Grandpa isn't going to be too happy about my not being at the cottage, but I must do this. And if Gramps can go with his gut instincts and decide I'm not ready for truths, then I can go with mine and determine my next move myself.

Pushing my shoulders back, I hold Ari's careful gaze for a moment before glancing away into the water.

"No, Oscar," I say, my voice steady and low. "We aren't. Take her all the way north."

CHAPTER TWENTY-NINE

The intricate detail of the arches in the viewport is magnificent; I trace the patterns as I sip my cup of tea in between yawns. The vessel plows through the early morning blue-green waters. Faint natural light trickles through the depths. The current is choppy and waves heave over the sub as it cuts through the endless environment, the propeller back to optimum performance.

Soon we'll be halfway across the country. Jojo's almost back to her stellar self, playing with the unattainable juicy bone as the projection teases her. I managed to wash her last night and change her dressing. The wound is healing nicely, thank goodness.

I hope Gramps isn't worrying. Whatever decisions he's made so far, I have no doubt they've always been, as he said, with my best interests at heart. I can feel that in my bones.

Ari.

All I've ever wanted is to know the truth. No matter what. No matter how difficult or complicated something is, I've always believed a starting point for fixing it would be to have the whole bloody truth. Not knowing has *always* seemed worse. But . . . ever since I've found out Ari's one of them, I wonder if I've been wrong. If it might not have been better that I didn't know. Because this feeling since spotting him in the water yesterday is too much. I forget for a moment and then suddenly it comes rolling back, hitting me with full force and engulfing me to the point where I question what I'm doing, if I'm out of my mind traveling with him, and if I shouldn't just ask him to leave.

A team of square-shaped eco-bots drifts on the current outside, their lights blipping away as they gather environmental information. Several plaice bob along with them, and the group drifts on past the viewport.

Ari insists he's been *himself* all along. But he's not what Anthropoids are like, so that can't be true.

And then I can't help but think back on the Anthropoid who attacked me in the engine room . . . how it paused for one brief moment. Paused and looked at me with *sympathy*. And how, along with the hatred and rage on its face, there was very definitely also a hint of pain etched there. Suffering. What does it mean?

And Ari's explanation of their past . . . of what transpired at the labs when the PM first set eyes on the Anthropoids. It's *so* different from the official account; if our government's record of the event were false, surely there'd be *some* trail of the truth? I can't wrap my head around it.

The government has lied about other things, too.

They have. They do. But I can't do anything about it. I just wish I could forget all this, dammit. *All* of it. I want to block it out. I *need* to. I need to focus fully on Papa.

I yawn again. I didn't sleep well. After dinner last night, I collected all Ari's things from around the sub and set the guest room up for him. I didn't mind before. But now I really need to know he has his own space, that he won't be in mine too much. The soothing, low music I thought he sometimes listens to is actually a wooden sax he plays, and I put that away for him, too. It never occurred to me that Anthropoids might play musical instruments. . . . Just after midnight, I woke up to him crying out, sheer panic in his voice. I recognized Lance's name. He also called out to someone called Freya. I stood outside his room, listening. I never considered Anthropoids might dream. . . . He sounded distraught but quieted down after a few minutes, and I crept back to bed.

Sleep still evaded me, though, and it wasn't just Ari's shocking identity on my mind. I couldn't stop thinking of the government's massive lie about living on the surface.

How can we ever feel safe and secure about anything else they do or say?

Relaxing music plays in the saloon. I finally finished unpacking yesterday. Personal items have been placed throughout the sub. The place looks perfect. It would *feel* perfect, too, if I could just forget what Ari is . . . Until I've found Papa, I need to at least *try*.

I finish my tea and look out again. "Oscar? Where are we?"

The Navigator appears, wearing a satin floral dressing gown. "My dear, we are approaching York."

My mouth falls open. *York.* Territory I never, not once, ever imagined I'd actually cross. I'm here, in the wilder waters of Great Britain. Outside of the safe capital.

As I gaze out at the current, it shifts suddenly, a shadow descending. I stiffen, taking a step back. A flexible sheet of some kind materializes in the depths ahead. It drifts toward us, until it settles right on the sub's bow. *Whoa!*

I peer harder. It's a piece of the material that connects the groups of solar panels up on the surface. I shake my head. It's not obstructing the very front of the viewport, and it isn't entirely opaque either—more a gauzy material. But still, it's not good. We'd be oblivious to anything approaching from that side until it was too late. I move closer and can see where it's got caught. Hmm, a simple nudge would do it. . . . I stare into the turquoise waters. The cleanest I've seen. I picture the moon pool and will myself not to imagine the worst, to stop feeling so afraid.

I straighten and, wringing my hands, turn to the Navigator. "Oscar, tell me about the *Kabul*'s submersible."

I shift in the seat. The submersible is more spacious than Tabby's single-seated cockpit. It's shaped like an egg—a translucent egg on its side caged in titanium. The vessel rests in a smaller room, off the airtight chamber. Jojo wags her tail in the seat beside me. I pull the toggle switch toward me and power up the craft. Oscar's face appears above the dashboard.

"Salutations, my dear lady! Would you like a demonstration?"

"Hey, Oscar. Actually, I think I've got it now." I buckle up. "You passed my message on to Ari?"

"I did apprise Ari, my dear. One feels it isn't quite prudent to repeat his *exact* words, but I do believe he was somewhat scandalized at the news of you—"

The door slides open, and Ari climbs into the submersible beside me. He picks up a delighted Jojo and places her in his lap. I stare at him. And then at Jojo.

She makes contented sounds as he strokes her. I don't understand. How come she doesn't perceive anything wrong with him? Daft thing. Surely her senses should've picked up his identity from the moment she met him?

You mean like yours did?

Ari gazes ahead, his brow furrowed. "Oscar," he commands, "you will secure the moon pool door as soon as we leave. You'll remain stationary until we return. Any problem and you will alert us instantly."

"Alas! It distresses me to notify your good self that I am unable to take any security orders from you, sir."

Silence. Even *I'd* forgotten I'd taken away his primary rights.

Ari is still. "Then could you at least ensure you've taken them from Leyla?"

I sigh. "Oscar, please carry out the security requests. And tell Ari I know what I'm doing. I don't need him with me for this. It's just for a few minutes, for goodness' sake."

Ari strokes Jojo. "Oscar, tell Leyla I *know* she can take care of herself. She's demonstrated so. But this is why I am here. I promised her grandfather I would keep an eye on her. Especially when she insists on leaving the safety of the *Kabul*."

I fold my arms. "Oscar, explain to Ari why we can't have a partially obstructed viewport."

Ari pauses, before clearing his throat. "*I* can do it . . ." he says quietly. "I could just swim to it and free it. You won't be placing yourself in any danger then."

I grimace. There it is again. Another reminder. I just don't want to be reminded. I straighten with relief when loud bleeping offers a distraction.

Soon the submersible is through the hatch and inside the smaller chamber. I don't feel a thing as my body gradually acclimatizes to the pressure of the water outside, and before I know it, we're through the safety hatches. The hefty moon pool door releases. A robotic arm above us carries us over and places the sub down in the large opening, right into the water. I stare at the depths, taking deep breaths and doubting my decision.

It's an opening into the unknown.

I fiddle with the joystick until I can delay it no longer, and push it forward. *Bismillah.*

The submersible descends into the abyss below.

Small wings emerge from the vessel's sides. I hover a couple of meters beneath the shadow of the submarine. The small craft rocks in the higher currents. I look around in every direction. The *Kabul* overhead makes it difficult to see much.

Once Oscar's assured me the moon pool door is closed, I move out of the submarine's shadow and make my way around to the front.

The sheet is larger than I first thought, with most of it hanging below the vessel. It takes several nudges and tight maneuvers before it's dislodged from the viewport and slinks away. I turn around, take the strange waters in, and hold my breath.

It's the first time in my entire life that I'm sat in a submersible outside of London. I'm actually here in waters I've only ever before viewed on maps and screens.

A slight tremor runs through me as I glance out at the unfamiliar territory. But there's something else, too. Faint light breaks through the waves here and there. The water isn't as murky as I expected, with optimum visibility. The blue-green depths are clear all around us. A craving takes hold, rippling through and flooding my whole being until finally every cell tugs at me with longing.

I've missed speeding in the water terribly. Would it be so wrong to just escape all the confusion by doing something I love for a few minutes? I wouldn't be wasting too much time—we're already out here.

"Oscar?"

"My lady?" The Navigator hovers above the dashboard.

"I'm taking the submersible for a swift sprint. Keep the *Kabul* right here, and we'll be back soon."

"Very well, my dear. Bon voyage!"

Ari shakes his head, his mouth set in a straight line.

"I want to know what it's like out here," I say. "I *need* to feel it."

Leaning forward, I ensure Jojo's strapped securely to Ari's chest and silently curse the rush of color to my cheeks as my hands brush against him. *Oh great.* I'm completely losing the plot.

I slide the joystick forward, and we descend.

The welcome hint of civilization greets us as the seabed comes into view. The solar spheres on the surface light up the depths, bathing the city in a gentle blue-white incandescence. Illumination pulses and beams from structures, traffic, and the lit-up orbs rooted deep into the ground below. Though the Path of Light is now seventy years old, thanks to the ingenuity of Old World engineers, the huge orbs remain our main source of light along the seabed.

There are far fewer submersibles around here than in the capital. It would make for a fab racing ground. My heart expands as I move the throttle all the way forward and the sub speeds up. *Freedom.*

I navigate the city. Oh, how I missed this. Ahead, the well-lit white train station is vast. Its high-dome center and eight terminals sprawl out on the seabed like some never-ending octopus.

I sail on the current, circling old high-rises and office blocks, and loop-the-looping a dilapidated walkway, much to Jojo's delight. I flip the vessel several times. When I right the craft, I feel Ari's gaze on me and turn to him.

His face is relaxed, his eyes bright beneath the thick, dark lashes. The corners of his full mouth are slightly curved up, softening his sharp angles. Shoulder-length hair, damp from his shower, falls in waves around his face. Heat radiates through my chest, warm and blissful.

And then I suddenly imagine him with gills.

I draw my head back swiftly, gulping away the warm feeling. What on *earth* is wrong with me? He's one of them!

I shake my head and force myself to focus on the surroundings instead of Ari's expression just now.

For just a brief and glorious moment, I'd forgotten. He wasn't one of them, and things hadn't changed between us. I sigh and press on.

The sub dives into a street of individual and clearly wealthy homes, all the exteriors cast in gold and titanium. Each dwelling is designed to resemble a house from an ancient era. They totally look like Old World homes that just miraculously never decay. Some even have mock chimneys and picket fences around them, reminding me of Camilla's house. The chief historian's home also has a coveted late Second Elizabethan park bench in the front garden.

Jojo barks. She stiffens in Ari's lap and growls.

"Over there." Ari points.

"Oh my God, are they Anth—"

"*No,*" he says curtly, then runs his hands through his hair, sighing.

I frown and bite back a response. Traveling with him is going to be a very *long* journey.

I move the sub closer. Next door to the Victorian-style home is a house with mock Tudor beams along the exterior. The garden features a washing line, complete with clothes hanging and swaying on the current. Beside the washing line is a bench. In the center of this bench sits a child holding on to a doll's pram. They rock the pram back and forth. On the other side of the garden, another child holds on to a kite, swinging their arm to and fro as the kite drifts along. A toddler sits on a tricycle, knees rising alternately as they pedal.

I clear my throat. "Projections?" I whisper.

But they aren't projections either. I move in closer. The sub hovers above the garden.

"Dolls . . . Oh my God, they're dolls." I shudder. "But why? Why go to all that effort? They'll have paid mechanical labor a *ton* just to have that done."

"They refuse to accept the reality," Ari says, his voice so very low now and dripping with scorn. His eyes turn cold, his mouth pinched. "They live in the Old World."

I shake my head, my mouth open. "What a strange and utterly sad place."

"There are many more like it."

Something moves inside the pram. A bulky, ghostly pale creature that looks like a gigantic insect rises out of it. Its huge shell is made of overlapping segments, and its antennae twitch away. It drifts toward the toddler on the tricycle and feasts on a fish trapped in the child's hood. The toddler continues to smile and pedal. *Bloody hell.* I grimace.

Wiping my clammy palms, I push the throttle all the way forward and speed down the street and around the corner.

And stop in my tracks.

A light beams down in front of us. A lone submersible, its small wings resembling the airplanes of old, tilts as it descends. The fluorescent-checkered design on the body glimmers.

The police.

Oh hell. Have they spotted me? As slowly as possible, I duck down and reverse. I turn just as laser beams flash all around us to indicate an inspection. *Damn.*

"We can't be stopped by coppers," I say. "We just can't." And then I realize: If they stop us, Ari probably has even more to lose than I have. My chest tightens.

He shakes his head. "Why do you have to be so stubborn? You could have been safely back on the sub." He lifts his chin. "You're my responsibility, so let's do things my way now."

I straighten in my seat, gripping the throttle and joystick. "Let's bloody not."

The coppers are just visible behind me when I push the throttle all the way forward and set the propeller at full speed. I pull back on the joystick, and the sub rockets out of their way.

A quick peek behind. *No.* They're on my tail.

I wipe my sweaty palms and race on, before diving toward the city seabed. Lights flash in an underground tunnel as a train whooshes through. I dip lower, ducking *beneath* the tunnel. Curse the sub's ground and fore lights. Whichever I select, it casts illumination around me and will attract attention. I need something more discreet. The sandstorm beam.

I select the sharp but short beam and switch all other lights off. *Oh crikey.* It will have to do, though. Using only the beam's limited glare, and the muted glow coming from the tunnel above me, I glide on as fast as I dare. My stomach heaves. I focus on the ocean floor as I skim it. Are they still following me?

I come out from beneath the tunnel, and Ari curses as we both spot another police car in the distance. They really are determined, dammit.

"Let's try this once more," I say.

I ram the throttle and set the propeller at full speed. Jerking the joystick back, I soar above the police car. I keep rising until the current becomes too volatile for the submersible, then I speed away.

When I can no longer see anyone behind me, I dive. My pulse races. I keep the joystick pushed forward until I'm just above the seabed. At last I balance the craft and pause to check on Jojo. The puppy's all right. I turn to view the surroundings and jolt. I hold my breath until I understand where we are.

It's an ancient theme park.

Huge arches of rusted metal tower in the murky depths before me. To my side a hefty sign, too oxidized to decipher, hangs precariously off another twisting frame that trails onward until it's out of sight. Below me, the bulky carcass of a sea creature is lodged in a vehicle lying on its side, a giant ice cream sculpture sticking out from the roof of the van.

We rise a little, swerving sharply to avoid a falling corroded sheet, with its faded image of a huge wave of water still just visible; the sign sinks below, finally giving in to the environment. All manner of frames loom in every direction; some are broken, others carry on, disappearing into the cloaking depths. I stiffen as tiny pulsing lights move erratically in the space ahead. Eyeballs. I rise higher.

I'm above the roller coaster now and speed along its track. Seaweed wraps itself around the construction and fish forage in the rusty crevices. A quick glance over my shoulder: the blip of a light. An Eyeball on my tail.

I loop under and over crisscrossing structures. The craft zigzags in and out of a long horizontal frame that still has a row of cars on its top and swerves around a vertical grid. Pole after defiant pole looms in the cloudy vastness. More lights—I need to hide.

I take a quick scan of the area. Nothing that would conceal us. The pulsing of the Eyeballs grows brighter, closer.

I peer below. The sub's ground light picks up giant cups. My gaze darts to the ride next to it. It has several toddler-size vehicles around the edge and enough room in the center for the sub, if I'm really careful. I inch the vessel right into the middle of the cars. Movement to my left catches my eye; there's something in the vehicle next to us.

A huge overturned shell tilts to one side, and a single, slimy tentacle reaches out from beneath. Bright suckers run along its dark, glossy arm as it unfurls and feels the water around the car. The tentacle retreats, and the shell moves once more to hide the octopus. *Please just stay there.* Octopuses are so bloody clever and known to be extremely stubborn if they attach themselves to your sub. I really don't fancy carrying one back to the *Kabul*.

I take deep breaths—*one, two, three*—and switch everything off. Total darkness. I gulp.

"Hey, baby, you all right?" I whisper to Jojo, and reach out to comfort her; the dark can be paralyzing. My hand catches Ari's instead, and I jerk it back at once.

Get a grip. Thank God he can't see my face, because it's roasting.

Minutes pass. The odd light still pulses here and there. My heartbeat whooshes away. It's such a *dense* space. Something flickers and moves past the sub. *Hold on.*

I mustn't let the dread in. Not now. I can't afford to.

My shoulders rise and fall. Again, something unidentifiable passes by. I sit on my hands. A sense that I'm sinking claws at me. Just about anything could be lurking in the cloaked waters, watching us. Waiting to swallow us whole, to cloud the depths with our blood. I shudder, my breathing loud. At last, the pulsing lights recede.

I let out a shaky breath. "It's time to go." My voice is small. Everything feels tight—my face, hands, stomach, chest. My thoughts. My palms are sweaty, and I wipe them on my thighs before powering up. The sub's fore light illuminates the surroundings and startles some passing dab that swiftly bolt away. I summon the Navigator.

"Oscar, coordinates for the *Kabul*, please."

He appears, tilting his head. "The submersible is connected to the submarine, my dear. If you select the house icon, the *Kabul* will guide you home to her."

Home. Where is that anymore?

What is Ari's home like? I frown; who cares?

The water ahead is clear. I relax a little and only now realize just how tense I was. I initiate the tracking device and follow the route back.

Ari gestures to the water. "There is nothing to fear," he says quietly. "It's the same environment. It doesn't change when you can't see it. It's still water, creatures, people in vessels. That is all. Nothing else."

Well, of course you *wouldn't be afraid of the environment!* I want to spit out.

Instead I hold back my words and look ahead.

He's wrong.

You might not be able to see the dread, but it exists. It visits me in dark places. And has done so for as long as I can remember.

CHAPTER THIRTY

I fold the paper Theo wrapped my brolly in—Christmas Day seems like a lifetime ago—bending and molding it into shape, my still-strapped fingers mildly annoying. Jojo's just eaten and lies snuggled up beside me in the viewport. The cozy glow from an orange Lumi-Orb on the floor beside us fills the space, the small sphere's light warming the evening. League after league of the dark waters roll by as we press on. This morning's excursion in the sub could have had serious implications. . . . I need to be more careful. The news plays in the background.

A gulper eel swims up to the windows; its lengthy tail glows bright pink at the tip as it whips the water in the sub's light. The long creature spies some shrimp, and its humongous mouth opens wide, trapping a good deal of water along with the catch. The unwanted liquid spills out through its gills as it gulps the meat down. My tummy rumbles. Ari is in the galley. He wanted to prepare dinner and suggested I rest.

Do Anthropoids never feel tired?

I can't think too much on his identity without panic and confusion gripping me, and then it's all I can do to distract myself from the fact. But I do know that what I saw in him previous to finding out his secret hasn't gone away. I'm not sure what this means.

How can I think anything *positive* about him still, when he's one of them?

The news on in the background is as gloomy as ever.

A corner shop was robbed at midday on its route through Liverpool city center; a passing bot spotted it and alerted the authorities just in time. The elderly shopkeeper was given medical assistance, and the vandalized vessel towed to safety. Next there's a vote for which Old World ruin ought to receive special renovation treatment—Windsor Castle or Syon House.

How can your sense of nostalgia render you so shortsighted that you at once spend millions to stop the unstoppable disintegration of ruins, while also happily believing you'll be leaving them behind very soon, to return to the surface? I mute the news and put on soft music instead.

Ari enters with dinner and places the large tray of food down in the viewport. Delicious smells waft around the saloon.

He points to the tray. "I chose at random."

"Thank you."

We both sit to eat.

He tucks into the saffron rice and lamb korma, gesturing to the food. He clears his throat. "Your mother was from Afghanistan." It's a statement more than a question.

It catches me off guard. "What?"

I can't help visualizing the scene. An Anthropoid boy speaking to a human girl about her family, where she comes from.

I am a human being, he'd said yesterday.

I'm so tired. So many thoughts and feelings and I don't have a clue what to do with them.

If small talk gets rid of the suffocating awkwardness that's sprung up between us since the discovery, then it's most welcome. *Anything* to make this situation less uncomfortable. The confusion I've felt since is beyond exhausting.

"Yes . . . from Kabul. Hence the sub's name."

He nods. "I like the name."

I think for a while, then continue. "Papa's also of Afghan descent, but he was born here. Mama came here in her late teens, fell in love with Papa, and stayed." I realize I'm smiling for the first time in what seems like forever.

His expression warms as he watches me. And I know the answer to the question he asked me yesterday: I'm not afraid of him. Even though it goes against *everything*—because *how* can I not be afraid of an Anthropoid? But I'm not afraid of Ari.

Should I be, though? Everything the Anthropoid Watch Council has ever said about them says I ought to be terrified of him.

But . . . he put himself at risk, on full display as an Anthropoid, to free the sub so we could escape the attack. Escape the Blackwatch.

What might've happened if he'd put himself before me? If he'd refused to enter the water so his identity could remain secret? I shudder at the thought.

He also had the chance to just swim away from it all, but he stayed. *It* stayed? Color floods my cheeks as my use of *it* to refer to Anthropoids hits me. I might not understand much else right now, but I do know Ari is very definitely not an *it*.

"You're a Muslim," he says, interrupting my thoughts. "My granddad was a Muslim; he was Mauritian."

Mauritian. I did wonder about his skin tone. And a Muslim in his family! "Yes. Are you religious in any way?"

I know that even among religious people—and much to the government's disappointment—opinions regarding Anthropoids and religion are split. Many religious leaders insist that despite their evil characteristics, the Anthropoids are human beings in the eyes of God and therefore can be saved from . . . their barbaric ways.

I gulp; why am I thinking about this now, dammit.

He shrugs. "Mum and Dad are agnostic, and I . . . I guess I am too."

"I see. Have you always lived in the Faroe Islands?"

He seems taken aback whenever I ask him something. He stares intently at me now before lowering his gaze and rubbing the back of his neck. Why? What did I say?

We are silent again for several moments. I can feel Ari's gaze fall on me once more, but I can't bring myself to meet it. Is there any point to all this? Will I ever see him as human?

He clears his throat and his voice is low, his words slower than usual. "My parents lived in London, years ago, before they had us, but then moved to the Faroe Islands."

"I see. And 'us'?"

Again, he flashes the same wary look; he's uncomfortable talking about his life. Why?

"Me and Freya, my little sister."

So Freya—who he called out to in his nightmare—is his sister.

"You don't like me asking you any personal questions, do you?"

He chews slowly as he contemplates the question. "I've never been asked a personal question by your kind before," he finally says.

Oh. So *that's* why all the hesitation.

He tilts his head in consideration then. "The name McQueen?"

"That's due to my great-grandpa Kasim—Papa's American grandfather. In Papa's family, future generations carry the paternal surname, and so we're the McQueens."

He nods. "Have you been to Afghanistan?"

"No. Papa said we're going to go one day, inshallah. He's been several times since he and Mama married. I have grandparents and cousins who I've never met in person. I want to see Mama's home. Afghanistan's rolling hills and old riverbeds are covered with kelp forest, and the mountain ranges, wow—just imagine driving through them. Now that I've finally left London, I want to go *everywhere*. One day I'll race around all the biggest mountains in the whole world. And through the Grand Canyon in America—even though it has Old World Heritage Status, so it's illegal to visit the site. My mate in New York's done it twice and always taunts me.

And I *know* I can beat his time." *Please, God, stop me talking.*

There's a tug at the corners of his mouth. "I think you could beat him, yes. You—you speak of the future." A hint of wonder surfaces in his gaze, brightening his eyes further.

"Well, of course . . ." *Don't you?*

He looks away, his brow furrowed. His jaw clenches and a hard expression breaks through. He stays quiet.

Oscar appears, straightening a flower in the pocket of his coat and breaking the sudden, awkward silence. "My lady, are we to continue on during the night, or would you prefer I establish a safe location where the *Kabul* may remain stationary until the morning?"

I clear my throat. "Stationary, please."

Oscar adjusts the satin cravat around his neck. He inclines his head as he looks on us both. "Ah, who, being loved, is poor?"

Heat burns through me. I clench my jaw and stare at the Navigator. If only you could tase a hologram. He simply smiles back.

"Oscar, you misunderstand. But that's all right."

He raises his eyebrows and waves his hand in the air. "My dear, women are meant to be loved, not understood."

Argh! "That will be all, thank you."

He finally bloody disappears.

"I'm sorry," I say to Ari. "He says the daftest things sometimes. It's maddening."

Ari's lips twitch. "I like him."

My mouth falls open. He actually *likes* someone!

He shifts, indicating the fried flatbreads. "So, what are these?"

"It's called a paratha. These ones have a cheese stuffing."

He raises his eyebrows and tries a piece, nodding in appreciation as he scarfs the food down. Thank goodness he eats normally. I'd hate to look greedy, even though I am.

"And these?" He inspects the kulche ab-e-dandaan.

"Dessert. Melt-in-your-mouth almond biscuits—utterly yummy. Try them."

Ari takes a bite and proceeds to stuff the whole biscuit into his mouth. I realize I'm staring at him. And he's staring right back.

He smiles hesitantly, and oh my—his whole face changes. All the sharp edges, the hardness, the fixed suspicion, it all slips away. Everything about him is soft, gentle.

Except Anthropoids are neither soft nor gentle.

I dip my head, my hair hiding my face, and continue to eat, deep in thought.

We chat as we sip cups of kahwah afterward.

He rests his gaze on me. "Are you feeling better? Your wounds, do they still hurt?"

"Not anymore."

His face darkens.

I shrug. "The main thing is, we survived it."

His eyes shimmer as he stares at me. I try not to stare back, but it's impossible. Neither of us speaks. I actually do not know what to say. Or what I even *want* to say.

And then the muted news screen behind Ari flickers, catching my eye.

I leap up, staring at the image. It's Camilla Maxwell, the chief historian's daughter. What has she done? I command the soothing music off and the volume for the news on.

"A truly sad, sad day for all Britons," the newscaster says. "Messages of condolence have been flooding Westminster all day, and Lord Maxwell himself will issue a statement later."

My legs start to quiver.

"For those of you who have just joined us, it has been confirmed that Miss Camilla Maxwell—that's our esteemed Lord Maxwell's daughter—went out to Camden Town on New Year's Eve, parking on its seabed. With a seventies Lastar, she blasted a hole into the side of her submersible. Miss

Maxwell is dead. Another victim of the seasickness."

An icy cold tentacle wraps itself around my heart and squeezes.

I shudder by the porthole in my bedroom, trying to focus on folding the paper model in my lap.

Camilla suffered from the seasickness. She drove all that way to the marshes knowing what she intended to do. She aimed at the sub's body knowing what would follow. Did she drown, or did the pressure crush her? What went through her head after the shot, in that split second before the horror began?

My insides lurch as I picture her final moments again.

How can we hope to survive where such hopelessness exists? Poor, poor Camilla. All I can see is her enthusiastic self back at Clio House, her blond ponytail bobbing up and down and her face glowing whenever she chatted about a story or script for the historical reenactments. *Damn* the seasickness!

I grind my teeth; sod the stupid paper model. I grip the half shape and rip it to pieces. There's a knock at the door.

"Enter," I snap.

Ari stares down at the torn paper and back at me. My bottom lip quivers. I swallow past the lump in my throat.

He pauses and then joins me on the floor by the porthole, a few feet away. We stare out at the glimmering darkness. Minutes pass in silence before I speak.

"Camilla was so incredibly gentle and good and kind. It's so unfair. It's unfair that the seasickness keeps taking all these people. It's so frustrating that we can't help them. Papa always tried comforting any sufferers —lifting their spirits. But how do you fight such an invincible sense of hopelessness?"

When I turn to him, his eyes are clouded, his face pinched. Ever since we heard the news, he's been struggling with something. As if he's unsure what to say. He clears his throat. "Where did the hopelessness come from?"

"The water brought it, of course. Every time a scary creature comes too close to the city—"

"It's their natural habitat. And people are safe in their homes and vessels."

"Every time the water conspires against us, when it tries to—"

"Nature. Nothing sinister," he finishes.

"Every time there's a bloody earthquake and—"

He looks away, clamping his jaw shut.

"Just because *you're*—you're not afraid of the environment, doesn't mean it's any less terrifying for others." I turn to the porthole. I'm not in the mood for this. Why are we going on about the water, when Camilla's dead? "She was a really talented writer, you know," I say. "On the morning of the marathon, she told me a recent story she'd submitted had been rejected because it was an original; they only want retellings. I wish they'd accepted her story, that she'd seen that happen." My heart sinks as I suddenly recall the premise of her story. A little girl trapped inside the mouth of a monster. . . .

We both peer out into the dark and shifting environment.

"Why does everything have to revolve around the Old World?" Ari asks quietly after a while. "What if new ideas were encouraged instead? We revere the Old World buildings. We are always looking back. What if the Great Briton of the Day was one of the many worthy people to have been born *after* the disaster? Those dolls today . . . Why are we creating mock Old World scenes in the water?"

I can't believe it. He's just listed everything I find bewildering and frustrating.

"Yes," I say. "Exactly. I've always found it a bit *creepy*, all the obsession for the Old World. I've never understood the intense reverence for its ruins, for instance." I press on my temples and look out at the water surging past as we make our way north, to wherever the coordinates for Papa will lead us.

So much to try and make sense of.

I can't get Camilla's face out of my head; her fixed, melancholic expression during the marathon. Why didn't I see it?

What could you have done?

I suddenly gasp and Ari turns to me. "Tabby!" I say. "She's going to be so upset. . . . Oh, I hope she's all right. She battled with the seasickness a few years ago—came through it, thank God. But it's all going to surface again. Oh no. Ari . . . will people ever feel truly hopeful again?"

I look away, staring into the water ahead. Ari still watches me, studying me.

The question hangs in the air between us.

CHAPTER THIRTY-ONE

I sit up in bed, heart thumping and soaked in sweat. I was back in my nightmare, the one from years ago. As ever, I'm standing by a window, looking out at the water. Watching and waiting. And then something so utterly foreboding stirs in the void. I shiver at the memory now.

I don't know what woke me up, but thank God it did. I shift around in bed, when a guttural moan reverberates off the walls. Ari. He's having another nightmare.

Scrambling out of the bed without thinking, I throw on my robe as I rush to his door and command it open. I edge into his room. A red Lumi-Orb burns, casting a dim light in the space.

I move closer. Ari looks asleep. My breathing is still too fast from my own dark dream; I take deep breaths and slowly come to my senses. What on earth am I doing entering his private space uninvited? What was I thinking barging in here like this?

I turn to go when his head twitches as if agitated. What should I do? On the cabinet next to him is his favorite knife. And the paper seahorse I made him. *He saved it.* He mutters something, and I lean over.

"Ari," I whisper. Nothing. "Ari, wake up. You're having a nightmare. You need to wake up." Still nothing. I reach over and shake his shoulder.

He lashes out. He grabs my arm, pulling me close, and sits up. In an instant, he has the knife in his other hand. I tremble.

"Ari! It's just me. You were having a nightmare. You're all right now."

He stares at me, blinking rapidly. The knife slips from his fingers, back onto the cabinet. His chest rises and falls as he breathes heavy and fast. He looks around the room and swallows. "Sorry," he whispers, eyes wide as his grip releases my arm.

He shifts back against the headboard, and gradually his breathing calms down. I sit on the edge of the bed and meet his gaze. His eyes are two golden orbs, and in the red light of the room, he's *mystifying*.

Against my will, I breathe in his smell. It's difficult to pin it down. Especially because I've never actually smelled woodlands, mountains, and the rain. But it's wild and raw and warm. And heartening. Is this *Ari's* scent, or an Anthropoid thing?

I want to ask him about the nightmare. I really want to know what plagues his dreams. I shouldn't ask, though. There's so much about him I don't know, that I've no *right* to know. But the way he automatically reached for his knife . . . That was *practice*. What kind of life do you have to lead that your first instinct on being awoken is to reach for a weapon? I feel so heavy just watching him now. I have to know.

"What is it?" I whisper. "Why do you have the nightmares?"

I'm not expecting an answer.

He lowers his eyes and twists the covers in his hands as he speaks. "We were all out by the rift—my family, friends, cousins, on our way to a family wedding. I was ten. We were attacked. An ambush. Most of them died. Cousins and friends. All children and teenagers. I was one of the few who escaped unharmed. Freya was not so lucky. She took a hit and lost her leg. Too many died. I couldn't help." He opens his mouth to say more but shuts it again. His shoulders rise and fall as he stares into the space.

"I'm so sorry," I whisper. Horrifying images fill my head. "I'm truly sorry. Who—who attacked you?"

A muscle flexes in his jaw. "A pack of savage soldiers sent by Captain Sebastian. Like always. And I couldn't stop them."

"Are—are you *sure* it was the government, though? Maybe—maybe they thought *they* were under attack?"

He shakes his head and stares at the ceiling. "They felt threatened by an unarmed family on their way to a wedding? Threatened by a group made up of mostly children? And it *was* the government. It is *always* them. When you have been treated like animals, hunted and slaughtered for decades, you come to know your tormentors." He grinds his teeth.

Weddings. Children. I've never once even linked these words to the Anthropoids.

"I'm really sorry. And what could you have done? You were too young."

"I should have done *something*." He shrugs.

"You're being unfair to yourself."

"You blame yourself for the attack on the sub. You made a mistake. We all . . . we all make them." He pauses then, deep in thought.

My mistake hurt us all.

"What do you fear most about the water?" he asks, in his low, rich tones. "How can you enjoy racing through it and also fear it?"

I fix my eyes on the russet covers.

"Please," he says.

I shrug, my face warming. "I don't know . . . I've always *loved* being out in the water, but it also terrifies me. I especially really hate the poorly lit areas, and anyplace I'm not already familiar with. I just imagine all sorts when I'm in that situation. I—I tried to overcome it once, with a freefall. Let myself drop through the depths, trust in my instincts. But"—I shake my head—"it didn't exactly work out."

"Leyla . . . look at me. Please." His voice is so husky, so deep.

I raise my gaze to meet his.

He opens his mouth, then pauses before speaking, as if unsure whether to go on. "They're fake. The earthquakes—they're not real."

I stare at him. "How do you mean? How the bloody hell can you fake an earthquake?"

"Because it's true. They're planned explosions. I saw one with my own eyes in London. A civic sub arranged one of the 'quakes.'"

"Stop, please. I really can't take any more right now."

"Why would I lie? You need to know they're fake. The water itself isn't as scary as you think, Leyla. . . . You've just been conditioned to believe it is."

"Please, Ari. The earthquakes can't be fake. They've *killed* people!"

"You don't trust me?"

I *want* to. I *did*—before I found out his identity. I search his face. He wouldn't lie about this. But it's too confusing. It's all too much. All I can think lately is *why, why, why.*

I stand. For all my desire to learn the truth, right now I honestly don't think I can take on any more. These revelations are far bigger than me, and I just don't know what to do with them. Each one is strange and terrifying.

My throat hurts. I swallow but the lump remains. "I—I hope you get some restful sleep."

He holds my gaze, twisting the beads around his neck, and nods.

I return to my own room and bed, looking up at the ceiling in the dim golden light.

Anthropoids feel pain.

We've always been told they don't, and that's why they're oblivious to ours. But it isn't true. Because Ari was in pain recalling the incident that took so many lives. The look in his eyes . . . I find myself wishing I could make the pain go away. I shake myself; I should focus instead on what he said.

Would the government *really* fake earthquakes just to keep us fearing the water? *Why?* It seems too far-fetched. It simply can't be true.

Is *anything* true anymore? It's a world full of deceit and uncertainty. What does the future hold for people governed by secrets and lies—and fear? Do I even still care about the truth? Lately, the truth's been one horrifying reveal after another. How is it better? Why did I so desperately seek it?

I hate them. I absolutely, truly hate Captain Sebastian and the Blackwatch. To take Papa as they did . . . And the attack on innocent people in the Faroe Islands—to hurt *children* like that. I shudder at the horrific images forming.

And where will it all end?

It feels like I'm circling the edges of one of the many whirlpools that sprang up all over the globe after the disaster, sucking in anything and everything in their way. But I have to keep my mind clear.

I *must* find Papa before Captain Sebastian catches up with me.

CHAPTER THIRTY-TWO

A ri walks over to the seating area and eyes the reports I'm reading. "Government funding?"

I glance up from the digital files hovering over the table laden with breakfast food. Something feels different today with Ari. After last night when he told me what caused his nightmares, he seems less guarded. And yet we both seem to be more aware of each other, which is maddening.

"I was thinking about stuff last night . . . after you told me about the earthquakes. I couldn't sleep. And well, one of the things that drives me up the walls is the worship of crumbling buildings. Did you know the government spends a *ton* trying to keep old London propped up? Well, I *thought* it was just old London, but I've found out this morning it's *everything* old—all over the country, an obscene amount of funding goes toward maintaining Old World buildings and structures. Look." I swish the funding reports in his direction. "It's something that's always done my head in. So I got up early and started reading the public records. One thing led to another, and before long I was staring at the annual expenditure reports the treasury releases. When you compare where the government is actually spending, against more urgent requirements like the funding for seasickness, the results are pretty rotten."

"The Underground . . ." Ari says, opening up another file.

"I haven't got to that yet, but I'm not surprised." I'm about to turn back to the page I was scanning, when my eye catches the one Ari's skimming. *Urgent: Bakerloo Line.* "Wait, what's it saying about the Bakerloo line?"

"They asked for funding—repeatedly. Many sections of the Underground have," Ari explains as he continues reading. "The Underground tunnels haven't been touched since the Old Worlders built them, soon as they heard of the coming disaster. This report warns of a catastrophe if the Bakerloo line doesn't receive funds for immediate, major structural rework."

My stomach rolls. "What year was that report filed in?" But before he answers, I see it for myself. And gasp.

"What is it?"

My heart sinks. "Terence Campbell, the twins' dad . . . A year after that report was filed, a year after the Underground pushed for the means to carry out repairs, was the Bakerloo line incident, killing so many—including Theo and Tabby's dad. The government was *warned* this would happen, and yet still they allocated the money toward upkeep of the old structures instead. I can't believe it."

Ari's expression hardens. "I'm sorry."

Vivian without a husband, and Theo and Tabby without their dad. Adequate funding would've prevented the accident and his death. Not to mention everyone else who perished in the tunnel.

Why does the government do this? I just don't understand why they would willingly ignore the dangers and flow the funds into futile projects.

I pour warm drinks for us both. The *Kabul* pierces the dark-blue waters, toward the undisclosed location. Despite the coordinates, it's proved impossible so far to know exactly *what* we're headed for—all the maps are coming up with nothing.

"Oscar?"

The Navigator appears. He's looking seriously dapper, with a lavender cravat wrapped around the upturned collars of a formal shirt. "My dear lady. Pray how may I assist?"

"You look pretty ace."

He dips his head. "Ah, one can never be overdressed or overeducated, my dear."

"Oscar, exactly where are we now, and can you please run another check for anything at our intended location?"

The Navigator nods, and his reply is swift. "My lady, we are now approaching those Scottish gems, the Shetland Islands. There is no structure at all at the precise location of the registered coordinates."

I sense Ari tense beside me. He gets up as I instruct Oscar to run the coordinates again.

Same result—there's nothing there.

"But there has to be *something* there. Maybe," I say to Ari who's now pacing the room, "just maybe, it's not a fixed structure? It could be a sub they're keeping Papa on, which is why it doesn't show up on maps?"

Ari pauses and looks at me the way he did that night in the Den. When he wanted me to guess the truth about him. He opens his mouth as if to speak but closes it again.

Oh no you don't. "Tell me."

He curls his hands into fists by his sides. "There *is* a structure that doesn't show up on maps . . . but it's not good." He clears his throat. "Leyla, if we keep heading in the direction we are, then there's a very real possibility your father's in Broadmoor. Because it doesn't show up on any systems."

"Huh? There's no such place. It's just a rumor. Ari, everyone knows Broadmoor's only a rumor—it *has* to be!"

"I'm sorry," he says. "But it exists. You mustn't worry though, the coordinates might not take us there."

I clutch my stomach. *Broadmoor.* The famed top secret prison where *anything* goes. It actually exists. . . .

Ari rubs the back of his neck, his expression taut.

Is it possible Papa's in there? What state might he be in? I swallow away the horrific possibilities. I can't go losing it now. Why put Papa in a top secret prison, though? What do they think he's guilty of? I fold my arms and straighten. Horrific as it is, if Ari's right, then I have an exact location now. Which is what I wanted, and needed. *Think.* My mind races.

"Oscar, the information we downloaded at Cambridge . . . is it enough to be able to contact them?"

We're on the same side; it's not what you think. Jas's words to me when the place was under attack. What did he mean? And is the Den even still standing? Did they survive the attack, or am I about to speak with the Blackwatch? I gulp and shake the doubts away.

"There is indeed a point of contact one may try, my lady."

I take a deep breath. "Oscar, contact Bia."

Ari whips his head around to face me, but I turn to the communications screen, sticking my chin high as I straighten. It's a long shot, and she *must* believe me.

Without warning, Bia immediately comes into view, the Den visible in the background with its screens hovering around. *Oh phew.* They survived. She narrows her eyes, her brow creasing.

"I am not finished with you. You have something of mine." She leans to the side to read something; presumably trying to track me. "And where are you, girl? Why didn't you head for King's—"

"You knew where my papa was and didn't tell me."

She purses her mouth and her eyes flicker. "What? What do you know?"

"I know he's in Broadmoor, and I'm going to do something about it." It's worth a try. But curse the waver in my voice.

Bia shakes her head. "What good would it have done to tell you your father's being held there? This is above you, girl."

My gaze darts to Ari. My cheeks burn now, and heat creeps along my neck. I breathe hard and fast as the truth finally drops.

It's true. Papa *is* in Broadmoor.

I finally know . . . I know where my papa is.

Ari nods slowly, understanding, as he takes in my expression.

Bia waves her hand. "I do hope you're not thinking of doing anything rash," she says, "because we already tried everything. We even made three separate attempts at breaking into the prison—and not just for your father. We have other business there. Each time, we've suffered considerable damage. We've never got past their first line of defense. But we have someone on the inside now, and we all just need to sit tight until we have a foolproof plan. Do you understand?"

I catch my breath. Hope is the strangest and most magical thing . . . It really is. It shows up at totally random and unexpected times, and can bloody well knock you for six.

I take a deep breath and cross my arms. "No. I'm not waiting anymore. I'm going to go in. From everything I've ever heard about this place, my papa doesn't have much time. You have a choice, Bia."

Her face tightens. "I don't think you underst—"

"No, I don't think *you* do. I'm going in, like I said. So now it's up to you. You can either explain to my papa and grandpa why you let me go near a top security prison without a clue, or you can send me everything you guys have on the place. I mean, *everything*. Because I *am* going in, and nobody is stopping me."

I end the communication. If I had to speak to her a second longer, I'd have crumbled. If she refuses to help, Theo could hack into their systems—I've no doubt. But I'd have to message him to ask, and risk getting him into trouble.

Ari's gaze finds mine and I hold it. He scratches his jaw and stares away into space.

I peer out of the viewport. I know where Papa is. Finally. *Finally.*

My papa is alive, and I know where he is!

A wave carries me away, cradling me as we roll toward translucent waters. It's still a rough sea, but with the current so much clearer now, I am definitely one step closer to being with him again.

A memory surfaces. Years ago, Papa and I used to play hide-and-seek— back when we lived in Westminster, before they cleared the government housing of most of its scientists and instead allocated the homes to families of historians and anyone employed in defense. Papa was in our sub, and I'd borrowed one of the twins' vessels as usual and gone off to hide behind the sprawling structure of Civic House. I'd become distracted though and careened off course. Once I realized I was lost—for what seemed like an eternity, but I now know must've been only minutes—I'd been too terrified, too frozen to think of contacting Papa via the Bracelet. I'd finally managed to focus and alert him to the problem.

But what if I did *get lost, Papa? How would you ever find me?* I asked afterward, trembling and consumed, as usual, by the dread of hidden places and wilder waters.

He'd chuckled. *You're not going to get lost, Pickle. You, my little Kabuli peree, were born to* rule *these waves—to create mischief and laughter and joy in these depths. Now trust in God and stop worrying!* But on seeing my expression, his brow had creased, his hazel eyes imploring as he wrapped his arms around me and I could breathe in his calming citrusy scent. His voice dropped to a murmur. *Don't you know I would sail every current, ride every wave, and dive into any depth, until I found you? But I won't have to because it isn't going to happen inshallah. I'm not going to lose you, Pickle.*

Ari startles me when his voice brings me out of my thoughts and back to the present. "What are you thinking?" he asks, as he places a tray of warm drinks and snacks beside me in the viewport. "It's not a good idea. You heard Bia. They have already tried, several times."

It's early afternoon now, and we've both been engrossed in the requested info, only pausing when necessary. Jojo's curled up on the sofa feeling lazy after her lunch.

Bia came through for us within the hour, sending whatever she has on the wretched place along with warnings and pleas not to do anything stupid and to just sit tight until we hear from her again. There's *everything*. . . . Blueprints of the place itself, security measures, routines, it's all here. The layout of the files makes the information a headache to decipher, though.

"That's because Bia's lot only headed in with submersibles," I say. "We have a *submarine*. We can do more. The *Kabul* has seriously impressive firepower. We can do this! We just have to believe we can. And we have to trust each other. . . ."

He holds my gaze, his own suddenly so intense I might get lost in it.

I swallow. "Oscar?"

"My dear lady?"

"Oscar, grant Ari full primary rights."

I have to go with my gut now. All I have left are my faith and hope. Ari looks stunned; he opens and closes his mouth several times before we both look away, reaching for our warm drinks. We take a sip and pull disgusted faces at the same time.

"*Tea*," Ari says, shaking his head.

"Bitter poison," I say, reluctantly swallowing the coffee and swapping the cup for my beloved tea. I glance at the info again and screw my face up. "Why are the prison files in such a *weird* design?" God, I hate technology. "Please separate the files for me; I want to focus on the prison's defenses."

Ari's mouth twitches, and he gets to work sorting through the trench of information, swishing the interior defense file over to me while he concentrates on structure and exterior security.

It takes a good amount of digging around before we share our findings.

"Did you know they have mostly *robot* prison officers?" I ask him. "Bia's lot have found a weakness, though—they have a reboot switch at the back of their necks in case of an emergency. Takes them thirty minutes to restart fully and they're useless during that time. Of course you'd have to somehow get behind them in the first place. . . . You?"

"The security . . . I have never seen anything like it before," he says. "There are no hatches, only a single moon pool. Apart from opening at random intervals for a few minutes—to allow for the movement of security and supplies—the pool is otherwise opened only once a week for a few hours to allow for new prisoners, supplies, and shift changeovers. The next one is at dawn tomorrow." Ari rakes his fingers through his hair. "I don't think the *Kabul* should go anywhere near the area. It—"

"We go in tomorrow."

"*What*—"

"I'm not waiting another week now that I know Papa's in that hellhole. The way in opens up for a few hours at dawn, so that's when we try."

He swears. "You will never survive their defenses! And if you do, you face capture and the same fate as your father. Why do you have to be so stubborn?"

"Because my papa might be dead in a week's time! I don't trust Captain Sebastian or the Blackwatch at *all* anymore. And that's if they haven't already done something to him. . . . What if he's been hurt? What if they hurt him?" I swallow, looking away. "We must have the Medi-bot ready just in case—" My voice catches in my throat; I stare out into the depths, wringing my hands. What might Papa have gone through? "I didn't come this far to let fear stop me from trying," I say. "We can't waste time. We need to go over everything: our firepower, what sensory devices we'll be using, how we get past any security posts we come across—the list goes on. We just can't afford to get it wrong." I take a deep breath to stop my insides from quivering.

"I think your father will be okay," Ari says gently, though there's still tension in his voice. "If he's as strong as you, then he'll be holding on."

We spend the next few hours assessing the *Kabul*'s weaponry and capabilities, and absorbing all the info on the prison.

My throat and chest feel like rocks have been stuffed into them, and I keep shivering.

Thank God I have Ari with me. And the fact he thinks it's a reckless idea but is trying to make it work because I really need it to . . . it just makes my heart expand.

I *understand* why he thinks it's such a rash plan. It's Broadmoor—the security's on another level. But I'm truly desperate. It's all or nothing now.

I *have* to make it work.

CHAPTER THIRTY-THREE

"W hy's this dolphin acting so weird?" I ask Ari, peering out of the viewport. It doesn't perform any stellar acrobatics, or blow bubbles to please us. Is the creature ill?

He looks up from the seating area, where the prison's blueprints hover. "It's not a free dolphin. Look closer."

The animal seems almost lifeless, showing only a detached interest in the sub.

I exhale. "I give up. Tell me!"

"Border patrol," he replies, as he opens up and zooms in on various holographic files. His face darkens and his voice hardens. "A whole army of sea creatures, mostly dolphins, guard Great Britain's borders. The dolphins are born and raised in captivity. They know nothing but the training forced on them."

I shudder and stare at the animal. The poor things . . . I place my hand on the window. No reaction. The creature moves away through the late evening waters.

I jump when Oscar materializes.

"My dear lady, the craft is on our tail again. This time they are traveling far too close for one's comfort, and they insist upon communication."

Ari glances up from his files, his face set. "I'll take care of it."

I hold my hand up. "Erm, no, thank you."

Whoever they are, they don't give up easily. They've followed us relentlessly since late afternoon, no matter what we try and do to shake them off.

It isn't the first vessel to get in our way out here. The *Kabul* only just managed to sneak around a security base over the Orkney Islands, when a private sub attempted to block its path. I sent them a warning by way of light firepower. They yielded immediately. Now isn't the time for obstructions. I want to get as near to the prison's location as possible so we're ready to move in at dawn. Besides, I've yet to see a single vessel that doesn't look dodgy.

This particular sub is especially determined to be noticed, though. Even out here where there's no one around for leagues.

"Send them another warning, Oscar. A bigger one."

"A most equitable response, my dear—and one already conducted."

My eyebrows meet. "And they still persist? Who on earth are they?"

Ari jerks his head up. "If you hit their propeller, you'll send them spinning below. Problem over. Oscar, damage their vessel."

I scowl in his direction; maybe I should cancel his primary rights again. I turn to the Navigator. "Totally ignore that, Oscar. Accept communication request."

Ari mutters something.

The screen comes to life. "Coo-ee! Only us! Just spreading the good word."

It's a group of missionaries. I shake my head, unable to control the grin spreading on my face. Even here, in the middle of nowhere. Ari walks over, his eyes narrow, hands on hips.

The immaculately dressed group offers warm smiles. A woman in a fuchsia hat waves at me and clutches her chest. "Oh, look at you, lovely. Thank you for agreeing to chat! Tell us, child, what do you think happens to your soul when you d—"

"You're about to find out." Ari bares his teeth. "Go now, or I'll sink you all."

I swing around to face him, my mouth open. He refuses to look at me.

His shoulders rise and fall, and his nostrils flare as he glowers at the jovial group. "Why bother us? You could have endangered our vessel. Trouble us again and—"

"Hold your tongue," a suited man says to Ari. "We risk life and limb in the wilderness, to reach those without direction. We offer to show you the way down here and this is how you respond?" The agitated missionary straightens and addresses me. "Blink twice, child, if you need rescuing. He's clearly beyond saving—headed straight for the fiery bosom of his mistress's—"

A woman hurries forward and whispers in his ear. Seconds later, communication is cut. Oscar confirms the vessel has sped away. *What the—*

A sense of foreboding rises from the pit of my stomach.

Ari glances at me. "Don't feel sorry for them. They could have harmed you." His eyebrows meet. "What's wrong?"

"You think *I'm* stubborn? Missionaries never, ever give up that easily. . . . Something's wrong."

Jojo barks and sprints toward me; I scoop her up. "What is it, baby?"

Ari's hands curl into fists by his sides, his eyes fixed on the viewport behind me. My insides lurch at the possibilities. I turn and gasp at the sight, covering my mouth.

It's all flesh and wires. A small head and bulky body. It's difficult to tell exactly what it once was. Only its face and flippers remain intact.

The corpse of the animal rotates in the vessel's harsh lights. I stumble back and hug Jojo tighter. The creature's midsection is missing. Inside the cavity of muscle and tissue, cables are all that remain. The wiring hangs out of its body, floating in the current. A small titanium contraption is strapped to its head, still flashing away.

"Oh my God," I whisper. "What is it? What on earth is it?"

Ari's eyes turn cold. "It was once a sea creature. Before the government decided to use it to its advantage. There are so many others like it."

I look down, shaking my head. "Poor, poor thing. But why did those people flee from it?"

"*That's* not why they left. . . ." Ari's voice is grave now, his tone low.

Jojo starts whining. A cold chill sweeps through me as I lift my head back up, hugging the puppy close.

In the distance, a great, lengthy shadow looms. A wall of hazy darkness. A wall that's alive, moving. It's a *group* of something. . . .

Ari hurries back to the files. "Move away from the window! Tell Oscar to turn around *now*." His tone is urgent. His hands swish through the air as he scans further files as fast as possible. "We need to retreat at least a league. Until it's time."

"Why?"

"Because we're here. Whatever they are, they belong to the prison. It's Broadmoor's first line of defense."

CHAPTER THIRTY-FOUR

I sit up in bed and check the time. One a.m. An hour before my alarm is due to go off. We'll soon head out in the hope of being at the prison when its moon pool opens up.

None of it seems real. Is there really a chance I might see Papa again in just a few hours? What state might he be in? My insides quiver. I mustn't make any mistakes.

The plan fills me with dread: We'll blast our way there, and then Ari will exit the *Kabul* in the submersible and head into the prison itself after Papa. It's a totally bonkers plan. But I'm low on choices. I shared it with Bia, and once she realized I wasn't budging on it she promised their guy inside would cause a distraction—a big one, and help in any other way they could in order to give Ari more of a chance to enter and leave safely with Papa. Both Ari and I have memorized every detail of the prison's interior security measures and prepared accordingly.

Deep, melodic notes sound as the sax echoes in the submarine. Ari's awake. I shuffle out of bed, wash, and read the Qur'an, praying for forgiveness.

I know if I hadn't killed it, the Anthropoid would've killed me. But I'm personally responsible for a life leaving this world. Anytime I dwell on any of it, it's too much.

Jojo's still asleep in her Bliss-Pod when I'm done and I head for the galley. Emerging with two hot chocolates, I cock my head. Ari's up in the small platform at the very top of the vessel. The music switches now to an incredibly sad piece as I make my way up. Such a low, forlorn tune that makes my heart ache. Can sound cry?

He glances at me as I crouch down at the top. His gaze is empty, distant.

Something's on his mind. And whatever it is, it's not good.

Ari puts the wooden sax down. I pass him his drink. A crimson Lumi-Orb casts a warm glow over the space. We sit in silence, sipping the hot, sweet liquid. Above and all around us the dense waters lap against the 360-degree translucent dome. Tiny creatures pass by, their lights pulsing away in the night.

He turns to me. "You mustn't go any farther from this point. Stay here in the submarine and wait for me. I'll take the submersible. I promise to do what I can to bring your father to you. Don't go anywhere near the place. *Please.* Their weapons are too many, too harsh." His voice is hoarse.

"And how do you think you're going to get past all their security and anywhere *near* the prison, without the *Kabul*'s firepower? Ari? What's wrong?"

He hesitates and faces the water before answering. "Did you see the news?"

My throat goes dry. It can only be bad. I shake my head.

"It was another attack. This time on a small community hiding out in Leeds. It was . . . bodies everywhere . . . Even children, babies."

My hand flies to my mouth.

"They went after them with everything. Ripped whole families apart . . . They'll stop at nothing. What they did in the Faroe Islands . . . It was cold, calculated slaughter." The tension is visible in his muscles, the strain showing in his jaw. He hangs his head.

My insides sink. Images of mutilated bodies flash before me. *Anthropoid* bodies. Anthropoid families. And I feel . . . pain. My heart actually hurts for them.

If Ari is one of them, then not all of them can be barbaric and evil.

He's silent for too long. When he finally speaks, his voice is barely audible. "Please. If you stay behind now, you have some chance of survival. We don't know how bad it might get. It's too dangerous."

Does he really think he stands a chance in one submersible, when Bia's lot have tried and failed with everything they had?

"Ari, I'm not staying here in the submarine while you head off in a submersible to face all the different security measures they have. You *know* that's no plan. No, we fight our way past all their defenses until we're near the prison itself. *Then* you get into the submersible and head down into the prison, while I defend the *Kabul* until you're back with Papa. Their guy inside is expecting you. We can do this."

He stares into space. His eyes are so beautiful and so utterly, unbearably sad.

I move closer to him. "I'll be all right," I say quietly, nudging him with my elbow. "We have to hope for the best."

"I daren't hope, Leyla. It abandoned us long ago." There's a shadow over his expression.

"I don't believe that, Ari."

He swallows, his eyes softening. I stare at him. Amber-gold eyes peer back from beneath thick, dark lashes as they search my own. He looks down and brings up his palm. There's a flattish pale-pink rock in it.

"It's a flint tool," he says, taking my hand and placing the rock in it. "From Mesolithic times. Thousands of years old. I found it one day when I was out . . . you know. In the water."

I nod eagerly, suddenly overcome with the need for him to know it's okay to mention himself actually *in* the water. *What's happening to me?*

I gaze on the rock in my palm. The oldest thing I've ever held is a 1950s vinyl record at one of those Days Past events held by the Royal Preservation Society.

The tool is carved into a point and smooth where it hasn't been chipped.

Specks of white dot the pink. *Thousands of years old.* My face warms, and my eyes prickle. I close them.

Sometimes, when I'm hovering in a place with a specific history, I close my eyes and imagine I'm in that moment in time. It's truly astonishing just how real and overwhelming it can feel. The sudden conjuring of a bygone person, place, or era.

Those lives were more than the buildings they inhabited or things they touched and used.

So much of us here and now—no matter where or how on the earth we're living—binds us to those gone before. And sometimes . . . just sometimes that connection ripples and reverberates, more stunning and infinitely more sentient than a thousand solitary nows.

Whoever carved this flint tool made the most of whatever they had, and when they hunted and built fires and secured shelter and stayed warm and cooked and had relationships and nurtured life and worried and loved and believed and mourned—I could scream from the magic of it all.

How we never stop seeking, never stop dreaming.

Never stop hoping.

Hope isn't measurable or conditional; it's not for anyone to try and control. It's ours—*all* of ours—boundless, as wild and unfettered as the waves. And always has been.

I open my eyes and meet Ari's. He wears the most *tender* expression. If I blink, tears will fall, I'm certain. "Have more faith in people, Ari," I whisper.

His shoulders rise and fall. He brings his hands up and cups my face, his touch gentle and warm. "I have faith in you, Leyla."

I smile and he lets out a breath. His eyes flash brighter than I've ever seen them: heart and soul and fire. He brushes my cheek with his fingers, and my breath catches.

We both jump when his Bracelet bleeps.

It's time.

CHAPTER THIRTY-FIVE

I pace the viewport in the control room as I stare at the unidentifiable huddled mass ahead. No matter which way the submarine turns, the gloomy, wall-like body moves to block its way.

"What are they?" I ask.

Ari stands still and keeps his eyes on the obstacle. "We must move forward." His face is all hard angles now, his stubbled jaw clenched and every muscle rigid. "We have to move now or we'll miss the opening of the moon pool."

He's right. "Oscar? Stay alert. And move on."

The *Kabul* presses forward.

Jojo's in her Bliss-Pod in the corner of the room. I selected the music function and set the pod on rocking mode. Together they'll hopefully distract her from whatever might unfold.

As the submarine advances, the shadows come into focus.

Ari's brow furrows. "Manta rays. So many . . . and so organized."

The dense wall disperses as the huge rays separate. They advance toward the sub. Ginormous wingspans block most of the light trickling down from the solar spheres. The gloomy creatures swim up to the viewport. An inky eye sits at either side of their wide heads.

"Poor things. I think they've been brainwashed into working as camouflaged Eyeballs, you know?"

A ray opens its mouth. *All* the rays open their mouths at once.

"Get away from the window!" Ari bellows.

I stumble back as he tugs on my arm. The view outside grows blurry. The water flickers.

Ari pulls me away. "Oscar, tear them apart—*now!*"

"No, wait. It's not their fault! We can—"

The submarine shudders. I stand rigid as the creatures all hover in the depths, their mouths open wide.

"Oscar!" Ari yells again for the Navigator. He groans and hurries to one of the control screens. "They're basically just machines now," he shouts in my direction. "Remotely controlled to block and attack us. It's us or them!"

A bleeping goes off in the vessel: warning of an incoming attack.

"Oscar!" Ari growls.

The Navigator finally appears.

"We have hostile visitors," Ari shouts at him. "Defend the *Kabul*!"

The Navigator flickers in and out of focus, his words inaudible. Another alarm sounds in the room. The sub heaves. Ari swears and takes over control of the firepower. I seize manual control of the navigating. The *Kabul* fires. Lasers whiz through the depths and several rays are hit. Blood clouds the water as the creatures sink slowly out of sight. My hand flies to my throat. I'm suddenly in my recurring nightmare, where a forlorn and desperate red fills the water before me and I know something so utterly terrible has just happened.

The vessel tilts as they fire on us, and I jolt into focus, concentrating on navigating.

Outside, a formidable blockade still remains. "I'm reversing a little," I say, and pull back several meters.

Ari runs a sequence on the control panel and turns to the water to watch. Before the rays have a chance to catch up with the sub, a low *boom* echoes and spreads from the *Kabul*. I glance out and cover my mouth.

The water wrinkles around us. The animals freeze in position. And then, oh my God, they *implode*. I cry out. The rays are nothing more than fragments of flesh and technology as they spread in the ensuing ripples. Waves unfurl from the spot and hit the *Kabul*. I shake myself and return my focus to the screen as the vessel rocks again.

Oscar appears beside me. "I do believe I am back in service, my dear lady. I daresay I was most flustered. Momentary blip, but all has been rectified."

I'm trembling all over. "Oscar, check for damage."

The submarine is fine, and all systems are working smoothly again. We move on through the drifting debris. I stare at the body parts around me. My chest aches for the creatures they once were. I check on Jojo; she's fast asleep, thank goodness.

The sub speeds through the surge the implosion left behind. On and on, drawing closer and closer to Papa. Something drifts into the edge of my vision. I look up.

"Oscar, a drone! And another one! Above and to the right."

"Already being taken care of, my dear."

The long, ghostly machines come into view. No viewports, no portholes. They glide effortlessly. One of them suddenly tilts and rushes toward the sub. I step back. The drone erupts into a ball of fire. Oscar takes care of the second one in the same way.

The water is aflame now, a shifting kaleidoscope of fire and metal and debris.

The sub presses through and onward.

I furrow my brow as I look out. The windows . . . They seem to move. I peer closer. The acrylic appears to bend and pucker in places. Unease creeps over me. What is it? Something in the water? But there isn't anything out there.

"Oscar? I think you need to see this."

"Highly cunning bots, my lady. Able to blend in anywhere. Inspired by the camouflage skills of certain sea creatures. A most devious foe."

A bleeping sounds in the room. "Oscar, that's the oxygen alarm!"

"Yes, my dear, we must act swiftly. They aim to paralyze our systems by accessing and scrambling them. Their first point of attack is often to impair oxygen levels, and it would appear they have already made a start. We cannot terminate them until they are detached from the vessel."

"Ari, you should check the atmosphere control equipment manually, too, just to be sure," I say. "I don't want to risk abandoning this station in case Oscar has another navigating blip."

Ari rushes out for the engine room.

The water ripples all around us. Seconds later, the windows are clear. "They're gone, Oscar!"

"Not quite, my lady. They are in the water now, watching us. They remain hidden, but they are there. As you will see."

The water seems to shudder. The center pulses, sending waves in all directions. And then there they are, bobbing in the resulting choppy currents. I gasp.

An army of small and transparent mechanical contraptions, each no bigger than a large hand, *fills* the water. At the heart of each one is a fist-size cluster of technology. The blobs are manic. They rise and dive, and dart to and fro as they watch the sub, desperate to cause some serious damage. The alarm continues.

Laser power flashes from the vessel, attacking the bots. The blobs jerk, twisting around in the waves. Some fall, but not enough. They regroup, making their way toward the sub again.

"Oxygen levels are being affected, my dear. The bots must be destroyed to break the connection they've made with the *Kabul*'s equipment."

"Take them out, Oscar." I hold my breath and stand still.

I watch as a spray of shots leaves the vessel and explodes among the bots. The explosion produces a dark, murky substance. On contact it dissolves their jelly-like encasement and penetrates the tech inside. The blobs writhe around. Small prods and wires stick out as the contraptions struggle. One by one, they fall below.

At last, the water is clear again. The alarm goes quiet.

I wrap my arms around myself. "Oscar, check the sub's oxygen levels."

"We're okay," Ari says as he returns from the engine room and hurries back to the control panel. "The connection wasn't sustained long enough to cause any lasting damage."

Phew. The *Kabul* plows on.

"Oscar, how much farther?"

"Around one league before we arrive at our location, my lady."

The obstacles are never-ending the closer we get. An oily liquid obscures the viewport when bots disguised as a shoal suddenly turn on us. It takes a while for the *Kabul*'s windows to self-clean. More drones appear. They release a substance that shrouds the surrounding waters.

"Thermal imaging, and terminate the drones, Oscar!" I shout. "And keep moving on. How far now?"

"Half a league until we approach the prison, my dear lady."

Half a league. And the closest military base is over fifty leagues away. Even if the prison's management suspect a breakout attempt now and decide their own security won't be enough, we should have enough time to go through with the plan and speed away before backup arrives. Half a league and then Ari can descend in the submersible and get Papa out of there.

If all goes well.

Humongous mechanical devices appear out of nowhere. Almost as big as small submersibles, they try to stall the vessel with wave generators. My insides heave. The sub rocks but pulls through the turbulence.

Ari consults the files hovering in the viewport. "We're over halfway through their defense walls."

I shake my head as I tap the screen, checking engine, propeller, and firepower status, just to be sure. Will we make it?

"A quarter of a league, my dear," Oscar announces.

"Good, just keep her moving forward, Oscar." I pace the viewport.

What's going on at the prison? Has Bia's inside person caused the distraction yet? She seemed really confident their guy would come through. During previous breakout attempts, they've faked a structural emergency and a technical wipeout; both proved insufficient in causing the required distraction but never came into play anyway. Bia's people have yet to get past the extensive security.

I suggested a full-blown riot this time. We need for it to be as chaotic inside as possible.

The water ahead looks clear. For now. The craft pushes through the current, which has becoming increasingly choppy. And then the view darkens.

They appear suddenly, looming in the distance. A pod of *enormous* whales. At the same time, strange jellyfish drop from above the vessel and rise out of the depths. I cry out and narrow my eyes. The dangly creatures remain deadly still. Their bells, tentacles, and muscles all pulse away, their clinical white lights illuminating the water.

Ari rushes to the viewport. "Bots."

"How can you tell?"

"I've come across camouflaged bots my whole life. These things were *never* alive."

I grimace. The shadows at the back grow bigger as the "whales" creep closer. The "jellyfish" near and hover in front of us.

I shake my head. So much I was totally unaware of, tucked safely away back in London.

"Erm, Oscar? I think we need to hurry." I wipe my palms dry as I keep my gaze fixed on the visitors. "They don't look too friendly."

The "whales" are huge dark submersibles designed in every way to resemble the real thing. A narrow slit in the tip of the vessels, exactly where a whale's mouth would be, is all they use for a window. They fire on us, golden-yellow blasts charging straight through the water toward us. The "jellyfish" now draw closer. The *Kabul*'s own firepower meets theirs head-on and the destructive forces explode as they clash.

Everywhere you look the current flares brilliant and bright, smoke and sparks spiraling in all directions before succumbing to the overpowering waters. The sub shudders.

"Oscar!" Ari shouts. "Blast them out of our way!"

"I have activated the shield, sir. The bots are seeking to impinge on our systems, and they're also rather tenacious trackers. The shield ought to suffice in preventing this."

The water ripples as the *Kabul*'s digital defense shield goes up. The jellyfish swim around the vessel, desperately trying to find a way through the blocking waves. The whale-like subs draw closer. And closer. The *Kabul* battles away, countering the firepower. All around the viewport the water lights up as our arsenal shoots through the current and explosives collide.

Thank goodness Theo had upgraded the vessel's defense systems!

I gasp as further movement catches my eye. "There are more of them." A wave of ammunition surges at the submarine from both directions. The vessel lurches. Alarms blare on the sub. I cry out as I stumble back.

All I can think of is us falling into an infinite abyss below, and every accursed creature we've ever been warned about, ready to emerge from the darkest depths to feast on us.

Oscar flickers. "I bring bleak tidings, my lady. We are outnumbered. The *Kabul* will not survive this attack."

No. *Papa.* I pull myself together. "Get a bloody grip, Oscar!" I shout. "Fight for your vessel, dammit!"

Another alarm. The craft abruptly tips forward. Ari's thrown against the windows. I scream. Jojo's Bliss-Pod slides across the floor.

Ari clutches his head and tries to catch his breath. The sub shudders again.

"Go!" he yells at me. "Grab Jojo and leave. They're distracted. You might survive if you take the submersible. Get *out* of here!"

Every part of my body quivers. I sway as I stagger to the main control panel. "Let's try rising and—" Something catches my eye, and I turn around.

Small circular crafts emerge from the depths and into the chaos. I squint; they seem familiar.

"Ari!" I shout, just as the sub rocks again. I grab hold of a locker handle to steady myself. "Look!"

The compact subs open fire on the large whale-like vessels. They lock into battle with one another.

"Oh my God. It's the people from Cambridge! It's Bia's lot!"

Ari runs to the main control panel. We both work away on the planes and propeller, stabilizing the *Kabul* as the new arrivals distract the prison vessels. At last, the submarine is steady again and the ominous swaying and alarms cease.

"Oscar!" Ari beckons.

The Navigator appears. "Please accept my most sincere and humble apolo—"

"Reverse a little," Ari shouts at him. "We're too visible! All defenses up, and attack with everything we have!"

The sub reverses. All at once, there's chaos. The current grows turbulent and visibility is challenging. I stare at the sight before us. Further crafts and weaponry have now joined the battle. And it's hell.

The water fills with drones, submersibles, and robots of all kinds—many of which are disguised as sea creatures. The "whales" fire missiles in every direction, and the "jellyfish" latch on to vessels. Lasers bounce everywhere I look. The manned prison's crafts are all a uniform rocket-like shape. Bia's people are in the compact circular subs I saw in Cambridge.

I can't take my eyes off the scene. It seems unreal. Like those ancient computer games Old Worlders loved so much. Will we survive it? We *have* to.

There's a communication request. Ari and Oscar pick off targets as I take the call. It's Charlie. I turn the volume up, listening to him as I run a 360-degree scan of our surroundings.

"Bia's gonna kill you!" he shouts from his sub. "You put her in a very difficult position. This is the farthest we've ever made it—thanks to yer sub taking hostiles out—but it's still an impossible task. You'll never get out alive!"

"I'm not leaving without Papa! Do you know if the door's open?"

"It's not gonna happen, Leyla, not today! Nobody can make it through that. Don't let yer friend do it. It's a death trap! They're tracking everything, locking on to anything they find and blasting it to smithereens. We'll try again another day, promise. For Neptune's sake, get the hell out of here!" He cuts off.

What? No, no, no. Papa's right there. Today. *Now.* Just below us. He might never make it to "another day"! And next time the prison will be even more prepared. I didn't come all this way to just leave without him! After all that, it can't end like this. It just *can't.* My heart is trapped in my throat, rigid and restricting. I gulp for air.

I glance at Ari; he's busy overseeing both attack and defense. Charlie's words ring in my head. *Don't let your friend do it. It's a death trap!*

There must be another way . . . There *must* be!

Think, dammit. I look out. Death and destruction everywhere.

My racing heart misses a beat when I see it: a terrifying and reckless idea. An unchartered, ferocious wave that carries a little hope deep within its fold. I'll never get another opportunity like this. I know that. I take deep breaths, cursing the sudden trembling in my legs.

It's the unknown. . . . It's everything wrong and horrifying. My throat hurts, my chest aches now. I can't do it. *I can't, I can't, I can't.*

But I'm finally *this* close. Am I really going to give in to the fear now? My hands shake and I clasp them. Time's running out.

I clear my throat and force the words out. "Just—just checking something in the engine room," I call out.

Ari barely acknowledges, busy conferring with Oscar on the best response to a group of fishlike bots surrounding the vessel's bow.

I hurry out, looking over my shoulder and grabbing a small bag as I leave. My heart pounds away and an icy chill sweeps over me as I head for the moon pool room.

CHAPTER THIRTY-SIX

I climb into the submersible, my movements clumsy and weighted.

"Lock the door behind me, Oscar. Don't forget. You mustn't leave it open a second longer once I'm away."

I rummage through the compact bag I helped Ari pack, ensuring everything I might need is still here.

"I assure you, my dear lady, the *Kabul* will be secured the moment the craft is clear of the moon pool."

I open and close my hands. I shift in the seat. Everything trembles: my arms, legs, hands—whole body. I wipe my palms on my legs again and look up. Ari's standing beside the vessel, his eyes narrowed. Frustration flames their depths.

"What are you doing?"

"He's *my* papa. It's my responsibility. I haven't come this far to leave without him. Charlie said they're locking on to anything they find. You can't go out into that; you'll never make it down, never mind back. And I can't compete with the sheer number of vessels, or their firepower. But I can try and do the one thing they won't be expecting." I clear my throat. "I will—" I swallow my doubt and lift my chin. "I will fall through it all."

His jaw slackens and his eyes widen. "Leyla—"

"Think about it. With my power off, they can't lock on to the submersible. And if they spot me, they'll just assume I've been hit and won't see me as a threat. And I really need to go now or I'll be locked in there once the moon pool door closes again."

His eyes are whirlpools of protest. "I *promise* we'll try again; we'll come back when—"

"Ari, you're just going to have to trust me—and hope for the best. I'm not leaving this place without my papa. And this is our best chance of seeing this through."

"Okay. Then let *me* go. It doesn't have to be in the sub. I can *swim* down there; we are fast, Leyla. Let me—"

"And then what? If you go in without a sub, how will you bring Papa back?"

He throws his hands up in the air.

"Ari, we're wasting precious time!"

He leans in. Just when I'm expecting more objections, he nods, though unease lingers at the corners of his mouth. My heart skips a beat as we lock gazes this close. Just beneath the fire in his eyes is something else. . . . He's at once veiled and blazing bright.

"What?" I ask. "What is it, Ari?"

"If you panic, it could be fatal," he says. He lowers his voice to a whisper now and rubs the back of his neck. "I need you to come back, Leyla."

My insides flip. I nod, wishing we had more time.

"Alert me if you need my help," he continues. "Tell me instantly, and I will be down there. If anyone can do this, you can. The fear . . . it's only in your mind, remember. There's nothing terrifying in the spaces you can't see."

"Yes." I nod away, trying not to think too much about it.

Ari moves back to meet my gaze. "You're confident you are familiar enough with the prison's plans? And what weapons are you taking?"

"I know the layout and where Papa's cell is, and I read your own notes, too. I have my brolly for any human guards." I gesture to the small bag. "I have the tools. They don't normally use the robot officers until midmorning, but there's always the chance they might call on them earlier—especially if Bia's guy is successful with creating a distraction. Hopefully none will cross my path, though. And I already have all the files—including the prison's blueprints." The sub lurches. "I have to go," I say.

He looks at me once more. "You can do this, Leyla." He nods and strides out of the room.

I lock the door and I'm soon through the hatch and inside the adjacent compact space, acclimatizing to the pressure outside.

Okay, time to go. I take several deep breaths. The hatch releases, and I'm now through to the moon pool.

I can do this. It's similar to the marathon out there. Just a bunch of obstacles and challenges, that's all. I push forward on both the joystick and throttle and the craft nose-dives a little. It immediately rocks in all the turbulence. The door closes above me. My heart stutters.

It's *nothing* like the marathon.

It's a massacre. I cry out at the onslaught of vessels, robots, and firepower all around me. Flames from bulky shapes and shadows burst into being, burning bright for one brief moment before fading to nothing. I shift in my seat, taking it all in. *Focus.* I gulp and straighten, peering into the depths. Somewhere directly below me is the prison.

And its only entrance closes again soon.

Each time my failed attempt at a freefall pops into my head, I have to shake it away. The terror is still too fresh. I take deep breaths. I can do this. *You won the London Marathon!* There's nothing to fear; the dread is all in my mind.

The constant shifting of the waves in all the action decreases visibility. I grit my teeth and check the depth gauge. The craft's wings retract, folding against the sub's body.

I move into place so I can fall just close enough to the prison, and grimace as I cut the power. *Bismillah.* My body tenses. *See, nothing to it.*

My insides heave at the sudden drop.

The compact sub plummets through the void, hurtling toward only God knows what.

Flickering chaos. Lights. Fire. Lasers. Crafts whooshing past me. Froth. Bots darting by. Flashing "jellyfish" tentacles.

I'm falling, falling, falling. And the dread just keeps on rising.

Anything could happen. I'm plunging through a great big nothing, and just about *anything* could be hiding down there in the veiled abyss, deep in the shadows where only terror slithers, waiting. *Oh God.* A familiar feeling tries to surface—the eternal fear clawing, trying to drag me down with it.

I'm not going to make it. I'm going to die. Papa will remain locked up forever.

Papa. His words echo in my head now.

Don't you know I would sail every current, ride every wave, and dive into any depth, until I found you?

I force myself to focus. The submersible spins on its way to the ocean floor.

I gulp for air, cursing the queasy sensation taking over now. My heartbeat thrashes away in my ears, my chest. My body jerks in every direction as the craft rolls. My stomach churns. I scrunch my face up; I should never have had that warm drink. Fixing my gaze on the seabed is impossible; I just don't know what I'm looking out for.

A glimmer of something else—a dark surface. It can only be the bottom. I shiver. The flashing chaos lessens around me. The shadow sharpens as the seabed pulls me closer. There are no lights there to guide me. I keep my eyes locked on the darkness as it grows closer. *Wait . . . wait for it. . . .* At the last possible moment, I power back up and skim the pitch-black rugged terrain. The altitude warning light blinks away.

I take long, deep breaths to combat the dizziness; I need all my focus now. I spin around in the seat, twisting my neck in every direction as I peer out.

I made it. . . . I actually managed to fall through it all without being hit—and without letting the dread conquer me!

Hazy silhouettes move far above me, but there's nobody down here. I inhale and blow my cheeks out as I try to navigate the structure. It looks like a giant, sprawling rock, designed, like the Trading Post at Cambridge, to resemble a natural part of the seabed. I pull back on the throttle and the craft slows down. I circle the entire structure—nothing. I shift in my seat and groan. Somewhere is the entrance to a moon pool. But *where*? The ground ripples. I peer closer and shudder.

Enormous arachnids scurry along the seabed. *Ugh.* Dark, webbed spiders dragging some kind of tail behind them, and spindly white spiders with the longest legs, like they're on stilts. Two of the ghostly spiders are fighting. One raises its legs and swings at the other, pushing it back. Into nothing. The spider vanishes. It literally disappears before my eyes. Into the rock.

I press my face against the dome, and there it is: the tiniest hint of a glimmer. They're concealing the entrance using a projection. My pulse races.

I take a deep breath and charge into the rock face.

I pass straight through the projection and find myself in an enclosed passage. Ahead, light trickles down through the waves. The moon pool!

I speed toward it, then pull back on the joystick and forward on the throttle. The sub rockets through the pool. A robotic arm lowers toward me. My heart beats faster and faster. I peer out in every direction. I don't have long.

Nobody's around in the moon pool room or smaller chamber, and I'm soon through all the hatches. I grab my brolly and exit. Curse the trembling. I wipe my sweaty palm and reach for the door's release.

I shiver. I'm in a long, freezing-cold corridor. A siren wails away. The stench of damp and rot is suffocating, scratching at my throat.

I turn, and before I've taken a single step, a towering prison officer lunges toward me out of nowhere, baton raised. I stumble back, about to lift my brolly. The baton pauses mid-strike and falls out of his hand. The officer looks startled, before slumping down in front of me.

A large woman steps out from behind him, a small laser weapon in her hand.

It's another prison officer, and she doesn't look happy.

"What in God's name are ya doing here?" she asks. "Where's the rescue party? Ya can't be serious? I'm risking me bloody position—me *life*—here, and they send in one wee girl? Where's the rest of 'em?"

I snap out of shock, and find my tongue. "You're . . . you're Bia's guy?"

"Aye, ya catch on quick, lassie," she says, shaking her head. "Name's McGregor. I've done me bit." She jabs her thumb upward. "It's madness up there. A bit *too* chaotic—sent management into panic. They ordered the door shut, so I've been risking everything hanging around here, keeping it open manually. What kept ya? Never mind—spit out yer plan, and make it quick."

My pulse races. "Get up to Papa's level—I have the plans, I know which cell it is. I break into it. I grab Papa, and we run back down here via the east-wing staircase. We—"

"Stop right there." She holds a hand up. "There'll be no running around once you've got yer old man. The inmates on that cellblock can barely walk, never mind run. You'll be wanting one of *those*."

She points to a stack of wheelchairs against the corridor's wall. I swallow, trying not to think what it all means, why they can barely walk, and quickly reach for the stack.

"Not yet!" she says. "It'll slow ya down. They have them on every level, and there are ramps at both ends of the corridors. And you'll need this." She passes me a card. "It'll open the cell a lot faster than whatever ya had in mind. Now scoot or you'll be locked in here; I don't know how long I can fool them keeping this door open. Ya shouldn't come across too many guards, if any at all—I've made sure those on watch are tied up on the higher levels. I've risked me neck for this little stunt, and ya better not let me down, lassie. See ya back here pronto. Now go!" She disappears inside the small chamber, shutting the door behind her.

Oh God. I look in every direction, spot signs for the ramp, and holding the shaky brolly out in front of me, I run. At last, I'm almost at the ramp.

Unfortunately, raised voices suddenly carry from that direction. My heart sinks. I peer around a corner where three prison officers stand arguing. The door leading to the ramp is just past them, and already open.

"Nothing to do with me," shouts one. "I don't work on the top floor, west wing."

"And I'm on me break, mate," says another. "After one hell of a watch. So—"

"I don't give two friggin' hoots *whose* watch it is!" bellows the third and loudest voice. "It's a goddam madhouse up there, and you two are hiding your ugly mugs down here. So I'm asking you once more nicely, get your arses back upstairs and help them bring it all under control—before the ruckus spreads prison-wide!"

The men go on arguing about being expected to help when it isn't their fault or problem. I rack my brains.

"Oscar?" I whisper into my Bracelet.

He appears before me, and I instantly instruct him to speak quietly.

"Oscar, I want you to distract the people around the corner so I can pass unnoticed behind them. Act all authoritative, all right? And quick, we don't have long."

Oscar flicks his hair and straightens his plush brocade waistcoat. "I shall not let you down, my dear," he says, his voice lowered. "But I implore you to relax. Life is too important to be taken seriously."

"Right, then . . . Go, Oscar. And remember—all authoritative now." I chew on my lip.

The Navigator tilts his head and turns the corner. I grimace. The guards hush immediately. I peek around the wall.

"I say," Oscar begins. "Would any of you handsome gentlemen care to take a walk with me through the rose gardens on this rather fine day?"

What the— Oh, I'm doomed!

Except they can't take their eyes off Oscar. Their mouths fall wide open. I creep along behind them.

"One should always be searching for new sensations," Oscar continues. "Be afraid of nothing, I say!"

I'm through the door in seconds and racing up the ramp to the second floor. I look down to ensure the bag's still around my waist, when I crash headlong into someone.

It's a prison officer rushing down in the opposite direction. Her eyes widen and she instantly brings her wrist up to her mouth. There's no time to think.

I move back just enough to raise my brolly, and tase her until she drops.

I sprint on, exiting the ramp on the second floor. More damp and gloomy corridors.

The siren continues to sound. Footsteps approach. I press back into a wide doorway, narrowing my eyes. The wet walls glisten. Slimy wormlike creatures creep out of cracks in the wall opposite and gorge on the filth growing on the surface. I hold my breath. The footsteps fade and I bring up the plans for the second floor. I'm really close.

I cover my nose at the stench. The cold and damp claw at my throat. Grabbing a wheelchair, I pause outside the door on the very end. I drop the card twice, my hand trembling as I try to scan it.

At last, the door clicks open. The cell releases an icy breath. I step inside and stand frozen. I shake my head as my gaze sweeps the bare and impossibly small cell.

It's empty. After all that . . . the cell's empty.

A great gloom stirs inside me, a shadow spreading. A bucket in a corner and a few gray rags on the concrete slab against the wall are the only things in the mold-ridden room. There's an overwhelming stench of decay.

Something moves among the rags.

I furrow my brow and look again on the empty, cold slab. I creep toward it. No . . . Oh my God. *No, no, no.* My lips and chin quiver. The "rags" are a person. I cry out, then quickly muffle the sound with my hand.

I turn the skeletal frame over and burst into tears. It's Papa, and he looks . . . lifeless. I cover my mouth to stifle any noise. "Salaam, Papa," I manage, choking back a sob.

Nothing. His eyes remain closed. Has he been drugged? I place my head against his chest; he's breathing, thank God. I recite a quick prayer over him.

It takes a while, and several stop-starts, but I finally manage to secure Papa into the wheelchair. I open the cell door. My stomach drops to the floor.

A robot officer blocks our path, a long, sleek gun in its hand. *Oh hell.*

"You have made a category one mistake, intruder," it says.

The tiny red eyes look me up and down. Lights pulse away all over its body as it insists I follow it. I freeze. What can I do? The bloody moon pool door could shut at any moment!

I slip my hand into the small bag around my waist. "Oscar?"

The robot turns as the Navigator materializes beside it in the corridor.

Now! I sprint from around the wheelchair and am almost behind the mechanical officer when it grabs my hand. I can't reach around to its neck!

"Oscar, help me!"

But there's not much the Navigator can do.

I point the brolly at the robot and flinch as I press down on the tase button, aiming for the raised section in its chest. Thankfully I don't feel anything, but the robot relaxes its grip on my arm, its movements jerky.

I jump on it before it can recover.

I wrap my legs around its middle, reach behind for its neck, and stab repeatedly with the tool in my hand. Nothing. I struggle with the guard until I have a better view of the back of its neck. I swap the tool for another one from my bag, and slide the finer point carefully into the opening in the base of its neck. The robot pauses and its lights flicker. It drops its weapon.

I jump down just as the central compartment in its torso opens, revealing the tech inside. The lights go out, and the robot freezes in position. I grab the wheelchair and am about to rush off, when I glance again at the opening in its chest. I pull out and pocket what I think might be chips but could actually just be rubbish, and race away with Papa.

I retrace my footsteps, praying the entire way down the ramp that we don't meet anyone. Luckily, nobody crosses our path except for the still-unconscious officer I'd tased on my way up. Exiting the ramp, I head for the chamber room. The door's locked. Where's McGregor? I swipe the lock with her card.

It refuses to open.

She's been rumbled. It's the only explanation.

My legs almost give way. I open up the tool bag and, remembering the instructions in Bia's files, fiddle away with the lock. Nothing. I try again but it isn't working. On discovering McGregor, they must've activated a locking system Bia's lot weren't aware of.

I stand, trying to think. "Oscar!"

The Navigator materializes. "Oscar, see if you can override the access system here. We need to get to the moon pool!"

The Navigator scans the access panel as I walk around and look into the chamber holding my vessel. Nothing. I peer past it, through its doors and into the moon pool room. That's empty, too. The moon pool door's still open, phew. But how do I get in!

And then surely my heart stops.

Because as I watch, a hand reaches out of the moon pool.

I can't stop staring. Another hand, two arms.

And then a body hauls itself out of the water and onto the floor.

An Anthropoid.

And it isn't Ari.

I stumble back. "Oscar . . ."

"Alas, my dear lady, I cannot seem to access this—"

I turn and grab the wheelchair. "Oscar, *leave* the damn lock. We need to hide! You may go now!" The Navigator disappears.

I scan the corridors around me and aim for a supply cove big enough to fit the wheelchair in. My heart won't stop thrashing around inside my chest. I check on Papa and his condition hasn't changed, his head lolling almost lifelessly to the side. I clasp my hands and lean down to whisper. "Inshallah, not long now, Papa."

I risk edging my gaze around the wall. And freeze.

The Anthropoid stands still in the doorway to the chamber. It's dripping wet and casts its eyes in every direction. It's tall, slim, and muscular, with short bright-red hair. I swiftly duck back behind the wall.

"Oscar." I place him on silent the moment he appears. "I need you to go back toward the chamber and to escort anyone you see there upstairs. Keep them occupied and out of the way until I summon you again. They are hostile; you will switch to safe mode as you converse with them. Say whatever you need to, to get them to go with you. Is this understood?"

The Navigator nods, and I take him off silent. He disappears around the corner.

I peek at them, and after a brief exchange, the Anthropoid actually nods and follows Oscar away from the chamber. What is it doing here? Before the Anthropoid leaves, it turns to the door and fiddles with the access panel. *No, don't lock it again!* They both leave, and I slowly wheel Papa out from behind the cove. We edge down the corridor and it's empty. I check the door to the chamber and the lock's been destroyed. They wanted to ensure they could leave again. But what are they doing here in the first place?

I use the wheelchair to push the door open and hurry inside. They could be back any moment. And the moon pool door will shut any minute now!

"McGregor?" I call out. Nothing. *Please be all right.*

I place Papa in the sub; his limp frame slumps into the seat. Soon as he's secure, I turn to run around to the driver's side.

And stop in my tracks. My insides fall to the floor.

The Anthropoid stands inside the chamber, not five feet from me.

My hand automatically reaches for my arm, and I grip the brolly. My legs start to quiver. I can't take my eyes off them.

It's a guy, around my age I think. He watches me, eyes narrowed with a hint of . . . *surprise* in them. He isn't like the ones who attacked Brighton Pier. His eyes aren't cold at all. The surprised expression now switches to one of concern. *Why?* What's he doing here?

And I have the strangest sense I know him from somewhere. . . .

He opens his mouth but before he can get a word out, voices sound from elsewhere, urgent, and headed in our direction.

"Go!" the Anthropoid urges, his pale-green eyes wide now as he sticks his head out of the chamber room door. "I will hold them off, but we don't have long. Get in your sub and *leave!*"

"Who are you? Why would you help?"

He whips his head around to me. "I'm a friend. Look, you'll just have to trust me!"

Trust. After they boarded the sub and attacked us. And after all the lies the government has been telling. I'm expected to just trust not only a complete stranger but an Anthropoid, no less. What does trust even mean anymore?

What I *do* know is right now there's no time to waste.

And that I trust Ari.

I nod and scramble around to the driver's seat, jump in, and start the vessel up. I want to start moving but I can't help looking back again.

The Anthropoid struggles with two human guards. *Oh no.* The guards will be in here any second, and I'll have failed Papa! Everything needs to speed up! I shoot Papa a glance, and he *really* doesn't look well.

The Anthropoid really is struggling, dammit.

Something inside me twitches.

What might they do to him? I try to block out the thought and concentrate on the craft, but it's impossible. I glance again at Papa, scream inside, and grab my brolly.

The guards don't see me exit. I crouch low. The moment I'm visible in the doorway I lift the brolly and tase the guard who isn't directly touching the redheaded guy. They all turn to me, eyes wide. There's no time, though. So I press down harder and don't lift my finger until he drops. Just as the remaining guard is distracted looking down at the unconscious man, the Anthropoid punches him hard and he drops immediately. Then several more voices echo from down the corridor.

"Okay, now we really have to go!" the guy yells, and we both rush back into the chamber.

I jump in the craft and I'm soon through the first hatch, willing the acclimatizing program to hurry up. Finally, we can move on. No sooner does the submersible enter the moon pool room, though, than a sixty-second countdown sounds around the space: The entrance is about to close. Oh my God, I'll be locked inside Broadmoor! *Come on!*

The mechanical claw grabs my vessel. I peek out and spot the Anthropoid. I gesture for him to go before me, but he refuses. The claw places me inside the pool at the count of five. Diving, I level the craft beneath the pool just as the door above me closes. *No.* Where's the red-haired guy?

I spin around in my seat until I spot him. *Phew.* He'd clung to the top of the sub. He slides off now, hovering there in the gloom, before darting out of sight. I gulp as I scan the water. Visibility is reduced, with dark shadows swaying all around. The dread doesn't have a hope in hell of surfacing here and now, though.

I have my papa with me. And we're going home.

I exit the projection and speed to the side. I can't rise without power, which means they can lock on to me if they catch me. I check on Papa again, ensuring he's as secure as possible, and stare at him. Three months. In just over three months his hair is graying, his face sunken and lined, and his color . . . Oh, it would've broken Mama's heart to see him now! I look away.

He's here at least. At last, he's with me.

Taking a deep breath, I turn the sub on and select the house icon that will lead me to the *Kabul*. I mutter a prayer as I pull back on the joystick and forward on the throttle.

The sub rockets through the current. Though we aren't in the heart of the battle, hostile vessels and bots, fire, smoke and debris all whoosh by me in every direction. *Please, please, please.* I hold my nerve, dodging attacks just in time, rolling and swerving to avoid all the firepower around me.

Keep going.

The submersible hurtles up through it all, past the dreadful shadows of the "whales" and the menacing shapes of the "jellyfish" bobbing away in the depths.

Until finally I spot the heartening lights of the *Kabul*, blinking on the current. *Home.* My chest warms at the sight.

I must be only meters away from the moon pool when I'm hit.

No. The submersible jerks as I scan to catch the source of the attack.

There are two of them, the rocket-like subs of the prison guards hovering in my way.

"Ari, I'm hit!" I shout into my Bracelet. "I'm right here—I can see the *Kabul*!"

The craft jerks erratically. Just when I've somewhat stabilized it, both subs fire on me.

I duck and dive, and the firepower keeps coming. I roll to avoid a laser beam, when a bright light flashes. A dull *thud* rocks my craft and it shudders. The alarm sounds. *No.* I shiver. The submersible's taken a serious hit this time. The propellers slow down. I slide the throttle forward, but the vessel won't speed up and I'm moving at seahorse speed.

Don't stall. . . . Oh God, please don't stall.

The sub lurches. *No, no, no.* After all that, everything's slipping away from me. "Hang in there, Papa." Cold nausea rises inside. I'm vaguely aware of activity around the *Kabul's* moon pool, behind the prison guards.

One of the prison's subs moves toward me. We'll never survive another hit. As the craft creeps closer and I watch, it jerks, its nose rising and dipping erratically. Something comes into view behind it, but when I peer closer it's gone. What's going on? The sub lurches again, and once more I sense something flash by, but it's too fast to register. A pole of some kind has been rammed into the rocket-shaped craft's propeller, and finally the sub stalls, before spinning away.

The second craft is damaged in the same manner and suddenly the way ahead is clear. The shape whizzes by the front of my vessel now and slows down just enough for me to realize it's an Anthropoid. It's Ari.

We are fast, Leyla, he'd said. I blink. *Wow.*

With the continued protection from several of Bia's vessels, Ari darts beneath my stalling craft and nudges the submersible the short way to the moon pool, and then upward.

I'm through the pool, and finally up and in the chamber. Decompressing feels like an eternity, but at last we're done. I exit the sub, legs trembling, to find Ari briskly toweling himself dry. Our eyes meet and the hesitancy in his eases, his posture relaxing. And then we snap into action.

"Oscar!" I call out. "Close the moon pool door. *Now.* Secure the submarine and head west at full speed. We don't stop for *anyone!*"

I rush to the passenger door of the submersible and gently edge Papa toward me.

Ari hurries over. His solid arms sweep into the craft and I step aside. As he helps Papa out, I initiate a full diagnostics program on the submersible; hopefully any damage to the vessel can be repaired.

Ari stops, catching his breath when he looks at Papa, alarm crossing his face. His shoulders rise and fall and his eyes flash with rage as he scoops him up.

We head for the second guest room I've prepared. I message Charlie and tell him I want Bia to let Gramps know we have Papa. She'll find a way to do it without anyone else listening in. I know Grandpa will tell the twins.

The *Kabul* turns and speeds away from the chaos.

The Navigator appears, tilting his head as I make Papa comfortable on the bed. "Might I welcome the gentleman Hashem on board the *Kabul*, my dear lady?"

Warmth radiates through me at his words. Tears prickle my eyes. I could hug him to bits. "You may, Oscar."

The corners of my mouth dare a slight lift.

CHAPTER THIRTY-SEVEN

In the evening, I wipe Papa's brow to help cool him down. Without the layers of filth, he looks more like himself. It took Ari and me over an hour to wash and change him, his skeletal state demanding the gentlest handling.

The Medi-bot has diagnosed him as severely malnourished and dehydrated. He also has several viral and bacterial infections, and a high fever. But he'll be all right.

Papa's with me and he's going to be okay. It's too good to be true. A dream.

We've found a safe place far west of the prison, with no security bases for leagues around. We'll keep our heads down until Papa's out of the worst and then decide on our next move.

Bia's still waiting to hear from McGregor. I really hope she's safe and that she's not been rumbled by the prison guards. Charlie messaged me, asking if Papa had come around and if he was speaking yet. They're desperate to know everything. Gramps is aware of what's going on, and he's somewhere safe, thank goodness. I feel a tug at my heart; I miss him so much. I understand now why he thought it best to keep Ari's identity from me. I would never have left London with him if I'd known what he was back then.

Jojo went totally barmy when she recognized Papa. We have to hold her whenever she visits him; she can't contain her joy.

The Medi-bot bleeps. I replace one of the drips. Soon Papa will be up and about. And just wait until he sees the *Kabul*. He's sure to love the sub as much as I do!

Back in the saloon, Ari stands in the viewport, facing the water. Right in front of him is a dolphin. I hold my breath, watching them. The sea creature is attentive and relaxed. Anytime Ari waves his hands a certain way, the animal responds, moving its head and fins. It's as if they truly understand each other.

I sigh. "The dolphin, it's the same one, isn't it? I'm certain I saw it back in London and again following the vessel when we first set off. You know it?"

Ari turns from the windows, his eyes bright, and beckons me. I join him in the viewport. Jojo rushes over, mesmerized, and I scoop her up.

"Leyla, meet Skye," Ari says. "Yes, she insisted on following me to London, all the way from my home in the Faroe Islands. Skye, this is Leyla."

"Hey, Skye." I wave and hold up Jojo, who barks happily.

The dolphin flaps a fin and I laugh. I peer into the water and find myself imagining Ari in it, playing with the creature. I turn to him.

I open my mouth and then close it again, color warming my cheeks. But I need to know. "What does it feel like, Ari? How does it feel to swim out there? Do you ever feel afraid?"

His expression brightens as he meets my gaze, and a small smile tugs at the corners of his mouth. My stomach flutters at the sight of him. He's washed and shaved and his face is all sharp angles again, his smooth, dark-gold skin glistening where it's still damp.

His eyes shine. "When we know a place is safe, then being at one with the ocean, moving with it, is the best feeling in the world, Leyla. It feels free. Like you with your racing, yes?"

"Yes," I say, breathlessly. "That's how racing makes me feel. That's why

I love it so much. It's freedom and endless possibilities."

He holds my gaze a little longer, tentative affection flashing in his own, before gesturing to a tray of warm food he brought in for us. "You don't like it when it turns cold. So, how's your father doing?"

The gentle evening waves lap at the windows as we sit to eat in the mellow apricot glow of the Lumi-Orb. Jojo tucks into her own bowl. Spicy scents waft from the biryani, warming the room.

"He's resting," I say. "It'll be a while before the fluids and medicine kick in, but at least we've started. It could've been even worse."

I sigh. Papa's with me, and he'll be all right. Jojo's fully recovered. Neither Ari nor I are hurt. The *Kabul* survived the onslaught. And we're well away from any security bases and borders. My heart expands. There's very real magic in feeling safe.

"I can't believe he's with us," I say, chewing the rice. "I'm so worried I'll wake up tomorrow and this will all have just been a dream, you know?"

He nods slowly, a gleam in his eye. "You did it. You never gave up." His expression turns abruptly somber then. "You're okay? You weren't hurt?"

"I'm good, thank you. It could have gone wrong so many times. . . . I can't *believe* how lucky we were." I'm stunned we did it; my legs still haven't stopped trembling. "Are you all right? You were . . . amazing, you know— in the water? Thank you so much."

His eyes shine and he nods in reply.

Jojo's full and curls up beside us. We finish eating and sip warm drinks as we sit side by side on the cushions, gazing into the calm current outside. Even in the darkness, it's clear from the sub's fore lights that the water is different this far north, so much clearer. It must look beautiful in the daytime and natural light. Maybe we can climb a little in the morning and see it.

I recall watching the sun reflected in the current, the intensity of the moment. An experience Ari wanted to share with me. I'm acutely aware of how close we're sitting now.

Once we've finished our drinks I sneak a peek at him; he's staring into the water ahead, his thoughts somewhere far away.

He turns to catch my gaze. "You've found your father," he says. He clears his throat. "I must think about returning home now."

I swallow and nod. "Oh. Of course . . . I have Papa back, and your family will be waiting for *your* return."

He was only ever here because Grandpa didn't want me to be alone. He should be home. I try to imagine the sub without his presence but it's impossible. An ache spreads in my chest. I try to picture him back home with his family. The red-haired guy back at the prison pops into my head, and my eyebrows shoot up.

"There was a guy at the prison. He swam up through the moon pool and—"

I said "guy." Not "Anthropoid." I know Ari's noticed, too, because the most tender expression lights up his face.

"Jack," he says. "That's Jack Taylor. I thought you might need help and contacted—"

"Oh my God—"

"I was worried. I'd never forgive myself if—"

"No, I mean oh my God—*Jack Taylor*! I *knew* he seemed familiar! But what the hell? He *died* in the last London Marathon!"

Ari watches me as my mind races. How they never found Jack's body . . . How his little sister, Becca, *always* speaks of him as if he's still alive . . . Jack is *not* her imaginary friend!

"Oh my God, he never died, did he? He was an Anthropoid!"

I can't believe it. Is the whole *family* Anthropoids? And who *else* might be one? Thoughts gather and swirl inside my head until it's all I can do to shake it.

"There's just so much I didn't know, Ari. . . . And so much more I need to learn."

He reaches into his pocket and produces one of the chips I swiped at the prison. I'd handed my findings over to him, to check if he could glean anything from them.

"One of them is useless, and I haven't tested the third one yet," he says. "But this one is full of files."

My eyes dart from the technology to him. "I'd forgotten all about them; I thought they were probably rubbish! Maybe it holds Papa's prison file?"

He shakes his head. "The prisoners' files need a pass code, so they're inaccessible. Sorry. But there's information on Bia."

"What?" I straighten. "Show me."

Ari brings the info up. Not a document, but a whole *file* on her. *Bia Achebe.* And then a list of her crimes. My pulse races as I read on. There's so much more to Bia and her group.

None of which I would've guessed about them.

From what I can gather, Bia's lot have been wanted by the Blackwatch for years. And Captain Sebastian has *especially* been on their case, never easing up. They keep outwitting the authorities, though. According to the file, the group have tried, several times, to "expose the government's sensitive action undertaken to preserve our heritage and ensure our survival," but so far have always been successfully blocked. A paragraph from a piece penned by the group, that Bia tried but failed to have released, catches my attention:

> . . . *Furthermore, the government is solely responsible for the existence and spread of the seasickness. The fear this administration has dedicated itself to promoting is the cause for this epidemic of malaise. Such dangerous and delusional behavior is unacceptable from our leaders. We have concluded the government is incompetent, acting out of fear. Their policies—all created in a state of fear—have and will cause irreparable harm unless abolished with immediate effect. We*

shall continue to monitor the authorities and to make their
failings known. They were elected to act in our best interests—
that is their job. The government works for us. We will not be
silenced. Look around you. Forget "No past, no future," and
ponder, if you will, "No truth, no future." Resist.

There's a sour taste in my mouth and my stomach quivers.

I turn to Ari. "They're right, aren't they? The seasickness is *not* something linked to the water. Oh my God . . . What if all those sufferers, all those who've taken their lives—Camilla included—what if they could've been saved if so much fear didn't exist? What if the illness *isn't* inevitable? It exists because of how we think and feel . . . and how we think and feel has been informed by our leaders." My face heats. "How dare they, though. How *dare* they do what they do, and then turn around and blame it on innocent people? They accused Papa of doing what *they're* guilty of!"

Ari nods away, his gaze soft and encouraging as he watches me.

Bia's words make so much sense. Fear is stopping those in charge from even *contemplating* us staying down here for the foreseeable future; they want us to return to what we once knew. At all costs. But how can you want something so much that you don't care about the facts anymore? So many Explorers and scientists have reached the same conclusion—that returning to the surface anytime soon is impossible—and yet the government refuses to acknowledge the findings. Instead they push this hope and dream as the only thing worth holding on to, worth living for. Nothing else is worth caring about, or enjoying.

How can a small group of people think they know what's best for the majority without even asking us?

"We have to change the way we think, Ari."

"But I like the way you think," he says softly, his eyes brilliant and bright now.

My mouth falls opens and warmth radiates in my chest.

He leans back, raking his hand through his still-damp hair as if checking himself, and his cheeks flush. He turns his gaze to the water and clears his throat, nodding. "I agree. The seasickness isn't inevitable. It's a result of all the fear we're exposed to."

"Yes," I say, gazing into the current. "It makes sense. Wireless Man and his constant droning on about all the dangers, daily scare stories such as *Today's Terrors of the Deep*, the 'earthquakes,' everything. It all adds up. Couple that with the constant worshipping of the past and of *course* it's eventually going to make us ill." I rub my arms. "Anyway, I've yet to work out why they took him. Thank you," I say, my voice small. "For everything. I'm so sorry about, you know . . . the Anthropoids who boarded the sub—they really hurt you." I look up at him.

His reply is low, his voice husky and firm. "I would gladly do it again to protect you."

Oh. I swallow. My chest expands forever until I'm floating away. We fall very still. His gaze burns into mine and neither of us blink. His lips look *so* soft. . . .

Oscar appears. We both turn from each other and warmth floods my face as I force myself to focus on the Navigator's words.

"My lady, the notifications alert system has been triggered."

"What? Where?"

"On the news. At this very minute, my dear."

We jump up.

I command the screen on and freeze, all warm feelings instantly evaporating. Captain Sebastian is speaking, his ever-shifty gaze now piercing cold as he stares into the camera. Before I even hear his words, my eyes catch the text running along the bottom.

Wanted: Hashem McQueen. Leyla McQueen. Crime: Terrorism. Approach with caution.

Ari stiffens beside me. The PM's right-hand man is still speaking, but I'm mesmerized by the images. There's a picture of the *Kabul* while it was at the principal base in Mayfair. Then footage as a pack of cameras hovers inside the hangars. The police are everywhere. It cuts to Deathstar, the mechanic who'd been in charge of the *Kabul*, hurrying away from the manic Newsbots. Next, he exits a door, a metal pole in his hand and, oh my God, he *swings* at the cameras. There's a scramble with several police officers and Deathstar is tased; he slumps to the floor, subdued.

I cry out, shaking my head, vaguely aware of Ari clasping my hand in his own.

Then Papa's face and mine—it's my official London Marathon picture—cover the screen.

"A *handsome* reward," Captain Sebastian says, his eyes narrowed, his bitter expression unshakable. A venomous sea snake devoted to the hunt, anticipating its immobilizing bite. "Your country needs your help in finding and apprehending these treacherous criminals. Know this: Leyla McQueen and Hashem McQueen are currently this nation's number one enemy. As such, the safety of Britons is our top priority."

"Screen one off," I whisper, suddenly breathless. Everything's flip-flopping inside.

The screen goes blank and I stare ahead, not seeing anything. My pulse whooshes away in my ears; I can feel it all over my body. I shiver.

"Leyla . . ." Ari tugs my hand, urging me to return to the cushions in the viewport. I sit, while he grabs the nearest throw and wraps it around my shoulders. He kneels in front of me, clasping my hands in his. Tension sparks off his rigid posture, the muscles in his face straining against his skin.

A terrible, searing chill sweeps over me and I shudder. I take deep breaths and nod. "Papa . . . he's not safe. We're not safe. We—we have to keep moving. Yes, we'll just keep moving—no matter where—until we've sorted this out." *Sort it out how?* Hot panic rises up, threatening to burn me to nothing. I'd always hoped I could return to London with Papa once I found him. But so much has changed since then. . . . My world isn't even the same one as before.

We sit there in silence, Ari in front of me, my hands in his. Finally my pulse calms, and I sort through my thoughts. I need to take control of the situation, make a list. First thing, Ari must go home immediately. He's already put himself at risk too many times for us and needs to return to them safe and sound.

"I can do it." I look at him. "I'll—I'll drop you off home first. And then I need to look after Papa and me. Thank God for the *Kabul.* . . . I'd never have made it a single day using public transport. With this sub, though, thanks to Theo's modification, I have a chance. All I have to do is keep hiding, only moving when necessary, you know? Yes, I can do this."

Though his eyes are heavy now, there's a small tug on his soft lips as he watches me and nods, before looking down at our entwined hands. When he lifts his gaze, the spark has returned. "*We* can do this."

I stare at him. He can't mean it. Would he really do that for us? "No, you've already done enough. This is my problem now. I can look after myself, after Papa. I *can*. We might be hiding for *ages*."

His amber eyes are imploring now. "I know. But I *want* to stay. I can't leave you like this. I can help you; let me help you. You're *fugitives* now. And there's a substantial reward for capturing you. They know it was you behind the breakout. They're not going to stop until they've taken you in." He tilts his head, jaw rigid as he considers something, his eyes glinting as they dart to the blank screen. "We need to make sure that never happens."

A scratching inside, sharp nails clawing as panic tries to rise again. But I push it down, down, down, and focus on Ari instead.

My heart expands as I take him in. There's always a perfect radiance around him, reflected in his eyes, on his brown skin. He's an ocean of coppery-gold bioluminescence, but infinitely brighter, and ten thousand times more mysterious than the deepest pockets of the earth.

It's incredibly selfish, I know, but I *want* him with us. He's been a light in the darkness.

I nod, and a wave of relief swamps the edges of the dread. *Ari's staying.*

"All right. Yes, we can do it," I say. "All we'd have to do is evade them until Papa's better and we know exactly what's going on. We're not clueless, and we have the *Kabul*. I know we can do it."

He nods as he watches me intently. "*You* could do anything you put your mind to, Leyla," he says, so incredibly softly now. "You must not worry."

I can't tear my eyes away from him.

His expression is dazzling. His face, mystifying in the soft apricot light, reflects the ripples of the waves lapping the viewport. The only sound to be heard is the comforting thrum of the *Kabul*, and the *thump-thumping* of my heart.

My mouth goes dry. I'm drifting into a dream as I stare into the honey-colored specks in his eyes. His face relaxes, and he moves closer. I hold my breath. His face is inches from mine now. My fingers hover in the air for a moment before they edge forward and touch him. I trace his thick dark eyebrows, a tiny scar at his temple, his high-bridged nose and the smooth, sharp jaw. My fingertips slide all over the deep-bronze skin of his face, tracing every honed angle, every cryptic groove. A rich blush burnishes his skin. I catch my breath.

He's just so utterly beautiful.

Ari reaches out, his dusky fingers weaving themselves in and around my hair and along its length. He gently brushes his palms across my face before cupping it. I stare at his mouth.

He leans even closer, sealing the distance between us. A sigh escapes his lips just before they touch mine. Soft, gentle. It's like looking right into the very heart of him. I'm *falling* into him. Down, down, down. As if we've held hands and jumped together into some sweet, swirling vortex. I never want it to end. It's a magic I never even knew existed. At last we slowly, gently come up for air.

His eyes blaze bright and unbound as they bore into mine. A glittering truth, daring to be discovered. His shoulders rise and fall, and a tidal wave of tenderness lingers at the corners of his mouth. He sighs as he pulls me to him. I bury my face in his chest, breathing him in as he wraps his arms around me. It's a dream.

I'm not alone. We have the *Kabul*. Papa is here; my papa is *home*.

All will be well, inshallah.

I am now armed with so many truths.

What's the worst Captain Sebastian can do?

CHAPTER THIRTY-EIGHT

O n the third morning after Papa's rescue, I make my way to his room first thing, as usual. Jojo's already there. Licking his face, the cheeky mutt.

"Oi, you muppet," I whisper. "Told you not to bother Papa. He's asleep."

Except he isn't. Papa's eyes—once bright hazel but now dull and distant—flutter open and shut. He moves a thin, shaky hand. I lift it and place it on my face, cupping it with my own.

Life. It flashes in his eyes. *Finally*. I shudder.

His lips move and I lean in. His familiar zesty, herby smell is gone, but it will return.

He repeats himself, a croaking sound escaping his throat. "Pickle?"

"Yes. Salaam, Papa." My voice breaks. "It's me." Hot tears well in my eyes until I can't hold them back. They leak, spilling over my cheeks. "You're safe now."

What did they put him through? I swallow, pressing my lips together to stop myself from openly sobbing. I chat quietly, telling him how Grandpa and the twins are doing.

I don't mention how I can't communicate with them, or how the authorities have labeled us "wanted." I don't say how despite such vast undersea distances, it's suddenly as if the world's too small, and finding safe passage and locations for us to hide out in is what consumes me now.

These aren't the *only* things happening. I tell him about the *Kabul*. I speak of Ari.

"You're going to really like him, Papa. He helped us so much. Jojo loves him. He's been taking care of everything so I can look after you. Oh, and we have a ton of books now. I'll bring some in for you soon as you're up to it. Real Old World books—and the paper smells lush!"

Papa's breathing slows as he falls asleep, with Jojo now curled up at his feet.

I rush into the saloon to share the good news. The whole world should know Papa woke up, but Ari will do.

My heart soars at the view outside. The water is so much cleaner here than in London. Clear cobalt-blue waves lap at the tip of the vessel as light from both the sub and the early morning solar spheres throws illumination across the mystifying vastness before me, reminding me the world isn't as small as I suddenly fear. All around, the water is undivided, boundless. As if even time and space have no significance here. I let out a breath; it's so perfect. I move closer.

A creature hovers in the far distance. It's the dolphin. Skye seems to be struggling with something. Another sea creature swims toward her. I peer harder. It isn't a creature. It's Ari.

I stare as he swims up to Skye and liberates her of a piece of fishing net, sending it sinking into the depths. I shake my head as I watch him gliding through the water.

A human who can breathe underwater. It's miraculous.

He turns and swims toward the sub. When he's near enough to spot me in the viewport, he pauses a moment, before drifting closer.

How was I so frightened that first time I saw him in the water that I rejected him? It's just him. It's *Ari.* He's beautiful. He looks so . . . *natural.* All that pressure and he shows *no* sign of it. My lips part as I watch the water flow freely in and out of his mouth.

Tentatively he swims right up to me. I place my hand on the window and smile. A memory stirs somewhere. Ari's posture eases and his face softens. He mirrors my action, covering my hand with his on the other side.

The elusive memory is alarming now. Strong and insistent. What is it, though? Why can't I recall it? I look at Ari and he too looks a little dazed. He keeps glancing at our hands and back at my face. *Same!* I mouth. And then the absurdity of it makes me laugh.

A veil lifts off me. So many things I suddenly want to ask him. So much I still don't know about him, about his kind, about his life! About their history and what he told me of their problems. *I'm ready*, I want to say. *I'm ready to hear everything!*

Ari gazes at our hands and smiles as he watches me grinning.

And then surely my heart stops.

It happens so fast.

It happens so fast I barely understand what's happening.

I stop breathing the moment I see the net. Thick and wiry and unforgiving. It drops around Ari and draws shut.

I stare at him, numb. His face contorts with rage as he struggles inside the trap. I gasp. Tears spring to my eyes; I can't breathe. I yell and reach out to him, but it changes nothing.

Ari is hauled up through the current like an animal, toward the shadowy gloom of a vessel far above us.

I scream and beat my fists on the window. Skye appears, clearly distressed as she glides through the water after him. She too disappears out of sight.

I glance up through the waves, squinting desperately to see some sign of Ari, anything.

Nothing.

It's hard to think anymore. I can't get Ari's face out of my mind.

Oscar was unable to trace him. All day the *Kabul* sped in every direction, but nothing. It's now early evening. I want to curl up on the floor every time I replay what happened. The look in his eyes when he realized what was happening . . . It's too much. I can't *bear* it.

What do they do to Anthropoids they take alive?

Ari. The staggering strength. The way he cocks an eyebrow. How the muscle beside his mouth twitches and his eyes dance when he's amused. The way his gaze turns darker and his face clouds when he's worried. The amber flames that flicker in his irises. Someone very much alive.

Someone who made me happy.

I can't stop quivering inside. The tightness in my throat makes breathing painful. Ari should be *here*. Not dragged through the current as if he's an animal.

What to do now? I can't just stay numb forever. I *must* find a way to focus.

Except . . . *How* can we treat each other like this, though?

I peer out into the melancholy waters of the North Atlantic Ocean. I reflect on the strange truths that unroll before me and stretch eternally all around. Strange, maybe. But truths nonetheless.

Fear has immobilized us.

And it might be turning us into monsters.

Fear of those different from us has caused the slaughter of so many innocent Anthropoids. Fear of the water, and of moving on—of change—has caused needless human deaths. The fear is all-encompassing, a deluge smashing into the deepest chasm inside us all. Into the gaping gulf the floods created *within* us. The dread breathes in the palpable darkness that sweeps all around us, ceaselessly tugging away—I should bloody know. I thought hiding in London forever would help keep me safe. From the unknown. From life.

We'll do anything to hide in a familiar past, hoping it'll save us, distract us from facing this world. But trying to hold on to the Old World leaves nothing for here and now—only fear. And the seasickness is just one of the side effects of that.

I think *this* is why Papa was really arrested. I'll know for sure once he's recovered, but I think he suspected the truth, looked into it, and was caught—taken away without any explanation or trial. Left to rot in a septic stone cage. I'm *certain* his "crimes" are discovering lies about the government, and trying to do something about it. And I am *so* proud of him. I straighten.

Maybe if we weren't bombarded with the endless promotion of despair, we might think and feel differently about our lives.

Imagine if we actually looked forward to the future . . . If we could go to the moon, then I'm sure we can bloody well survive on our own planet without the constant dread. There's still so much to look forward to.

We're living, deep down in this liquid abyss, beneath impossible pressure and in the darkest depths, on a sphere covered in water, rotating in a galaxy inside a cosmos within a never-ending infinite space. We with our skin and bones and muscle and hearts and souls and minds and hopes and dreams, are still *being.* We're *alive.*

We aren't untethered from existence. The universe still acknowledges us, wraps us in its glittering, expanding embrace. The moon still tugs away. The sun rises and sets as ever, sustaining us even now. They didn't abandon us down here.

We abandoned ourselves.

But enough.

"Oscar?" I whisper through my aching throat.

The Navigator appears, draped in a purple velvet cape. "My dear lady?"

"Oscar, are you able to track Ari's heartbeat in the water?"

Ari was wrong on New Year's Eve. The truth *can* set you free. I won't let it cage me. I mustn't let fear determine what I do with truths. Even though I *am* scared. Absolutely terrified.

The Navigator inclines his head. "Ah, it pains to admit one's shortcomings, but no, regrettably not, my dear."

I peer into the water. Where's Skye? Oh God, I hope they didn't manage to hurt her when she went after Ari.

"And what about thermal imaging?"

"Alas, the sea is awash with living things, my lady. The gentleman Ari would not be the only form of life to radiate heat."

Living things. Gentleman. Form of life.

"Oscar? You know where the Faroe Islands are, don't you?"

I can't make any mistakes. Not a single one. If I do, the authorities will be onto me. I recall Captain Sebastian's words and shudder: *Know this: Leyla McQueen and Hashem McQueen are currently this nation's number one enemy.* It's too dangerous to return to Cambridge—not only for myself but for Bia and her people, too. Besides, we're close to the Faroe Islands.

The Navigator bows his head. "My dear lady, you need only give the word."

I have to find Ari's community, his family. Hopefully they'll know how we can help him.

"Turn north, Oscar. We head at full speed for the Faroe Islands, in search of some simple truths."

The *Kabul* sets course and speeds up.

"Oh, but, my dear," the Navigator says, "the truth is rarely pure and never simple."

I look down and swallow. I nod, then take a deep breath and straighten. "But . . . there's always hope, Oscar. *Always.*"

THE END

*That which is far off
and exceedingly deep,
who can find it out?*

Ecclesiastes 7:24

ACKNOWLEDGMENTS

The Light at the Bottom of the World has been a labor of love and a personal lesson in determination. Creating this story remains one of the most thrilling, most satisfying, and hardest things I've ever done. Life delivered some unbearably difficult times during my writing it, but working on it in the background remained a constant passion—and refuge. It's gone through innumerable drafts, but I got here, and I'm endlessly grateful to everyone who played some part in this journey I chose to embark upon.

Thank you first and foremost to my beloveds, Aswila, Mariam, and Ibrahim, for all your unwavering support, patience, understanding, respect, and enthusiasm throughout all the years it took me to write and publish this story. You proved my fiercest champions. May you always find the light in everything you ever encounter, inshallah.

Much love to the rest of my family, and infinite gratitude for your support.

All my appreciation and love for my agent, Rebecca Podos. Thank you for loving and believing in my story, Becca. Thank you from the bottom of my heart for believing in me. I'm so grateful for all your support, encouragement, and guidance.

Huge thanks to everyone over at Hyperion: My editors, Laura Schreiber and Augusta Harris, the conjurers of my gorgeous cover—the talented artist Mike Heath and Hyperion's lead designer, Marci Senders—copy chief Guy Cunningham and his brilliant crew, proofreader Meredith Jones, managing editor Sara Liebling, Christine Saunders in publicity, Elke Villa and the whole marketing team, Molly Kong, Emily Meehan; and to everyone else at DBG, much gratitude.

Endless thanks to Michael O'Donnell (aka Moose), who at the time of my writing this story was a research scientist at the University of Washington's Friday Harbor Laboratories. Moose was so very kind, patient, and enthusiastic with any questions I had relating to the science of my fictional underwater world.

I'm indebted to Adam Wright, who at the time of my writing this story held the position of CEO at DeepFlight. Adam was wonderful and considerate in answering all submersible-related questions. He went above and beyond when he also generously gave me a mini tutorial via Skype, covering the basics of driving a submersible!

Much love and my deepest gratitude to Courtney Kaericher, an amazing critique partner and wonderful friend. Thank you so much for your endless enthusiasm, support, and patience, Court. I can't wait for the world to read your beautiful words!

All my love and appreciation for my niece Juwairiah Khan who zealously read the earliest (and worst!) drafts of this story. You'll always be a queen to me, Jojo.

I'm so grateful for my wonderful friend Tracey McNaughton. You've been here from the beginning, Tracey, and never wavered in your support and enthusiasm. Thank you!

I'm incredibly lucky to have encountered so many amazing souls during this journey. You all absolutely rock. I feel especially grateful for: Samantha Shannon, Marieke Nijkamp, Sabaa Tahir, Sam Copeland, Joanna Hathaway, Laura Weymouth, Sajidah K. Ali, Angie Manfredi,

Rachel Strolle, Justin A. Reynolds, Anna Bright, Deeba Zargarpur, Meredith Ireland, Heidi Heilig, Ausma Zehanat Khan, Tehlor Kay Mejia, Shannon Chakraborty, Candice Montgomery, Louie Stowell, Nadine Jolie Courtney, Sangu Mandanna, Diana Urban, Nafiza Azad, Sarwat Chadda, Claribel Ortega, Kat Cho, Naseem Jamnia, Saba Sulaiman, Kiki Nguyen, Tasha Suri, Carissa Taylor, Adiba Jaigirdar, Karen Strong, Cindy Baldwin, Heather Kassner, Fadwa, Diana Sousa, Swapna Krishna.

Heartfelt thanks to *all* my early readers, and especially to the following kind and generous folk for their insightful feedback: Laura Weymouth, Maria Hossain, Eric Smith, and Carissa Taylor. Carissa, you read countless random chapters and scenes in the early days, and I'm indebted to your unbelievable patience, support, and kindness.

For their brilliant editorial skills thank you to Tehlor Kay Mejia and Estella Mirai.

So much admiration and respect for those Muslim SFF authors whose works I've been lucky enough to discover so far, and who inspire me with how they've paved the way writing their fantastical, diverse stories. They are: Sabaa Tahir, Saladin Ahmed, G. Willow Wilson, Shannon Chakraborty, Ausma Zehanat Khan, Sami Shah, Nafiza Azad, Tahereh Mafi, Samira Ahmed, Hafsah Faizal, Karuna Riazi. I can't wait to explore the other stories already out there, and urge all lovers of sci-fi and fantasy to check out the phenomenal works by these brilliantly talented authors.

Likewise, it's also been heartwarming to discover the inclusive, stunning, and refreshingly new SFF narratives hitting our shelves from authors of color. A few firm favorites I've had the honor and delight of reading over the last year or so—and which I wholeheartedly recommend—are:

The Belles by Dhonielle Clayton, *A Blade So Black* by L. L. McKinney, *Opposite of Always* by Justin A. Reynolds, *Empire of Sand* by Tasha Suri, *Dread Nation* by Justina Ireland, *Girls of Paper and Fire* by Natasha Ngan, *The Storm Runner* by J. C. Cervantes, *They Both Die at the End* by Adam Silvera, *We Set the Dark on Fire* by Tehlor Kay Mejia, *Wicked Fox* by Kat

Cho, *A Spark of White Fire* by Sangu Mandanna, *Binti* by Nnedi Okorafor, *Rebel Seoul* by Axie Oh, *The Girl from Everywhere* by Heidi Heilig, *The Star-Touched Queen* by Roshani Chokshi, *Forest of a Thousand Lanterns* by Julie C. Dao, *The Wrath and the Dawn* by Renée Ahdieh, *Labyrinth Lost* by Zoraida Córdova, *MEM* by Bethany C. Morrow, *Shadowshaper* by Daniel José Older, *The Serpent's Secret* by Sayantani DasGupta, *Want* by Cindy Pon, *A Ruin of Shadows* by L. D. Lewis, *The Reader* by Traci Chee. I've gone blank now, but there are, of course, so many, many more exciting and authentically inclusive SFF tales out there by authors of color, and it's been incredibly heartening and inspiring to discover them.

To all booksellers, librarians, educators, bookbloggers, bookstagrammers, reviewers—anyone who has ever helped to promote my debut novel in any way and strived to put it in the hands of readers: Thank you. I'm deeply grateful for every single one of you.

Unwavering love for the city of London, where a story lingers in every alleyway, on every bridge, and in every lookout. You are undeniably the best and most inspirational of them all.

Finally, thank you, dear reader, for picking up this book. For selecting a science-fiction story with a British Muslim lead. For choosing to follow my beloved Leyla into her underwater world. I appreciate you more than you could ever know. May you always find the light in everything you do.